THE NATURE OF A LADY

Books by Roseanna M. White

LADIES OF THE MANOR

The Lost Heiress
The Reluctant Duchess
A Lady Unrivaled

SHADOWS OVER ENGLAND

A Name Unknown
A Song Unheard
An Hour Unspent

THE CODEBREAKERS

The Number of Love
On Wings of Devotion
A Portrait of Loyalty

Dreams of Savannah

THE SECRETS OF THE ISLES

The Nature of a Lady

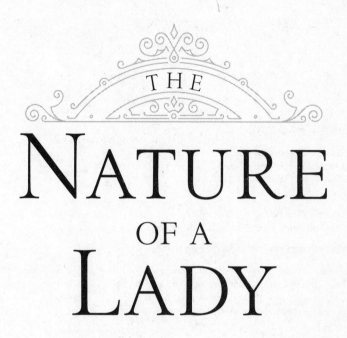

THE NATURE OF A LADY

ROSEANNA M. WHITE

BETHANYHOUSE
a division of Baker Publishing Group
Minneapolis, Minnesota

© 2021 by Roseanna M. White

Published by Bethany House Publishers
11400 Hampshire Avenue South
Bloomington, Minnesota 55438
www.bethanyhouse.com

Bethany House Publishers is a division of
Baker Publishing Group, Grand Rapids, Michigan

Printed in the United States of America

Library of Congress Cataloging-in-Publication Data
Names: White, Roseanna M., author.
Title: The nature of a lady / Roseanna M. White.
Description: Minneapolis, Minnesota : Bethany House, [2021] | Series: The secrets of the isles ; 1
Identifiers: LCCN 2020052226 | ISBN 9780764239205 (casebound) | ISBN 9780764237188 (trade paperback) | ISBN 9781493431472 (ebook)
Subjects: GSAFD: Love stories.
Classification: LCC PS3623.H578785 N38 2021 | DDC 813/.6—dc23
LC record available at https://lccn.loc.gov/2020052226

Scripture quotations are from the King James Version of the Bible.

This is a work of historical reconstruction; the appearances of certain historical figures are therefore inevitable. All other characters, however, are products of the author's imagination, and any resemblance to actual persons, living or dead, is coincidental.

Cover design by Jennifer Parker
Cover photography by Todd Hafermann Photography, Inc.

Author is represented by The Steve Laube Agency.

21 22 23 24 25 26 27   7 6 5 4 3 2 1

To all my readers named Elizabeth.
The sheer number of you inspired this tale of mistaken identity,
and I pray you enjoy it.

The Isles of Scilly

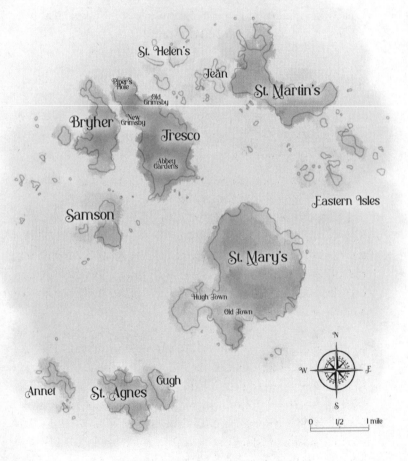

St. Helen's

Teän

Piper's Hole

St. Martin's

Old Grimsby

Bryher

New Grimsby

Tresco

Abbey Gardens

Eastern Isles

Samson

St. Mary's

Hugh Town

Old Town

Annet

St. Agnes

Gugh

N

W   E

S

0   1/2   1 mile

Cornwall due East 28 miles >

Prologue

He was a prince at sea. That's what John Mucknell shouted whenever battle was upon him.

Even before he'd stolen the East India Company ship, against whose deck his feet were now braced. Even before he'd presented himself and the *John* to the exiled Prince of Wales, offering their services against those blasted Parliamentarians who had taken over their country. Even before he'd been knighted and named vice admiral of this new royal fleet.

Pirate fleet, the enemy said. Mucknell's lips twitched up as he watched the enemy craft close in. He was a prince at sea, a cockney. And, yes, a thief and a pirate. But it was the blighted Roundheads who had forced him to these straits. When his rightful sovereign was forced to barricade himself on an island to escape his enemies and found himself in desperate need of supplies, what course of action was there but to rob the ships passing by? And if the richest prizes were usually from the East India Company, under whose banner Mucknell had worked and kowtowed for so many useless years . . . shame, that.

7

"Admiral?" His first mate slid to his side, keeping his voice low. "There's no way we'll be able to slip by them into the harbor."

"Nay." Mucknell didn't even need to raise his spyglass to see that three Parliamentarian ships had completely cut off the path to his base in the Isles of Scilly, off the coast of Cornwall. He'd met the *Constant Warwick* once already today, near Land's End, and they'd both gotten in a few good shots.

Shots that had left them both weakened. But the enemy had now rendezvoused with the *Cygnet* and the *Expedition*. And Mucknell's fleet . . . well, they were pirates. There'd be no help for him, unless he could lure the enemy into range of the isles' batteries, but that wasn't likely.

"Our course of action, sir?"

The wind blew, snapping the sails taut overhead and lifting strands of hair from Mucknell's shoulder. His mouth ached for a sip of rum, but he'd not indulge it, not until this crisis was well past. His fingers twitched over the pommel of his sword. His mind, sharp and fogless, spun through what he knew.

His hold was loaded with the booty from a significant haul—one that the Prince of Wales would be most eager to receive: much-needed supplies of food and cloth and metal, casks of wine, spices.

Silver.

Mucknell's fingers traced the circle of the pommel. Silver and more silver. Some of which he'd decided wouldn't be among the cache he turned over. He'd branded his own name on the crate, making it clear to his men that this one wouldn't be off-loaded with the rest. It was a man's right, after all, to take a fee. And his would be the pieces already engraved with his wife's name, as if they'd been made for her.

His gaze flicked toward St. Mary's Island—so close, but too far to be of any help. Was his Lizza there, watching from a lookout? Or at their house on Tresco? She never breathed a word of her distaste for his new career. She just went where he asked her to go. Uprooted herself from their comfortable, if bare, life in London and followed him here to the very edges of England.

In moments like these, he knew she deserved better than a scoundrel like him for a husband. But she'd never say such a thing. Not his Lizza.

He'd get that silver to her. And the rest of the supplies to his prince. He'd outfox that triple-strength enemy bearing toward him. Somehow. He'd win. Because Vice Admiral Sir John Mucknell might be a pirate, but he was blamed well the best pirate these waters had ever seen.

As the closest of the enemy ships drew near, he pulled out his sword and held it high—the signal all his men would recognize as their cue to man their stations. And he shouted the words that were their battle cry.

"I am a prince at sea! I am the proudest man upon the face of the earth. I am an Englishman, and were I to be born again, I would be born an Englishman. I am a cockney. . . ."

He could feel the tension in the air that whipped around him, feel the energy of his men as they laid hold of their ropes and ammunition and torches and aimed the twenty-one guns on the starboard side toward the enemy, who had spilled the wind in her sails to slow and meet him. He could feel his crew waiting for his final cry.

"And that's my glory!"

1

More beauty than Lady Elizabeth Sinclair had ever thought possible beckoned to her—a turquoise sea, blue sky wisped with soft white clouds, birds cartwheeling through the air, islands studding it all with the promise of life she'd never had the opportunity to examine up close. The only thing standing between it and her was a woman whose eyes were growing worryingly watery.

The last thing she ever wanted was to make her mother cry. Or at least, that had always been the case before. Just now, something else had stolen that "last thing she wanted to do" ranking.

The last thing she currently wanted to do was give in to her brother's machinations to marry her off to his school chum. Which meant she might have to harden her heart to her mother's distress. "Mama . . ." She sucked in a breath only to find it as shaky as her mother's. Hardening her heart was easier decided than done. "It's only a summer."

"I know." Her mother pasted a wobbly smile into place and gave Libby's fingers a squeeze. She'd scarcely let go of them since they debarked the train and made their way to the ferry. "And it'll do you good. I know that too. Even so."

11

She didn't need to voice her concerns. She'd done that already a dozen times since Libby came to her with this plan a week ago. They'd never been more than a few miles apart. Libby had never been on her own—and even though she technically wouldn't be alone now either, a lady's maid who was only two years Libby's senior wasn't exactly a full-fledged chaperone. She'd know no one on the islands. She'd be lonely. What if something happened to her? What if something happened at home? Or with her sister? Proper young ladies simply didn't run off to the Isles of Scilly for the summer by themselves.

The thing was, Libby had already proven herself an absolute failure at being a proper young lady. And when her brother had announced at breakfast eight days ago, with that frustrating "I know what's best for you" look, that he'd spare her any further embarrassment and arrange a match with Sheridan, her options for the summer had shrunk considerably.

It wasn't that Lord Sheridan wasn't a good man. It was just that she didn't really like him. He went ever on about archaeology. And she went ever on about the nature that his digs upended. And it only took about five minutes for both of them to be either bored out of their minds or seething at each other.

For the life of her, she couldn't determine why Sheridan would have agreed to her brother's plotting. Maybe he hadn't yet. Maybe Bram meant to inform Sheridan of his brilliant new plan in the same heavy-handed way he'd informed her. Though why a marquess would feel any obligation to obey an earl, she couldn't imagine.

Sheridan would object, if given enough time to really contemplate what Bram was demanding of him. That was how it always worked with Sheridan—he'd go along, follow her brother mindlessly for a while, and then he'd get that look on his face and declare, "I say, old chap. That is, what were you thinking of? That won't do."

She just had to give him time enough to come to the conclusion that she'd make him a lousy wife before her brother could get wedding plans made to the point that neither could back out without damaging their reputation. The summer to think about it—that was what Sheridan needed. She'd never seen him take longer than three months to wake up to Bram's manipulations.

Never in her life had *she* disobeyed her brother though. Or, before that, their father. The very idea of it made her stomach squirm like the beetle she'd found digging its way through the garden at the inn this morning. But Bram had finally pushed her too far. It was one thing to inform her that she *would* be fitted for a new wardrobe for the Season and set up rules for what she could do when wearing it. It was quite another to simply state that he'd decided on a husband for her.

Mama sighed and turned her face into the breeze, toward the ferry. Her blinking was too quick to bespeak anything but a continued struggle. But her voice sounded steady—if a bit tight—when she said, "You're going to have such a lovely time exploring and cataloguing. I only wish we knew someone on the islands. There are surely a few of our acquaintances holidaying there this year."

Libby shot a look over her shoulder at her lady's maid for fortification. Mabena Moon gave her that same muted grin she always did when they were in company with anyone else in Libby's family. The one that everyone assumed was merely a polite acknowledgment instead of a sign of shared secrets. "I won't be alone, Mama. Moon's entire family is there. You read the telegram she got in response— they're most happy to keep an eye on me."

A beat of silence descended, punctuated by the ringing of the bell on the ferry calling all passengers to board. Her trunks were already stowed, her ticket purchased. All she had to do was walk up the gangplank and the adventure would begin. An entire summer on England's most unique island chain. A subtropical climate that produced plants she'd be able to see nowhere else in the country. Birds her eyes had never beheld. Seals. Ocean creatures she'd not even learned the names of yet.

She could almost hear her magnifying glasses calling to her from her trunk. And her microscope sang a siren's song in her ears. She had fresh notebooks waiting to be filled. Pencils in every shade, sharpened and expectant. Watercolors snug in their cases. A book on the classifications of life on the Isles of Scilly on the tip-top of her trunk, so she could snatch it out the moment she arrived in her summer cottage.

Then it struck—the tidal wave of uncertainty. What did Libby know of the world, of independent life? She'd never been away from home, not really. She was barely twenty. And if she couldn't get on in the society in which she'd been raised, how did she expect to get on there, with strangers?

Her fingers were the ones to tighten around her mother's this time. "Are you certain you don't want to join me?"

Mama chuckled and released her hand. "Had I not promised Edith I would be with her for her lying-in, I would be there in a heartbeat."

Mention of her older sister, the eldest of the three Sinclair children, made Libby's lips twist into a wince before she could stop the reaction. Another reason this holiday had sounded so alluring when Mabena whispered the suggestion after Bram's high-handed declaration last week. Her other option, if she didn't want to spend the whole summer scowling at Sheridan across the breakfast room at Telford Hall while she waited for him to come to his senses, was to join her mother at Edith's.

And none of them were ever happy when she and Edith were in the same room. "Give her my love. And if you wanted *not* to include her judgment on my holiday in your letters, I'd not complain about the lack."

With another chuckle, Mama stepped back, folded her arms across her middle, and nodded toward the boat. Even with emotion waging a war against the composure on her face, Augusta, Lady Telford was the image of a grace Libby could never make herself aspire to, despite admiring it in her mother. "Enjoy yourself, my darling. Try not to ruin too many dresses. And do make an effort to see who from our acquaintances are summering there and send me a wire with their names. I'll make any introductions I can through telegrams and letters."

"Yes, Mama." She'd make an effort. It would be a paltry one, but Mama wouldn't honestly expect anything more from her. Libby grinned, leaned over to kiss her mother's cheek, and waited.

Mama swallowed. Gave her another smile that was trying too hard. "Off you go, then. Don't miss the ferry. Moon, I'm trusting you to see my daughter is well cared for."

Mabena's nod was solemn. Though when Mama waved them on-ward, Libby exchanged a grin with her maid that nearly gave way to a squeal of excitement. Mabena must be excited to see her family again. And Libby . . . Libby could hardly believe that she'd actually pulled this off. She'd actually let a cottage for the summer without her brother's knowledge. She'd actually get to put a few leagues of distance between herself and the society that had decided she wasn't quite what they were looking for in an earl's sister.

Another call from the ship's bell had her and Mabena both pick-ing up their pace, each clutching the smaller bags they carried with one hand and using the other to hang on to their hats, since the wind was greedily trying to steal them. A laugh spilled from Libby's lips as they charged up the gangway at a pace too quick to be ladylike.

But that didn't matter. Not now. They were on their way.

Once aboard, Mabena let out a gusty breath of relief. "There, now. We made it. And not a moment too soon."

Indeed, with a final *clang*, the gangway was taken in and the ferry pulled away. Libby took up position at the rails so she could wave to Mama. Her mother blew her a kiss and shouted something that was lost to wind and water slapping the hull and the steam engine's chug and clamor. Good wishes, no doubt, to match her brave smile.

Libby held her place for a minute more and then spun to take in the world. St. Michael's Mount, its causeway currently under water, jutted out of the sea to her left, the ancient castle reigning over the small town of Marazion. Gulls swooped and called. And likely count-less fish darted beneath the waves, if she could but see them.

Beside her, Mabena chuckled and placed a restraining hand upon her arm. "Easy now, Lady Elizabeth. We don't need you falling in to get a closer look."

Libby shot her friend a smile. "No more of that—not this summer. It'll just be us, Mabena. No one even needs to know that I'm Bram's sister. I think . . . I think I'll just be *Libby* until we go home again. Libby Sinclair. No 'my lady' nonsense."

She expected a smile of pleasure. A nod. Quick agreement. Instead, thunder flashed through Mabena's deep brown eyes. "That will never do, my lady. You *are* His Lordship's sister. You can't just pretend otherwise. And I had better not either, lest I forget myself when we go back to Somerset."

For a long moment, Libby just listened to the splash of water as the boat sliced through it, wishing one of her magnifying glasses could help her see what this heavy thing was inside her chest. Wishing there were a Latin name for the feeling of disappointment—no, discomfort. No . . . she didn't *know* the word for this feeling that always seized her when someone disapproved of her.

Which was all the time, lately. She could all but see her sister's perfect face looking at her in utter dismay, hear her voice saying, *"For heaven's sake, Elizabeth, can't you just be a proper young lady for a day in your life?"*

Mabena's sigh joined the wind jostling them for elbow space at the rail, and she leaned closer until their shoulders just brushed. "You know it isn't that I don't want to be so informal, my lady. It's just that it would be so easy to do that I honestly do fear I'd forget myself when we go back again. And I don't relish losing this position when your mum or brother realize we're friends. We walk a fine enough line as it is."

She knew that. She did. As indulgent as Mama was about the microscope and slides and endless supply of sketchbooks, she wouldn't budge on some things—the lines between the classes high on the list. Loyalty and some affection between a lady's maid and a lady was acceptable. Friendship was something else. Friendship required equality, and *that* she'd never grant.

Were she a braver girl, Libby would defy that unspoken dictate and argue the point. She'd declare that she didn't care who Mabena's parents were or where she was from, they *were* friends and that was that. They understood each other. Shared a fascination with the natural world—something Libby couldn't claim about any of the gentlemen's daughters she knew. While they recoiled in horror at a worm or an insect, she leaned in for a closer look. They were too different.

In those ways, Mabena was much more like her. But in others, they were different too. She *did* need to protect her position—something Libby never had to worry about. She'd better remember that and help her guard it. With a matching sigh, Libby nodded.

"Now, you needn't look so sad, my lady. St. Mary's is one of the prettiest places on earth, and you're going to have a fine time cataloguing every creature and plant you can find. Don't worry so over a trifle like what name I'll call you." Mabena's eyes, when Libby looked over at her, flashed with laughter. "Perhaps I'll just take up calling you *Mea Domina*. That's your Latin designation, isn't it?"

Libby laughed and then leaned over the rail again to watch the world swimming by beneath them. Not that she could see much through the froth of their wake, but the glimpses were fascinating. She ought to have convinced her family to spend more time at the seashore. How lucky Mabena was to have grown up with such variety of life at her fingertips. "I'm looking forward to meeting your family. They'll be there to greet the ferry, right?"

"Ah . . ." Mabena cleared her throat in a way Libby had never heard her do before. She lifted her gaze from the water to her friend's face. It had a strange look upon it. A bit sheepish. A bit . . . guilty? "It was a friend of mine who sent that telegram, my lady, not my mother. My family's all on Tresco. We'll be summering on St. Mary's. Not that the two aren't close enough to go between—by boat—and I'm sure you *will* meet them, but they're not down the lane as I led your mother to believe."

"Then why . . . ?" She didn't even know what to ask. Where to begin. She felt no stab of anxiety over realizing there *wouldn't* be a family a few paces away to see to her comfort and care—that hardly mattered. But hadn't Mabena's idea for a visit sprung from the desire to see her family again?

"Tresco's too small to support as many tourists. We'd never have found a place to let there at such a late date." The twinkle returned to Mabena's dark eyes. "And besides—there's a reason I left the isles. Being near family is all well and good, but being able to breathe without them asking if you find the air satisfactory has its merits too. A bit of distance between us and them will be a good thing."

She could hardly argue with that, given her reasons for wanting this holiday. Perhaps Mabena had a brother like Bram. Not that she'd ever mentioned any siblings. Or really spoken much of her family at all, come to think of it.

"We've nearly two and a half hours on the ferry. Why don't we find a place to sit? You can get out a sketchbook."

An obvious ploy, but given the beauty surrounding them, she decided to let herself be redirected. There would be plenty of time over the summer to pry a bit more information out of her maid. For now, it was enough to soak in this new world surrounding her. And easy enough to get lost in it.

She'd filled three pages with sketches of the birds and fish she glimpsed and was putting down a rough image of the Isles of Scilly themselves, emerging from the sea, when they chugged into St. Mary's Sound. She closed her book and tucked it and her pencil back into her bag as Mabena pointed to the sights visible from their course.

"That opening there is Porthellick Bay. And there, that giant pile of rocks—that's Giant's Castle."

Libby's lips turned up at the whimsy.

The narration continued with a list of names Libby would never be able to keep straight, at least not until she'd explored them for herself. Finally, they docked at the quay in Hugh Town with a whistle and a clang of the bell.

Mabena patted her arm. "Just sit tight for a moment, my lady, while I direct them on what to do with our trunks. I've arranged transport for those, but we'll walk to the cottage through the town from here. I thought you'd enjoy that."

"Perfect." And indeed it was. She happily sat and soaked in the bustle until Mabena signaled her to debark, and then she happily strolled through the quaint little seaside town by her maid's side, trying to catalogue absolutely everything she saw. Squat little houses of granite, flowering shrubs hugging their corners. Shops with darling little signs dangling outside them, proclaiming the wares within. Oceanic birds swooping and calling overhead.

It only got better when they left the town behind and took to the road meandering along the seashore. Grasses bent in the steady wind, and she spotted heather unlike any she'd seen before. Rocks cropped up here and there, promising ample places to sit when she explored. And the sky overhead stretched blue and promising.

Soon, cottages came into view, their sizes varying. Near the larger ones she spotted families of obvious wealth, playing at a seaside holiday. From these she averted her face and hoped against hope that Mama was wrong and none of them would recognize her.

Mabena pulled a folded slip of paper from her pocket and, fighting the wind at every step, opened it. She checked something about their surroundings, though Libby had spotted no road sign to tell them where they were, but her maid nodded and pointed toward a lovely small cottage at the end of the lane. "There we are. Our home for the rest of the summer."

Was there something odd in her voice, or was the distortion just from the wind? Libby put it out of her mind for now and focused on the granite building abutting the old garrison wall that her friend indicated. The location was ideal—they'd have views of the other islands, the water, and the town down below. Even from here she could spot a path to the water through the high grasses. And best of all, there were no other houses sharing walls or gardens. She'd have privacy to do whatever she pleased.

As they neared, she spotted a woman of middling years rounding the corner, shielding her eyes from the sun to watch them approach.

"That would be Mrs. Pepper, I imagine. The landlady." Mabena nodded in satisfaction. "With our keys and no doubt something to sign to let the place officially. I told her which ferry we'd be on." She darted a glance at Libby. "Could we give her your name? If I mention mine, my family will hear of it before the tide goes out."

"No objections from me." It was properly exciting, actually. A holiday cottage, let in her name. She could hardly have helped smiling even had she wanted to as she strode to the matronly woman awaiting them. "How do you do?" she said the moment she was near enough. "Are you the landlady?"

The woman gave a brisk nod, her eyes taking them in with a few quick darting glances that seemed to dismiss Mabena in a second and measure Libby from her new hat to the shoes she'd already muddied. "Mrs. Pepper. You'll be the young miss who wired about letting the place, then?"

"I am." More or less. She smiled anew. "Elizabeth Sinclair."

"Another Elizabeth, is it?" The woman turned with a baffling huff of frustration and waved for them to follow her to the door. "May you be more dependable than the last. That one left me high and dry after sweet-talking me into promising her the whole summer but letting her pay week by week, she did. And then vanished before the second month is out, as good sense should have told me she'd do."

Libby blinked at the woman's back . . . and at the deluge of information she had absolutely no need of. "Well, how fortuitous that we were able to take over the vacancy, then. I was quite afraid we'd decided on our plans too late to find anything half as lovely as this."

"All I needed to know, miss, is that the money you wired to the bank yesterday came through without a hitch. Here." She opened the front door for them and held its key up, which dangled from her fingers. "You mentioned catering, aye? My daughter or I will bring a basket once a day with all the fixings you'll need. I trust your maid can discern what to do with it."

Mabena's hum vibrated with irritation, but Libby didn't look back at her to see if she was glowering. She simply took the key ring. "Yes. Thank you."

"She'll take any laundry you have for us at the same time. Mind, that's extra. You pay by the article, as you would at any fancy hotel in London."

She'd never stayed in a fancy hotel in London—they had a townhouse, after all—but she saw no reason to point that out. Mama had sent her ample funds to see her through the summer. "That sounds reasonable." She tried to peek past Mrs. Pepper into the house. It was the size of their gardener's cottage at Telford Hall. It wouldn't take long to explore, but she'd like to get about it so she could get everything where she wanted and escape back to the out of doors.

Apparently, Mrs. Pepper was no more eager to dawdle. "The lease is on the table, miss. Read and sign it at your leisure, and Kayna or I will fetch it back tomorrow when we bring your meals. There are supplies enough in there now for this evening and breakfast. And a few little guidebooks, if you've a curiosity about the place. If you need anything more, your girl can find us at the corner of Garrison Lane and Well Lane. Mr. Pepper or I will see you have anything you need."

Because her bank's wire had gone through without a hitch, no doubt. The woman certainly didn't seem to welcome her with anything like warmth. But that was all right. Libby didn't need her for a friend. Clutching her valise in her hands, she smiled again. "Thank you, Mrs. Pepper. I'm certain we'll find everything perfectly satisfactory."

"Good." With that, the woman finally cleared the doorway and strode away.

Mabena let out a huff. "The Peppers. Never much got along with them."

Having no commentary on the family as a whole, Libby merely grinned and charged into her new home, while Mabena announced that their trunks were arriving and she'd oversee their being brought in.

The living area was small indeed. But prettily decorated, and the windows looked out over the bay and the wall of the garrison. Adjoining it was a tiny little kitchen with a table right there among the shelves and the stove. It would be like sneaking down for a midnight biscuit, only for every meal—eating right there in the kitchen. She hurried to look at the other rooms, finding the necessary and bathtub and two bedrooms of nearly equal size. She chose the one with the harbor view, affording her a lovely sight of the other islands.

It had a small desk by the window, which would be perfect for her microscope. It hadn't space enough to hold all her art supplies, but she could designate part of the chest of drawers for that. She moved to it now and opened the top drawer.

And froze. Inside were blouses. A lovely shawl in heather blue. And a book lying open on the top, pages down. *Treasure Island*. Libby picked it up, her brows knotting when she saw the pages had folded on themselves. Her stomach twisted. The book had clearly been dropped into the drawer, not *placed* there. She smoothed the pages, her frown increasing. Was that handwriting amid the printed words?

What had Mrs. Pepper said about the previous occupant? That she'd "vanished before the second month was out." Vanished . . . but left her things behind.

"In here, then."

At Mabena's brusque voice, Libby moved the book behind her back, not ready to have it snatched away just yet. Mabena was looking over her shoulder as she entered, clearly leading someone in. Though when she turned back around, her gaze seemed to take the situation in with startling speed. She frowned. "What's this? You can't have unpacked already. You hadn't clothing in your valise."

Libby rocked on her heels and shrugged. She should probably show the book to Mabena, but she'd rather examine it first. "Not mine, but the drawers are already full."

Mabena's huff sounded irritated. But her eyes sparked with . . . something. Curiosity? Or did she feel the same uncanny dread that coursed through Libby's veins? Regardless, she stalked over to the dresser and simply scooped out the stranger's things. "I'll take care of it. And of your unpacking. Go on outside. I know you want to."

Because it was expected of her, Libby grinned. But she felt a bit guilty as she slipped by the stevedore and out the door, clutching the book to her stomach once she was past.

Everything always made more sense out in nature. And *this* . . . this could use a good dose of sense. Currently, it had none.

2

Oliver Tremayne leaned forward as far as he could, the oars two wooden extensions to his arms. He breathed in as he bent, exhaled as he leaned back, his arms—the wooden parts of them, anyway—slicing through the crystal waters as his gig skimmed the top of them. *Faster. Faster.*

Sweat poured down his torso, soaking his shirt. He looked up, sighting the beach that would be their finish line. "Almost there, lads! We'll take them this morning!"

From the bench behind came a chorus of cheerful grunts as other arms-and-oars matched his pace. Oliver grinned through the exertion. He enjoyed a solitary row too, but there was nothing like a five-man gig to really set one flying over the waves.

"Look alert!" This from Enyon in the rear. "They're gaining on us!"

It was all the incentive his team needed to reach farther forward, dip the oars in faster, and then throw themselves back again with all their effort. They would *not* be losing to Casek Wearne's team. Not this time.

He didn't dare look over to glimpse how close the other gig was.

He didn't have to. He knew if he did, if they were in view, he'd see what he least wanted to see: Casek Wearne's smirking face.

From the shore came cries and pumping arms and an entire choir full of voices shouting for whichever team they'd pinned their hopes on this morning. A few of them *always* rooted for Oliver's. A few others, always for Casek's. Most, however, made a great show of sounding out the rowers' conditions of a Wednesday morning and deciding on whom they'd wager a pint or a pudding that day.

Thanks to Enyon's bloodshot eyes, most had bet against Team Tremayne. Which had been all it had taken to wake Enyon up—his old friend hated losing like Oliver hated the blight that had been feasting on Mamm-wynn's prized roses.

The nearer they drew to shore, the less he could ignore the second gig. He could hear their oars slicing the water, off the beat of his own. He could see their prow when he leaned back. He could feel the tingle of competition in every nerve ending. *Not today, lads. Not today.*

With a last surge, he and his crossed the line, ahead by only two yards, amid the raucous cheering of half the crowd. Oliver made no attempt to quash his smile as he jumped out into the surf with his teammates and pulled the gig up onto the sand. They'd lost the last two races. High time they set things right.

"Good show today, lads. Good show." Jowan Menna, esteemed tender of the famous Abbey Gardens, took hold too and helped pull the gig out of the water. His eyes caressed the lines of the boat with nearly as much love as he gave the blooms when counting them in the Gardens each January. Nearly.

Oliver stowed his oars. "You ought to take a turn again soon, Mr. Menna."

The gardener chuckled. "I think I had better leave that to you young stallions."

Enyon barked a laugh. "You can outrow all of us, and well you know it, old man."

Though he demurred, there was no denying the gleam of satisfaction in Mr. Menna's eyes. Though twice Oliver and Enyon's age at fifty-two, he was as stalwart as the granite slabs of the island's cairns. He turned his smile on Oliver. "I've pruning to get to so can't linger long. You'll drop in later?"

"Of course. I would appreciate some time in the garden while I compose my sermon." Sometimes it was still odd to realize everyone had accepted him in place of his uncle behind the pulpit of St. Nicholas's—that he was their official vicar instead of just a lad who always listened to their woes.

Enyon slammed into his shoulder with a victory whoop, nearly knocking him back into the surf.

And Casek Wearne sneered at him. "Luck. Nothing but luck. If that one wave hadn't—"

"Stow it, Caz." Matthew Hart nudged Casek out of the way—one of the only fellows on the islands big enough to successfully pull that off. But then, the two burly men were cousins. "They beat us fair and square. Today." He winked over in the general direction of Oliver and his team. "But we'll take them next week."

"Especially if Enyon shows up so ragged again." Enyon's mother frowned at him, even as her younger son—on Team Wearne—handed her his discarded cap to hold while he wrestled his shirt over his sweaty arms. "Were you up all night carousing, Enny? It isn't like you."

It wasn't, at that. Oliver frowned at his friend too, awaiting his answer. Usually nothing could interfere with Enyon's sleep. He wasn't one to stay out too late at the pub, and the allure of a good book never fazed him a bit, though that was something that had kept Oliver up too late a time or two . . . hundred.

Enyon ran his fingers through his black hair, smoothing the damp locks away from his forehead, and yawned. "Of course not. It was—" He stopped, cutting a glance at Oliver.

Why at *him*? His frown dug in deeper, even as his hands accepted by rote the mug of piping hot tea someone passed him. Old Mrs. Gillis always had it ready for the racers when they got back. "What?"

"It's nothing. Probably. Just . . ." Enyon shrugged and cast his glance out at sea. "I couldn't sleep. Kept hearing . . . things. Not sure what, but it was coming from the direction of Piper's Hole. Reminded me of those old ghost stories." Though he laughed, it was rusty. And the gaze he sent back to Oliver said he knew very well how that sounded. "You probably think I'm mad."

Casek snorted a laugh. "Well, if anyone knows mad, it's him."

Oliver's muscles tightened across his shoulders, as did his fingers around his mug. It had been seven long years since he'd last plowed his fist into Casek Wearne's nose. He recited *"The vicar oughtn't to get in tussles"* so often it had become a silent mantra marching through his mind whenever he was near him. But if Casek kept insulting Mamm-wynn, wisdom may yet lose the battle. "Watch yourself, Wearne."

"Or what?" Casek shouldered his way close—too close—and ignored the mug of steaming tea held out to him like an invitation for peace. "Will you have your mad old grandmother put a curse on my head?"

Oliver jerked toward him, not entirely sure he was in control of his arms and legs, so involuntary did the lunge feel. But a big hand, rich soil forever staining its cuticles, landed on his chest. And another matching one on Casek's, pushing them apart. Mr. Menna's stern face came into focus. "That'll be enough, lads. Let's not give the tourists anything to laugh about, aye? The vicar and the headmaster, of all things."

Oliver sucked in a long breath, fingers so tight around his mug that it probably would have snapped had it been one of Mamm-wynn's delicate teacups instead of the stout ceramic Mrs. Gillis brought to the shore for them. He met Casek's taunting gaze. "She's off-limits, Wearne. You ought to know that. If you had a shred of decency—"

"You've never given the Wearnes any credit for that, though, have you?"

Mrs. Gillis stepped into the space Mr. Menna had made between them, pressing the hot mug to Casek's chest. "Let bygones be bygones, both of you. And you, have a bit of respect. Mrs. Tremayne's mind may not be what once it was, but it's no fault of anyone's. It comes with age."

The comfort, if that's what it was meant to be, settled over Oliver about as comfortably as sackcloth. He edged back, glad the gig had been pulled totally clear, out of his way. He wanted to say his grandmother's mind was just fine, thank you very much. He wanted to say that anyone who thought otherwise just didn't understand how to listen to her anymore. He wanted to say that if he failed to give the Wearnes any credit, it was because they'd gone out of their way to prove they didn't deserve it. Casek with his constant taunting. And worse still, his twin brother's treachery two years ago.

It was their fault Oliver's family was fractured. *Theirs*. But none of them had ever been man enough to admit it.

Too much to say here and now, with not only half of Old Grimsby but also a collection of holiday-goers watching. He shook his head, handed his mug back to Mrs. Gillis, and strode off. Enyon shouted after him, but he ignored him. He'd go home, bathe, eat. Pray. And likely then need to pray some more to rid his spirit of this creeping fog of frustration. Pay a visit to the Floyds, who were both ailing. Help Mr. Menna in the Gardens while his sermon percolated through his brain.

Forget Casek Wearne. Again.

His gaze tracked, as always, to the hill above town, where Tremayne property came into view as it tumbled down into the sea. Well, not that it was technically theirs—the Duke of Cornwall owned all the Scillies. But some long-ago duke had granted the Tremaynes a permanent lease of this little slice of heaven, and for generations it was where they'd all chosen to stay, rather than on the small estate on the mainland that they *did* own. That other land produced enough in rents and income to provide what Tresco couldn't. But this was where the Tremayne heart had always belonged.

And that hill was where Morgan had always stood to watch the morning races—or sat, if it was a bad day. He'd always been there, always cheering for whichever team Oliver was on. And when Oliver reached the crest, he'd always say the same thing. *"I daresay my little brother is the best athlete in all of Cornwall."*

More brotherly pride than any truth, but Oliver had given up arguing with him long ago. He'd just laugh. Clap an arm around Morgan if he'd been standing or take hold of the handles of his wheelchair if not. They'd go together back to the house, where Mamm-wynn and Beth would be just stirring, where Mrs. Dawe would have breakfast ready on the sideboard.

But Morgan wasn't on the hill. Would never again be on the hill. And Beth wasn't inside mumbling about whatever odd dream she'd just had. And Mamm-wynn . . . He frowned when movement on the hillock did catch his eye—the flutter of a shawl in the ocean's perpetual breeze.

What was Mamm-wynn doing out in the morning damp? Muttering something that was half frustration and half prayer, he kicked his pace from walk to run, feet eating up the well-worn path through the waving seagrass.

She looked like a wren perched there, slight and small and so dainty he was afraid she might just spread her arms wide and let the wind carry her off. His chest squeezed tight, so tight he could scarcely breathe.

What would he do when she left him too?

Not yet, Lord. Please. But she was ninety-five last February. It would happen. Someday it would happen. And how Beth could leave now, knowing how fragile their grandmother had grown—

No, he mustn't think that way either. His sister had a right to live her life. And if that meant a summer away, rubbing elbows with the incomers visiting St. Mary's . . . well, he didn't see the allure. But he prayed every day it would be enough to satisfy her. That she'd come home in September and forget all her fool ideas about needing something more, something bigger, something *else*.

She was always after the *else*, Beth was. Despite it always disappointing her.

"Mamm-wynn." It emerged breathlessly as he crested the hill and neared her.

His grandmother smiled and held out a hand toward him, all delicate bones and paper-soft skin. Her eyes were clear. It eased him some. Until she asked, "Where's Beth? She isn't where she ought to be."

The tightness turned to heaviness, weighing him down until he was sure he'd sink straight through the sandy soil and all the way to bedrock. "She's just over to St. Mary's, Mamm-wynn. Remember? She wanted to spread her wings a bit this summer."

"My little rosefinch, always wanting to fly." She smiled, though it fluttered down into a frown. "Are you certain she's there, Ollie?"

"Of course I am." Though even as he said it, worry slithered through him. She was supposed to write twice a week—it was his one request. He'd sworn he wouldn't even step foot on the big island from May until September unless it was necessary for business, that he'd give her this semblance of independence so long as she wrote to him every Tuesday and Friday. A quick note to say all was well.

It had been a perfectly reasonable request, hadn't it? Better, as he'd pointed out, than simply asking all the neighbors who boated between the islands for an update on her.

So why had it been two weeks since her last note?

He cast a gaze in the general direction of St. Mary's, but glowering at the island wouldn't make his sister remember her word. So, he wrapped an arm about their grandmother instead and guided her back toward the house. "Let's get you back inside. I can hear your cup of tea calling to you."

She chuckled and let herself be led. "All right, dearovim." Leaning close, she whispered, "You were always my favorite."

His lips pulled into a smile. She'd always said it to all of them—and loud enough for them all to hear. And somehow, they each believed her too. They were *all* her favorites, Morgan and Beth and him. Her favorites of all the people in the Scillies, in England, in the world. That was what made their little house here all they ever needed. What had helped Morgan never to rail at how his infirmities kept him home. What made Oliver eager to hurry back during each holiday from university and take up the mantle of the church here, rather than looking for a living elsewhere, when his uncle stepped down four years ago. What made Beth . . .

He sighed at the circuit of his own thoughts. He didn't know what made Beth do anything these days. Baffling creature. She too had insisted on going to the mainland for her schooling. But why hadn't her experience taught her all she needed to know about the society to which their father's family technically belonged? They'd never accept the Tremaynes. They'd always snub them the moment they realized their mother's side wasn't quite so sterling. They'd always look down on them for being too much a part of the islands, not present enough in London, their holdings too modest to be of any account. In her year away, she'd only ever made one friend worth mentioning. So why her constant yearning for a Season? Why, *why* the insistence to get away again this summer?

Mamm-wynn reached over and patted his stomach, hugging him from the side as they walked. "You're fretting, Ollie. What does the Good Book say about that?"

He breathed a laugh. "Somehow, it's always easier to quote those passages for another than live it for myself. Especially when it comes to Beth."

The moment he said her name, he regretted it. Mamm-wynn's eyes clouded over, and her gaze wandered to the sea. "Where is Beth? She isn't where she ought to be."

This time he sighed. "No. She isn't." And if she had her way, she'd probably charm some visiting nobleman who was holidaying on St. Mary's and let him take her away forever, leaving them. Drawn like a moth to some flame he couldn't even see.

"There you are!" Mrs. Dawe rushed into the garden, worry drawing lines out from her mouth as she came to his grandmother's other side and gently took her other arm. "You had me right worried, Mrs. Tremayne, vanishing on me as you did."

Mamm-wynn straightened her spine, raising herself to her full height—all five feet of it. "A lady has a right to take a morning stroll when she wishes." She cast a mischievous little grin Oliver's way, which shored up a few of the sagging places in his spirit. "And to watch her boy best those Wearnes in the race."

Blessed laughter tickled his throat, spilled into the sea air, joined the calls of the gulls cruising overhead. He leaned down to place a kiss on her too-soft cheek. "I had better get ready for the day." His gaze sought Mrs. Dawe's.

She nodded, a promise in her eyes. "Go on, then. The missus and I will get settled with some tea and porridge, won't we, dearover?"

He let her lead his grandmother inside, but Oliver hung back for a moment more. Turned, scanned the coastline, the water, the smaller isles beyond. So beautiful, this place where the Lord had planted them. The loveliest spot in all the world. He could live out his life here and never regret a day of it.

His gaze snagged on a flutter of something white against the rocks of Samson Island. It looked too random to be a bird—probably just a bit of rubbish that had washed up on the rocks and that the wind was now playing with. Some local would boat over and snag it free, dispose of it properly. They took pride in their islands, did the Scillonians. But for a moment, the way it blew called to mind the stories Tas-gwyn Gibson had used to tell all the children huddled about his knees. No one on all the isles could weave a yarn like his mother's father. Tales of pirates and ghosts and . . .

He frowned. What sounds had kept Enyon up last night? He wasn't the kind to be spooked by a piece of snagged rubbish on the rocks . . . though granted, of all the lads on Tresco, he *did* have the richest imagination. They'd all played no end of jokes of him when they were younger, just to make him run in fright. But that was ages ago, when they were boys. He wasn't so impressionable now.

Oliver pivoted back to the house, to the bath, to breakfast. He'd add another stop to his outing today, that was all. The Floyds. The Gardens. And then he'd find his best friend before he came home.

3

ome. Mabena Moon stared out the window of their rented house, still not able to believe she was back. Feet once again on the islands she swore they'd never touch until the last whisper of *him* was gone from them for good. Back once more where everyone would know her name. And her family. And her business. Back where every turn and every step carried a memory.

Her fingers knotted in the heather-blue yarn she'd scooped from Lady Elizabeth's drawers the day before, even as her eyes stayed on the view of ocean and sky and islands. Mrs. Pepper hadn't taken the time to recognize her yesterday—but other Scillonians wouldn't be so oblivious. They wouldn't all be fooled by the neatly pinned hair that she'd once let fly free in forever-tangled curls. They would look past the prim and proper clothing expected of a lady's maid that she never would have donned before she left. *A wild soul*, that's what her neighbors used to call her.

She stroked a thumb along the pattern of the shawl she clutched like an anchor. Maybe she was—or had been. But that was in a different life. She wasn't that Mabena anymore. She was just Moon now. Trusted maid of Lady Elizabeth Sinclair, sister of the Earl of Telford.

A jagged nail caught in the yarn, and she let out a sigh. All right, so obviously some of the old Mabena lived on, otherwise she never would have given in to that anxious beating of her heart last week and convinced Libby to come here for the summer. But she'd been worried, when the letters stopped after that last startling one.

And she'd been right to be worried, clearly. Where the devil had Beth gone? She should have been *here*, in this very place. This beautiful shawl that Mrs. Tremayne had knitted for her ought to have draped her shoulders, not been left in a drawer. And while Mabena had once been the sort to follow a whim wherever it took her, hardly caring if her family knew where she'd gone, Beth had never done the same. Oh, she'd adventured aplenty, it was true—but never without letting her family know. Yet here Mabena was, in the house Beth Tremayne had let for the summer but then vanished from.

Her pulse quickened again. Something was amiss. She could only pray, if her prayers weren't as out of practice as her rowing, that it was something as simple as an unplanned trip to the mainland. But Beth hadn't mentioned anything that could lure her there in her last letters. Which left Mabena with her fears of something . . . *else*, though she didn't know what it might be.

And since the blighted islanders couldn't be trusted to care for the hearts of their daughters—Mabena was proof of that—what choice did that leave her but to come home and look after Beth herself?

"Mabena?"

She looked up to find Libby in the threshold of her room, a smile on her face and a few books in her hands, including her sketchbook and pencils. "I'm going to follow that path down to the shore. Perhaps wander a bit."

She didn't invite Mabena along. And Mabena couldn't blame her. There was nothing like exploring a new place unhindered—and there was no safer place to let a young woman wander than along these shores. She couldn't get lost, there was no traffic to speak of, and the islanders had long ago learned to keep a watchful eye on visitors. So, ignoring the stern image of Lady Telford's face that flooded her mind, she nodded. "I'll have luncheon ready for you at noon."

Libby's grin was pure bliss. "Don't feel obligated—I *can* make my own sandwich, you know. If you want to go over to Tresco today to see your family, you're welcome to do so. You know I'll be perfectly content here."

She'd meant to take a few days first, get used to the idea of being in the Scillies again before taking that final step home. Maybe even give the gossip time to reach Mam and Tas. *"Mabena's back! Though she doesn't look much the wild soul we knew. Serving some tourist as maid, of all things."*

Not that her parents didn't know what she'd been doing. They'd sent Ollie after her the once, to try to talk her home, to show her that she needn't subject herself to such a life. As if Mabena gave a fig about what he might say, just because he had an official title to make his ever-offered counsel more legitimate. He was still just Ollie.

Did he realize Beth had vanished? She couldn't think so, or he'd have been here. He'd have collected her belongings and taken them back to Tresco. Every local in the Scillies would have been out scouring the beaches and caves for her.

She folded the shawl. Maybe she *would* boat over to Tresco today. Just to hear what any gossip was concerning Beth. She'd say nothing—not until she knew more. If Beth just wanted some independence and to escape from the prying eyes of the people who had known her all her life, Mabena wouldn't be the one to ruin it for her.

But if there was cause to worry, she'd know it before the day was out.

She nodded to Libby. "I may, at that. Thank you, my lady."

Libby hugged her pile of books to her chest. "Totally selfless of me."

She laughed—she couldn't help it. Libby was definitely not like any other nobleman's daughter she'd ever run across. Which was possibly the only reason she'd survived two years as a maid. "Oh yes, I'm certain of that. Get on with you, then. And take your key, as I'll lock up behind myself when I go."

"Already have it." Patting her pocket in proof, Libby pivoted away. "Have fun!"

"You too." Mabena shook her head in amusement as Libby darted away, her hair in a thick braid of honey blond better suited for a girl of sixteen than a young lady of twenty, and her clothes simple enough that she'd blend in more with the locals than the tourists.

And she was, without question, about to have a brighter day than Mabena would.

Telling herself the reason she lingered was to watch the lady safely reach the beach below, and not because of any lack of courage when it came to facing her past, Mabena sat a few more minutes at the window, worrying the shawl. Beth's favorite shawl, ever since her grandmother had finished it before she left the isles for finishing school. She wouldn't just leave it behind if she went somewhere.

Anxiety feasted on her insides again, forcing her to her feet. Enough dillydallying. She wasn't back for her own sake—she was back for Beth's. Setting Mrs. Tremayne's handiwork on the chair she vacated, she snatched up her straw hat and pinned it in place, wishing its brim were a bit wider so she could dip her head and hide beneath it whenever someone too familiar came into view.

And *that* was an inevitability, even here on St. Mary's. She didn't know everyone here as well as she did those on Tresco, but she knew them still. With only two thousand or so residents on all the isles combined, the only strangers she'd ever see here were the tourists.

The moment she stepped outside, pulling the door shut behind her and locking it, Mabena dragged glorious salt air into her lungs. She may not have missed the nosy neighbors while on the mainland, but she had, without a doubt, missed the isles themselves. The perpetual symphony of water lapping shore. The cry of countless birds. The scents of sea and plants and . . . yes, the Polmers' bakery, which was tantalizingly close to this seaside cottage. Perhaps she'd just slip in and . . .

No. She knew the Polmers too well. And *he* had always gone there every time his feet touched the soil of St. Mary's. She'd avoid such places, at least for now.

She'd avoid Hugh Town altogether. Instead of the road into the village, she chose the sandy track that wound its way through the high grasses, hugging the shoreline. It would deliver her to the quay, where any locals with boats would be, ready to charge tourists a modest fee for a little tour or ferrying to another island, or come over for their own purposes. It wouldn't be difficult, either way, to find someone to take her the rest of the way home.

Maybe Enyon would be here—it was Wednesday, after all. He could well have come over with a fresh supply of painted knickknacks and framed photographs for the tourist shop. Yes, Enyon was likely, and she wouldn't object to riding home with him. Or with Matty, if it came down to it. Matty went between the islands nearly every day in the summer. Or there'd be a lad or two—too old for school and home already from their morning of fishing—come to get the latest supplies from the ferry. That could be her best option, as the adolescents who clamored for those tasks might not look closely enough to realize they knew her.

She reached the quay, her gaze drifting over her options. Any of the ones she'd named would do, so long as they could take her over now and not make her wait hours on end. She'd just find someone ready to shove off, like whoever was in the little blue sloop far to the right. She picked her way over the smooth rocks and sand, trying to identify the bloke merely by the backside he was presenting her as he leaned over, into his boat, to stow something.

Her lips turned up. A game she and Beth had played a time or two when they were but giggling girls themselves. Though from this distance, all she could tell was that whoever-he-was was a man full-grown, not a slip of a lad yet to come into his breadth. He wore rather standard island garb, though neat enough to make her think he wasn't a fisherman. Trousers in brown, a crisp white shirt with sleeves rolled up past the elbow—revealing well-muscled forearms, at that—a knitted waistcoat in tan, and a flat cap on his head that wouldn't be stolen by the first stout breeze. Could be any number of men.

But it wasn't, she saw as he straightened and turned, once she was too near to find a hiding place. It was, blast her luck, a Wearne.

There was nowhere to hide, unless she wanted to dive into the surf and take shelter behind a boat. Her only option was to pivot on her heel, which she promptly did. Running would only gain his attention—so she would just act like any other half-lost tourist and meander about for a few minutes, until he was on his way. He'd never know her from behind, not with her hair combed flat, pinned neatly, and covered with the hat. Not with this prim gown of dark grey encasing every inch of her. Not with—

"Benna?" A laugh and pounding feet over the rocks and sand. "Mabena Moon!"

Drat and blast. She came to a halt—she'd never outrun him, not in a thousand tides—her hands curling into fists at her sides. For one moment, she allowed herself the indulgence of eyes squeezed shut. But then she dragged in a breath and spun again to face him.

Only Casek, at least. Not Cador. Small blessings. Though they looked enough alike that she couldn't make herself smile over the difference. "Caz."

Her greeting, hard as the granite stones of Giant's Castle, did nothing to wipe the grin from his lips. Ollie had always hated that grin—a smirk, he called it, and he seemed to think Casek only ever donned it to taunt him.

He may have a point, in general. But as Caz strode her way, gaze sweeping over her as if she were half-apparition, she knew the look had nothing to do with Oliver Tremayne. "Mabena Moon," he said again, this time with disbelief in his tone. "Didn't expect ever to see you back here."

She lifted her chin. And fought the sudden urge to pull off her hat and toss it to the waves so she could feel the bolstering strength of the wind in her hair. But she'd just have to settle for righteous anger. "And why, I wonder, is *that*?"

Casek halted a few feet away, hands raised in truce but that grin still playing at the corners of his mouth. "You can't blame me for what Cador's done, can you?"

She folded her arms over her chest. "I don't see why not. You Wearnes were always the all-for-one sort."

He snorted a laugh. "As if your own family's any different?"

A lift of her brows was the only answer she'd give him to that one.

He didn't seem to require any other. Just chuckled, and it sounded like *his* always had, a deep rumble of surf on stones. "What are you doing home, Benna?"

She debated half a dozen answers before deciding on the one that would seem to have the least to do with her. With a hand waved in the general direction of the cottages, she said, "My employer's holidaying here. She's given me the day to see my family, so I thought I'd find someone to take me to Tresco."

That steady look of his didn't shift any, though his eyes danced like the light on the waves. "If you think for a moment I'll believe that you just let your . . . *employer* decide to come here without exerting any opinion on the matter, then you don't give me near enough credit. Mabena Moon lets no one else decide something for her."

She hoped her blink, long and slow, was as disdainful as she meant it to be. "I'm a lady's maid, Casek Wearne. I've no right to exert my opinion."

Why did anger dance through the light in his eyes? He shook his head. "Why've you gone and done such a fool thing, anyway? You're better than that."

"Am I?" Perhaps her words came out with every ounce of bitterness she felt—and she let them. "Your brother would disagree."

"My brother's a blamed idiot, as everyone well knows." Casek's brows could hike upward with every bit as much disdain as hers could. "But as I'm *not*, I won't for a moment believe your *employer* dragged you here against your will. You'd sooner resign whatever position you found than return. 'Not until the sun falls into the sea'—isn't that what you said when you stormed off?"

"Might have been." And she'd meant it at the time. Still would have, if not for that last letter from Beth—and then the cessation of all letters from Beth. Some things were more important than her own mangled heart. "But as I certainly didn't come home to discuss my business with a Wearne, I'll just find another way over to Tresco, thank you, and—"

His bark of laughter interrupted her, and he waved a hand at the quay, filled with boats anchored in the shallow water but currently empty of people. "Take a look around, Benna. Unless you want to wait for someone else's leisure, I'm your option just now. So . . ." He took a diagonal step back and held out a hand with a flourish toward his sloop. "Allow me, my 'ansum."

She looked first to the paths leading here, willing some other acquaintance to come whistling her way. None. Which was just her luck, wasn't it? Her fist squeezed tight again until her nails dug into her palms, and she sucked in a long breath. She'd like to declare that she'd sooner swim home than ride with him, or "borrow" one of the other crafts—something she'd done a time or two over the years. But this blighted dress was too restrictive to allow for rowing or sailing.

And this was for Beth. So, she hissed the breath out again and jerked forward, lifting her skirt out of the way and taking some small pleasure in the way her stomping steps sprayed a bit of wet sand onto his trousers. "Fine. But because you're the only option."

His chuckle drove home what every Scillonian already knew—that Casek Wearne never lacked for confidence, and no one else's opinion of him ever made a dent in it.

She gathered her skirt a little higher to prepare to step into his boat, squealing a protest when hands landed on her waist and she was hoisted into the air. Though her feet were on the bottom of the boat a moment later and he let her go again, it didn't keep her from spinning round and smacking him in the arm. "Brute."

He was grinning. Of course. "Just helping a lady, that's all. You look so prim and rigid in that getup, I thought you'd need the assistance."

"You're lucky I'm lady enough to refrain from punching you square in the nose." It still had a bump on it from when Ollie had done so when they were nineteen, and she wouldn't mind adding another. Though it wouldn't be half so satisfying as delivering the blow to his brother.

"I'm utterly terrified." He climbed in after her, pulling the anchor

39

up as he sat. His hands then found the rigging, and within a minute he'd caught the wind in the newly unfurled sails, and they were off.

Just to poke at him, once they were in open waters, she asked, "Who won the race this morning?"

His scowl was all the answer she needed, which brought laughter to her lips.

He settled into his seat with his hand on the tiller. "We'll take them next week. Especially if Enyon keeps losing sleep because of ghost stories."

"Ghost stories?" She wasn't sure whether to be curious or simply amused. "I thought he'd outgrown such tales."

"Apparently not. He was going on this morning about hearing something in Piper's Hole and seeing lights from his window." He shook his head, but then he glanced over his shoulder, back toward Hugh Town. "There were rumblings in the village about something, too, though. Shadows on the shore. Dogs barking at all hours. Mr. Gibson, as you'd expect, was quick to launch into tales of pirates and smugglers."

He would. It softened her. She'd have to make certain she was at his house at teatime so he could tell her a few tales too.

Her feet bumped against a box, and as she looked down at it, she finally thought to wonder *why* the headmaster of Tresco's school was over on St. Mary's of a Wednesday afternoon. "Third term isn't over yet. What are you doing here?"

"Had to pick up the new slates we'd ordered." His eyes lit in a way she still had a hard time reconciling, even after knowing him from the very day she was born. She never would have taken him for the sort to get excited about academia. And likely he wouldn't have developed said excitement for it either had he not been in perpetual competition with Oliver. Through their childhood, they'd always been locked in a struggle for the highest marks, the top spot in the class.

Mabena shook her head. "Headmaster." Not at all what she'd expected of him. Of course, the role she'd imagined for him was *pirate*, and there weren't too many of those positions available these days. Though if his job brought him to St. Mary's regularly to fetch items for the school . . . She tried to keep her tone casual as she asked, "Are you over here often, then?"

"Once or twice a week. Why?" *His* tone went taunting. "Hoping to see me while you're here?"

"Right. That's it."

He made an exaggerated wince. "Cut to the quick by the lady's sarcasm, as always. Some things haven't changed, at least, I see."

But how to address the things that had without rousing more curiosity than she wanted from him? She went for a chuckle and cast a look back at St. Mary's. "I thought to run into Beth by now. She's summering on St. Mary's, isn't she?"

His hum wove through the wind, tangled with the sounds of water against hull. "Much to Tremayne's annoyance." He smiled as he pronounced that. "Went over sometime in April, I think, so she could have her pick of cottages before the incomers started pouring in."

The part she knew. What she didn't was where she was *now*. "She mentioned it in a letter. Said Ollie had promised to let her have her privacy and not so much as step foot on the big island unless it was absolutely necessary." It was the sort of promise the whole of Tresco must be chuckling over.

Casek certainly did. "That's right. When last I saw Beth, she seemed properly pleased with that—which I assured her I understood completely. I'd want to escape him at the first opportunity too."

Mabena snorted a laugh. "And she no doubt was quick to retort."

"She *is* a Tremayne."

That she was. "When did you last see her? Do you know which cottage she'd let?" Better to make it sound like she was simply looking for a friend.

His heavy brows drew together. "Must have been . . . what, a fortnight ago? Perhaps three weeks. Walking along with a few tourists—wouldn't even acknowledge me, though that's no great surprise. She's taken one of the cottages along the garrison wall, I think."

She kept her own hum even, relaxed. Cast her gaze out to sea and tried to identify the flash of wings gliding toward Samson. "I'll have to introduce her to my employer. She'll enjoy making friends with an earl's sister, I daresay."

This time his snort sounded far too derisive. "Just like a Tremayne. Always has thought herself too good for the likes of us normal Scillonians, hasn't she?"

Mabena shot him another granite look. "No. Only you Wearnes. Because she has sense."

The familiar barb served to bring his smile back to his lips anyway.

They sailed in silence for a few minutes, her mind whirling with all her questions. Nothing too terrible could have happened to Beth, surely. If it had, everyone would know it and they'd all be talking. And Casek Wearne would be the first to spout off about any failing of a Tremayne. No, her vanishing must have been quiet. But how? Why?

And why hadn't Mrs. Pepper gone to Oliver for the next rent payment rather than simply reletting the room? That made precious little sense either.

"I'm in too deep, Benna. The waters are closing over my head."

Her pulse skittered as the words from Beth's last letter flitted through her head again. Mabena and Beth had gotten themselves trapped in one of the caves once as the tide came in. They'd been tagging along with the older boys, though they oughtn't to have been. They'd been trying to stay out of sight and ended up too far into a crevice when the tide turned. They'd screamed and cried as the waters rushed into the crevice, certain they'd drown. Would have, had Oliver and Enyon and Cador not rescued them.

It wasn't an image Beth would use lightly.

"Aren't you going to ask?"

She started at Casek's voice, blinked to refocus her gaze on him. "Ask what?"

The look he sent her probably did wonders for keeping squirming adolescent boys in line. "About Cador."

The mere sound of his name in her ears—one that hadn't filled them for over two years—brought her chin up and made her fingers

42

dig into the splintering wood of her bench. "What could I possibly want to know about *him*?"

He chuckled. "All right, so you're too proud to ask. But you no doubt want to know."

No. She didn't. Though she couldn't unclench her jaw long enough to tell him so.

"He's in London now. Says that's where all the writers of any substance gather. His first book of poetry was published about six months ago."

So he wasn't here. No risk, at least, of running into the person she least wanted to see. Or catching a glimpse of him at a pub or in a gig or walking hand in hand with—

She turned her face away, wishing she could unknot her shoulders. Wished she could summon the polite words to her lips that would prove she didn't care. *I wish him well.* Or maybe, *Your mam must be proud of him.* But when she opened her mouth, what came out instead was, "I hope the critics rip him to shreds."

She never was any good with polite.

4

There. Libby squinted at the drawing, finally satisfied that she had the storm petrel's webbed feet drawn proportionately. And the distinctive bump on its beak too. According to the guidebook that sat open beside her, its pages weighted with rocks to keep it open, the *Hydrobates pelagicus* she'd been sketching must be an adolescent, given the narrow white bar on its upper wing.

She smiled, remembering its awkward shuffle when it had landed briefly on the shore and the fluttering, nearly bat-like movement of its wings as it flew. It didn't hold a place in the hierarchy of nature as a strong bird, a fast bird, or a particularly beautiful bird.

But it was hugely migratory, the book said. That small fellow—or lady, one couldn't tell gender at a glance—would see South Africa. Mauritania. Turkey. It would dive in waters she'd never touch, feast on jellies and small fish round the world, and somehow find its way back here again next year.

How lovely it must be to know your place in the world without ever having to think about it. To feel no need to defend yourself to your peers just because your flight wasn't soaring like an eagle's or your dive as deep as a murre's. To simply eschew walking on land most of the time when your feet weren't suited for it.

How lovely to just be who you were meant to be.

Who God made you to be. That's what Mama would have said. Libby sharpened her pencil to a fine tip, leaned close to her page, and added the small claws at the tip of each web. Satisfied with the addition, she sighed and looked up. The last thing in the world she ever wanted to do was disappoint her mother—and even worse, make her worry for her immortal soul. But much of what the vicar at the village near Telford Hall espoused from his pulpit made no sense to her. It contradicted the things her own eyes observed.

She didn't see creatures in need of a God to form every claw and beak and feather and dictate to them how they must work. What she saw were creatures capable of adaptation—creatures that evolved to fit whatever environment they were in. Creatures that fought and killed and ate and were eaten, that mated and reproduced and defended their young.

Breathe the word *mated* around the ladies of society, though, and one would be shushed with horrified glances. Which she knew first-hand. Their husbands may talk of breeding horses and dogs, but a lady wasn't to speak of such matters.

Libby pushed aside the rocks holding down the guidebook's pages and snapped it closed. Mama said each person was designed by the loving hand of God too, fashioned in their mother's womb, known before they were born. But if so, then why—*why*—had she been made to be so ill-fitting an addition to the world in which she'd been placed? Why was she strapped with expectations that chafed so terribly?

Asking her to dance and flirt and attend musicales and teas was like asking a storm petrel to walk confidently on land or dive a yard beneath the surface. She wasn't suited for it.

And now she'd ruined her lovely morning with the very thoughts she'd hoped to leave behind her on the mainland. Frustrated with herself, she closed her sketchbook. She'd put down images of two birds and three beetles as well as a detailed diagram of the flower to her right that she'd yet to identify. The birds she'd found in the guide-book, so she'd been able to write their Latin names, their common names, and her own descriptions of them. The beetles she'd look up when she was back at the house, where her entomology book was still

45

in her trunk. The flower . . . she didn't yet have a book to teach her about the flora of the Scillies. She'd poke about the shops in Hugh Town sometime in the next few days though. Surely there would be a bookshop that had something. Or a local who could teach her.

What she needed was a botanist. Her lips tugged up a bit as she stacked the guidebook on top of the sketchbook. Perhaps one *particular* botanist. The man who had quite literally stumbled upon her in the gardens of Telford Hall two years ago, while she'd been flat on her stomach, watching a caterpillar spin its chrysalis on the underside of a leaf. She didn't know his name—there'd been no shortage of people coming and going in those days, offering their condolences to the family after Papa's death.

Comfort, for her, had only been found out of doors. Away from the mourners. The guests. The black dresses and veils. The whispers of what a shame it was that Lord Telford had lost the ongoing battle with consumption at that particular time, when it meant postponing her coming out. As if she could care about presentations and balls and gowns when her father lay dying. As if she ever would have cared anyway.

So, she'd been hiding from them all, as she did every chance she got, in the gardens. Mabena had only just been hired, and she'd won a place in Libby's heart by covering for her and helping her slip out. She'd hunkered down to watch the caterpillar, her sketchbook under her hand and the Latin names flowing from her fingers.

When she'd heard the startled footsteps behind her, she'd thought for sure she'd be in trouble—there she was, the daughter of the house, lying on her stomach in the gardens. But instead of a horrified gasp or a quick rebuke, polished black shoes had come into view seconds before the owner of them had crouched down beside her.

He must have been a friend of Bram's, given his age. But her brother hadn't called her in for any introductions, which meant he wasn't of a society that he deemed acceptable for her. Probably a school chum who had heard about his loss and been in the neighborhood. She didn't know. And it hadn't mattered.

All that had mattered was that he watched the caterpillar with her for five silent minutes. And then had touched a finger to the leaf and told her how the plants in the Brassicaceae family were the favored food source of the *Pieris rapae* when they were in their larval stage. He'd answered her questions about the mustard plant's reproduction. Then told her about the neighboring stalks and stems too, while she sat up and took frantic notes.

She didn't know who he was. But he'd brightened an otherwise miserable time in her life, and she thought of him every time she wondered about a plant whose name she didn't know. The Botanist—her version of a fairy godmother . . . or god*father*, as the case may be. Or perhaps god*brother*, if such a thing existed, as he was far too young to be a parental figure.

Were he here, he'd tell her about the flowers nestled among the grasses. He'd examine her sketch of them and perhaps correct a small detail she'd gotten wrong. He'd provide the Latin names and tell her about the cycles of blooming and seeding. Probably then enlighten her about the commercial flower trade that she knew provided much of the Scillies's livelihood and how each bloom had made its way here.

But he wasn't here, of course. So she'd have to settle for finding a book.

Her fingers traced the debossed design on the cover of the other book she'd brought out with her. Certainly not a treatise on flora. No, *Treasure Island*. She'd glanced through it yesterday afternoon but had been too aware of all the people about to really look overlong. Now she had it all to herself.

Handwritten notes were all throughout the pages. In the margins. Occasionally between the lines, or circling words. The script was feminine, leading her to guess that it was another something left behind by the Other Elizabeth, whose things were scattered through the house.

It took only a few minutes of note reading, however, to realize that she had no context to make sense of all these scrawled words. They certainly had nothing to do with the story. Well, the little sketch of a pirate vessel, fully rigged, could have been, she supposed. And the treasure chest. But the words made no sense at all in that context.

Some of them seemed to be almost a laundry list, though she had no idea what sort of laundry it might refer to. The items were just odd abbreviations—like *cnm* and *svw*—with tally marks beside them.

She flipped to another page, her gaze traveling over what was, at least, full words. A poem, it seemed.

> What a lovely Tuesday afternoon
> But it's Wednesday, sir, I fear
> No matter, that, for the sky is blue
> And the waters crystal clear

How funny, given that it was Wednesday today. Smiling a bit over that, she turned another page. And frowned. *Once upon a time, there was a princess. She lived on an island of rocks and bones, with no one to keep her company aside from the fairies.*

Why in the world would the Other Elizabeth write a fairy tale in the margins of another book? A fairy tale that seemed to stretch on for quite a ways at that. She flipped several more pages, and all the handwritten words on them seemed to be part of the same story.

"I beg your pardon. Elizabeth?"

Libby started at the voice, smacking the book shut and turning on her rock. She didn't know the voice. Or at least she didn't *think* she knew the voice. She couldn't. Anyone who knew her would call her *Lady* Elizabeth. Still, she turned before that thought could process, curiosity eclipsing the surprise.

A man probably in his thirties stood a few feet away. He looked wind-blown, cheerful, and utterly normal in his holiday clothes—shirt with sleeves rolled up, grey trousers, no waistcoat or jacket. Middling brown hair, brown eyes, average height. The only thing remarkable about him was his nose—prominent and a bit turned up at its tip. Well, that and the satchel pulling down his shoulder. He was entirely unfamiliar.

He didn't seem put off by her lack of greeting though. Merely smiled and said, "What a lovely Tuesday afternoon."

What? Did he just say . . . ? Before she could think better of it, she heard herself reciting the next line of the poem. "But it's Wednesday, sir, I fear."

He chuckled and looked to the sky as if it had a calendar printed upon it. "So it is. Here you are, then." He reached toward her rock as he opened the satchel, sliding a huge, paper-wrapped something onto the surface a foot or so away from her books and pencils. A *heavy* something, from the looks of it. Smiling all the while, as if it were perfectly normal for a complete stranger to call her by name, exchange a line of a handwritten poem with her, give her a gift, and then just tip his cap. "Cheerio."

She blinked. "Good day." What else was she supposed to say? She could protest, she supposed, that she had no idea what he was about. But then he'd probably take that parcel back, and she couldn't deny a sudden, rather sharp desire to see what was in it. It was a rather enormous thing to be carrying around in a shoulder bag.

Curious indeed.

He whistled as he turned and tromped back through the sand and grass toward the path. A minute later he'd disappeared over the garrison wall. Libby watched him until he was gone, cataloguing everything she could think to note about him. Then, making herself ignore the parcel for a moment more, she grabbed her notebook and opened to a page at the back, jotting down her observations about him.

She scribbled down the words they'd exchanged as well as the clothes he'd been wearing. And finally the words *Brown paper–wrapped parcel, round, approximately nineteen inches in diameter. Tied with white string.*

There. She'd examined it all scientifically. She rather felt she'd earned the curiosity now as she reached for the parcel. The . . . rock? It certainly felt like one as she hefted it, which made her mouth twist. The last time someone had presented her with a rock, it had been Sheridan. And the rock had supposedly borne evidence of some ancient civilization that he claimed had once lived at the location of Telford Hall. She'd stared at it for a solid five minutes and noted absolutely nothing of interest. Had it contained a fossil or impression of a leaf, perhaps she would have seen the allure. But chisel marks or whatever caught his eye? What did that matter?

If this was more of the same . . . Well, no way to know until she opened it. A tug on the string, a folding of the paper. And she frowned again.

It definitely wasn't a tool-marked rock. It was, without question, a cannonball. A very large, very heavy cannonball.

Setting it down on the rock before her, she picked up her pencil again and described it as best she could, adding a couple sketches from the various angles that revealed wear.

A cannonball. Utterly boring, except for the mystery of the delivery.

There would be a simple, innocent explanation—there always was. And no doubt Mabena would help her determine what said explanation was later, when Libby showed her. But in the meantime, she might as well enjoy the oddity.

The growling of her stomach reminded her that the sun was directly overhead and there were luncheon fixings in the icebox in the cottage. Since she'd no doubt managed to get a sunburn on her nose already, despite her straw hat, she'd be wise to obey her stomach and go inside. At least for a while.

Perhaps tomorrow she'd bring a picnic lunch with her, like some of the other families along the beach had done. For now, she hefted the lead, grunting a bit at its weight. It had to be nearly twenty pounds.

Ten minutes later she was sitting at the little table in the cottage, her lunch on a plate before her. Never had she been gladder that she regularly horrified her sister by slipping down to the manor's kitchen and helping the cook. When she was little, the sole appeal had been pilfering snacks. But it was rather handy now to know how to take care of herself. Heaven knew if Edith ever found herself alone in a kitchen, she would just stare at the icebox, waiting for it to deliver food on a silver platter.

No, that wasn't fair. Edith would never allow herself to be alone in a kitchen to begin with.

She'd tucked away half of her sandwich, her nature journal open on the table before her so she could review her morning's work, when a knock on the door drew her attention up.

It couldn't be Mabena back already, not if she'd gone over to Tresco. Which meant Mrs. Pepper, probably, or her daughter. Perhaps a temporary neighbor.

She wiped her hands on a napkin—refraining from licking her fingers as a silent nod to Invisible Edith—and moved to the door. When she opened it, however, she didn't find a woman, as she'd expected. She found a man, this one dressed in the rougher garb of a fisherman.

And he looked her over as if *she* were the one who didn't belong in her doorway, his brows knit. "Elizabeth?"

Her brows no doubt mirrored his. "Yes. And you are?"

He started at the question, frown deepening. "Here." Somehow she didn't think that was his answer to her question—she'd never heard of Here as a surname, though what did she know? Perhaps it was Cornish. But he held out an innocuous-looking white rectangle, marking the word as command instead of answer.

An envelope, that was all. With *Elizabeth* scrawled on the front.

Was he just a courier? But who in the world would send her a note with no address on it, only her name? Mabena, perhaps? But she would have put *Lady* Elizabeth on it—unless she was trying to obey, at least in small part, Libby's desire to go unnoticed.

She forced a smile and took the letter. "Thank you, Mr. Here. Oh—here." She reached into her pocket and fished around for one of the coins she always kept there for such purposes.

Pressing it to his palm earned her another look of supreme consternation. "Em . . . thanks?"

A strange courier. Maybe the Scillonians just always ran errands for each other, as friends, and didn't expect tips for it. That would be rather lovely of them, wouldn't it? Her smile feeling a little brighter, she said, "You're welcome. Good day." And closed the door.

Not until she turned back to the table, gaze falling to the envelope, did she look closely enough to recognize that this was most assuredly not Mabena's handwriting. It was, in fact, masculine rather than feminine. But what *man* would be writing to her? The only one she could think of was Bram, but it wasn't his hand either. And he never called her Elizabeth. He had, in fact, been the one to nickname her Libby when they were children.

She flipped it over, looking for some clue. But all the turn revealed was that the envelope was sealed. No indication of who had sent it or from where.

Her gaze flicked to the table, where the lead ball rested on its paper. Where the book sat with its odd notes in the margins. Where some other Elizabeth's possessions invaded Libby's world.

The envelope wasn't for her—of that she was suddenly quite certain. Whoever the previous tenant had been, she was still getting deliveries, as surely as her belongings had still been in the drawers. And while curiosity pricked, Libby set the envelope on the table beside the cannonball without opening it.

It was one thing to have unwrapped the paper and string when she didn't realize it wasn't meant for her. It seemed somehow different to unseal a letter intended for someone else. And though she was many things of which society disapproved, she'd never been the sort to go snooping through someone else's post.

When Mabena got back this evening, she'd tell her all about the two strange men with their unsolicited gifts and see what *she* thought they should do about it.

In the meantime, she still had half a sandwich and a beach full of creatures and plants she'd yet to explore. Putting aside the other questions—and the marked-up book, too, since it only bred more of them—she finished her lunch and gathered a new armful of supplies for her afternoon. She'd spend an hour or two out collecting a few specimens for closer inspection and then get her microscope out later. She'd already determined that three o'clock would be the perfect time to set up the device at the desk by the window, when the light would be streaming inside in quantities ideal for reflecting off the mirror.

It was enough to make a girl positively giddy. She'd only had the microscope for a few months—Mama and Bram had given it to her for Christmas—and she'd already examined the cellular structure of everything she had even a mild curiosity about at Telford Hall. But who knew what might beg for a closer look here?

Armed with a basket full of slides and containers, pincers, and a scalpel, she all but skipped back down the path to the shore. She'd get a sample of the seagrasses and see if they were any different from the kind that grew at home. Perhaps she'd find a small jelly washed ashore that she could look at. For that matter, looking at water itself under magnification could reveal the most fascinating small oddities in it. How would seawater appear, as opposed to the fresh variety from the small lake at Telford Hall?

She spent a happy two hours collecting a variety of samples, blissfully ignoring the laughter and shouts from other tourists along the beach. None of them cared a whit who she was or what she was doing, which suited her perfectly. There was no brother to scowl at her and warn her to adjust her hat before she burned even worse. No sister to chide her for crouching down in an unladylike fashion. No mother to beg her to come and sit with her for a while.

Though she had a feeling she'd miss that last one in another day or two. Time spent with Mama was rarely anything but pleasant.

And, she granted as she winced upon brushing her hand against her nose, a *few* warnings about better protecting her skin from the sun might not have gone awry.

But no matter. Bent on enjoying her new freedom to the full, back at her desk, she let "Chorus of Furies" spill from her lips at top volume as she set up her microscope, angled the mirror to send a brilliant ray of illumination through the slide and up into the eyepiece, and lined up her samples. Microscope work always brought *Orfeo* to her mind and her lips, much like painting did *Carmen*. Bram teased her mercilessly about her propensity to sing opera while she worked, so she usually hummed it instead of outright singing. But Bram wasn't here to poke fun, so she let her chest and throat expand fully through "*e lo spaventino gli urli di Cerbero.*"

She opened up the correct notebook to a fresh page and twisted the cap off her fountain pen, using it as a baton to conduct herself into the final bars, her favorite part. "*Seun Dio no—*"

Before she could get out the piercing final word, a knock pounded its way through her one-girl opera. Her hands froze in midair, the right one raised, ready for the downbeat that would go along with the final "*e*."

Her cheeks went hot. What if whoever was at the door had heard her? Her finale turned to a squeak that faded into a moan. She lowered her pen-turned-baton-turned-pen-again, tossed it to the desk with the notebook, and scurried to the front door.

If it was another delivery for Other Elizabeth, she would just have to be truthful. Tell him she wasn't who he was looking for. Ask him to kindly inform all other nameless givers of oddities that they ought to direct their deliveries elsewhere for the rest of the summer.

She pulled the door open, fully prepared to greet her latest visitor with an apology for not being who he sought. But the words froze on her lips as surely as the closing bars of "Chorus of Furies" had.

It was a man, yes. But he wasn't altogether unfamiliar. And he didn't lift his brows and ask if she was Elizabeth.

No, he frowned as if the whole weight of the islands had crashed down upon his brows. "Where's my sister?"

His sister? Libby blinked, blinked again. Opened her mouth, but no words would come. She could only stare at the too-long hair, nearly black; the too-dark eyes, drowning in worry; the too-often imagined lips, not speaking now of plant species.

He'd come. Somehow all her wishing had made him appear. The Botanist. Here, at her door.

But no. Well, yes. The Botanist, to be sure—she'd recognize him anywhere. But obviously it wasn't her wishing that had conjured him. She gripped the door and gathered together all the facts as they'd been presented to her. They created a picture with many holes, but a few indisputable facts. "Is your sister by chance called Elizabeth?"

5

Oliver couldn't breathe, try as he might to suck island air into lungs well accustomed to gulping it in after a jog or a row or a quick climb from sea level. But air wouldn't come, and it had nothing to do with the run from the quay. And everything to do with the fact that the young woman standing in Beth's doorway wasn't Beth.

His fingers curled into his palm as he tried to make sense of it. But there was no sense to find. He'd gone about his morning as planned. Visited the Floyds. Puttered in the Abbey Gardens with Mr. Menna. Tried and failed to track down Enyon. Finally made his way home for tea with Mamm-wynn, ready to put everything aside and enjoy a rest.

But his grandmother wouldn't eat or drink. She just kept worrying the edge of her shawl. And when she looked at him and said, "Beth's not where she's supposed to be, Ollie. She's gone," the strangest feeling had come over him.

He'd crumbled his biscuit instead of eating it and just stared at her. *Mad.* That's what he heard in his ears, in Casek Wearne's voice. His grandmother was mad.

But he couldn't quite believe it. Not with those unwritten letters haunting him when they should have been sitting on his desk. Not with his own uneasiness nipping at him. He'd set his teacup down and forced a smile for Mamm-wynn. "I'll just check on her, shall I?"

Her eyes hadn't brightened though. If anything, the clouds in them had flashed lightning. "You won't find her, lad. But go anyway. See what you can learn."

He'd jumped into his sloop, the rigging melding with his hands. Straight here to St. Mary's, to the cottage along the garrison wall that he knew should have housed his sister. His fist upon the door. A hundred excuses ready to crowd their way to his tongue when Beth scowled at him and demanded to know why he'd interrupted her summer after he promised her independence.

But it wasn't Beth. *It wasn't Beth.* It was another young lady of a similar age, with similar golden hair in a similar braid, wearing a similar white blouse and a similar grey skirt. Similar—but not Beth.

"Is your sister by chance called Elizabeth?" The question echoed in his brain long after she finished asking it, too many thoughts knocking about with it for him to make sense of the words.

He knew her, this girl who wasn't Beth. Sort of. Had met her before, anyway, though in that first second of shock his muddled mind couldn't think where. All he knew was she wasn't one of his sister's friends—if he'd met her in Beth's company, he would have made a comment on how they looked at once alike but different. But that wasn't the image elbowing its way to the surface of his mind. No, it was . . . a garden.

He shook it off and focused on the here and now. "She's Elizabeth, yes—though we call her Beth. Are you . . . visiting her?" But that made no sense. If she was a friend of Beth's after all, she wouldn't have to ask him what her name was.

The girl stepped back from the door and waved him inside. "I think perhaps you'd better come in."

He hesitated a moment. As a vicar, he visited people all the time when otherwise a proper gentleman shouldn't; he served as a chaperone more than he needed one. But she probably didn't know that, so shouldn't she be unwilling to let a veritable stranger inside?

There was no duplicity in her eyes though, simply concern. For whatever reason, she must not be considering questions of reputation. And so long as he only stayed a few moments, no locals would question his presence here. He *was* a vicar, and one concerned for his sister to boot.

With a nod, he crossed the threshold and looked around, his gaze searching for any hints of Beth. "Forgive me for intruding. And thank you for granting me time to sort through this." He could feel his brows knitting into what Beth and Morgan had always jokingly referred to as his scholar's frown—the one he tended to wear when puzzling through a text, trying to solve a tricky problem in arithmetic, or striving to understand the mysteries of God. But try as he might to smooth it out now, it was no good. "My sister . . ."

"Isn't here, I'm afraid. Mrs. Pepper made mention of her leaving without a word, so she relet the place. To me. And my maid."

"What?" Though he'd been trying to catch a glimpse of anything that was Beth's scattered about, he spun now on his heel to stare at his makeshift hostess. "What do you mean, leaving without a word?"

Where did he know her from? It was right there, just behind his worry. If she was traveling with a maid and renting a holiday cottage, she must be a gentleman's daughter of some sort. But who? Was she the younger sister of one of his friends from school? Or perhaps of the society he very occasionally rubbed elbows with in Cornwall, when duty demanded it?

She closed the door with an artless shrug. Not the sort he often saw gentlewomen give, designed to draw attention, saturated with guile, studied. No, this was simply a shrug. Refreshingly honest. "I really don't know. But she left her things here. Moon gathered them up—I'm not certain what she did with them, but they're probably in her room."

Moon—Mabena. Recognition slammed him hard. The girl from the gardens of Telford Hall, whom he'd met when Mabena's parents had begged him to go and see if she was all right in her new position—and more accurately, see if he could talk her into coming home.

He hadn't known, when he stumbled across the girl sprawled in the dirt, that she was the daughter of the house. But he'd pieced it together in the time since, given the subtle information in Mabena's letters home.

Now he sucked in a breath and executed a quick bow. "Forgive me, Lady Elizabeth. My shock has eclipsed my manners. I didn't realize you and Moon"—it took every ounce of self-possession to remember to call her that rather than Mabena—"were holidaying here this summer."

Was that disappointment that sagged her shoulders? Why? She even let out a little breath that rang of frustration as she tucked back a tendril of hair that had slipped free of her braid. "You seem to have me at a disadvantage, sir. You know my name, but I don't recall ever learning yours."

No, their hour-long walk through the gardens at Telford Hall hadn't been cluttered with such unnecessary things. For all he'd known at the time, she could have been a governess, a maid enjoying her half day, or even a daughter of one of the many visiting families. He hadn't known, when he'd let himself be prodded to Somerset, that he'd be stumbling upon a funeral, and certainly not that he'd find the bereaved daughter covered in garden dirt. Though *had* he known at the start, he would have simply assured the Moons that Mabena would get on well enough with her.

He inclined his head. "Forgive me again. Mr. Oliver Tremayne, of Tresco."

"Tresco?" Her spine snapped straighter, and she darted a look toward the window. And presumably the islands beyond it. "But . . . then you're not one of Bram's friends. He knows no one here."

Bram? It was logic more than knowledge that told him she must mean her brother. He shook his head. "No, I've never had the pleasure of meeting Lord Telford, aside from the few minutes he granted me when I arrived at your home at so unfortunate a time." He, too, motioned, but toward her door. "I'd merely come to make certain Mabena Moon was well. Her parents asked me to make sure she was all right."

Her brows drew together, making the piercing amber of her eyes all the more striking. She regarded him with the same expression she'd been giving the chrysalis in her garden—that if she could only study it long enough, she'd unravel all its secrets. "Why would her parents ask that of you?"

There were more reasons than he knew Mabena would want him to share, so he offered the simplest one. "I'm the vicar on Tresco. And one of the few Scillonians with ties to the mainland. I'm frequently called upon to help in such ways."

He probably should have introduced himself as Mr. Tremayne of Truro Hall, as he'd done with her brother two years ago. But it wasn't who he was, not really. He belonged to Tresco, not to their estate on the mainland. And her frank eyes demanded the real truth, not the nominal one.

She nodded and then glanced around her as if looking for something. "I . . . I expect she'll be back any minute. Moon, I mean. She went over to Tresco to visit her family—but perhaps you know that? Is that what alarmed you, made you realize we were here where your sister should be?"

It was his turn to shake his head. "I haven't seen her. I came because . . . well, because my sister was supposed to be writing to me twice weekly, and she hasn't been. I was growing worried. For good reason, apparently. You say Beth's things are still here, but Mrs. Pepper said she left without warning?"

"That's right."

Where could she possibly have run off to? He'd ask Mabena when she returned. She and Beth had always been the best of friends. If anyone knew . . .

Wait. What was Mabena doing back here, renting a cottage on St. Mary's, anyway? Striving for a casual countenance, he summoned up a smile for Lady Elizabeth. "I didn't realize Mabena Moon would be coming home. I'd have thought her parents would have mentioned it."

"Oh, it was a last-minute decision." She shifted away a bit, her gaze skittering to the wall and then down to the floor. "I . . . wanted a holiday, and Moon had told me how lovely the Scillies were. We considered ourselves rather fortunate we found a cottage with a vacancy." Now those brows and the piercing eyes frowned anew. "It seems a bit less fortunate now, considering. Why don't you sit, Mr. Tremayne? I'd like to show you something. Perhaps you can help me make sense of it."

She didn't wait to see if he obeyed, just hurried off in the direction of what must be the bedrooms. Oliver looked over the kitchen and living area, trying to imagine Beth here, making her own meals and filling the space with her constant movement. He couldn't quite picture it though.

She'd always been independent, to be sure. She'd once boasted she could spend a week on one of the uninhabited islands without any help, and their father had granted her permission to prove it. She had, indeed, been quite well and happy, fishing for her meals and exploring. But that had been ages ago. In recent years, Beth had been more inclined toward drawing rooms and garden parties than survivalist skills. It was what had brought her here, after all—the promise of society on holiday. He moved into the living area and sat.

Lady Elizabeth reappeared a moment later, her arms full of books and parcels that were just a jumble until she spread them out on the low table beside a cannonball—a rather odd decoration, but he supposed Mrs. Pepper could have thought it would be charming. Though even then, he wasn't certain what he was looking at. The only familiar item in the collection was a worn copy of *Treasure Island*. He reached for it, teeth clenched. Make that *his* worn copy of *Treasure Island*. He recognized the inkblot on the back and the nick on the bottom right corner, where his pen knife had slipped one day. "She left this here?"

And why did she ever take it to begin with? She'd borrowed it as a child, yes, but she'd long since returned it. It had been on the shelf in his bedroom for the past decade. Or so he'd thought. He flipped it open to where his name, written in pencil on the end leaf, was barely legible through the smudging of time.

"Flip a bit further, if you will." Lady Elizabeth sat beside him on the sofa, a whiff of salt and sea and a hint of citrus reaching his nose. She leaned closer, clearly anticipating his obedience.

He turned a few more pages and let loose an involuntary shout of horror. "She's written in it! I'm going to box her ears! What sort of monster marks up another person's book?"

"It isn't hers?"

"No—but it's her hand that's ruined it, that's for certain." He turned a few more pages, knowing well that his exasperation came out in every breath. "Why would she even take this from my room?"

He didn't expect an answer. If there was one, it may in fact lie in the words Beth had so rudely scribbled into the margins, but he was too annoyed to read it. He was too annoyed, just now, to even wonder where his sister was. She'd better hope she was far, far away from him, though, because if she was anywhere nearby . . .

"I'm not certain as to the why, of course," Lady Elizabeth said. She reached for the book, turned it to page seventeen, and tapped one of the horrific notes. "But that one there. I'd just read it when I was down at the beach this morning, and then this fellow came along and said the first line to me. I was so startled, I just repeated the second. And then he gave me that."

Oliver's gaze followed her hands—not the white, pampered fingers one expected of a lady, but with short nails, ink stains, calluses, and enough traces of dirt under her nails that he was reminded of how much he'd liked her on their walk—to the table. No, to the cannon-ball.

He frowned. It had to be an eighteen-pounder, given the size. Too big for most of the ships that would have historically made port here, but the wear on it suggested it had been underwater. "Who did you say gave it to you?"

"I didn't. And I don't rightly know. Just some chap who asked if I was Elizabeth, recited the first line of that poem there, and then handed it to me after I said the second line."

"How very odd." He reached over and rubbed a hand over the pocked surface, then pulled it closer to the side of the table. "We see a lot of old ordnance around here. But not often examples that show water damage. I wonder if it could be from a wreck."

"A shipwreck?" She leaned closer to examine it, though surely she'd already done so. She seemed utterly oblivious, however, to how close that put her to him. Something of which most society ladies would be keenly aware at all times.

Oliver's lips twitched a bit in the corners, despite the situation. It was no wonder he hadn't guessed upon their first meeting that she was the new earl's sister. He went somber again. "I cannot think why Beth would have been receiving something like this—but that's your conclusion, I presume? This fellow mistook you for her?"

Another honest, artless shrug. "I don't know what else to think. They certainly aren't intended for me, but these men were looking for an Elizabeth."

"Men—plural?"

She lifted up an envelope and handed it to him. It was a standard size, nothing special about the paper. The only thing of note was the name scrawled across the front. *Elizabeth.* But that in itself was odd, wasn't it? "None of her friends call her Elizabeth, only Beth. And any strangers ought to be calling her Miss Tremayne. So why her given name?" He flipped it over. "You didn't open it?"

"Of course not. It clearly wasn't intended for me." She darted a glance toward the brown paper underneath the cannonball. "That one wasn't marked, and I really had no idea . . . and then it was so *heavy.*"

His chuckle scratched his throat as if it were made of pebbles. "I don't blame you, my lady. I would have opened it too."

Her smile took him back two years to that afternoon garden. It was filled with a dose of sunshine, the wonder of creation, the joy of questions still needing answers—but squeezed around the edges with the creeping vines of sorrow. Once he'd eventually realized with whom he'd had a conversation, he'd assumed the sorrow had been over her father's recent death. And perhaps it had been.

But if so, she hadn't yet managed to banish it, because those vines were still there. And while he loved a nice ivy-covered wall as much as the next person, far too often vines were parasitic. Damaging. And sorrow was the same—it could sneak into the cracks of a person's spirit and make them widen. Steal the nutrients needed. Compromise the foundation. Choke the very life out of a person.

And if there was anything worse than seeing a beautiful, healthy specimen killed by something that should have been removed by a careful gardener, he didn't know what it would be.

Seemingly of its own volition, his hand lifted, as it would have done had she been any other islander instead of an earl's sister. It landed on her shoulder, slid the length of her upper arm, and cupped her elbow. Something he'd done countless times with countless parishioners, all of whom had long ago learned not to be startled by the touch.

She clearly didn't know it. Her eyes widened, her gaze sprang to his. But even then, when colored with surprise, the sorrow was there, twined around her.

"Why are you sad?" The words emerged as a murmur as his fingers found their places around her elbow. One could tell much about a person by their elbow. Whether it was plump or bony, tight or loose, how much tension they carried there. Hers spoke of youth and strength without pretention. Pointed, the muscles leading to and from firm. Covered with simple cotton.

She sucked in a long breath. Sometimes—rarely—people would look away when he asked such questions. Evade the answers they didn't want to face. Sometimes—rarely—they would laugh away the basic human yearning to share, to be understood. He didn't think Lady Elizabeth Sinclair would be the type to do either of those things.

And he was right. Her chin sank down a few degrees, but she didn't break his gaze. "Because . . . I was planted in a garden in which I don't belong. And I don't know how to flourish there anymore."

He shook his head, his fingers tightening around her joint. "You are exactly where you need to be. The only place able to nourish your spirit."

Her gaze wandered away then, but she wasn't so much looking *from* him as looking *to* something else. Something not in this room at all. Seeing, perhaps, the family that clearly indulged her. The home in which she'd passed so many happy years, discovering new joys even after all this time. Even her presence here, so far from her family, spoke of their love for her—otherwise they never would have let her come and explore.

She let out the breath she'd drawn in, just as slowly. "Maybe. But I can't stay there forever. Expectations, you know."

He did. Oh, how he did. They were their own set of vines, left all too often to squeeze and constrict and kill. But they too could be controlled. Trained into safe places. Used to climb instead of pull one down. "I have found that when a transplant is necessary, finding a new place for the plant ought indeed to be undertaken with great care. Sometimes the shock is too great for it, and it won't survive. But other times . . . other times it will flourish in its new environs far more than it ever did in its old."

She blinked, her gaze falling to the floor. "How do you ever find such a place though? And how can you be sure you're not consigning the plant to destruction?"

"There are never such certainties in life." One never knew when a boat would overturn in a storm and steal one's parents. When disease would eat away at one's brother. When madness would steal one's grandmother's mind.

When the promise of *else* would lure one's sister away.

He gave her elbow a gentle squeeze. "This is why we don't transplant anything until it's necessary. But sometimes it is. And so, we learn what we can and make the best decision possible, do the work to the best of our ability, tend it with care. And we pray, trusting that the Master Gardener will bless our efforts."

She looked at him again, her brows lifted, and, finally, a shaft of welcome amusement bloomed in her eyes and on her lips. "You pray for your plants?"

"Each and every one of them." Both human and botanical.

She clearly understood the duality, given the sparkle in her eye. "Where exactly is your church, Mr. Tremayne?"

"I like to say all the islands are my cathedral, all the people my parishioners." He gave her a grin. "I always sense God the best outside in His creation. But if one is being specific, I'm the vicar at St. Nicholas's in Old Grimsby, on Tresco." His uncle still lived in the parish house next to it. There'd been no need for him to move, not since Oliver was happy enough to stay at home. And now . . . now home, and its perpetual lease, were his anyway.

Her smile was as sweet as nectar, though the vines hadn't gone away. "Perhaps one Sunday this summer Moon and I will find ourselves on Tresco in time for services."

"You are always welcome." He let his gaze fall back to the envelope he still held. "She'll box *my* ears if I go opening her post."

"Turnabout, then. If it was your book she wrote in."

He liked the way good humor brought a lift to her alto voice. It made another smile tickle his lips, though thinking of Beth and strange letters by unknown carriers and odd writing in his book made him too aware of the heaviness.

Mamm-wynn had been right. Beth wasn't where she ought to be. And yet here was something delivered to her. Well, let her box his ears for opening it, since it would mean appearing again to achieve the feat. He used a finger as a letter opener and ripped the top of the envelope. Peered inside, breath caught. Drew out . . .

A letter. "It's about the cannonball."

Lady Elizabeth had made no show of not watching him read. Her nose was scrunched, brows drawn together. "Does it say anything helpful?"

"I don't know if it's helpful or not. It says, 'What we can verify for you is that it is indeed an eighteen-pound shot and that few ships that used Scilly as a base in the era in question were so equipped. But there is no way to verify the exact year or the exact ship, so it's of no interest. Please focus upon the items in the *Canary*'s manifest.'" Oliver blinked at the page. "Manifest? Have you come across anything resembling a ship's manifest?" And what was the *Canary*? He couldn't recall any stories of a ship by that name, though that hardly meant anything.

Lady Elizabeth caught her lip between her teeth and shook her head. "Not that I've seen. Unless there's one written on something in invisible ink." She topped her jest with a crooked, uncertain smile.

"Mm." He grinned back. "Probably unwise to put every paper in the house to a flame to test it. I don't fancy burning up everything—that's what happened last time I tried such a trick." And his mother hadn't been exactly pleased with him when he'd dropped the candle in shock and burned a hole in her favorite tablecloth either.

"You've used invisible ink?"

At the note of pleasant wonder in her voice, Oliver's grin grew. "With Beth and our brother, Morgan. We were pretending we were pirate princes—and princess—evading our archnemesis in port."

Her frown twitched a bit at the word *princess*, but she banished it with a wistful smile. "What fun you must have had."

Why the wistfulness? "You've a sister, haven't you? And a brother, of course."

And like pollen on the breeze, her wonder blew right off her face. "Edith never liked the same games I did. Nor, for that matter, did Bram. They played together, but I was always left behind, it seemed."

Mother never let him and Morgan get away with neglecting Beth—try as they might. "And so you went outside and made a friend of nature instead."

The way she blinked up at him, clearing the memories from her eyes, said his observation startled her—at least for a moment. Then she relaxed again, even smiling. "I suppose I did. Well." As if finally realizing how close to him she sat, she scooted away and motioned to a few other items on the table. "I haven't yet had time to go through all these, but I found them in my room with the other things. I thought at first they were just part of the furnishings, but are they your sister's?"

Glancing over the collection of papers and books, he could only say the truth. "I have no idea." Before he could suggest they thumb through it all together, the door gusted open.

And the wind herself blew in.

6

Mabena blew inside with a stiff sea breeze that had won the battle with a few of her hairpins. She summoned a laugh to her lips, ready to deliver it on cue to Libby, if she were inside, though it was entirely possible she was out enjoying the afternoon on the island.

The laughter died on her lips when her quick scan delivered not only Libby on the sofa, but Oliver Tremayne himself. She pushed shut the door and mentally scrambled for what she meant to say—to each of them together, and separately. She'd thought she'd have another day or two to decide on what story to give them both. But here they were.

"Mr. Tremayne. What a pleasant surprise."

Apparently *not* the story Ollie had been expecting her to tell, given she'd never in her life addressed him as "mister" anything. And the arch of his brow called her on it—though he turned said arch toward her alone so that Libby couldn't see it. He might not approve of her decisions, but he wouldn't take her to task in front of an outsider. "Miss Moon. How lovely to see you again. I had no idea you were coming home for the summer."

She heard the accusation as clearly as she would the bells in St. Mary's tower come Sunday. She could only hope Libby didn't. "Lady

Elizabeth needed a holiday. Didn't you, my lady? And I told her there was no lovelier place in all of England than the Scillies."

Libby didn't *look* particularly suspicious. Just curious, which was nearly as bad. "Mr. Tremayne's sister seems to be missing, Moon. Beth—she was staying here before us. It was her things we found. Do you know her? Well, of course you know her. I mean . . ."

Mabena's heart might as well have stopped beating. Oliver knew, then? That Beth had vanished into thin air? She hadn't counted on that either. She'd rather hoped she'd be able to poke around a bit without alarming him or his grandmother. Without shining a light on whatever secrets Beth had been hiding.

Hiding from him. From everyone here. When Mabena blinked, she could see those hastily scrawled words. *"I don't know what Ollie would say if he knew, but it wouldn't be good. I can't let him find out."*

Mabena hadn't a clue *what* Beth didn't want him to know. But still, it was a trust. And she'd not break it. Not now, at any rate, when the answers to Beth's whereabouts could be simple.

She pasted on a look of mild concern that she moved between the two on the sofa. "Beth Tremayne is the Elizabeth who Mrs. Pepper was so put out with? But that makes precious little sense. What was your sister doing here for the summer instead of at her own home, sir?"

His nostrils flared the slightest bit at that *sir*, and he cleared his throat. "That is what Lady Elizabeth and I were just trying to discern—because clearly she was about something more than the holiday she said *she* wanted." He motioned to the table.

Mabena frowned at it while she unpinned her hat. "What's all this, then?"

Libby pushed to her feet. "There are a few other things I'd like to check too, in my room. I don't know if they were Beth's or just came with the house. Mr. Tremayne can tell you what we know while I look—and put away my microscope."

"Microscope?" Oliver stood, being too much of a gentleman to do otherwise. Though with an eagerness that said he might just leave Mabena to inform herself while he went to investigate the lady's toy.

Had the lady not been there, Mabena would have laughed out a "Down, boy," as if he were the wolfhound he'd had as a lad.

Perhaps he heard her silent jest even through her still lips, because he glanced her way and relaxed. A bit.

Libby was already angled toward the bedrooms. "The light isn't very good for its mirror out here right now, but I can bring it too, if you like. Not that it will help us with the question of your sister, but . . ."

But she'd heard the note of eagerness, obviously. And where it made Mabena want to roll her eyes, it would make Libby thrum her own note of it. Quite a chord they'd make—or part of one, anyway.

"Ah." Usually Ollie would have been quick to agree. But it took him a long moment to say, "That would be lovely, if you don't mind. I haven't seen one since my university days."

Libby smiled, bobbed her head in a half-shy acknowledgment, and scurried into the bedroom.

Oliver spun on Mabena, making it quite clear why he'd hesitated but decided to ask—to buy him a few more minutes to question *her* as the lady gathered things up in the other room. "What in blazes are you about, Benna?"

"Exactly what I said. She wanted to visit, so we came."

His eyes, nearly black, snapped at her. "Don't lie to me. I know very well coming here couldn't have been her idea."

Everyone knew her so well, did they? First Casek Wearne, and now Oliver Tremayne. She planted her hands on her hips, then huffed out a breath. They had a point, after all. "Fine." She shifted a bit so she'd see the moment Libby reappeared in her doorway. "If you must know, Lady Elizabeth had a rather urgent need to escape her family. And I knew of no other place to recommend she go."

There. That had enough of the truth in it that he ought to hear it in her voice and believe her.

Which he must have done, given the way he frowned and eased closer, darting a glance at where Libby had gone. "What? Why did she have to escape them? She wasn't in any danger, was she? Hurt in some way?"

69

That was Ollie—always ready to play the hero.

No, it was more than that. Always quick, so quick, to care. This time her exhale was more sigh than huff. "Nothing like that. Her brother was trying to convince her to marry his best friend, Lord Sheridan—a marquess. And the lady wanted nothing to do with his plans. That's all." Libby wouldn't be happy she'd shared that, probably, given her inclination toward privacy. But she couldn't very well let Ollie worry over her too, could she?

His shoulders eased back down to a normal position, rolled back. He nodded. And reached for her elbow. "Mabena—"

"Oh no you don't." She leapt away from his touch. "None of that elbow-magic of yours, Oliver Tremayne. I'll keep my heart to myself, thank you."

He breathed a laugh and slanted a look at her that made his next words redundant. "I don't need your elbow to know your heart."

Probably true, but still. Everyone in the Scillies knew that when Oliver Tremayne took hold of your arm and looked deep into your eyes, he saw right down to your soul. A few of the old biddies whispered that it went beyond the natural. Mabena didn't know about *that*, but she granted it had made him the easy choice to fill the role of village vicar. Everyone had already loved him. Trusted him. *Wanted* to share their secrets with him and receive in turn his encouragement and counsel.

But Mabena wasn't in need of any spiritual guidance, thank you very much. She just needed to know where Beth was. "Can we focus, Ollie? She'll be back out any moment."

"Certainly. You can begin by explaining why you don't want your employer to know that we—"

"Because," she said with exaggerated articulation, just to interrupt him, "it would raise more questions than I care to answer about what took me to her home in response to their advertisement about a position. Beth, if you recall, provided my recommendation."

And why was the look he gave her bordering on sad? Or worse, disappointed? "Benna."

"Don't chide me. That's a bed I made long ago, and I'm happy enough to lie in it. So play along, will you? Pretend I'm just another parishioner."

He opened his mouth, but before he could argue—which was clearly what he intended—Libby appeared in her doorway, her arms full of scientific whatnot, giving Mabena the perfect excuse to rush forward. Away from Oliver Tremayne. "Oh, my lady! Let me help you with that before you drop something."

Libby relinquished a basket full of papers she was juggling, though she kept the microscope firmly in hand. At least the grin she gave Mabena assured her that she hadn't heard any of the furious whispering. "How was the visit to your parents, Mabena? You weren't gone all that long."

"I wanted to be back in time to help prepare dinner." She smiled too, though it didn't feel as effortless as Libby's looked. "And there was much fussing, as anticipated." A few too many tears in her mam's eyes, too, and Tas had threatened not to allow her to leave again as he held her tight to his chest in an embrace as strong as a bear's. She'd not struggled free either. Just closed her eyes and breathed him in—salt and sea and sawdust. For a moment, she'd actually entertained the notion of letting him convince her of coming home. *Staying* home. Going into his shop again to watch him craft the vessels that connected the islands. Helping Mam weave her silver and stones and the occasional gem into jewelry to sell to the tourists.

Running into Wearnes every time she turned a corner.

No, the memory of the hour she'd spent in Casek's boat had been enough to remind her why she'd left to begin with.

"I came back with other holiday-goers staying here on St. Mary's." *Not* with the obnoxious headmaster of the National School. She turned, aiming a smile at where Oliver still stood. "You know what would make the trip faster? If the locals would invest in a few of those motorboats to run the tourists around."

Oliver snorted his opinion of that. "Right. And we should all bring automobiles over from the mainland too and string electricity."

71

"My next suggestion."

He shook his head. But any levity the idea brought faded as his gaze caught on the basket in her hands. He met them halfway into the sitting room and took it from her, reaching with a frown to pull out a book. Specifically, a well-worn Bible. Mabena couldn't readily recall if it was Beth's or not, but Oliver clearly recognized it. He set the basket onto the low table before the sofa and stood there, flipping through it.

Libby put her microscope and slides onto the table, which left Mabena with little to do other than examine the strange collection. Some of the items made perfect sense for Beth to have brought here—books, paper, clothes. But others made her frown. A small concretion. A ragged edge of parchment. From the basket, a piece of driftwood that looked like it came from a board rather than a branch.

Items Beth had collected over the years as she explored the islands. Of sentimental value, yes . . . but why bring them here just for the summer?

Oliver set the Bible down, holding up in its place a piece of paper. Perhaps it had been tucked into the pages. He flipped it over to check the back, revealing the front to her. *Oliver*, written on it in Beth's hand.

Mabena's breath caught. A note? Would it have some explanation? Or was it just Beth pouring out her frustrations in something she'd decided not to give him? Or, perhaps more likely, one of the letters she was supposed to send him twice a week. Unfinished, maybe.

Oliver sank onto the sofa, flipping open the paper. As his eyes darted back and forth across the page, Mabena lowered the slip of parchment she'd been holding to her side. "What is it?"

His brows were as low as a bank of storm clouds. "I'm not entirely certain. What do you think?"

He handed it over far too casually, in her opinion, something unlikely if they were the mere acquaintances she was trying to pretend they were. But Libby didn't seem to think anything of it, just came to Mabena's side to look at it with her. Always more curious than polite, that was Libby. And much as Mabena had the sudden urge to shield the letter from her, she squelched it. It would give away too much about how invested she was in what Libby would think only a mystery.

Oliver,

I know you'll be unhappy with me, and I'm sorry for that. I only meant to have a bit of fun, find a new story to tell, perhaps earn a bit. But it's certainly not fun now. I can't undo the last month, but I can try to put a stop to the trouble brewing, anyway. Only, I can't do that where I've been. But I know you're not going to like the plan I came up with, and so . . . well, so I'm not telling you.

I know it's cruel of me to leave you guessing, and I'm sorry for that too. I assume Mrs. Pepper will return this and everything else to you, and no doubt you'll worry. Try not to. I can't say more than that—I know well you'll interfere. You won't be able to help yourself. Just trust me, big brother. Please? And if you would pay Mrs. Pepper for the cottage when she comes to you, that would be lovely. I'll need it again soon.

If all goes well, I'll be back home and annoying you within a few weeks. I've tried to put a few safeguards in place in case anything goes awry. There are no guarantees, of course, when one is dealing with this sort of thing, but . . . but I can't in good conscience let it go unanswered. Even if it is unlikely I'll prevail against them, I have to try. I owe it to him.

If you get this before Johnnie's funeral, tell his mum I'm sorry I wasn't there. He was a sweet lad.

Beth

Mabena's frown was no doubt every bit as thunderous as Oliver's. "Johnnie?"

"Rosedew." Oliver's voice was low; no doubt he was remembering that Beth wasn't the only one who would regret missing his funeral.

Mabena had helped watch him for his mum when he was little. Ages ago. He would have been, what, sixteen by now? "Had an accident two weeks ago, in Piper's Hole on Tresco. He must have slipped, went down hard and . . . No one was with him, but a few of his chums found him next morning." He shook his head, sorrow thick on his face. "His mother's a wreck. Poor lad."

She very nearly reached for *his* elbow. Funerals were, she knew, his least favorite part of the job. And it would be worse when it was that sort of funeral. "A couple weeks ago? Then this must have been written before the funeral but after the accident."

"Must have been. I—" He was interrupted by a knock upon the door.

Libby huffed. "If it's another someone looking for your sister, Mr. Tremayne, I'll let *you* talk to them." She spun to the door before Mabena could thrust the letter back to Oliver and insist she ought to answer all knocks instead. It wasn't fitting for a lady when Mabena was there.

But Libby, of course, never thought of such things. She merely pulled the door open before Mabena could get out so much as a squeak of protest, revealing a glowering Mrs. Pepper with a basket as big as her scowl.

"Mrs. Pepper!" Libby's greeting was pure sweetness—and perhaps relief at it being someone who knew who she was, more or less. "How—"

"Was that a man's voice I heard?" Their landlady pushed her way in. "I hadn't thought it necessary to set down the rules for you, being well bred as you clearly are, but—oh! Mr. Tremayne!"

The woman's demeanor changed as swiftly as lightning when she spotted Oliver. Mabena rolled her eyes—she couldn't help it. It was annoying and convenient both how he had that effect on people.

He'd folded the letter in the moments when she and Libby were turned to the door, and he now smiled warmly at the old biddy, holding out a hand toward her. "Hello, Mrs. Pepper."

She put her hand into his, setting her basket down to a gentle rest on the floor. "How good it is to see you again. I thought I'd not get the chance once your sister went home. Are you here on business or for a visit? Calling on Mr. Gale? He made mention of seeing if you would consider filling in for him one Sunday here, if that cough of his doesn't improve."

His smile didn't so much as falter, though his mind surely snagged, as Mabena's did, on that *once your sister went home*. "I'll certainly be paying a visit to Mr. Gale. He did send me a note just yesterday, yes. And I told him I'd be happy to fill in for him at St. Mary's soon. I'm going to encourage everyone at St. Nicholas's to simply come over here with me."

"Oh, we could have a meal together afterward, the whole parish together." Mrs. Pepper positively beamed at him. "And we do so love to hear you now and then."

"And I relish the time with you all as well." He patted her hand, which still rested in his. "And how is Kayna, ma'am? And your husband?"

He had a way of asking those simple questions in a way that made it clear he actually cared about the answers. Where normally people would give a polite, simple answer, with him they responded with the truth. Hence Mrs. Pepper's long sigh. "I do worry for Henry. He tries to do too much, never admitting he isn't as young as he used to be. And Kayna hasn't been quite the same since she lost the last babe."

Mabena drew in a sharp breath. She hadn't even known Kayna Pepper had married, much less that she'd lost a child—or more than one? Was that what "the last" indicated? Perhaps she oughtn't to have told her parents not to bore her with island gossip. Then she wouldn't feel quite like the world here had spun away from her.

"I've been praying for her and Thom every day," Oliver said, his gaze never leaving the woman's eyes.

She sniffled. "I know they'd appreciate it if you stopped in while you're here. Poor Mr. Gale hasn't been well enough for his usual visitations."

"Absolutely. And I'll make certain to say hello to your husband as well before I go home for the evening."

Mabena was about ready to shake him—or Mrs. Pepper—to draw them back to the question of Beth. She had to curl her hands into fists to control them but didn't quite manage to keep her feet still. She shifted from one to the other.

Oliver finally glanced at her, then back to the older woman. "Forgive me, Mrs. Pepper, but did you say Beth left for home?"

For a moment, her face went utterly blank. The kind that bespoke genuine surprise at the question. "Two weeks ago, wasn't it? Right after poor Johnnie Rosedew. I thought at first she was just going to Tresco to be there for the funeral, but she took an awful lot with her. And when she didn't come back—well, I knew you'd talked her into staying home. Though I must say, I was a trifle peevish when she didn't bother letting me know she was done with the place. Had I not happened to see her leaving with all her things . . ."

Oliver's frown dug its way back into his forehead as she spoke. "She didn't come home." He said it so simply. Clearly. So very briefly that even Mrs. Pepper must have heard how the words haunted him down to his soul.

"What? But of course she did! Where else could she have gone? I watched her for a good five minutes, and she was clearly going in the direction of Tresco."

In lieu of a reply, Oliver shook his head, the muscle in his jaw ticking. He was likely clenching his teeth in that way he did when it took everything in him not to respond to something. Usually one of Casek's taunts. He let go of her hand.

Mrs. Pepper lifted her newly freed fingers, shaking, to her lips. "But—no. The weather's been fine, the currents normal. She was too able a sailor to get lost or go astray or get caught out, otherwise I never would have countenanced her going round alone as she did. Nothing bad could have happened to her. Not like your parents. Or Johnnie."

Not like your parents. Or Johnnie. The Tremaynes, who had also known the tides and currents and weather as well as any other Scillonian but had still been caught out in a storm and drowned. Johnnie, who had known the dangers but had slipped on the wet rocks of the cave, presumably, and taken a fatal fall. Just two of many tragedies to steal the islands' people in her memory.

With the greatest of care, Mabena uncurled each finger from her palm. There was no need to assume the worst. Not given that letter, opaque as it might be when it came to Beth's reasons for going. The going was still part of her plan. As was coming back. Soon. Any day, given the timing. "A few weeks" was up, or nearly. And if she'd left with a boatload of things but those things *weren't* the items she'd brought here, they were likely supplies. Food, necessities. Beth, wherever she was, was well provisioned. She was fine.

They just had to be patient for a little bit longer.

Though it must have cost him dearly, Oliver summoned a smile to his lips. "She's off on an adventure, no doubt. That's what the summer was meant to be for her. But I didn't realize she'd left you without notice—and didn't pay her rent, I assume?" He motioned toward Libby, who jumped a bit at the sudden attention.

Mrs. Pepper turned to her as if just remembering she was there. "Oh. Yes, I'm afraid so. And when Miss Sinclair contacted me inquiring about vacancies . . . well, as I said, I was a bit peevish at your sister's abrupt departure. I'm sorry for that."

"Quite all right. Beth clearly isn't using the place, so Lady Elizabeth might as well." Oliver motioned next to the odd assortment on the table. "I'll just collect the rest of her things, I suppose. The lady informed me she'd left a bit in the drawers."

Mrs. Pepper's gaze flew between Libby and the belonging-strewn table. "*Lady*—forgive me, my lady, I had no idea!"

Libby sighed. Had she been a bit more like Mabena, she would have sent Oliver a glare for letting her secret slip. Though how she really expected to keep her family a secret for long, Mabena still wasn't certain. As it was, however, Libby chased the sigh with a small smile. "There is nothing to forgive, ma'am."

"Oh, but—allow me to help." Mrs. Pepper bent, hoisted the basket again, and bustled toward the little kitchen. She still didn't so much as glance at Mabena. "Shall I whip you up something for your meal?"

"No, no. We can see to it ourselves. You needn't bother—"

"It's hardly a bother to help, Lady Elizabeth. Won't take me but a few minutes. The good vicar can entertain you while I work."

The good vicar looked caught between amusement at suddenly going from guest to host and concern at the focus moving so quickly from Beth. He transferred that all-seeing gaze of his to Mabena again. "Would you fetch the clothing she left? Lady Elizabeth said you'd already moved it to your room."

The idea made her shoulder blades edge together. There had been some comfort in having Beth's clothing there, mingled among her own. "Are you going to carry it all about St. Mary's with you while you visit Mr. Gale and the Peppers?"

"A valid point. I'll have to come back for it all." He looked out the window, toward the lowering sun. "In fact, I'd better be on my way or I'll never have time to pay those visits and make it home before dark." He turned to them again, darting a look at Mrs. Pepper.

The old biddy was so busy poking about in the kitchen that she didn't even notice that she'd inconvenienced him.

"Well, you needn't entertain us. Sir." Mabena tried to keep her smile casual. Helpful even. She just wasn't certain she managed it.

Oliver sighed. "I know. It's just . . ." He surveyed the strange collection on the table again. And this time, it was she who could read *his* mind. It was just that Beth was gone, and he had no idea of where or how to find her. No idea if she was truly in trouble or merely chasing a lark. No idea if he should let her do whatever it was she meant to do or scour every inch of every island looking for her.

Perhaps Libby had been able to read those thoughts as easily as Mabena had. She edged forward, the slope of her shoulders hinting at her usual bashfulness, but determination bringing roses to her cheeks. "Don't worry, Mr. Tremayne. We'll help you find her. Won't we, Moon?"

Mabena nodded and turned a bit more toward Oliver—a bit more away from Mrs. Pepper, who'd spun at the familiar surname. "Of course we will."

78

Oliver's smile was small and sad. "I appreciate that. But you're here for a holiday, my lady. Enjoy your time. This needn't be your concern. Wherever she is, my sister has proven she's quite capable of taking care of herself."

Libby's chin edged up a bit. "I believe it was made my concern when people mistook me for your sister. It could well happen again, you know. I'm involved—let me help."

He must have heard that underlying note in her voice as clearly as Mabena did. The one that said no one ever let her help with anything, and she craved it. Craved being useful—in something real, not just one of the dressed-up causes her mother championed that was more about parading around in a fancy hat and being seen making a difference than about actually making a difference.

Ollie, of course, was helpless against such a plea. He didn't have it in him to deny anyone the chance to do good—at least not unless that someone's last name was Wearne. "I will certainly welcome your assistance then, my lady. As long as it doesn't interfere with your holiday."

Libby's smile was somehow both bright and sympathetic as she folded her hands before her. In that moment she looked like what her family had always begged her to be—a demure young lady capable of putting anyone at ease. "I assure you, sir. It is no inconvenience at all."

And that, it seemed, settled it. Mabena didn't know whether to be glad that she now had her employer's approval for any poking about she wanted to do . . . or to resent the fact that her quest was no longer her own.

Ollie saw himself out, and Mabena went to her room to gather Beth's clothes. With the shawl wrapped around her hands, she decided it didn't matter how she felt about it. The only thing in the world that mattered was finding Beth.

7

Blessed sunshine greeted Libby on Friday morning when she rose, bringing a smile to her lips and making her jump from bed and fly to the window. She pushed up the sash, breathing in the scents of salt and green life and a world washed clean by the rain she'd been none too happy with yesterday. It had pounded the island all day, keeping her in when all she really wanted was to be out. After Mrs. Pepper left the other evening, Libby had insisted Mabena sit down with her so they could write up a plan, and most of that plan included tasks that required going about St. Mary's asking after the missing Beth Tremayne. *Not* sitting at home twiddling their thumbs.

Though to be sure, they'd put their day to use. They'd gone over every inch of the cottage, finding a few more items that were more likely Beth's than the Peppers'—books on the islands' history, mostly, that Mabena had thought were from the Tremayne library. At Libby's insistence, they'd catalogued them, along with the items they'd already sent to Tresco with Mr. Tremayne. She'd even transcribed all the notes in *Treasure Island* before he left, including the entire fairy tale—not that it had been finished.

Mabena had sighed at the list-making, but in Libby's opinion it brought a bit of much-needed order to the situation. They now knew exactly what Beth had deemed not important enough to take with her on her task—or, in the case of *Treasure Island*, what she'd dropped without realizing it, which was Libby's suspicion. Perhaps that didn't tell them what she *had* taken, but it was more information than her brother had when he came here. She glanced again at her transcription of the fairy tale.

Once upon a time, there was a princess. She lived on an island of rocks and bones, with no one to keep her company aside from the fairies. All her life she'd danced with them to the tunes they played on their magical pipes, the tunes echoed by deep voices from the rock itself. One day, however, the music stopped.

The princess, concerned for her fay friends, set out to find them, only to discover that every fairy on the island had vanished. Far and wide she searched, high and low. In the treetops she found no friends . . . but there was a house in the boughs she'd never seen before, one made of wood creaking and ancient, bearing the name of the fairy king over its lintel. In the pools she found no friends . . . but there was glinting metal winking up at her from the depths, the very shade of the fairies' eyes. Not to be tempted, the princess pushed onward. In the forest glens she found a wonder that dazzled her eyes. Trees with fragrant bark peeling in fairy-wing curls. Crocuses with petals like fairy gowns. Purple-spiked flowers like fairy crowns. But none of her friends were there.

She kept on, toward the far-looming mountain from whence it was said that all fairies came. But the closer she drew to the rugged rocks, the heavier her feet grew. And the louder came the voices that used to sing along with the fairies' pipes. The very bones were singing, inviting her to sing with them. She knew, though, that to give in—to sing that song—would mean becoming naught but bone herself.

So heavy were her feet by the time she climbed up the first rock that she could scarcely go any farther, and the winds blew cold now against her. Shivering, the princess tucked herself into a cleft of the rock and cried for her lost friends.

Still, the voices sang. "Look toward the birds," they chanted over and again. "Look to the birds, Lizza." The princess tilted back her head and watched an eagle soar overhead. But no help came for her from his widespread wings.

Libby stepped away, trying to shake the words of the story from her mind. She took in one more breath of the lovely air and then spun back toward her room. She'd dress, make a cup of tea, perhaps grab a bite to eat, and then go back to the beach. The day of rain had allowed the slight burn on her nose to lessen, so another day of sun on it shouldn't hurt too badly—and this time she'd be certain not only to wear her hat, but to keep it adjusted to actually protect her.

She also meant to obey Mama today and greet the other families staying in the cottages dotting the island. Though, granted, not for the reasons her mother wanted her to. Rather, she meant to ask them all if they'd seen or met Beth. Mabena, meanwhile, would begin canvassing the locals in Hugh Town and Old Town, maybe going so far as Little Porth and Trenoweth, if there was time. If not, then Trenoweth and Pelistry would both be her assignment for another day.

It was a fine plan. A helpful one. Mr. Tremayne might have said that they needn't go out of their way, but he could only be in one place at a time. Surely it would be to his advantage to have them asking questions too.

She dressed quickly and put her hair into a utilitarian braid that the wind wouldn't be able to ruin in a matter of minutes. Today she meant to test the temperature of the water too. She had a bathing costume packed away, and she wanted to put it to use.

But for now she opened her door as quietly as she could, hoping Mabena had taken her advice and meant to sleep late. *She* deserved a holiday too, and there was no reason at all for her to be up at the crack of dawn just to assist Libby.

When she stepped into the living area, though, she saw her friend already at the stove, and Mabena greeted her with a grin. "I tried, my lady. It was no use. The sun seemed to work its way through my curtains and find my eyes within minutes of rising."

She didn't look at all unhappy with that, so Libby smiled back. "Sly thing. Did you sleep well?"

"Mm. Well enough. You?"

"Perfectly." She moved to Mabena's side to measure out their tea.

"I mean to go down to the beach as soon as I can so I'll have a bit of time for collecting before the other tourists arrive."

"Good. I hate to think that you've promised away all your time." Rather than shooing her from the kitchen as Mrs. Pepper had done on Wednesday night, Mabena handed her a spoon. "I'll start at the bakery this morning and pick us up a few treats as well. I daresay Beth frequented the place while she was here."

Libby spooned out the tea leaves and stole a sidelong glance at her friend. "How well do you know her?"

Mabena lifted a single shoulder in a shrug, but somehow it didn't look quite right. "Well enough, as I do everyone on Tresco, especially those of an age. We always got along. She is, in fact, how I learned to dress hair and whatnot. She provided my recommendation when I applied for the position with you."

Libby set the spoon down again, frowning at Mabena. There had been a strange undercurrent between her and Mr. Tremayne the other night, to be sure. But not the sort that came of having been employed by his household—*that* undercurrent was one Libby had plenty of experience with. No, it had been something else. Something she'd told herself not to wonder about.

But she had the hardest time not wondering about things. "I didn't realize."

"No reason you should have. What would we like for breakfast this morning?"

And now she was changing the subject. Libby let her, but she filed away the question for later examination. There were questions Mabena clearly didn't want her asking, and that was all right. She didn't need to know everything about her friend's past. But if she was so determined to keep that past a secret, why had she invited Libby to the Scillies for the summer to begin with?

Libby mentally reviewed the contents of the icebox and larder. "That bacon looked lovely. Perhaps with toast and eggs? I intend to do a bit of walking today, so something more than porridge sounds good."

"Perfect. I'll handle the eggs and bacon if you would tackle the toast. I've a fire lit in the stove already. No electric toaster here, I'm afraid."

"Not a problem." Their cook at Telford Hall had been rather excited to get the device last year from a small company in Scotland, but it wasn't as though they'd even had electricity for most of Libby's memory. Papa had resisted having it installed, quoting "needless expense" as the reason, but they all knew he just didn't like making any changes to his ancestral home. Bram, however, had always been one for the latest and greatest. He'd had both the country estate and their London townhouse wired soon after Papa died.

She could rather see Papa's point though, especially here on St. Mary's, where so much was as it had been for centuries. There was a charm to the unchanging. To watching and learning the rhythms of nature and seeking to be part of them, rather than to rule them. To gliding over the waters with the help of the wind or oars rather than churning them up with an electric motor.

"I should like to learn to sail while I'm here. I'm a decent hand at rowing already, thanks to our lake."

Her sudden declaration was met with a moment of silence before Mabena's clattering of pans commenced again. "And you went from toasters to sailboats *how*, exactly?"

Libby grinned. "The old ways versus the new. There's no reason I can't learn, right?"

Mabena shook her head. "No reason, but don't get any fool ideas about sailing around by yourself in search of puffins or seals. It takes more than a summer to learn all the waterways."

"Don't worry. I'll take you with me on those adventures." She flashed her another grin. "How do we find a boat? Can we rent one?"

Mabena sighed. "We can, though I daresay we needn't. My father builds them. I've had a small sloop of my own for years, and he's already promised to get her ready for me. The *Mermaid*."

"Oh!" Libby's eyes went wide. "He builds boats? Fascinating. Could I see his shop sometime?"

Mabena chuckled. "He would be honored to show you about, I'm certain."

"And we need to see the Abbey Gardens soon. So obviously we should just plan an outing to Tresco."

"Obviously." Mabena thankfully looked amused rather than annoyed at the thought of introducing Libby to more of her world. Good. "Perhaps we could even plan to stay overnight. I know my parents would be thrilled."

"Perfect!"

They chatted about whether the fine weather was likely to hold and what days would be best for that trip while they cooked. An easy, companionable conversation, followed by an easy, companionable silence while they ate.

She'd always liked breakfasts best for this very reason. Even when her company was Bram and Mama instead of Mabena, it was such an *easy* meal. The one where her brother often had a newspaper open before him to mask his usual morning silence, where they could each come and go at their leisure, where there were no expectations. Certainly no evening gowns or perfectly coiffed hair like at dinner.

When she was finished, she took her own plate to the sink, washed it, and stacked it neatly back in the cupboard with the others. After fetching her notebook, pencil, and hat, she said, "All right, then. Down to the shore I go. Feel free to find me whenever you're bored of town, Mabena."

Mabena, still at the table with her tea and the last half of her toast, smiled. "I'll just look for the girl on her belly in the sand, studying the root systems of the grasses."

Chuckling, Libby snatched up one of the remaining pieces of bacon for the walk. And then another. "A fine idea." With a wave farewell, she let herself out and aimed directly for the path down to the beach. She had a feeling she and that path were going to become the best of friends before the summer was over.

"Meow."

Her feet paused near the garrison wall even as her gaze skittered around, looking for whatever child had made the cat call. And she was a bit surprised to find not a sweet little lad or lass poorly imitating a feline, but an actual feline poorly imitating itself. It was a tiny thing, striped and white socked, its fur matted and scraggly. And when it emitted another "Meow," Libby couldn't suppress a giggle. It really did sound more like a person trying to mimic a cat than an actual kitten. "Hello there."

It came a few steps closer, peering up at her with wide golden eyes. It meowed again, and again as she took another step toward the path. She glanced down at the bacon in her hands. "Ah. I suspect I know what you want. Well, you certainly seem to need it more than I do. Here you are, little darling."

She broke off a few small chunks of the bacon and tossed it to the kitten, grinning when it scarfed it down as if it were starving. Which, given the ribs she could make out through the fur, it may well be. Poor little mite. She crumbled the rest of the strips and tossed them down a few pieces at a time.

A tabby for certain, she decided as she looked for and found the distinctive M on its forehead. And a lovely one—or it would be, if it weren't so scraggly. Fur of what she suspected was a nice brown with those dark grey stripes, and white markings under its chin, down its chest, and on two of its four feet. It reminded her a bit of one of the stable cats they'd had when she was younger. Though it had been too wild to ever let her come near and pet it, it had been her favorite one to watch.

"You seem friendly enough." She crouched down, and the kitten came immediately over to her, trying to climb up onto her knee. It was either too small or too weak to manage it, but she gave it an obliging scratch behind the ears and smiled at the loud rumble of a purr. "Yes, I think you're simply a stray, not feral. But I'm afraid that's all the bacon I've brought out with me. See?" She showed it her palm.

It licked her, its sandpaper tongue making her laugh again. "All right, little darling. I'm going down to the beach. But if you're still here when I come back, I'll see what else I can find for you to eat. Hopefully when Mabena's not at home. She prefers dogs," she said in a stage whisper, just in case her voice was carrying toward the open windows of their cottage. She stood again, after placing the kitten's paws back on the ground.

"Meow."

Still smiling, she started down the path, not exactly surprised when the meowing followed her. But the kitten would no doubt tire of the walk and turn back to the shelter of the grasses it must have been hiding in, so she pressed on. And though she caught glimpses of the little tabby several times as she catalogued the flora and fauna over the next couple hours, it did indeed seem more inclined to the grass than the beach.

Around midmorning, her solitude evaporated into the wind-blown laughter and shouts from other holiday-goers bent on seizing the sunny day after twenty-four hours of rain. Though she sighed a bit, she also told herself that this was exactly as she had planned. She could do this. She didn't really *want* to . . . but it wasn't about her. It was about Oliver Tremayne and his missing sister.

Closing her notebook and tucking her pen into her pocket, she started toward the nearest cluster of people. A woman who looked a decade or two older than Libby, sitting in a chair that a man she guessed to be a servant had carried down for her. An older man—the woman's husband, most likely—was setting up a badminton net, the wind carrying to her his boasts that he'd "show the young pup how it was done."

The "young pup" was a lad of about twelve, by her estimation, who was grinning and playing a game of keeping the birdie in the air with his racket. A girl, perhaps eight or nine, was on her knees in the sand, happily digging, while another woman—a nanny, most likely—tried to put a discarded hat on the girl's head.

A normal family, by all appearances. Nothing to make her stomach clench. Libby made certain her feet kept to their easy, strolling pace and took her near to the mother. What was she really to do though? Just stop at her feet and say hello? Demand to know who she was? If she knew Beth Tremayne? Or the Sinclair family?

It had sounded so simple on paper last night when she made the plan. But when put to the test, Libby never had the faintest clue how to interact with the people who were supposed to be her peers.

The woman, however, didn't seem to have the same problem. She was calling out a cheerful "Good morning!" the moment Libby was close enough.

Smiling back was not difficult. "Good morning." She paused a polite distance away, making a show now of surveying the scene. "A lovely day for a family outing, isn't it?"

"Oh, it's perfect! I'm so glad I convinced my husband to get us out of Manchester for the summer." The woman stood and came nearer. "Mrs. Giles Haversham. Victoria."

"How do you do?" Libby opened her mouth, ready to give Mrs. Haversham the same name she'd given Mrs. Pepper. But no. If she wanted to be the best possible help to the Tremaynes, she had to earn people's trust. And, dash it to pieces, she'd do that better with her title. "I'm Lady Elizabeth Sinclair."

And indeed, the woman's eyes flashed brighter. "How do you do? Newly arrived on St. Mary's with your family?"

Libby nodded, not bothering to correct her on the "with your family" bit. "Have you been here long?"

"Just since Monday, but it's a charming place."

She wouldn't have encountered Beth at all then. Double dash it. "It is indeed. My maid is from Tresco, so I've made her promise to play tour guide for me. Though I was also hoping to find a few other holiday-goers who had been here longer and could tell me which spots they've most enjoyed."

There—that was a rather skillful fishing for information, wasn't it? As subtle as any of the drawing room conversation Mama had tried so desperately to teach her.

"You may want to talk to the Myer family, then. They're letting a house to the north and have been here since May."

Perfect. She chatted a bit longer, until the little girl called her mother over to show her the haphazard sandcastle she'd built, and Libby seized the opportunity to wish them a good day and walk on.

She introduced herself to six more neighbors over the next two hours, and it got a bit easier each time to approach the lady of the family and say hello. They were all friendly enough, though none had been here more than two weeks. And the Myers, she discovered when she happened across their next-door neighbors, were already gone for the day, having hired a boat to take them to St. Martin's for some bird watching.

Bird watching. Her heart thrilled at the mere mention. She'd have to make time for that at some point as well.

Walking back wouldn't take nearly as long as walking this far had done, since she wouldn't feel the obligation to do more than wave a cheery greeting at all the people she'd just met, so she decided to press on a bit farther, past the Myers' cottage. She'd go so far as that stone one up ahead and then—

"Libby? Lady Elizabeth, is that you?"

She froze, telling herself she was surely imagining the familiarity of the voice. Though of course she wasn't, because otherwise how would the voice have known her name? But really, what were the chances that Charlotte Wight was here, now?

Very good, apparently, as proved by the young lady who ran toward her, laughing, arms outstretched, as if Libby were the very dearest of long-lost friends. She drummed up a smile but didn't manage to get her own arms raised before Lottie swept up to and over her like the tide, crushing her in an embrace.

"I can't believe it!" the young lady squealed directly into her ear. "It's been ages! You look just the same though."

From anyone else from the finishing school where Libby had met her, it would have been a catty insult—young ladies weren't supposed to emerge "just the same" as they were when they matriculated. But Lottie hadn't a cruel bone in her body. Libby had to grant her that much.

Lottie didn't, however, give her any more time to reply than she ever had. Laughing, she linked their arms together. "I was just telling my mother how I hoped I'd find a friend, because otherwise this was bound to be the most boring summer in history. Well. Not the *most* boring." She leaned close, her blue eyes twinkling. "There's some rather pleasant company to be found of the gentlemanly sort. Lord Willsworth and his cousin, Mr. Bryant, are here. You know them."

Did she? There was a possibility, she supposed, that they'd met in London during the Season. "Er . . ."

"Willsworth is a viscount. He'd be a perfect match for you, now that I think about it. He's a patron of the sciences—you're still interested in that nonsense, I suppose?" Wheeling them about, Lottie led her toward a cluster of chairs and a giant umbrella, under which Mrs. Wight was stationed, her nose in a book. "I prefer his cousin anyway. Mr. Bryant is positively dreamy—and worth more per annum than his cousin, though he doesn't come with a title. Your family, I think, would prefer the viscount. Which is absolutely perfect. Unless." She halted again and turned eyes now wide on Libby. "Is your brother here with you?"

Given that Lottie actually paused for a response this time, Libby cleared her throat. And felt as though her words emerged at a crawl, compared to the breakneck pace of Lottie's. "No, I'm afraid not."

Lottie's lip poked forward into an exaggerated pout for a second, then she laughed again and tucked back a strand of mahogany hair that the wind had teased free. "Of course not. He's no doubt in London for the Season proper. It's just as well. As big a coup as it would be to land an earl, I should probably be more reasonable than that. Neither my dowry nor my name is likely enough to interest your brother."

Libby just blinked at her. Truth be told, she had no idea what might interest Bram in a future wife. He'd been far more concerned these last two years with finding someone willing to put up with *her* for the rest of her life. She'd been an utter failure last Season. And the Little Season this spring hadn't gone any better. She'd begged Mama and Bram to stay at home after they returned to the country for Easter. Her mother had been happy to visit Edith instead, and Bram would simply travel to and from London whenever he wanted to be there for Parliament.

As for what of that to say to Charlotte Wight, she had no notion.

But Lottie never minded that Libby hadn't a clue how to keep up with her conversation. In fact, Libby had always suspected that was why the talkative girl had latched on to her during their shared year at the academy. Libby was one of the only ones who didn't fight her for a part in the conversation.

She was also always so exhausted by her after an hour that she'd hidden from one of her only friends at school more often than she was comfortable admitting. But really, when only one side did all the talking, could they even properly be called friends? Lottie knew precious little of her, other than that she was fond of "that science nonsense." And that she had an earl for an older brother. The thing all of society most cared about, it seemed.

"But now the summer is absolutely perfect," Lottie was saying, unhindered as usual by Libby's lack of participation. "Mother, look who I found wandering the beach! Lady Elizabeth Sinclair! You remember Libby, don't you? From the Château Mont-Choisi?"

At the name of the elite finishing school that Mama had forced Libby to attend for a year, Mrs. Wight looked up from her book with bright eyes. "Oh, of course! How do you do, Lady Elizabeth?"

"Very well, thank you. How do you do?"

Before her mother could answer, Lottie had started up again. "Mother and I were just talking about the dinner party we've been planning for ages—it's a week from tomorrow. You must come. Mustn't she, Mother? She can be Lord Willsworth's partner. Mother was terribly worried that we hadn't anyone to pair with him, but this solves everything!"

Her head was starting to spin. A dinner party? No, no, no. This was *not* what she'd come to the Isles of Scilly for. The very opposite. "Oh, I—"

"Sinclair, did you say?" Mrs. Wight straightened in her chair and narrowed her eyes. "Lady Telford's daughter, correct? Why, I had a wire from your mother just this morning, dear, saying we ought to find you, that you were holidaying here as well. She heard that we were here from a mutual friend, it seems."

Libby sighed. Leave it to Mama to discover that even before Libby could, from hundreds of miles away.

Lottie was still grinning. "Where are you staying, Libby? I'll walk back with you so we can plot and plan. Is that all right, Mother?"

Mrs. Wight was already looking back at her book. "Of course, dear. And you know well she may come to absolutely anything we host—I insist upon it, as a matter of fact."

"Perfect. Come." Their elbows still locked together, Lottie spun them around and started them back the way from which Libby had come. "This direction, I assume?"

"Yes." She didn't really *want* to tell Charlotte Wight where she was staying. She'd learned the mistake of that when she'd shown Lottie her room at the Château. Once Lottie knew where to find her, there was never any guarantee of peace within the walls. But what help was there for it? Mama would no doubt wire Mrs. Wight the information if Libby didn't supply it herself. "One of the cottages along the garrison wall."

"They're sweet, aren't they? I've walked this way and was admiring them. We rented those three there. I must say, I'm highly enjoying the whole island—or what we've seen of it. We've been here only a week. We'd been in London since the new year, but Mother was tiring of it, and Father said there was as much to be accomplished here as there." She giggled, bumping their arms together. "He meant Mr. Bryant. We'd been introduced in late February, but he'd already been planning to summer here. Quite an avid sailor, you see, but he doesn't much like the motorized versions his set has taken to racing."

Libby was tempted to pray for an escape, though she wasn't quite sure the Lord would respect such a prayer. Why, oh why, hadn't Lottie already found another friend whose ear she could chatter numb?

"Do you know Lady Emily Scofield?"

Suspecting she'd missed whatever sentence or two connected the current question to the talk of sailing, Libby shook her head. The name sounded vaguely familiar, but she was fairly certain she hadn't made her acquaintance.

"Oh, I suppose you didn't meet her at the Château, since you only stayed a year. She came in the next year, and our paths have crossed a few times in London since then. Great patrons of the British Museum, the Scofields—and she's very pretty, and of course well dowried, so I expect she'll land whomever she fancies. But at any rate, she has another friend from a finishing school she attended before she came to Switzerland who's actually *from* here. Well, not here, St. Mary's. But here, the Scillies. She told me I ought to make her acquaintance, but I've had quite a time of it. Miss Beth Tremayne."

Though Libby's attention had wandered a bit through the initial talk, Beth's name drew her back with a jolt.

Which Lottie clearly noted, given that she hushed for half a second and turned her frank blue eyes on her. "Do you know her?"

"I've . . . met her brother." *Twice*, she nearly said.

"No! Which one?"

Libby's brows knotted. Had Mr. Tremayne mentioned a brother Wednesday night? Yes, that was right. One named Morgan, who had played pirate prince and princess with him and Beth. "Mr. Oliver Tremayne. The clergyman." The Botanist. The one who could pull her deepest heart to the surface with one well-aimed question and then look straight to her very soul.

Lottie nodded. "The younger. Well, now the only one. The older one passed away a few years ago, I'm told, but I didn't know when you may have met him. Quite a curious family."

She oughtn't to encourage the gossip. She could hear Mabena in her head even now, scowling over the audacity of a stranger thinking she knew anything about an islander she'd never even met. And it took only a syllable to get Lottie really going. But curiosity burned like the sun on the sand, making an "Oh?" emerge before she could stop it.

Lottie leaned closer. "They've an estate in Cornwall, you know—not very large, but well enough situated that the Tremaynes have always been somewhat accepted in society, when they choose to enter it. But they haven't often, not for generations. They've been *here* instead. From what Emily said that Beth told her, once upon a time they had a connection with the Lord Proprietor himself. Or was it the Duke of Cornwall? At any rate, their family was granted a permanent lease of a plot of land near the Tresco abbey, and ever since then, they've been here more than on their actual estate on the mainland."

While Lottie paused for breath, Libby said, "What's so odd about that?" She certainly couldn't blame them for staying on these beautiful islands.

Her friend gave her a look of complete shock. "They've scarcely been to London in *decades*! The current Mr. Tremayne's father, you see, didn't marry a gentleman's daughter—he married an islander. Which was frowned upon by fashionable society."

Lottie walked as fast as she talked, and already Libby could see the familiar lines of the garrison wall. "I don't see why that's all that curious either. Such things happen."

"Not outside the pages of one of Mother's novels—not very often, anyway. But regardless, he married this local girl, and they had three children. Morgan was the eldest son, then the one you met, Oliver. And Beth was the youngest. Then, a few years ago, the parents were killed when a storm came up suddenly and caught them out at sea. Their boat went down."

The wind snatched the breath right from Libby's lungs. "No!" So that's what Mrs. Pepper had meant when she mentioned how Beth wasn't like their parents. And now she was missing, after last being seen climbing into *her* boat? Oh, Mr. Tremayne must be an absolute wreck of worry, though he'd done an admirable job holding himself together.

Lottie nodded. "The older brother is a bit of a mystery, Emily said. Beth would never talk much of him, and he never once stepped foot on their estate in Cornwall, despite being the heir. He always sent the younger in his place." She gave an exaggerated shiver though the sun was warm and the story far from spooky. "I asked around a bit, and there's talk of him having been deformed. Like Quasimodo, perhaps. His family was clearly ashamed of him."

No, that couldn't be right. Libby couldn't imagine Oliver Tremayne ashamed of his brother, no matter what he might look like. The eyes that had drilled down to her soul hadn't been capable of looking on his own flesh and blood with anything but the deepest love. She was sure of it. "Charlotte."

The use of her full name, Libby had found during their shared year of finishing school, was able to pull Lottie back better than a longer chide ever could.

"Well, what better explanation do you have for why the eldest son and heir would never have anything to do with his own business? The younger went to university and joined the church as expected, but he never spoke of his older brother. Why, I ask you?"

"Perhaps," said a harsh voice from before them that made Libby look up with a jolt, "because he wouldn't sully the thoughts of his saint of a brother with such vitriol as *your* sort would offer."

For a moment, she scarcely recognized Mabena, snarling as she was, with her hat held in her hands instead of fastened in place, and curls wisping all around her face. But it was definitely she who stood before them. Clearly having come to look for Libby. And clearly having heard at least the last bit of their conversation, over which she was even more annoyed than Libby had known she could be.

Charlotte, of course, didn't look chastised. She just lifted her chin. "And who are *you*?"

"Someone who knew Morgan Tremayne from the day I was born, that's who. Someone who can tell you, as could any soul on the islands, that never was a kinder, more generous-hearted man ever born, unless it be his younger brother." Mabena lifted a finger and poked it in Lottie's general direction. "Shame on you for speaking so of the dead. You want to know why he never left the island? Because he *couldn't*, that's why. His health was too fragile. As if he were the only gentleman ever afflicted so! And you, to sully his good name on account of an ailment he couldn't help! I say again, shame on you. On *both* of you."

Though the words only made Lottie bristle, they cut Libby to the quick. She hadn't said anything bad about Morgan Tremayne.

She'd in fact been defending the whole family in her thoughts and one-word rebuke. But there was no deterring Charlotte Wight from conversation. How could she be blamed for merely being present while she gossiped?

All the same, she knew well if it had been the Botanist standing before them now rather than a neighbor of his, he'd be looking at her in just that way. And the thought of it made her chest go so tight she could hardly draw breath enough to say, "Moon, please. Charlotte meant no harm."

For the first time in fifteen minutes, Lottie released her arm. "You know this . . . person, Libby?"

"She's my maid." The words felt wrong. Why, when they were true? When Mabena wouldn't want to be introduced as a friend? But all the same, she felt the chafing of it. To Mabena she added, "Charlotte said a friend of hers—Lady Emily Scofield—recommended she find Beth while she was here this summer. Lady Emily and Beth are friends, it seems." She hoped Mabena would hear in it that *this* was the real reason she'd been listening. That was her whole purpose today, after all. To find anyone who might have met Beth. And while Lottie hadn't, it still seemed significant that she, too, had been searching for her.

Because if there was one thing Lottie was proving even now, it was that she was an expert at finding out all the gossip to be had about a person. That could be useful—though tricky to determine which parts were true.

Mabena didn't soften any. "Given what she clearly thinks of the family, I'm surprised she'd deign to obey her friend's advice."

Lottie crossed her arms over her chest. "Well, sometimes we must keep company with people we'd rather not, when there's no other option. Right, Libby?"

Though it may in fact have been true—and accurately explained *their* friendship—she clearly meant Mabena now, and the fact that Libby was "forced" to keep company with her. But never in a million years would she agree.

Her stomach ached. "Please don't."

Just like that, Lottie shifted back to her usual smiles, arms falling to her sides. She even laughed as she turned to face Libby. "You never were one who could handle conflict, were you? Or disapproval. Even from your maid, it seems. How *did* you survive in London, Libby?"

She wrapped her arms around her stomach, notebook still clutched in one hand. "Badly."

"Hence, I suppose, while you're summering *here* instead. Well." She took a step backward. "I've no need to get in a row with a domestic. You can deal with her impertinence as you will—or probably *not*, knowing you. I will get an invitation to you for the dinner party. You did bring a few appropriate gowns? Lord Willsworth favors greens, I think."

As if Libby had ever in her life dressed to please a man. Well, other than her father. And brother. But they hardly counted. She *had* to please them at least a bit in order to be let out of the house—and getting out of the house had always been part of the agreement for what she was allowed to do when back *in* it. Balls and soirees in exchange for microscopes and slides.

Devious men.

To Charlotte, she simply nodded. She would worry with viscounts and dinner parties another day. For now, she'd try not to burst into flame under Mabena's continued glare.

Her friend scarcely waited until Lottie was out of earshot before spitting out, "You know *that* person?"

Maybe the ache in her stomach wasn't dread and fear. Maybe she just needed lunch. She stepped past Mabena. "We were at finishing school together in Switzerland."

Mabena snorted her opinion of that. "And you let her fill your ears with such rot as she was spewing about Morgan Tremayne?"

"There's no stopping her from talking, and it wasn't as though I knew what she was going to say. I was only . . . I said I'd learn what I could. I thought maybe she'd found something useful, since she was looking for Beth too."

A snort was Mabena's only answer. They trudged in silence back up the beach, nothing companionable about it now. By the time they reached their path, even the too-perfect "Meow" and the emergence of a cute little striped face couldn't quite make Libby smile fully.

Mabena hissed. "Shoo. Go away, kitty."

Instead, the little darling fell in beside Libby, lunging playfully at her feet and then tumbling away. It drew out a breath of a laugh, despite the clenching of her stomach.

Mabena sighed. "You fed it your bacon, didn't you."

It wasn't a question, so why bother answering?

"Fabulous. You'll never get rid of it now."

"Really?" Perhaps she oughtn't to have sounded so happy about it. It made Mabena roll her eyes and storm ahead. But the kitten let Libby pick it up and cuddle it under her chin. So it was worth it.

8

The wind whispered in his ear, luring his feet toward the shore. Oliver would have obeyed it even if he hadn't been on the path already, his gaze set on Enyon's familiar form down at the water. "Ahoy!" he called when close enough that there was a prayer his friend would hear him.

Enyon straightened, turned, and lifted a hand in greeting. At his feet rested the little one-man gig he always used for a bit of pleasure rowing, which meant he hadn't been running all the way to another island, just about Tresco, or perhaps over to Bryher to visit his sister. Given the fine mist that had been falling all day, Oliver was a bit surprised he'd been out at all. Enyon had always preferred a sunny day for his errands, when one was to be had.

"And what brings the good vicar down here twelve hours before his next sermon?" Enyon grinned at him, wiping a hand over his face to rid it of the mist.

Oliver lifted his brows. "I'll have you know I've finished my sermon. Mostly."

His friend chuckled, then nodded toward his gig. "Help me carry it up?"

Rather than waste words on an answer, Oliver grabbed an end. The larger craft were kept anchored in the quay, but the locals tended to store their smaller boats well above the waterline overnight.

At Enyon's grunt, they lifted it in tandem. "What does bring you here though? You're usually not to be peeled away from your desk on a Saturday evening."

Sermons were not his favorite part of his job and required by far the most effort, perhaps because he spent far more time visiting parishioners and contemplating what truths he might work into a sermon *someday* than crafting one for that week. But after the last few days, he wasn't all that concerned with whether he bored the congregation to tears. "I've been trying to catch you up since Wednesday."

"Ah. Sorry. You knew I had to make that overnight trip to the mainland on Thursday, didn't you?"

Oliver blinked against the mist and moved for the boathouse used by half a dozen families. "I'd forgot, honestly. I've been a bit distracted, worrying over Beth." He wouldn't confess it to just anyone. But this was Enyon.

They slid the gig into its spot in the boathouse. When Oliver turned, he found his friend's face lined with a concern to match his own. "About what? Is she still plotting how to go to London for the Season?"

"No, nothing like that." He'd already decided when he sought Enyon out that he'd tell him everything he knew. But even so, he couldn't quite put into words what he felt in his heart. "Did you hear Benna's back?"

"Aye, Mam mentioned that she saw her at her parents' the other day, trussed up like a Christmas goose—her words, not mine. Does that have something to do with Beth?"

Though he shrugged, he couldn't shake the feeling that it did, despite the fact that Mabena hadn't admitted as much. Why else, though, would she appear out of the blue? "She says that her employer just wanted a holiday. But . . ." He dragged in a deep breath, trying to keep thoughts of Benna and Lady Elizabeth from crowding out what really needed to be said. "But Beth . . . she's not on St. Mary's, En.

Mrs. Pepper said she thought she'd come home. But obviously she hasn't. She's just *gone*. Has been for over two weeks now."

"*What?*" Enyon took his hat off and ran a hand over his hair in one practiced motion, putting the cap back on with the next. "What do you mean, gone?"

Oliver made a *poof* motion with his fingers. "Gone. Vanished. No one's seen her, nor the *Naiad*." And though he could well imagine her hiding *herself* for weeks on end, how and where was she hiding her sloop?

"And you're not banging on the constable's door? Organizing a search?"

He'd considered it. But . . . "She left me a letter, indicating she was vanishing on purpose. Told me not to worry."

"Likely."

"Right?" He shook his head and buried his hands in his trouser pockets to keep them from mirroring Enyon's hat-swipe motion. "I don't know what I'm to do. She's my baby sister. She isn't supposed to do this sort of thing."

Enyon's snort at least had a bit of amusement in it this time. He motioned Oliver to follow him, though surprisingly, he didn't head for the cozy, dry cottage he'd let for himself last year, after his second sister and her brood moved back into their parents' house when her husband took a job on the mainland. He turned instead toward the beach.

Talk about a true friend. Oliver breathed in the damp air, relishing the mist on his face and the shift of sand and pebbles under his feet. It soothed him as nothing else could.

"Sisters," Enyon drawled after a long moment, "apparently think they're *supposed* to do whatever will cause us the most disquiet. If you ask me, the Lord ought to have made us humans to be capable of only producing one gender of offspring each. Boys could have brothers, girls could have sisters. Nice and tidy."

Laughter stole its way from Oliver's throat. "I suppose He didn't mean for our lives to be so tidy. Even so, a *bit* tidier just now wouldn't go awry. I can't . . ." *Lose her.* But he couldn't say it. Putting words to the fear lent it credence. Gave it weight.

He wouldn't give that fear any more weight than he already had, just by thinking of it.

Enyon didn't ask him to finish his sentence. "Do you think she took the ferry? There's a world of possibilities as to where she is if she did."

He couldn't discount the possibility. She could have sailed toward Tresco just to make sure no one was watching, stowed the boat somewhere, and then secreted her way back to Hugh Town. "I spoke with the captain, and he didn't remember seeing her. But you know Beth. When she doesn't want to be noticed, she isn't."

Enyon chuckled. "Oh yes, I'm well aware."

Oliver let the tug of a smile have its way with his lips. "Do you remember the time we all decided we'd brave a night in King Charles's Castle? And she—"

"Aye, I remember." Enyon gave his shoulder a shove. "And I don't need you imitating yet again my shriek when she jumped out at me, thank you very much."

"Wouldn't dream of it." Though his lips nearly pulled back to disobey his claim. He settled for another laugh instead, and then a few paces of quiet.

Over and again he'd taken this band about his chest to the Lord. Begged Him to watch over Beth as Oliver couldn't do. Begged Him to touch Mamm-wynn and keep her healthy. Begged Him to somehow put to rights whatever had gone wrong.

He closed his eyes for a moment, just to be. Here. Now. With his best friend at one side and the ocean at the other. The beach beneath his feet. Home stretching up above him. To feel the rhythms that *hadn't* changed, despite all that had.

Oliver. He could imagine his name in the breeze—and he always heard it in Mamm-wynn's voice, in that way she'd whispered it when he was just a boy, standing on the bluff overlooking the shore. He'd gone out in a huff, angry that his parents hadn't taken him with them to the mainland when they went to check on Truro Hall. And his grandmother had come out to soothe him.

"You don't belong there," she'd murmured, taking his slight shoulders in her still-strong hands and meeting his gaze, holding it. *"It's here you belong, Oliver Tremayne, as surely as your father and his father and his before him. Listen—listen to the wind. Do you hear that? It knows you, lad. The islands know your name, as they know all of us who love them. Be content."*

He had been. Him and Morgan both. It had been enough for them, to know the islands and be known in turn. But Beth . . .

Maybe Mamm-wynn hadn't ever had that talk with her. Maybe she hadn't taught her how to hear her name on the wind.

"So . . . Benna, eh? Did she look as tight-laced as Mam said?"

Oliver opened his eyes again. Pushed thoughts of Beth aside in favor of the picture of Mabena that surfaced. "I scarcely knew her. You'd have laughed for a century. Her hair, Enyon—it was *tidy*. Straight as a pin, sleek, all tucked in properly."

Enyon laughed now at the mere imagining. "Blast, but I'm sorry I missed it. I'll be sure and catch her soon, before the isles get back into her. It's a sight I need to see before it vanishes. And the lady she's serving now? She's here too?"

A nod did little to sum up that surprise. "Lady Elizabeth."

"What's she like? Pretty?"

Oliver rolled his eyes. "Always your first question."

"Come on, Ollie." A sharp elbow found his ribs. "Help a chap out."

"She's . . ." He sighed. She wasn't the sort of pretty people expected of a young lady. That was for certain. No carefully styled hair or dress or posture. No colors chosen to bring out eyes or lips or complexion. She didn't have the bold bone structure of Enyon's oldest sister or the wild allure that had made half the lads on Tresco fall for Mabena. Her features weren't unpleasant, but they also weren't the sort to draw the eye. Yet she had the sweetest smile he'd ever seen, and her eyes had been as boundless as the sea. One couldn't discount that. "I'll let you be the judge when you meet her. I liked her too well to think of such things."

Enyon barked another laugh, gave him another shove. "Only you, Ollie."

He wasn't sure if it was a compliment he should thank him for or an indictment he should defend against. So he shrugged and narrowed his eyes. "Do you see that? On Samson?"

They both paused, Enyon lifting a hand to add an extra shield to his eyes as he gazed toward the uninhabited island. "I see *something*. Not sure what. Movement though. A bird?"

"Looks too big." Squint as he might, Oliver couldn't bring it into any better focus. "A deer?"

"It's white."

"Could be an albino."

"None of those over there that I've ever heard of," Enyon said.

"Anomalies could be born at any time." But there weren't that many deer left on Samson. The Lord Proprietor had tried to build a park there for them after he moved the last of the residents off it fifty years before, but even the deer hadn't wanted to live on the inhospitable scrap of land. They'd tried to wade to Tresco during low tide, and some of them had succeeded.

Enyon pursed his lips. "Definitely doesn't move like a bird. Or a deer."

"No. It doesn't." But it wasn't moving like a person, either, to be a tourist or a local strolling about—not to mention that dusk was falling and no one would be over there at this time of day. Probably. "I saw a scrap of something white fluttering in nearly the same spot the other day. Rubbish, I assumed. Could be that, tangled on driftwood."

"I'd have thought someone would have cleaned it up by now." Enyon shifted, darted a glance at him. "You know what it *looks* like. . . ."

A ghost—something Enyon had claimed countless times over the years when they spotted something on a distant island shore that they couldn't identify. And countless times over the years, the other lads had teased him about his rich imagination.

This time, Oliver just hummed and kept watching the slip of white. As he'd visited his parishioners over the last two days, more than one of the old-timers had been muttering about "Gibson's tales coming to life." And the tales his mother's father favored were always the ones with specters. Or pirates. Or, better still, both.

Oliver braced one elbow on the opposite hand and tapped a finger to his cheek. "What did you say kept you awake Tuesday night?"

"Ah." Enyon cleared his throat. "Noises. Coming from the direction of Piper's Hole—not that I went to investigate. Didn't sound like voices, nor like an animal, and it wasn't a windy night. I know it was probably just youngsters causing a ruckus, but . . . but, well, it was enough to keep me awake. Especially worrying if it was youngsters, after . . ."

After Johnnie. "Have you heard them again?"

His friend shook his head. "But I was gone Thursday night, and last night I was dead to the world after getting home. Why?"

"I don't know. Noises in the caves, something odd on Samson . . . Just makes me wonder if—"

"If all the old tales are true and it's a lady in white over there? Singing a haunted lullaby to her lost babe in the caves?"

Oliver laughed again. "I was going to say that someone was up to something. Maybe someone decided to revive our long history of smuggling."

"Hmph." Enyon made a face. "You're always so boring."

"My apologies. I meant to say that it's likely some beleaguered ghost, trapped on the shores by her love for a sailor who dropped her there in 1624 and promised to come back for her but never did."

"Better." Though he cocked his head to the side. "Who's that, do you think?"

"My fictitious sailor and his abandoned love? How am I to know? I just made them up."

"No, idiot." Enyon slapped his arm and then pointed at something just coming into view around the point of land, aimed at Samson. A boat, obviously, moving at a good clip.

A familiar boat, as most of them were. It took him only a moment to place it. "Casek." He spat the name.

"Ah. He must have spotted whatever it is and decided to see to it."

"At this time of day?"

Enyon lifted a brow. "Since when does Casek Wearne care if it's the wisest time to do something?"

Because he had a point, Oliver relented. And started walking again. "Did you investigate the caves later? See if there was any sign of people having been there that night?"

"There are *always* people in the caves. What would I have hoped to see? Besides." He kicked at a shell, eyes on the ground ahead of them. "I haven't had the heart to go in there. Not after I helped them haul Johnnie out."

He'd forgotten that Enyon, living so near, was the one Johnnie's friends had fetched to help them. He clasped Enyon's shoulder. It should have been someone else—anyone other than softhearted Enyon—to do such a task. "I can't blame you for that. And maybe that explains it. Maybe it was his mam down there, crying. Or young Harriet—she was sweet on him."

One of the clouds cleared from Enyon's face, at least. He nodded. "You could be right. Or even his friends, paying their respects at the place where he fell. The wind could have just been distorting their voices."

"I daresay. That answers that question, anyway."

"And Casek will clean up the beach on Samson. That only leaves finding Beth. And how I'm to get a glimpse of Mabena all prim and a look at this lady she's serving."

"The islands aren't that big. I'm sure you'll see them." As they'd see Beth, if she were here. When she wanted them to.

They walked onward, until Oliver's house came into view. "Come up?"

"Thanks—not today. Still have a few things to do at home. Luncheon after church tomorrow though? Unless you've already been spoken for."

"Only by Mamm-wynn. You're certainly welcome to join us."

As he did at least one Sunday a month. "Sounds good. Talk to you tomorrow, Ollie."

"Good night." He lifted a hand in farewell as he climbed the path up his hill and Enyon turned back the way they'd come.

Every step upward, though, made his heart weigh a little heavier. When he got inside, Mamm-wynn would no doubt ask him, as she had every other time he came home since Wednesday, if he'd found Beth yet. And, like every other time, he'd have to tell her no. He'd tried explaining that Beth was where she wanted to be—without sharing the worry his sister's exact words had buried deep within him—but Mamm-wynn didn't even seem to hear those assurances.

He couldn't blame her. He didn't believe them himself.

A few minutes later he was passing through the familiar doors of home, listening for an indication of where his grandmother was to be found. When he heard the strains of the piano, he followed the music with a smile. She didn't play much these days. Her hands were too arthritic, and her eyes had trouble reading music. But once in a while she would sit and play one of her old favorites that both fingers and mind had memorized long ago.

He slid as quietly as possible into the drawing room and sat in his favorite chair, just listening. The song wasn't exactly as smooth sounding as it had once been, but it still brought a smile to his lips. And when she finished, he applauded, as he'd always done.

She spun daintily on her bench, fluttering a bow and smiling. Not at all surprised, it seemed, to find him there. "That one was for you, Ollie. And for her, of course."

His smile flickered. "Who? Mrs. Dawe? I didn't think she cared for Bizet."

Mamm-wynn laughed. "No, not Mrs. Dawe. You silly thing. As if you don't know very well of whom I'm speaking."

Did he? *Should* he? She couldn't mean Beth. His sister had never enjoyed opera at all, even just the instrumental parts. It had always been a bit of a joke in the family. "I'm afraid I'm at a loss."

Still chuckling, she stood. "I won't tell her you said so, darling. Don't worry. Though really, a man ought to know his wife's taste in music."

His . . . wife? A stone took over where his stomach had been earlier. Not knowing what to say, he just watched her hum her way from the room.

Maybe she'd thought him his father. Though that scarcely brought any comfort. Whether she thought him someone else or thought he had a wife, the truth of it was the same: confusion had clouded her mind again.

He buried his hand in his hair and leaned on the arm of the chair.

He wished she'd just asked about Beth again.

9

Rain—or its weak, misty sister—had plagued them again for days, and while Mabena might have braved it on her own, she wasn't about to suggest that Lady Elizabeth Sinclair simply don a mackintosh and wellies and they go to Tresco as planned. Because Libby would do it in a heartbeat, and then Mabena would be parrying curious glances and outright questions all day as to *why* an earl's sister was prancing about in the rain.

It had taken her until church on Sunday for her to put aside her irritation over that too-chatty Charlotte Wight. She needed nothing to put her in another mood. Not when Libby, by her very desire to be forgiven for something she didn't even do, made her feel so very prickly in all the wrong ways.

And the thought of people smiling and laughing over her employer being so different from what they expected just soured her mood all over again. So they stayed on St. Mary's through the rainy days, talking to ferry captains and bakers and grocers and anyone else Beth was likely to have spoken to while she was here.

Not that any of them offered the slightest insight as to where she could have gone when she piled her boat full of stuff and sailed out of Hugh Town's quay. Like Mrs. Pepper, they'd all just assumed she'd gone home, and no one had seen her or her boat since. But they did confirm that she'd stockpiled enough food and whatnot to see her through weeks, when one combined her purchases from different stores. Wherever she was, she was well enough fed, and the weather had been mild.

When Tuesday dawned bright and promising, it took only one brow-raised half-smile from Libby to have Mabena sighing out her agreement over breakfast. "Yes, all right. Today we'll go."

Libby's excited squeal made her feel more like a heel than ever. A lady shouldn't be so blasted easy to please. Mabena almost wished, as she scrubbed their porridge bowls clean, that Libby were more like her mother—or even the ghastly Edith. At least then the Scillonians would exchange five words with her and have no question at all as to why Mabena kept her dress buttoned up to the chin and hadn't come home once in two years.

"Are you trying to scrub the enamel off that bowl, Mabena?"

The soft tease tried its best to pull a smile onto her lips. But the sour won. Mam would accuse her of having put vinegar in her tea instead of sugar. "Yes, that's it. Blighted enamel." She set the bowl atop its mate with too loud a clatter. And glanced up.

Mistake, that. It showed her Libby's pinched brows, and the uncertain curve of her lips. "Have I . . . ? Or perhaps you're embarrassed to be seen with me on Tresco? By your family?"

The sigh that heaved its way up took all the fight out of her. "Don't be silly, Lady Elizabeth. Perhaps it's the other way round."

It wasn't, exactly. A lady couldn't possibly expect her maid to come from anything grand. There was no reason to be embarrassed by her family. If anything, Libby would find the Moon home to be more than she likely expected.

But every time Mabena saw it, she still heard those vile words in her ears. "*You aren't enough, Benna. Your father's a blighted shipwright, not a gentleman or an academic. You—you're more suited to be a maid to the sort of woman I need than a lady yourself.*"

Blast that blighted Cador Wearne. She ought to have kicked him from the bluff then and there, straight into the Atlantic he was so set on crossing. With the rage he'd kindled in her chest, she probably could have kicked him all the way to those coveted academic circles of his precious London.

"Mabena?"

And now she was gripping those bowls like she'd as soon grind them into dust with her bare hands as put them away. She slid them into their place in the cupboard and forced a smile. "Sorry, my lady. Bitter memories keep finding me. This is why I haven't come back till now, I suppose."

And she wouldn't have come *now* if Beth Tremayne had the good sense to mind herself and not go disappearing. Mabena wasn't ready to face all this. Not by half. And now she was casting blame on her oldest, dearest friend.

She dragged a long breath into her lungs. "Let's bring a change of clothes. If I know you at all, one day in the Gardens won't be enough. You'll want to go back tomorrow, so we'd better just plan to stay overnight."

Libby looked ready to skip to her room. Such a simple thing really shouldn't bring an earl's sister this kind of joy. "Perfect. Where shall we stay? With your family? Or is there a hotel or inn or something?"

"My mam would be honored to have you—and may disown *me* if I tried to stay anywhere else."

"Meow."

Mabena scowled down at the striped nuisance winding about Libby's legs. She'd tried to forbid the cat from coming inside, but it had "slipped in" the other day when Libby held the door open—deliberately too long, if one were to ask Mabena—and had hidden under the lady's bed until Mabena had given up trying to force it out.

She'd capitulated. More because of the happy smile on Libby's face than because, really, it wasn't her decision. But nothing said she had to be gracious about it. "And what are you going to do with the cat while we're gone?"

"Leave him outside with food enough to see him through." Libby bent down and lifted the mite into her arms, laughing when the tabby tried to crawl onto her shoulder like a blasted parrot.

"You oughtn't to let him do that. He's trying to assert dominance over you."

Libby lifted her brows, more curiosity than challenge in her expression. "Really? How do you know?"

Mabena scowled. "It's what my mother always said. I don't know. Seems logical, doesn't it?"

Yet there the creature was, all but wrapped around Libby's neck as she shrugged. "I rather thought it was just their instinct to find the highest place to perch. But then, cats aren't my specialty. I'll have to do some reading about it."

And in the meantime, she apparently meant to wear the thing like a scarf. Mabena rolled her eyes and strode toward the bedrooms. "I'll pack for us. You try to convince the little monster to go back outside." Mabena had been trying for days, but the beastie wouldn't cross that threshold again for anything, even the promise of more bacon. "And name it, will you, if you mean to keep it?"

Libby grinned, as if the request were a sign that Mabena was softening toward it. Which she wasn't. She just knew that her companion would get cross eventually if she kept calling it "the little monster." And much as a cross Libby sounded amusing in theory, she had a feeling it wouldn't be half so fun in practice. *One* of them needed to be all sunshine, and it certainly wasn't Mabena these days.

"I'm fairly certain it's a tom, though it is rather difficult to tell on so small a kitten."

"If you say so, my lady. I haven't a clue."

"In which case, I was thinking Darwin."

Mabena paused. "Not after *Charles* Darwin."

"Well, he was one of the greatest naturalists of the modern era."

"There's controversy around nearly all his theories." Not that she'd known much about his theories until she started serving Libby, aside from the fact that most people on the isles considered them heretical.

"He was awarded the most prestigious scientific award in all of Britain! The Copley Medal isn't handed out to just anyone."

"Your mother would be appalled and think you were railing against the church."

There, a crack in Libby's smile. Though it brought Mabena no pleasure to widen it, not really. "Plenty of clergy thought his theories noble and not at all in opposition to biblical teachings."

"And others—the voices that won the day—thought they demanded a polarization of science and theology." Mabena shook her head. "You'll find the people here far more given to theology than science, my lady. Some may find it offensive if you name it Darwin is all."

Libby's sigh made her wish it were otherwise. "Very well. Darling, then. That's what I've actually been calling you, haven't I?" She rubbed a finger under its chin. "I was considering Darwin largely because it sounded similar. But we'll just stick with my original thought."

A tomcat named Darling. Though she shook her head, Mabena's lips finally twitched up into a semblance of a genuine smile. "Well, convince *Darling* to go outside. I'll have everything ready in ten minutes, and we can be off."

It was bound to be a trying two days. But they might as well get them started so they could get them over with.

Libby was far from the only tourist in the Abbey Gardens on such a gorgeous sunny day, which was a bit of a shame. She stepped from the Garden Lodge, past the artfully arranged figureheads of ships long since sunk or retired, and wished she had the whole place to herself so she could explore every bloom and leaf. The Lodge delivered visitors onto what they called "the Avenue," a winding path that led through the Gardens. She took the first turn it offered, into an area marked as "the Wilderness." Ferns abounded—identifiable as such, but far different from the varieties to which she was accustomed. She'd seen images of a few, but to behold them with her own eyes . . . Her breath caught with glee.

113

Behind her, Mabena chuckled. "You're going to be here all day, aren't you?"

"Come and find me in a week. Maybe a month." She intended to start right here by the door and move as slowly as necessary to take in absolutely everything.

"And this is why we came here even before going to my parents'." At least Mabena finally sounded amused again, instead of angry. Libby's stomach had been in knots for days, the way she had refused to come out of the mood Lottie had put her in. "Have fun. I'll take our things to their house and find you later. Shall I arrange for luncheon and tea somewhere, or just bring you a sandwich?"

"Sandwich. Please." Positioning herself as out of the way on the path as possible, Libby dropped to a seat on the ground, crossed her legs under her skirt, and opened her notebook. The Abbey Gardens had provided her with a little booklet that named many of the blooms, and between that and the gardener, she meant to put together an exhaustive catalogue. Though really, two days wouldn't be enough for such an undertaking, not even close. She'd have to start working on Mabena now to come here with her at least one day a week this summer. Or let her come on her own. There were tourists aplenty on the boats between islands. Surely that would be acceptable if Mabena didn't want to join her.

According to the booklet, the gardener counted the blooms every January, and this year there had been two hundred and eleven varieties, nearly all of them exotic and to be found nowhere else in England— other than when the seeds had been carried to the other islands in the chain. The Gardens were arranged like the empire itself, with species from the different colonies and outposts grouped together. Here, at the door, she was in Australia. As fine a place as any to begin.

She started with a sketch of the Gardens themselves from this vantage point. She always liked to get the wide view before she switched to the narrow. When she was back in her cottage, she would put color to it, but for now, black strokes on clean white paper would suffice.

"An artist, are you?"

She was nearly finished with this first sketch and ready to flip the page when the deep voice drew her gaze up. She smiled when she saw the older gentleman crouching down beside her. If she wasn't mistaken, he was the gardener, though she'd caught only a glimpse of him inside, where he'd promised to chat with each guest and answer any of their questions. It would hardly be fair to dominate his attention, but she knew well she'd have questions enough to keep him busy all day.

She flipped to one of the sketches she'd done the other day of the seabirds, complete with scientific names and her observations. "A naturalist. The sketches are just part of my observation and discovery." That was always the first step to learning, after all—observation.

The gardener nodded, appreciation in his eyes rather than condescension, which was the usual response she got from people. Especially men.

"Well done, indeed. You'll find a rich selection here in our Gardens, to be sure. Mr. Menna," he said then, a palm extended. "The gardener."

She probably ought to use her full name with title, but it seemed too pretentious for the setting. "Libby Sinclair. How do you do?" She put her fingers into his palm, liking him even more when he bowed over them even without knowing she was a titled lady.

"Wonderfully, miss. Thank you. Have you any questions yet? I do realize you've barely begun your exploration, but I'm happy to answer any inquiries."

No fewer than a dozen rioted for a place on her tongue, which made her laugh. "I could keep you occupied all day, sir. Here's the most important though—do you need an apprentice?"

He laughed, though there was nothing mocking about it. Just actual delight. "I've a bit of one already in the vicar. But I do enjoy talking about my gardens with avid pupils. You are certainly welcome here any time, Miss Sinclair, and I'd be most happy to share any knowledge with you that I have and you desire."

The vicar—he must mean Mr. Tremayne. He was the only vicar on Tresco, so far as Libby knew. And it made sense that he and Mr.

Menna would be not only acquainted but friendly. That certainly explained how he'd known so much about botany when he led her through her own gardens with such expert ease.

Though she wanted to glance around to see if perhaps he were here now, she instead kept her focus on Mr. Menna. Conversing with him was ever so much easier than chatting with the holiday-goers on St. Mary's. "That's very kind of you, sir, and I'll no doubt take you up on your offer. Though you ought to attend the other visitors first. I don't want to take up too much of your time."

He chuckled and leaned a little closer, dark eyes sparkling. "To be perfectly honest," he said in a whisper, "I'd prefer to spend a day with someone genuinely interested than with someone who only came because they were told they must. But we'll let that be our secret. I try to think of it as a challenge to interest those casual visitors and help them see the splendor all about them."

"What a lovely perspective." It certainly was healthier than growing frustrated when people didn't seem to care about the same things you did. Which was how she ended every single conversation with Edith. "I pray you open someone's eyes today, Mr. Menna."

"And I pray you enjoy every minute you spend here, Miss Sinclair. Don't hesitate to find me if you have a pressing question. Otherwise I'll certainly find you in a bit."

She smiled him on his way and turned to a fresh sheet of paper. Her first individual subject would be the *Alsophila australis*—a fern, so said its leaf, but far larger than the sort she saw at home. The stalk was as thick as the trunk of a sapling, and it was at least three feet tall.

It was like being in another world altogether. One she could happily get lost in. Where, she had to wonder, had Oliver Tremayne last been in these gardens? If Mr. Menna called him an apprentice of sorts, then he must spend a lot of time here. Had he ever knelt right here, where she sat now? Had he helped to plant any of these specimens in the ground or arranged the stones that guarded them?

And why did the thought of that make her fingers tingle around her pencil? She took a deep breath and focused on her work. First this fern, and then the ones neighboring it. As the morning went on, she had to scoot to a new position several times as the sun arched over her, warming her shoulders.

"There you are, dearest."

She may have ignored the unfamiliar voice if its owner hadn't stopped directly at her side, casting a shadow over her page. Libby looked up, the crick in her neck telling her as surely as the angle of the sun that she'd been here for hours already. Her prepared smile went genuine when she beheld the little sprite of a woman grinning down at her, as ancient as the stones all over the islands, from the look of her.

She didn't know why the woman spoke as if she'd been searching for her, but it was hard not to enjoy being found by such a face. "Good morning, ma'am." Had Mr. Menna sent the lady to find her? Perhaps it was his mother, and she'd offered to check on the odd girl who was sitting on the pathway, drawing. That must be it.

The lady held out a hand. "Come, dearover. I've been wanting to walk with you."

"Oh." Odd, but . . . "All right." She scampered to her feet, tucking the pencil into her notebook and the notebook into its usual place under her arm. She then put her hand into the old lady's, marveling at how soft her skin was, like the most precious paper. "Where shall we walk, ma'am?"

The lady's laugh was how Libby imagined a fairy's, if she ever bothered to think about how a fairy might laugh. Which she hadn't until now. "How many times must I tell you? You needn't call me *ma'am*. Just call me Mamm-wynn, dearest, like the others do. Heaven knows I've earned the badge, at my age."

She knew from Mabena that it was simply the Cornish word for *grandmother*. And she had no real reason not to call the woman by such a title, if it was what she preferred. Perhaps she considered herself the grandmother to everyone on the islands. But that "how many times" gave her pause for a moment. Had she confused Libby with someone else? If so, mightn't that someone else be upset if they found their grandmother hand in hand with a complete stranger?

Well, she'd try to catch Mr. Menna's attention as they walked. If the woman had wandered away from a group of tourists or her family home, he would surely know it and help her return the delightful figure to her rightful place. She gave the delicate hand an equally delicate squeeze. "Of course, Mamm-wynn."

"That's a good girl." Mamm-wynn patted her arm, her smile still as bright as the sun. And her eyes looked perfectly clear, not clouded with confusion. But then, what did Libby know of such things? Papa's parents had died when she was too young to remember them, and Mama's she never saw more than once a year, living on the other side of the country as they did.

"So, tell me, dear—what do you think of our islands, now that you've been here awhile?"

Did a week count as awhile? She tipped her face up to take in the blue sky, watched a gull circle, and then smiled as she took in the expanse of the garden again. "I think . . . I think I could spend the rest of my life here and never miss the mainland for a moment."

Only when she spoke the words did she realize how true they were. Perhaps it was a strange sentiment, given how much of the week had been spent indoors hiding from the rain. But every time she'd stepped outside, be it to the beach or into charming little Hugh Town, or onto the boat that had ferried them from St. Mary's to Tresco this morning, that same sense of contentment had overtaken her.

This place was more than the mere facts she'd learned about it before coming. It wasn't just an archipelago situated twenty-five miles off the coast of Cornwall. It wasn't just the host to exotic species imported from around the empire. It wasn't just six square miles of flower farms and sheep pastures and beaches.

It was something more. Something that made her wonder if she'd find here what eluded her in London, and even at Telford Hall.

Mamm-wynn hummed her approval of the answer. "That is just the way I felt when I first came here."

Libby looked down at the pixie of a woman. "You weren't raised here?"

"Oh no." The lady laughed again. "I was born and raised in Essex. It was my husband I took a fancy to first, when he was in London for the Season. That was . . . my, more years ago than I care to count. More than seventy-five! I was seventeen that spring, and he was the handsomest thing, with those snapping eyes as dark as midnight."

Her dreamy sigh made a grin tickle Libby's lips. She'd never been much for romantic fancies herself, but she couldn't deny the charm of hearing a woman in her nineties still sigh so over her husband. "And so you married him and he brought you here?"

"Quite so. I was uncertain at first, I admit it, when he said he meant for us to stay here. I thought it impossible that I could survive on such a small island." Another magical laugh, and Mamm-wynn tugged her toward a branch in the path that led away from the Australian plants. "But then we got here, and I stood on the hill overlooking Bryher and the sea. And I knew." She closed her eyes and drew in a long breath. "You know the value of names, don't you, dearest?"

"Hm?" The abrupt shift made her blink. "I . . . names?" Was this a rebuke for not giving Mr. Menna her full name, complete with honorary title? Had she somehow found her out?

But Mamm-wynn indicated her notebook. "You've written down the Latin names, haven't you?"

"Oh! Yes. Precise nomenclature is how we can identify and separate one species from another. When something is given a unique name, it's . . . well, it's like a tip of the hat, in a way, isn't it? It's us acknowledging that it is unlike anything else previously named. It is something unique."

Had she delivered that little speech to her own grandmother, she'd have gotten an owlish blink and then a stiff reminder that such talk wasn't likely to win a young lady a husband.

Mamm-wynn, however, nodded, sending a wisp of silver hair dancing on the breeze. "Exactly so. And it's the same with people. Names . . . they matter to us. They shape our souls in ways I've never fully understood. But have you pondered the power of them? That the angels instructed parents in what to name the children of promise—

John the Baptizer and Jesus, just to name the obvious two. The Lord renamed Abram. Sarai. Jacob. Simon Peter. Saul of Tarsus. Why?"

Libby let her gaze wander the path Mamm-wynn had put them on. "The Long Walk," Mr. Menna had called it in his introductory speech inside the Lodge that morning. Dozens of plants vied for her admiration—palms, aloes, gum trees, cacti, dracœnas. And she'd always much preferred thinking about them than theology.

But no one had ever put a biblical question to her in such a way. She let it roll about in her mind as they walked at a pace faster than she'd have expected Mamm-wynn to be comfortable with. "I suppose . . . I suppose because the Lord recognized an evolution in them." She darted a glance at her companion to see if she'd object to the choice of word like Mama would have. But her wrinkled face remained happy, so she pressed on. "They began as one creature—Abram or Sarai or Jacob or Simon or Saul. But through the events of their life, they became something else altogether. Abraham, Sarah, Israel, Peter, Paul."

Mamm-wynn nodded. "And that evolution couldn't go unnamed. Because the naming itself is crucial. Part of the change, don't you think?"

"Part of the acknowledgment of it, at the least."

"With a plant, to be sure. But people have an awareness that plants don't—they need to *know* their name." The lady splayed a hand over her heart and looked out along the Long Walk as if it took her through the years and not just the Gardens. "I needed to know mine. And I didn't, not fully, until I married my Edgar and came here, when I realized I hadn't just taken on his name. I'd truly taken on my own for the first time. And I could hear it in the whisper of the sea breezes."

She sent Libby another smile. "I always say that there are some born here. Some who visit. Some who leave. Others who stay. And it isn't because of circumstances or opportunities. When we stay, it's because the islands know our names, and they whisper them to us on the wind. But others—others keep their names locked away, held secret from the Scillies. And because they won't let the islands know them, they can never really know the islands. They can never love them."

120

As fanciful, certainly, as one might expect of a fairy. But a fairy who likened ideas to the Bible, so perhaps it wasn't just fancy. Perhaps it was something else entirely.

Taking in another sweet-scented breath, Libby tilted her head. Listened to the wind whispering through branches. "Do they know *my* name, do you think?"

Another pat of a featherlight hand on her arm. "How could they not, when you show them that sweet heart of yours?"

The thought made her lips curve in a way she couldn't ever recall them doing before, and she followed Mamm-wynn's gentle guiding toward another offshoot of a path. Perhaps she was only spending a summer here, but all the same she relished the idea that she could belong. By virtue of simply knowing and being known. Of loving it.

If that were truly how one knew when one was home, then it was no wonder she'd never felt so secure in London, where she felt the need to guard her true self at every step, every word, every introduction. And even Telford Hall . . . she'd always known it wasn't meant to be where she stayed forever. How could a daughter *not* know it, when from the time she was old enough to carry on a conversation, her elders spoke always of family alliances and good marriages and making a match that would benefit them all? They might as well have shouted, "Your role is to leave us as quickly as possible!"

How could one feel truly at home in a place always ready to foist one away?

"Here we are." Mamm-wynn drew her to a halt in front of a weathered slab of granite with two holes in it, one directly above the other. They were near the walled edge of the garden now, it seemed. Just beyond it was a building—a church, from the look of it. Which meant St. Nicholas's. Where Oliver Tremayne could be even now.

Libby focused again on the moss-kissed stone. "Where, exactly?" She'd seen similar stones around St. Mary's, sort of. Granite ones, certainly, and roughly the same rectangular shape, though this was by far the largest she'd beheld. Those others had only one hole though. And while most were simply garden decorations at this point, a few still had cords tied to the holes, the other end of which extended to the roofs. Anchoring the thatch, Mabena had said, to keep it from blowing away in the first good storm.

Mamm-wynn giggled and gave her arm a playful nudge with her shoulder. "As if you don't know."

Had Mr. Menna mentioned the stone that morning? Libby tried to recall, but she hadn't noted anything about a large slab of granite.

But the lady didn't seem to notice her silence. She let loose a happy little sigh and leaned into Libby's arm as if they were old friends. "I always loved hearing the tales of the Betrothal Stone. They're probably more fiction than fact, but even so. I wove a few of my own for my children. And when my dear boy proposed to his darling right here, I think I was every bit as pleased by it as Theresa was. And now you have your own story to tell!"

Libby's stomach flopped. Not exactly in the way it had when Mabena rebuked her and Lottie. But still, it wasn't comfortable. Clearly this lovely lady thought her someone else. Which was not only ironic, given the talk of the importance of names, but also distressing. She needed to find out where Mamm-wynn belonged and return her. Because as delightful as their conversation had been, she hadn't ever meant to have it with *her*.

That probably shouldn't make disappointment sink so heavily into her bones. But it had been nice, if only for a quarter of an hour, to call her Grandmother and feel as though she belonged there by her side.

Her smile wobbled now when she put it on. "May I help you home, Mamm-wynn?"

As if the mere mention of it sapped her strength, the lady leaned more heavily upon her and nodded. "I think that would be wise. Mrs. Dawe will be cross with me for sneaking out again." But she laughed. "I keep telling her that *someone* has to keep her on her toes."

Hopefully whoever Mrs. Dawe was, she wouldn't be cross with Libby for keeping her out instead of returning her the moment their paths crossed. But she hadn't known the lady had been sneaking anywhere.

And even if she had, she wasn't entirely certain she would have done anything differently. Even if the conversation had been intended for someone else, it had lit something in her.

"We had better take the shortcut." Mamm-wynn indicated another path.

"All right." Libby slid an arm around her companion's slight waist as they walked, the better to support her, since it seemed her energy was flagging with each step. They slipped out a small door in the garden wall that clearly wasn't used by many people, and Libby followed the subtle presses of the lady to know where to go from there.

They didn't walk far before they'd entered the gate of a quaint stone house that she prayed was where the woman actually lived. It was bigger than its neighbors, set apart, with a beautiful vista stretching down to the sea. Nothing nearly so grand as Tresco Abbey, where the Lord Proprietor lived. But beautiful. She'd have liked to take a moment there at the gate simply to pause and admire it—the way it looked as though the stones had sprung from the ground itself and clambered atop one another, moss acting as mortar; the way the sun glinted off the windowpanes and made them wink a greeting; the explosion of color in the flowers growing along absolutely every line and boundary and wall.

If this was where Mamm-wynn's Edgar had brought her when they wed, it was no wonder she had let the islands know her name. Who wouldn't want to live here? Perhaps it was only a fraction of the size of Telford Hall, but it would be perfect for a family to grow in.

The door opened as they approached it, and a worried-looking woman of middling age bustled out. "There you are! And what will Master Oliver say when he learns you've sneaked out again, Mrs. Tremayne?"

Mrs. Tremayne? Master Oliver? Libby nearly stumbled on the perfectly smooth flagstones under her feet. Had this lovely woman—his grandmother, no doubt—mistaken her for Beth, as the strangers had?

But no. Beth wasn't engaged or married either. She'd have no story of the Betrothal Stone to tell. Perhaps she'd mistaken her for a neighbor. A niece. Who was to say?

The worried woman—Mrs. Dawe, presumably—had reached their side and turned grateful eyes on Libby. "Thank you so much for seeing her home, miss."

She didn't have to force the smile. If this was what Mrs. Dawe looked like when cross, then she could only imagine her happy. "It was my pleasure, I assure you."

Mrs. Tremayne linked her arm through Libby's again. "We'll have some tea now, I think. Are you hungry yet, dearover?"

"Oh, of course! Come in, please." Mrs. Dawe—a housekeeper, perhaps?—waved a hand toward the still-open door. "A bit of refreshment is the least we can offer in thanks."

"Oh." She wanted to accept. Which might be the first time in her life she could say such a thing of an invitation from a stranger. "I'd love to, but Mabena Moon will be looking for me in the Gardens."

Mrs. Dawe chuckled. "Not for a while, she won't. Her mam roped her into helping her set up a new display in her shop, and they were nowhere near done when I walked by ten minutes ago. You've time to come in, and I'll send Mr. Dawe round to let her know where you are. Lady Elizabeth, then, is it?"

She liked the way Mrs. Dawe said it—as if it were simply a matter of fact, stated for clarity, not something to fuss over like Mrs. Pepper had done. She didn't at all mind nodding her agreement. "That's right."

"Lovely. You and Mrs. Tremayne can rest in the drawing room while I put the pot on and get lunch together. Master Oliver ought to be home soon too."

She wasn't sure what Mrs. Tremayne's wink was supposed to mean, but it made Libby's cheeks feel warm again. But then, she'd forgotten to pay attention to whether her hat was shielding her face from the sun, so it was possible she'd just been sunburned.

No one seemed to mind that Libby didn't say anything. She let the lady of the house lead her into the pretty little drawing room and didn't even mourn the time she wasn't spending in the Gardens.

The plants would still be there in an hour. For now, she would simply enjoy the time with the Botanist's grandmother.

10

Oliver paused, his hand on the doorknob as he looked over his shoulder at his uncle. "You'll let me know if you hear anything else?"

Uncle Mark gave him the same look he'd *always* given him when he asked what he deemed a ridiculous question. "Keeping it to myself wouldn't do much good, now would it?"

"No. But we've never encountered this particular problem in my memory. Perhaps you'll decide to combat it singlehandedly tomorrow."

His uncle chuckled at that and hooked his pipe into his mouth. He looked like he'd much prefer sinking into his favorite armchair and getting lost in that book by George MacDonald sitting on the end table than going about the village, speaking up against superstition. "By tomorrow it'll likely have blown over. It's just your grandfather Gibson, you know it is. He's been having a grand time, telling tales at the pub."

And Oliver would do well to drop in for a visit with *him* later and beg him to stop it already. He enjoyed Tas-gwyn's tales as much as the next person, but on the heels of Johnnie's death, everyone was jumping at every shadow. Or wail of the wind in the caves. Or flutter of white on the shores of Samson. New tales of a White Lady

125

haunting the cliffs had sprung up, and it was frightening enough that no one had dared venture to the island to collect that wisp of white, until Wearne had gone.

To his uncle he gave a nod. "Mrs. Dawe said she'd be making some fairings today. I imagine she'll send some around for you and Aunt Prue."

Uncle Mark grinned around his pipe. "Good woman, that Margie Dawe. We wouldn't object."

They said their farewells, and Oliver let himself out of the vicarage, into the bright June sunshine. That, aided by the joyful shouts of children nearby, eclipsed the worry at least momentarily and brought a smile to his face. He followed the sounds of laughter and small voices to the National School on the opposite side of St. Nicholas's, where the children must have been enjoying their lunch hour—and no doubt wishing the third term would end.

He leaned against the stone fence around the schoolyard, watching the enthusiastic game of cricket underway. He'd played many a game there himself, a decade or two ago. Always with Enyon at his side. Always with Casek on the opposing team. Always keenly aware of the fact that Morgan wasn't there at the local school with him but was home with a tutor. His mother, ever conscious of the "tarnish" she'd brought to the Tremayne name, had wanted to keep Oliver at home for his schooling too, saying the island's state-run school would do him no favors.

How glad he was that his father had prevailed. He'd claimed it far more important that Oliver have a place among his neighbors—and he'd been right.

"I said *stop it*." The voice cut through the ongoing game from somewhere nearby, though Oliver couldn't see the owner. It sounded like one of the Grimsby boys, though he couldn't be sure which one without seeing them. There were three, only a year between each, and when they ran in a line, one had the strangest feeling one was seeing the same person progressing through time.

"Aw, come on, Joseph. You're not scared, are you?" That answered the question of who the first speaker had been—Joseph was the middle step of the Grimsby stairs. And the mocking voice was his best friend, Perry Hill, if Oliver wasn't mistaken.

"Lay off him, Perry. No one wants to go down there. Not now. Not after Johnnie."

Not after Johnnie. He'd heard that phrase more times in the last weeks than he'd bothered to count, and each time it made something tighten in his chest. But where was "down there"? The caves? Piper's Hole in particular?

He took a few more steps along the wall until he could glimpse the tops of a few dark heads hunkered between the Cornish hedge and the stone wall, in what children had been using as a "secret" lair for decades. "Afternoon, lads."

Though they jumped at his voice, when they looked up, the three smiled at him. Two Grimsbys—only the youngest was missing—and the Hill. "Afternoon, Mr. Tremayne," the eldest Grimsby said. Nick.

He'd tossed enough balls for all of them that he didn't think they'd really mind his inviting himself into their conversation now. "How have you all been? After Johnnie, I mean." He met one gaze after another, and in each he saw the same emotions, though in unique combinations: pain, anger, uncertainty.

Perry clenched his fist. "I say it wasn't just a slippery rock, sir. No one was more sure-footed than Johnnie."

Johnnie was Perry's older cousin, and the lad had idolized him. Oliver tilted his head and held young Perry's gaze. "What else could it have been?"

At the direct question, the lad sighed and shrugged. "His head was busted. It could have been someone sneaking up on him, not just him falling and hitting a rock."

"Who would do that?" Joseph Grimsby shook his head. "Everyone loved Johnnie. *Everyone.* Forget it, Perry. *Please.*"

"Everyone from here loved him, but it could have been someone *not* from here."

Nick snorted, dismissive in that way lads always were when they had an extra year and so thought it came with extra wisdom. "Right. A pirate, like old man Gibson was telling us about. Or a smuggler. Because that's really likely."

Tas-gwyn again. Oliver didn't know whether to sigh or laugh. "Has my grandfather been telling tales to you lads too?"

Perry shrugged. "I'm just saying it wouldn't hurt to go down to the caves."

"No." Joseph punctuated the word with a fold of his arms over his chest. "I'm never stepping foot in those caves again."

"Me neither." And his older brother didn't seem the least bit ashamed of his decision. "No one is, as we've been telling you all month. If you want to go, you'll have to go alone. No one else has since they brought Johnnie out, and no one will."

"*No one* has? Or none of you?" Oliver feared for a moment that he'd sounded far too interested and would scare them back to the cricket game.

But these lads were closer to being men than that. Nick shook his head. "No one. Johnnie's mam said it must be cursed, and no one's dared go down there since. Especially after Enyon said he heard strange goings-on last week."

"Whole island's a bunch of cowards." Perry jammed the stick he'd been fiddling with into the dirt. "So what if it *is* his ghost down there? He'd only be haunting the place if he'd been murdered or something. Right, vicar?"

Was that what others thought too? All these ghost stories Tas-gwyn was telling—were they mixing up in the minds of his neighbors with the recent tragedy?

Oliver shook his head. Kept his face and his gaze soft. "No, Perry. I knew Johnnie. He was a good, God-fearing young man. However he died, he's not haunting the caves—he's at peace with the Lord."

Joseph's foot flashed out, connected with Perry's shin, and retreated again. "I *told* you."

Perry lunged, and a moment later the leaves of the Cornish hedge were shaking as the boys tumbled in a blur back into the yard, Nick somehow joining the melee too. Oliver sighed and considered vaulting over the stone wall to intervene.

Though before he had the chance, Casek Wearne came charging outside. "Grimsby! Grimsby! Hill! On your feet *now*!"

The tussle continued for half a second more, until the approaching footfalls of the headmaster must have convinced them that he meant business. Then they scrambled to their feet.

Casek stalked along the line of them but did nothing more than give them a scathing look.

Oliver realized a moment too late that the headmaster had set his path toward *him*. He ought to have walked away the moment the lads tumbled out of the bush, but his hesitation now meant that Casek Wearne was a foot away, sneering at him over the wall. "Stop harassing my students, Tremayne."

How could the man make him bristle so fully with five little words? His fingers curled into his palm. "Harassing them? Really?"

"This is school property." Though Wearne drilled a finger into Oliver's shoulder, which put said finger *outside* school property. "You're not welcome here."

Oliver backed up a step to keep himself from poking back. "Isn't it tiring, being such a blighter all the time?"

Casek looked as though *he* would vault the wall at any moment. But awareness of his audience prevailed. He too stepped back. Though he lifted his finger again, pointing it instead of poking. "Be ready to lose tomorrow, Tremayne."

And this was the example he was setting for his students? Oliver lifted his chin. "Good luck to you too."

"I don't need luck. Not as long as your teammates are so scared of a few ghost stories that they don't sleep anymore." He pivoted then and shouted something at the children—a warning of only ten minutes left of recess.

Oliver scarcely heard those words, so fully had his mind caught on the ones he'd spat before. Would Casek Wearne stoop so low as to play tricks on Enyon?

Undoubtedly.

But would he really leverage the tragedy of one of his former students' deaths to do it?

Oliver spun away from the wall, not sure even he could believe that. Casek Wearne was a blighter, without question, but he genuinely cared about his students. This stupid rivalry wasn't stronger than that, was it?

He sincerely hoped not. But he didn't know anymore where the Wearnes drew their lines.

When next he refocused, he saw his own house before him, though he'd intended to pay one more visit before going home. Apparently his feet had obeyed his stomach instead of his mind, and since he smelled something delicious wafting from the kitchen door, he followed its trail inside.

Mrs. Dawe met him with a tray and a smile. "There you are. In the drawing room with you, sir. Your grandmother and the lady are entertaining each other, though I'm not certain who's most amused by whom."

"The lady?" But even as he fell in behind her, he knew. It *had* been Mabena he'd caught a glimpse of before he went into the vicarage—he hadn't been sure. And she must have brought Lady Elizabeth with her.

But how had she ended up in his drawing room?

Mrs. Dawe chuckled. "While I was baking this morning, Mrs. Tremayne decided to take a turn through the Abbey Gardens and happened upon her. Lady Elizabeth was good enough to bring her home."

"Ah." He should probably be concerned that Mamm-wynn had slipped out again without telling anyone where she was going. But the banding around his chest didn't feel like worry for his grandmother. It felt suspiciously more like anxiety over what Lady Elizabeth Sinclair might think of her.

Casek Wearne's fault, no doubt. Last week's *"your mad old grandmother"* still irritated Oliver whenever the memory surfaced, and given that he'd just seen his snarling face . . .

Even before he reached the drawing room, he could hear them.

Two voices, laughing together, one as familiar as the wind through the Cornish palms, the other as novel as the long-headed poppy that bloomed in the garden for the first time that spring. A bit of the tension eased.

And it eased more when he stepped into the room and saw them perched on the sofa together, heads nearly touching as they leaned over something in their laps. A book of some sort. Hopefully a notebook, given that Mamm-wynn was writing something on it with a pencil. Lady Elizabeth watched her intently, her lips curved into an echo of her laughter.

His breath whispered out. He'd seen her feigning polite interest last week with Mrs. Pepper. This was something different. This seemed to be genuine pleasure with Mamm-wynn's company.

As well it should be. There was no woman in all of England quite like Adelle Tremayne. But how long until everyone forgot that, when she greeted them by the wrong name or spoke of events from forty years ago as if they happened yesterday?

"Here we are, ladies." Mrs. Dawe set the tray down on the low table before the sofa, beaming at them both. "And I've brought the young master in to share it with you."

"Oh good." Mamm-wynn motioned him closer and patted the space left on the sofa beside her. "I've been describing the flowers in our family garden for Libby, dearovim, but I don't remember their Latin names, only the common ones. You'll have to help us."

Libby, was it? And why not—Mamm-wynn was probably more the lady's peer than anyone else in the Scillies, having been born to a viscount's second son herself. Oliver took the proffered seat with a smile. "Of course. And how are you today, my lady?"

She met his gaze, revealing eyes dancing with light. "Absolutely wonderful. I do believe I like Tresco even better than St. Mary's, though I hadn't thought it possible." She grinned at Mamm-wynn. "Or perhaps it's the company."

She liked her. It should come as neither a surprise nor a relief, but . . . but he hadn't realized until then how much he *wanted* her to like

131

his grandmother. To like all of Tresco. "Both are without equal, to be sure."

"Oh, you." Mamm-wynn chuckled and tapped the page, on which were a few small but skillful drawings of the flowers from around their front door. "Latin."

He provided the names while Mrs. Dawe prepared a plate of sandwiches and sweets for each of them. Rather impressed that Lady Elizabeth didn't require any help in spelling the Latin, he made no objection when she flipped back to the pages dedicated to a few of the Australian specimens from the Abbey Gardens and asked for their binomial designations too.

They ate while they discussed the plants—since the Latin names led to which other varieties were related and how they managed to flourish so well in the Scillies—and he found himself rather liking the way Lady Elizabeth took actual, hungry bites of her sandwich, rather than the dainty nibbles he and Morgan used to tease Beth for attempting.

And why was he watching how she ate?

Mamm-wynn interrupted his thoughts with a hand on his wrist. With her other, she covered a yawn. "I think I'd better go and rest for a bit."

Mrs. Dawe sprang forward from where she'd been waiting by the door for that very announcement.

Mamm-wynn let Oliver help her to her feet, though she paused once standing, as she always did, to pat his cheek. "I don't imagine you two will complain about some time to yourselves."

Oliver frowned. Shouldn't she have instead been assuring him that Mrs. Dawe would return momentarily to chaperone?

Mrs. Dawe apparently thought so, given the baffled look she shot him. "Perhaps you ought to walk Lady Elizabeth back to the Abbey Gardens, sir, so Mabena can find her."

"Of course."

Mamm-wynn waved a hand at him as if she thought he should sit again. "Let them have their time, Margie. Don't you remember what it's like to be a newlywed?"

He'd never thought himself given to embarrassment, but Oliver's face felt alive with flames. As did his neck. And his ears. And—he spun, eyes wide and an apology ready to trip off his lips.

Lady Elizabeth was blushing too, but she was still smiling at his grandmother. "Have a lovely afternoon, Mrs. Tremayne. I hope to see you again soon."

His grandmother gave her a pointed look. He didn't know what it was for, but it seemed Lady Elizabeth did. "I mean, Mamm-wynn."

Mamm-wynn nodded. "Better. And I should think so. I won't nap *that* long."

Lady Elizabeth closed her notebook and stood as Mrs. Dawe ushered his grandmother out. He waited until they'd cleared the room, then faced her again. Spread his hands. "I am so sorry. I don't know what's come over her. She's . . ."

He couldn't say it. Could only spin his hands, searching for some other word.

Her fingers caught his, stilled them. "She's the most delightful person I think I've ever met. There's no need to apologize, sir."

Wasn't there? When his grandmother was acting as though they were married? He shook his head and let her lower his hands. "She is. But lately—I don't know where she gets some of her ideas. I certainly didn't . . . I mean, I hadn't said anything . . ."

She let go of his hands, though her smile didn't dim any. "I don't know where she got the idea either, but it does explain a few things she said to me in the garden. I thought she'd confused me with someone else?"

Was it a question of whether he *was* involved with someone—or, more likely, a question of what in the world Mamm-wynn had meant? Either way, he had to shake his head. "I can't think who. You bear a passing resemblance to my sister, but not so much that she'd mistake you. And even if she did, she wouldn't have then made *those* comments."

He motioned, as he spoke, to a photograph, framed and hanging on the wall, that they'd had taken a few years before. Their last summer with Morgan, though they hadn't known it at the time.

Feared it. But hadn't known it.

The four of them, all that remained of the family within these walls. The three siblings and their father's mother.

She moved over to it and studied it as intently as she did the Gardens. "No, we certainly don't look that similar. Your sister is very pretty."

She was, though he wasn't sure if agreeing with the statement would somehow imply that Lady Elizabeth *wasn't*. Which certainly wasn't true, was it? He still had a hard time putting words to the question, even when she was standing right before him. *Pretty* was such an arbitrary thing. All he knew was that he liked looking at her, talking with her. That seemed far more important.

She didn't wait for him to comment before adding, "And this is your older brother?"

"Morgan. Yes." Had Mabena told her anything about him? It was possible—she'd always adored him. Oliver slid over to her side to look at the familiar lines and planes of his brother's face. How glad he was that they had this reminder to keep the image fresh. "He died two years ago. The doctors weren't sure what it was that kept him ill for much of his life, but it finally won."

Her gaze was on him now, rather than the photo. "I'm so very sorry."

Perhaps eventually he'd be able to speak of him, to think of him without this tightness in his throat. "He was my best friend."

"Then he must have been a most remarkable young man."

He blinked away the memories and looked down at her. "How gracious you are to my family, my lady."

Her smile was as sweet as a spring breeze. "There's no grace involved. I *like* your family—or what I've met of you. It's only logical that I'd like the rest of them too."

He offered his arm. "To the Abbey Gardens?"

"Yes, thank you."

They paused for their hats on the way out but were soon in the sunshine again, and Oliver looked about, half expecting Mabena to come barreling upon them even now. "Are you here just for the day?"

"Until tomorrow. Moon said we'd stay overnight with her parents. Though even a day and a half won't be enough in the Gardens. I'm going to have to convince her to come back at least once a week."

"Indeed, if you mean to study the whole of the place. And you're interested in the fauna too, aren't you? You should really arrange for a tour to St. Martin's. That's where the bird-watchers tend to flock."

She chuckled at his pun. "I've been thinking the same. Is there an inn or something here? Moon said her parents would be offended if we didn't stay with them, but I don't want to impose upon them too often."

She'd clearly not met the Moons yet. "There is little her mother enjoys more than having guests—and you'll be the most important one she can claim, so I can't imagine she'd ever see you as an imposition."

She didn't seem entirely comfortable with the thought of being an important guest though. It hummed through her fingers and into his arm. "I'm looking forward to making their acquaintance."

Was she? Because she sounded a bit more like she was afraid of it.

She shook off whatever doubts plagued her over meeting the Moons and smiled up at him. "And how has your day been, Mr. Tremayne?"

With most new acquaintances, he would have equivocated and talked of neutral matters. But this new acquaintance already knew the gravest of his concerns. And his grandmother had embarrassed them. It seemed only fair that he give her the truth instead, so he drew in a long breath, let it carefully out. "Concerning, to be honest. You remember the mention of the young man who died in Piper's Hole a few weeks ago?"

She nodded. "Johnnie Rosedew."

He was a bit surprised that she remembered his full name, but she did like to categorize things, so perhaps it was natural for her. "That's right. Well, since then, a few locals have reported strange noises in said cave and supposed sightings of a White Lady on the coastlines. Which has led to a bit of speculation that it's his ghost rendezvousing with another."

"They actually believe such tales?"

He shrugged and led her toward the shortcut into the Gardens, through the back wall. "Most of them don't, not really. But sometimes the stories of the unexplained, the mysterious, the ancient are more compelling than the simpler explanations. And when you combine that with a community still reeling from grief and shock . . ."

Her nod looked thoughtful. And hesitant. "But as a man of science . . . ?"

"I know that generally there are logical explanations able to be discovered if one can collect all the data—though more often than I like, it's impossible to find what I know must be there."

He liked the way she looked up at him. With thought but curiosity. Respect but challenge. Perhaps he *shouldn't* like it quite so much.

"You said 'generally.'"

He looked forward again, to the world he knew so well. The one that, most of the time, he understood. But because he knew it, he also knew where it ended. Where the *else* that Beth was always seeking could really be found.

"I'm not just a man of science, my lady. I'm also a man of faith. The sort who says that God created an orderly universe, set rules in motion, and so we can understand them with study enough—but who also believes that a God who made such rules can also break them on rare, very special occasions. He can whisper the future to His prophets. He can send and heal plagues. He can raise the dead."

Her fingers went tight on his arm again, and when he moved his gaze to her, he found her eyes troubled. She kept them glued to the path ahead. "I struggle with that dichotomy, I confess." Barely did she confess it—the wind nearly snatched the words away before he could hear them. "I always hear everyone speaking of the mysteries, and they quote the verse where Jesus said no one knows what makes a seed grow. But we *do* now. Does that mean I'm faithless, because I see only those rules as necessary, rather than the hand of God guiding every seed from planting to harvest?"

"No." He reached over with his free hand to brush the fingers resting against his forearm. "Far from it. Humanity has grown. Our understanding has deepened. We know things now that Jesus couldn't have said to people nineteen hundred years ago, because they wouldn't have known what He was talking about. Some mysteries are no longer mysteries. That isn't a lack of faith, to say so. It's instead acknowledging that He created us capable of discovering nuances in the rest of creation. There is nothing wrong with that. Science and faith do not need to be at odds."

The pain that flashed through her eyes must be linked, somehow, to that sorrow they had spoken of a week ago. "Doesn't it? I want to believe you're right, Mr. Tremayne. But it seems that some rather loud voices on each side disagree with you."

They did, sadly. "Perhaps. But here's the thing."

She looked up at him, gaze expectant.

He grinned. "I'm right and they're wrong."

Her laughter joined the cry of the gulls overhead.

11

The morning air carried a chill in it that Libby hadn't anticipated, but one that made her smile even as she suppressed a shiver. Sunlight, soft as a kiss, shot the mist through with gold, encircling the island with a promise of another beautiful day. She crossed her arms to try to keep in what warmth she had, all but skipping beside Mabena on the path to the beach.

At every possible moment, she stole a glance at her friend. Never in their two years together had she ever seen Mabena Moon with her hair in anything but a tight bun, her clothes anything but the expected high-collared, long-sleeved grey dress. Even over the past week, she'd never caught her with more than a few stray curls blowing in the breeze.

Today though . . . today, Mabena Moon looked like someone altogether different. She wore a white blouse, its sleeves loose to the point of being billowy, and a simple brown skirt that looked soft and comfortable from endless washings. And her *hair*—she wore it in a braid much like Libby's, but with pieces slipping out in wild surrender to the tug of the wind.

Other animals underwent transformations, to be sure. The permanent metamorphosis of the caterpillar to butterfly; crustaceans molting old shells and growing or finding new; the shifting colors of the chameleon. There was always a purpose to such change.

Mabena had *said* that her purpose was simply being able to man the small sailboat in which her father was sending them back to St. Mary's. Her usual dress, she said, was too restrictive to allow her to manage the sails.

No doubt true. But something about the way her neighbors were calling out to her through the morning mist made Libby quite certain that *this* Mabena Moon was the one they all recognized. And that the other—the one Libby had thought she'd known—was the imposter.

"There she is!" a deep voice boomed even now, not seeming at all concerned with waking any of the neighbors *not* currently trekking to the water at the crack of dawn. "Benna girl! I scarcely believed it when they said you'd come home. Tresco isn't the same without you, dearover."

It was an older man who sidled up to them, arms outstretched and grin spread just as wide.

Chuckling, Mabena stepped to his side and let him enfold her in what looked like a bear of a hug. "Looks just the same to me."

"An imitation, that's all. You're the soul of us."

Mabena snorted at that and pulled away again. But her lips were curled up in a smile. She motioned to Libby. "Have you met Lady Elizabeth yet?"

Libby smiled too. There was something about how these islanders addressed her that she couldn't mind at all. Nothing changed in their gazes when they heard the title, nor in their manner as they nodded a greeting to her the same as they did to everyone else. The Moons, for example, had welcomed her into their home as if she were just one more daughter—they had two besides Mabena, and two sons as well—and had her laughing and relaxed within minutes. When they made her promise a few minutes ago that she'd consider their home her own whenever she came over to visit the Gardens, she'd had no qualms at all about agreeing.

This gent grinned at her as he shook his head. "Not yet, though I've heard she was about." He executed a short bow, more bounce than grace. "Fitzwilliam Gibson, at your service, my lady. You may call me Tas-gwyn Gibson, if you like. Most of the youngsters do."

Mabena poked him in the side playfully. "He's the island storyteller. Weaves a yarn that could have even *you* believing in ghosts and fairies, my lady."

Doubtful. But she wasn't above such an experiment, especially when it was an entertaining one. "Perhaps next time we come." Much as she wanted to spend another full day in the Gardens, they'd decided to sail back to St. Mary's by noon. According to the ache in Mr. Moon's big toe, they'd have a bit of a squall move in this afternoon, and they wanted to get home beforehand.

Apparently nothing could tell the weather quite like Jeremiah Moon's once-broken toe. Knowing that joints—and poorly healed fractures—did indeed respond to air pressure as accurately as a barometer sometimes, she'd seen no reason to argue with the claim.

Mr. Gibson grinned. "I'll prepare the best tale you've ever heard. Perhaps about the pirate admiral who once made his home in the very spot I now call my own."

"Allegedly." Mabena shot him a mock-stern look.

"No alleging about it! Why, did I not hear his ghost rattling about just a week ago?"

"I daresay you didn't. The wind, perhaps. Or rats."

"Bah." He poked her back. "You've no imagination, Benna girl. I'm telling you, it's Mucknell himself, his soul tied to the treasure he probably buried under my very floorboards."

Libby smiled at the banter. And at the allure of pirate treasure—something the Scillies no doubt had scads of stories about, as many buccaneers and smugglers had used the islands as their base over the centuries.

Mr. Gibson lifted a hand to another neighbor emerging from the morning fog. "Ho, Hank! Have you seen the lads yet? Who should get my wager this morning?"

Libby leaned a bit closer to Mabena. "Do they really wager on the races, when the vicar is one of the rowers?"

She chuckled. "The usual bet is a pudding or a pint." To Mr. Gibson she said, "As if you've ever bet on anyone but Oliver."

He sent her an arch look, belied by the twitching in the corners of his mouth. "I might do, if Enyon's still looking rough."

Hank—coming toward them from the waterline at a pace that said he had some pressing errand—didn't slow as he answered, "Casek's been snarling already at your grandson, so I imagine the vicar will be rowing as if his soul depends upon it."

Tas-gwyn Gibson was Mr. Tremayne's grandfather? Maternal side, clearly, given the different surname. Which meant the Gibson side of the family was the one that Lottie had been so quick to dismiss.

Surely even Lottie wouldn't have been able to resist the man's laugh though. Perhaps he wasn't landed gentry, but this was a fellow who was quite content with what and where he was.

Libby could learn a thing or two from him.

A minute later, the three of them stepped from road to path, following the echoes of morning greetings to the water. On the beach were ten men, ranging in age from late teens to early forties, gathered into two clusters. They were all moving busily around the two boats, long and sleek, resting on the sand.

At the first glance, she'd picked out the one form that was familiar—Oliver Tremayne, dressed in the cotton trousers and shirt of an athlete, a knit cap upon his head. He was giving a direction to another of the men, it seemed, pointing here and then motioning there. Whatever chap he'd been talking to nodded and spun to do something or another.

One of the men on the other team, a tall and burly one, shouted something that the wind garbled and stole before it reached Libby's ears. But she didn't need to hear it to know it must have been a taunt, given the way the four men around his boat laughed and the other five all stiffened, one spinning around with tense muscles.

Mabena nodded toward the chap that Mr. Tremayne restrained with a hand on his shoulder. "That's Enyon," she whispered. "Oliver's best friend."

Sometime over the course of the last twenty-four hours, Mabena had slipped from calling him *Mr. Tremayne* to *Oliver*. Libby hadn't pointed it out though she'd wondered at it. At least, she'd wondered until now, when she realized that Mabena referred to *everyone* near her own age by first name. Which made fine sense on an island the size of Tresco.

The only curiosity was why she'd greeted him so formally last Wednesday.

Libby nodded toward the burly one who seemed to be the leader of the second group. "And who's the boulder?"

"Casek Wearne." Her voice dripped disdain. "The headmaster. But Oliver's archnemesis long before that."

Libby felt her brows climb toward her hair. "I've never known anyone who had an archnemesis before."

"Yes, you have." Mabena flashed her a smile. "Those two ladies in London always out to steal each other's suitors. Lady Rose, wasn't it? And Lady Elvira?"

That seemed a different sort of rivalry. It was all catty words and simpering smiles and insults veiled as compliments. *"Oh, my lady, what a lovely gown! It suits you so much better than the one you wore last night."* Not shouts and posturing that looked like it could turn into a fistfight at any moment.

Males were such interesting creatures. No matter the species, they bore remarkably similar behaviors. Puffing out their chests, squawking, locking horns to determine who was stronger or faster or better, claiming territory—or females.

Somehow she hadn't imagined that Oliver Tremayne—it was a bit difficult to keep the *mister* in place in her thoughts when the Moons continually forgot it—would be one of two dominant alpha males vying for supremacy. He hadn't seemed the type when he was strolling with her through the Gardens, blushing over his grandmother's words, or peering into her very soul. Obviously she had a bit more studying to do before she could fully understand him.

It was a study she wouldn't mind, she had to admit—silently to

142

herself. During her time in London she'd never found the sport of man watching to be particularly engaging, but perhaps that had something to do with pomaded hair and tuxedos—unnatural plumage, to be sure.

This . . . this was entirely different. The ten men on the beach seemed somehow closer to nature and therefore their own true states. She could see muscles straining under soft clothes, grace in their movements that had nothing to do with choreographed dances. And, as she observed in another moment, the very bonds between them. These were men who interacted without pretense. Their friendship was true and their rivalries comfortable.

And Oliver Tremayne was one of them. A beloved one, whose directions were obeyed almost before he finished speaking.

Mabena stopped them right in the heart of a knot of onlookers, all of whom were watching, shouting, and making noises about the need for tea as they clapped chilled hands together. She wasn't the only one, it seemed, who'd expected the June morning to be a bit warmer than it was. The group made room for them without any comment other than cheerful, casual greetings. No one gave her curious looks. No one seemed surprised, as she'd been, by Mabena's loose hairstyle or flowing attire.

The rowers, at a signal she hadn't seen or heard, climbed into their boats—*gigs*, Mabena had called them. The onlookers all started cheering and whooping and calling out to the two teams, so Libby clapped along with them.

Oliver Tremayne glanced their way. His gaze snagged on hers for a moment. Didn't it? Or was he looking at Mabena, or at his grandfather? His mouth hinted at a smile for a fraction of a second. And then he refocused on his men, calling something to them that had them all taking up their oars.

A man nearer to them—Mr. Menna, it looked like—lifted a hand. Shouted something. Dropped his hand. And the oars dug in, pushing the gigs off, away.

The cheering continued until the boats were out of sight, rounding a promontory of land, and then it died down to jocular speculation on who would overtake whom and which lads looked in the better form today.

Libby leaned toward Mabena. "How far do they go?"

"A mile, then back."

And what were they to do in the meantime? She nearly asked it, had her mouth open to do so, when an answer of sorts seemed to present itself in the form of a rattle of pottery and a voice calling out, "Anyone going to help me, then?"

Libby spun, heels digging into the sand, to see an older woman stopped at the head of the path, where pavement turned to sand, her hand on an overloaded tray. Steam rose alluringly from a massive urn, and stacks of dozens of sturdy mugs told Libby what had been rattling.

Mr. Gibson and another man of a similar age hurried to her, each taking an end of the cart and carrying it down the path with what must be well-practiced ease.

"That's Mrs. Gillis," Mabena told her. "She's been bringing tea down on Wednesday mornings as long as I can remember. We all chip in a bit to help cover the costs—she's a widow on a pension, her only son a fisherman."

As the cart passed them, Libby spotted the jar on the lower shelf that had a few florins and pence in it already. She was quite glad she'd stuck a few pounds in her own pockets this morning, anticipating a stop in a bakery on her way to the Abbey Gardens after the race. There were no other paper bills in the jar, but as that was all she currently had with her, she'd just have to slip it in when no one was paying attention.

She followed Mabena toward the cart and, when Mrs. Gillis turned to her with a blink, as if trying to place her, offered a smile. "May I help?" The words tumbled off her lips before she could examine them too closely.

The widow didn't seem to find anything amiss in it. She just swept a gaze over her as if taking her measure and nodded. "You must be

Lady Elizabeth—and a lady ought to know how to pour a cup. You do the pouring, dearover, and Benna and I will pass them around."

A few simple sentences, a task to do—strange how it made her feel warmer.

Fifteen minutes later, all the cups had been filled, distributed, and some refilled, and the chill air had replaced the warmth of acceptance again, though it couldn't wipe the smile from her lips. She claimed a cup for herself and wrapped grateful fingers around it.

Something soft blanketed her shoulders, supplying a few degrees of relief. She looked first at the wool—purple, soft as a cloud, skillfully knitted—and then to the small, gnarled hands still positioning it over her arms for her. "Mamm-wynn! I didn't expect to see you out here this morning."

She looked from the old woman's smiling face to the space over her head—had she sneaked away again?

But a frazzled-looking Mrs. Dawe was a few steps behind, looking none too at home on the beach, a shawl of her own wrapped tightly around her.

Mrs. Tremayne chuckled. "I knew you'd be chilly, dearest. You never do remember a wrap."

True—but how did the lady know it? And how had she even known she'd be down here? Perhaps she'd spotted her from her house or garden as she and Mabena had walked by. "Well. Thank you." Holding her steaming tea in one hand, she ran the other over the lacework. "It's beautiful. Did you make it?"

"For you. It's your best color, I'd say." With a critical eye, she reached out once more to straighten it on Libby's shoulders. "Not like our Beth—she does better in blues and greens. But then, those spark color in her eyes, which are the loveliest grey. Yours, now—I have a string of amber beads just that color."

Libby didn't quite know what to say. She'd always liked purples— but the lady couldn't have made a shawl for her before they met, and she certainly didn't whip it up since yesterday afternoon.

Perhaps Mabena read her mind. She appeared before them, eyes wide and admiring. "Mrs. Tremayne! Another of your masterpieces! I'd thought you'd given them all away already."

Mamm-wynn chuckled. "I've a few stashed away yet, just waiting for their rightful recipients to come along." She flexed a hand with a sigh. "I certainly can't make them at the rate I used to do. I'll be lucky to finish my current one before autumn comes."

Ah. That made more sense. But she couldn't mean for Libby to keep such a work of art, could she?

Mabena must have thought so, given the weighty smile she directed to Libby. "Now you'll always have something to remember your first gig race by, my lady."

Mrs. Tremayne tucked her arm around Libby's and motioned toward Mr. Gibson. "Fitz is just getting warmed up, I see. Let's go and listen, dearest."

"All right." But first she turned to find Mrs. Gillis with her gaze. "Do you need anything else, ma'am?"

Mrs. Gillis smiled and shooed her away. "Get on with you, my lady. And thank you for helping."

"My pleasure, I assure you." It had earned her plentiful smiles and afforded her the chance to slip her contribution into the jar.

Mabena and Mamm-wynn led her toward a cluster of rocks the locals were perched on like so many terns, all listening with half-smiles and rapt eyes to Mr. Gibson, who stood before them, waving his arms in a way that made her hope the mug he held was nearly empty.

"There was no question about it," he boomed. "It was the pirate prince himself!"

"Pirate prince?" she whispered.

Mamm-wynn patted her arm. "Prince Rupert of the Rhine," she murmured back. "One of the Scillies's most famous temporary residents—during the Civil War and Cromwellian era. Though a nephew of the king, he served under Admiral Mucknell himself and was part of the pirate fleet."

A pirate fleet? She didn't recall learning about that in her lessons of the Civil War and the Parliamentarian era—that brief span when

England's king had been exiled and the Roundheads were in control of the government. But then, history had never been her best subject.

Not that Mr. Gibson seemed to be relying too much on an understanding of Scillonian history—unless Prince Rupert the Pirate really still walked the shores as a skeleton in the light of a full moon. She shivered and tugged her shawl closer. Skeletons couldn't do much walking without muscles and tendons and flesh to give them power, but that knowledge did little to detract from the story.

She was beginning to see Oliver Tremayne's point about a simple truth not always being as compelling as an interesting fabrication.

"There they come!" The shout came from closer to the waterline, where a lad in knee breeches had been keeping watch.

Mr. Gibson broke off and spun about. "Who's in the lead, Yorrick?"

"Wearne—no, wait! The Tremayne team's overtaking them!"

Mr. Gibson led the charge back into the sand, shouting, "Come on, lads! I've a fruit pie riding on your win! Put your back into it!"

Libby wandered onto the beach with Mabena and Mamm-wynn, watching the two crafts skim their way back over the waves. They had to be remarkably evenly matched, because from one stroke to the next she couldn't be quite sure who was in the lead, or who might be so in the next second. All the islanders were on their feet now, all voices cheering either for Wearne or Tremayne. Even Mabena was shouting the names of each rower on Team Tremayne.

Libby had never gone to the horse races, never cared much for the football matches Bram attended now and then. She'd never honestly been much interested in any sport. But there was something interesting here that she'd never accounted for when thinking of a game or competition—something that had nothing to do with the sport itself and everything to do with the community cheering it on. By simply joining in, bouncing on her toes in time with Mamm-wynn and lifting her voice along with Mabena, she became part of something.

It was a lovely feeling.

And it grew all the lovelier when Oliver Tremayne's team glided in a second before the other, the five men whooping their victory and jumping out into the surf with arms pumping the air and slaps on each other's backs. Oliver himself at the center of them all.

He was an odd sort of alpha. She couldn't help but watch the interplay with fascination. He wasn't the largest, probably wasn't the strongest—though he was clearly quite fit. If he was the dominant male in his group, it wasn't from his physical stature. No, it must rather be because of the way he laughed with the men, spoke to them, directed them with a hand on a shoulder or a gesture to the right or left.

Casek Wearne, on the other hand, must have won his place as captain of his gig from sheer muscle power. While his men laughed off their loss and joked easily with the winning team, he was glowering about it. At least until he glanced toward the shore. Something in their general vicinity must have caught his attention, because he straightened, and his face brightened.

"Benna, my lady—will you two take these to the winners?" Mrs. Gillis was shoving steaming mugs at them even as she asked it.

Libby took two, and Mabena somehow balanced three with total ease, though Mamm-wynn plucked one away from her. "I'll help too."

Mrs. Gillis had already turned to press a few others into delivering sustenance to the Wearne team, so Libby didn't bother replying, just struck out through the sand. The men saw them coming and met them a few feet away from the gig.

She couldn't even have said who took the mugs from her. She was too busy watching the care with which Oliver accepted the one from his grandmother's outstretched hands, the warm smile he gave his matriarch.

"Mamm-wynn. What are you doing down here?"

"Libby was cold. I had to bring her a shawl." She stated it simply.

But when his gaze shifted to her in a way that made her think—probably foolishly—that he'd been waiting for an excuse to do so, it didn't feel so simple. Libby trailed her fingers down the edges of said shawl. "She was my hero this morning."

His smile was certainly warmer than the sunshine just beginning to burn away the mist. "And how have you enjoyed your first gig race, my lady?"

She found herself grinning back. "I think I need to convince Moon that our weekly garden visits always need to happen on Tuesdays, so we can be here Wednesday mornings."

"Oh yes, you don't want to miss any of them. Our Ollie can't win them all, but they're always such fun." Mrs. Tremayne turned, then, to answer the greeting of one of Oliver's teammates.

Oliver shifted a bit closer to Libby's side. "Are you staying the day or . . . ?"

"We'll be leaving midmorning. We want to get back before the storm."

He shot a pointed look at the blue sky, brows raised.

Libby grinned. "Mr. Moon's big toe insists an afternoon squall will be coming."

"Ah. Well, no one argues with Jeremiah Moon's toe, to be sure." He'd taken his knit cap off at some point and now raked a hand through his damp hair. "Mr. Gale and I have solidified our plans for me to fill in at St. Mary's the Virgin this Sunday, so I'll be coming over on Saturday. I thought . . . that is, I know you said yesterday that no one else has mistaken you for Beth. But I thought I'd drop by when I get there. To make sure it's still the case. If that's all right."

"Oh yes. Please do." She bit her lip to keep any other assurances from spilling out. She could just imagine Mama across from her, waving a hand and telling her without words that she sounded far too eager. But . . . "We can show you the remaining things we found in the cottage, and you can let us know if they're Beth's—books, mostly. We weren't certain, so we didn't bring them."

"That will be lovely. Mrs. Polmer promised me a batch of sticky buns from the bakery that morning. I'll bring them with me."

"I could hardly turn that down. Moon brought two home the other day, and they deserve to have songs written about them." She smiled at his laughter, then bit her lip again. It had been on the tip of her tongue to invite him to return to their cottage for dinner Saturday night. But he'd probably already been claimed by a parishioner.

And *she* had been claimed by the Wights. Which was enough to eclipse the happy glow in her chest and replace it with dread. She didn't want to break out one of her evening gowns, have Mabena dress her hair, and spend the evening trying to remember the right thing to say to a viscount and his rich cousin. She wanted to lounge about in her braid and her cotton and talk about unfinished fairy tales and the slides she'd made for her microscopes and listen to his stories about whatever mischief Mamm-wynn or Tas-gwyn Gibson would have found by then.

"You'd better come with me, Mrs. Tremayne." Mrs. Gillis had appeared while Libby was trying not to say anything more. She flashed them each a smile and held out a hand toward the grandmother. "Mrs. Dawe said she needs to get the bread in the oven."

The lady turned placidly around, still chuckling over whatever Enyon had said to her, and put her hand in Mrs. Gillis's. "My toes *are* a bit cold." Though rather than walking immediately away, she instead held Mrs. Gillis there, facing Libby and Oliver, and gave a contented little smile. "Aren't you glad our Ollie finally found someone? And don't they make a handsome pair?"

Now Libby had to bite her lip to keep the laughter from spilling out at the way Oliver Tremayne's eyes yet again went wide with panic. "Mamm-wynn! We're not—Mrs. Gillis, she's—"

But Mrs. Gillis chuckled and winked at them. "I know, lad." Though to Mamm-wynn she added, "Aye, they certainly do strike a fine pair. I always did like seeing the dark and the fair together like that. Though as I've said many a time, Mr. Tremayne, you could do with a visit to my brother." She made a snipping motion with her hand, aimed at his hair. "Don't you agree, my lady?"

Her opinion, she suspected, was solicited solely to pressure him to the barber. But Libby shrugged and grinned up at him. "I rather like it long."

Mrs. Gillis tossed her free hand into the air and nudged Mrs. Tremayne forward. "Now he'll *never* cut it."

"Tremayne! Are you going to help with this gig or just stand there flirting all morning?"

Flirting? Were they flirting? Libby turned along with Oliver to see his friend's teasing gaze and raised brows, knowing she was the one blushing now.

Oliver grinned. "Well, if you're giving me a choice—I'll take the flirting."

His friend roared with laughter and waved him over. "Come on, Ollie. Some of us have work to do yet today."

She expected him to simply follow, but instead he looked down at her, eyes still sparkling with amusement, and his fingers cupped her elbow, squeezed. "I'll see you on Saturday."

Her stomach did a lovely little flip. "I look forward to it."

He released her and stepped away. Her elbow shouldn't have felt so cold after a short three seconds of warmth from his tea-heated fingers, should it? He pivoted, took his next step backward so that he was facing her. "And my lady? Purple suits you." His gaze brushed over the shawl before returning to her face.

The flip turned to a dance. "I know." She grinned. "Mamm-wynn already told me so."

She might have stood right there, watching him turn to his team-mates and listening to his laughter, until the tide swallowed her up, had Mabena not obscured her view and all but pushed her away.

For a moment she thought it genuine horror on her friend's face— but no, it was teasing. And her words were loud enough to be over-heard by all the men. "Now you've done it—you've let him work his elbow-magic on you. You're doomed now, my lady, to spill all your secrets to him."

The group all laughed, even Oliver. Though he also shouted back, "Watch yourself, Mabena Moon. I've known yours since I was three years old!"

Libby chuckled with Mabena as they started back up the beach. Maybe it hadn't been actual flirting, then. Probably not. After all, if it had been, she wouldn't have held her own. Nothing made her tongue tie in knots and her stomach start aching like flirtation. Well, unless it was disapproval.

Mabena bumped their arms together. "I think the islands have been working their charm on you. I've never heard you flirt so effortlessly."

"You mean it *was* flirting?" Laughter bubbled out. "I'd just convinced myself it must not have been! Oh, Mama would be proud."

Mabena snorted. "Aye—at least until she realized who it was that you'd managed it with."

She might as well have tossed a pail full of the cold Atlantic over her. "You don't think she'd like Mr. Tremayne?" Dash it all—and why did she ask? Why did it matter?

"Oh, she'd adore him. Everyone does. She just wouldn't like *you* liking him overmuch." Mabena sighed. "That Wight girl had that much right, my lady. Society won't accept his family, not fully, thanks to his mother and *her* family." Her lips curled up in a self-deprecating smile. "There are members of it in service, you know. And they all work with their hands."

"And what of it? It doesn't make a person any *less*."

"Most people would disagree."

"Well, they're wrong." She surveyed the group of islanders, all drifting back along the path, carrying empty mugs and laughing together. "Everyone *here* knows that."

Mabena's sigh was as gusty as the air. "Maybe. And maybe they respect him the more for his mother. But that's *here*. Your people, your place—"

"Mabena!" The voice was deep, clear, and totally unfamiliar. To Libby, though, the way Mabena stiffened said she recognized it perfectly well. And didn't mean to acknowledge it, since she lifted her chin and kept herself facing forward rather than turning to greet its owner.

Its owner didn't seem inclined to be ignored. His footsteps pounded, and a moment later he jumped in front of them, walking backward like Oliver had done a few minutes before. And yet not at all like Oliver.

Casek Wearne, that's who it was. Libby recognized his breadth if not his face, which she hadn't seen clearly before. And he barely glanced at her before directing the full wattage of his smile at Mabena.

He had nice teeth—straight and white. But the showcasing of them didn't soften her friend's posture any. "I hear you're going back to St. Mary's today," he said. "Do you need a lift? I've another delivery coming on the ferry and need to run over anyway. I'd be happy to take you and the lady."

Mabena's chin came up even more. "Tas has prepared the *Mermaid* for me, so I don't need to be relying on anyone else to ferry us about."

The rebuff just made his smile go lopsided, into a grin. "Good. What time are you leaving? It's been too long since I've watched you sail."

Mabena huffed. "Shouldn't you be over there telling Perry and Yorrick to hurry along to class?"

"They have an hour yet." Though he darted a glance, Libby noted, to the left, gaze searching until he found the two teenaged boys.

"Then allow me to rephrase it: go away."

"One more dagger to my heart." He splayed a hand over it. And also flashed her another grin. "The world's put to rights again. It was all wrong when you weren't here to insult me."

Libby pressed her lips against a smile. If ever she meant to make a study of flirting, she could pick up a thing or two from this fellow.

Mabena, however, didn't look amused. "It'll tip on you again at the end of summer, if that's so."

"Perhaps you should prepare me this time. You could start with a compliment."

"No. I couldn't." Her tone was absolute, genuine ice.

But Casek Wearne just chuckled. And tipped an invisible hat. "I'll see you around, Benna. My lady."

Libby offered only a neutral smile in farewell, since it seemed a bit odd to say good-bye to someone who hadn't even looked at her. She bumped Mabena's arm much like she'd done to Libby a minute before. "I think someone likes you."

Mabena didn't flush, much less smile. "No. He doesn't."

"Oh, come now! I may be no expert on such things, but even *I* could see—"

"It doesn't matter if he did. I'm not fool enough to get involved with a Wearne."

"Why?" She didn't really mean to ask, but the question just came so naturally to her that it slipped out.

"Leave it, Libby." Mabena slashed a hand through the air and took off at a half run, clearly intending to leave Libby in the dust. Or sand.

She drifted to a halt. It was the first time her friend had ever called her *Libby*. But she'd said it in anger. And then left her here.

"Don't take it personally, dearover." Mr. Gibson filled in the empty spot Mabena had left at her side, even slipping a companionable arm around her and chafing a hand over her arm. "You're not a true Scillonian until you've been snapped at by Mabena Moon."

She let him urge her onward. And rather liked the sensation of walking under the protective wing of a grandfather. Her own had sheltered her so a time or two. But not nearly often enough.

And to be honest, the comfort didn't dull the sting of the snapping. "She's never spoken to me like that."

"No, I don't suppose so. But then, you've never witnessed her history before, I daresay. Not safe on the mainland, far from it all."

She angled her face up so she could see his. Saw a bit of Oliver's jaw in his, which lent her strength for some reason. "She's never told me anything about her family. Or why she left the isles."

"She wouldn't. And a better man than me would probably say it was her story to tell, not mine. But as you have to live with her . . ." He bent his head down, eyes somehow both twinkling and shadowed. A play of fire and smoke, light and dark. Joy and pain. "You'll want to avoid further mention of the Wearnes. She has a history with them."

"With Casek?"

"No." He said it on a breath of laughter. "His twin brother—Cador. They were engaged, until he left her for a well-connected girl from London. Her father was in publishing, and he had dreams of literary grandeur, you see."

No. She didn't see at all. Mabena had been engaged? Had been tossed aside? And she'd never breathed a word of it? "So she left the Scillies?"

"That's right."

She faced forward again, watching her friend's back disappear behind another knot of people, then over the rise. Or maybe not her friend at all. Friendship required a certain amount of openness on both sides, didn't it? Maybe Mabena was no more her friend than . . . than Lottie Wight.

And how could she have left all this? The family, the community that knew her and loved her? The place that called her its own? Or maybe it didn't. Maybe Mabena was one of those born here but destined to leave. "Do the islands not know her name?"

Mr. Gibson chuckled. "More than that, my lady. They've always been her heart."

Her stomach hurt. How could that be, given her silence about them? "Then how could she leave?"

"Well." He didn't say the word like a storyteller. He said it like someone who had given the matter a lot of thought and reached a logical and unavoidable conclusion. "Because when the island is your heart, and your heart is broken . . . what are you to do but break ties with the island?" He patted her shoulder and then slid his arm from around her, so he could grip her elbow to help her over the final rise of sand, back onto pavement. "But she's back now."

Her feet wanted to drift to a halt again. Maybe even turn her around and run back down to the beach, where the morning had been bright and beautiful. "You think she'll stay."

"I know she will—though she's not ready to admit it yet."

But—but if Mabena stayed here, sent Libby home alone at the end of summer . . . If she was expected to just face her family again, face society again, face London again without anyone who understood her and championed her, if only in the privacy of her own room . . .

"Don't want to lose your maid, I take it?"

Her face probably looked as sick as her stomach felt. "I don't care about the maid part. But I don't want to lose *Mabena*."

"Well then. The answer's simple enough." He reached up and chucked her under the chin in the way Papa used to do. "You'll just have to stay too."

Even though there was no way Mama and Bram would ever allow it, the idea was alluring. Except that she had a sinking fear that Mabena would disagree. Loudly.

And she wasn't so sure she could handle hearing it.

12

Mabena may not much fancy the kitten who was once again stalking through the cottage as the promised squall raged away the afternoon, but she'd always liked puppies. And she felt as though she'd kicked one, the way Libby avoided her gaze and went out of her way to keep from crossing Mabena's path for the last eight hours, though she had still been steaming too much over Casek Wearne's audacity to really notice it when they were in the Abbey Gardens. But by the time they climbed into her lovely little sloop and started for St. Mary's, she could no longer ignore the slump of the lady's shoulders.

What a bore she was, to have stolen the morning's happiness from her with a few short words. But apologies had never been her strong suit. Not if they required words.

Perhaps chocolate could do the job for her. While Libby chased after the cat, who was making rather hilarious tiny ferocious hunter noises from her bedroom, Mabena put the kettle on and got out the powdered cocoa, milk, sugar, and salt.

She was just pouring it into two cups when Libby reemerged a few minutes later, a sheet of paper in her hands, which she took with her to the sofa. When Mabena slid the peace offering onto the table, Libby didn't even glance up.

Mabena huffed. She didn't *want* to apologize. She shouldn't have snapped at her, but she wouldn't have had to if Libby hadn't pressed. Always with the *why*. When would the girl learn that she didn't need the answers to everything? "It's your favorite. Don't let it go cold."

Libby reached out, wrapped a hand around the mug, and lifted it to her lips. Obedience. Not pleasure.

And what was Mabena now, her mother? She spun back to the kitchen and picked up her own cup. Though she didn't take much pleasure in the taste either. "What's that you brought out?"

A shrug, and she flipped it around for Mabena to see. "Darling found it under the bed."

A drawing of a coat of arms. Not one from any of the families in these parts though—probably something a previous tenant had dropped.

Libby set it on the table and went back to her book.

Mabena hissed out a breath. "Are you going to make me say it?"

Silence. The rustle of a page. A voice barely above a whisper. "I would never make you say anything."

Even though she *should*. Any other lady would probably have met her attitude with an ultimatum: apologize or be sacked. But Libby wasn't like any other lady. "My lady . . . I oughtn't to have snapped at you as I did. It wasn't your fault, nor you I was irritated with. All right? Please stop avoiding me."

"All right." Still the same small voice though. Mabena hadn't heard her sounding so . . . so insignificant since after her coming out ball last year. When Lady Telford had to threaten to cancel the order for the new set of encyclopedias if she didn't come out of her room and get ready for that night's musicale. When she'd been overwhelmed by all the expectations and other young ladies with their backbiting and the gentlemen who saw only pound signs when they looked at her.

Mabena couldn't think how her one flare of temper had resulted in *this*. But clearly a cup of chocolate wouldn't mend it.

What was it she'd even said? She'd only told her to leave it alone, hadn't she? And, yes, she'd stormed off—but it wasn't as though she couldn't find her way back to the Moon cottage. There were only so many streets, and they'd explored them all together Tuesday night. Besides, Tas-gwyn Gibson had caught up to her in about two seconds. He'd have kept her entertained on the walk home.

Leaning against the wall, she took another sip. Her gaze darted to the table, the drawing. Not from a family in these parts, but . . . it looked a bit familiar. She couldn't place where she'd seen it before though. Likely on something an incomer had. Or even, she supposed, a crest she'd seen on a carriage that visited the Telfords.

It was probably nothing, but it niggled, so she moved over to pick it up and studied it a bit more closely once she was in her spot again. Turned her eyes to the window, hoping realization would dawn, and frowned when she saw a man approaching their door, which might not have been anything worth noting if it weren't pouring. He wore a mackintosh and carried a brolly, but it took her only a moment to be certain that she didn't recognize him—the hair peeking from his hat was fairest blond, and there was no one here who could say the same.

Under his arm he clutched a parcel.

Mabena shot upright, slipping the drawing into her pocket. "My lady! A man's coming. With a package."

Libby's mug clattered back to the table. "For Beth, do you think?"

"I don't know." But the pounding of her heart said maybe, just maybe this one would have a clue that would tell them something useful. "You should be the one to answer the door, in case it's for Beth."

A mask of uncertainty settled over Libby's face. "You don't think I should say I'm not her? Ask him what he's about?"

And scare off any future deliveries? "No. Just play along with it."

"But . . ."

"How else can we help Oliver find his sister?"

Libby let out a breath. Nodded, even as footfalls joined with the pounding rain, and then a knock harmonized too. She stood, depositing the kitten on the sofa, and moved to the door. Mabena stayed out of sight, her fingers curled tightly around her mug.

"Hello?"

"Good afternoon. Elizabeth?"

Her heart raced, even as she tried to place the accent. Cornish, without question. But not quite the cadence of a native islander. But of course it wouldn't be a Scillonian—any native would know it wasn't Elizabeth Tremayne at the door.

"That's right. Though I wasn't expecting a delivery today."

What was she doing? Mabena's nostrils flared.

The bloke, however, sounded a bit confused. "It's Wednesday, ain't it?"

"Oh! Is it?" Libby chuckled, though Mabena heard the strain in it. The stranger likely wouldn't though. "I've lost a day somehow. Very well, then. Thank you."

A moment later the door swung shut again, and Mabena surged forward, sliding her mug onto the table. The parcel—a large manila envelope—was now in Libby's hands. "Why the question?"

Libby flipped the envelope over in her hands. "It was Wednesday last week too. I'd been wondering if there were no more by design or if the rain had kept people away, and then our absence. But this fellow came through a downpour. Which either meant that he'd been waiting for me to come again and saw our lights, or that Wednesday is simply the delivery day." She shrugged. "Not that two examples provide enough data to say for certain. But we at least know now that he'd meant to come today, not that he'd been put off by my absence."

Mabena smiled. "Sometimes that scientific mind of yours is rather helpful."

Libby's answering smile was weak, strained. "Sometimes."

Blast. That wasn't how she meant it to sound. Which normally Libby would know. But she didn't have time just now to soothe her. She grabbed her own hooded mackintosh from its hook. "You open it. I'm going to follow him."

"Mabena!"

But she was already dashing out the side door and hugging the garrison wall as she ran, grateful that the man had that umbrella. It not only obscured his view of people following him, but it also gave her something to keep an eye on.

A drizzle was never enough to keep anyone inside, but this sort of rain meant largely empty streets as she trailed him into Hugh Town. The fellow kept up a quick pace, which suited Mabena fine. She had no trouble keeping him in view while staying well out of his.

Somehow she wasn't surprised when he led her straight to the ferry dock, where the last trip of the day would depart within the half hour. She hung back under a helpful eave, watching as he purchased a ticket and then jogged up the gangway and onto the boat. She had no reason to expect him to debark again, but still she waited a few minutes. Just to be sure.

The rain eased up as suddenly as it had come upon them at noon, and her lips quirked with the lightening of the clouds. Tas had said the storm would blow over by supper. Looked as though he was right, as usual. She took another minute to listen to the *drip-drip* of water still running off thatch and tile and into the drains, but the blond bloke didn't emerge from the shelter on the ferry.

So then. She shook the water from her hood and let it fall. A shaft of sunlight bullied its way through a crack in the clouds, and even that little bit of it was enough to make the day remember it was nearly summer.

As she retraced her steps, she debated her next move. She wanted to go back to the cottage and see what was in that envelope. But she owed it to Ollie to let him know another something had been left for Beth. And if anyone from Tresco was on St. Mary's, they'd be making for their boats now so they could get home before dusk.

To the quay, then. She shrugged out of her jacket as she went, preferring the few stray drops to the heat of the mackintosh.

Of the boats bobbing in the tide, however, she spotted only one other than her own that belonged on Tresco. Of all the rotten luck.

"Looking for me?"

Why did it always have to be Casek Wearne? She turned slowly, fixing a scowl just so on her face. "Anyone but, actually. Is no one else from Tresco here?"

161

"Only you, my 'ansum." He wiggled his brows at her.

She rolled her eyes. "When are you going to stop this ridiculous act of yours?"

"When you admit you chose the wrong brother five years ago." He sounded . . . serious. And his gaze had lost the gleam of a jest. Now it just seared her, reminding her too much of the past.

She half-turned away. Better to look at his boat than him. "There was no choosing."

"Right." And there, the hard edge she was more used to hearing from him. "Because it was always Cador—had always *been* Cador."

"Or maybe it was because you only wanted to poke at Oliver. That's all it ever was with you. Your stupid rivalry, your need to prove you were better than him."

"Let's get one thing straight." His hand was on her elbow, turning her, anchoring her. No magic in it like Ollie's elbow touching, but the very fact that he didn't let go started a tingling there. Of irritation, that was all.

Maybe.

He leaned down, putting their faces a mere six inches apart. "There are many reasons I kissed you that night and tried to convince you to go with me to that dance instead of Cad. But Oliver Tremayne had nothing to do with any of them."

She hadn't thought of that kiss in years—her first, though she'd never admitted to anyone in the world that it had happened—and she didn't intend to start now. "And you expect me to believe that? That if it had been you I'd gone with, you'd not have just embarrassed me? Made a mockery of me?" She scoffed a laugh and averted her face. "That's not what Beth heard."

His hand slid down her arm, found her hand, even as he straightened again. "I don't know what she heard. But the Mabena Moon I know couldn't be embarrassed by the likes of me, even if I *had* tried that—which was never my intent. The Mabena Moon I know could turn mockery on its heel with one well-placed sentence. You'd not have feared that. No."

He edged closer, making her keenly aware of the fact that he was nearly a foot taller than she was. And it was just his usual bullying tactics, to tower over her now.

Well, he had one thing right. Mabena Moon wasn't one to cower before a bully. She tilted her head back and stared him down. "I didn't *fear* anything."

"No?" He had the same grin as his brother, nearly—but Cador had never worn it like Casek did. Mocking. Challenging. Not until the last.

No, even then it wasn't the same. At the last, Cador's smile had been cruel, pure and simple.

Casek shook his head. "Cador was the *safe* choice."

"Safe?" She spat the word. "Ha." If he'd been safe, he wouldn't have walked away as he'd done, grinding her heart into the sand with sadistic pleasure.

"Cad was the one who'd always got along with your family, the one who always tried to be everyone's friend. The one you didn't have to explain to anyone. But he was only those things for his own purposes." His fingers tightened around hers. "Didn't I try to tell you that? He'd always been selfish. Out only for his own interests—it just happened that those interests were you. Because he knew it would dig at *me*."

"This is absurd." She tried to tug her hand free so she could spin again and march away. Oliver could wait until tomorrow to get the message he didn't even know was coming. What difference would a few hours really make? She'd take it over to him herself in the morning.

For a moment, Casek held tight to her fingers. Then he released them abruptly, even stepped back, gave her room. "You said it was him you wanted—so I let you go. He broke your heart—so I let you go. But you're back now, and he's gone, and blast it, Mabena, but I'm not letting you go a third time. You're going to give me a chance."

Of all the . . . She whirled first one way, then back the other, waving her arms to force words into her brain. "You think you can just *proclaim* that? Has it never once occurred to you that I don't want *any* Wearne, ever again?"

"Nope. Never occurred to me. It's going to be different this time. You'll see."

She could only shake her head at him. Because there should have been at least a flicker of vulnerability in his eyes when he said something so daft, shouldn't there? But there wasn't. Just steel and fire and the whole blasted forge, his words the hammer meant to bend her. "How do these small little islands even hold your head, big as it is?"

He grinned again. "You can test me, Benna. Try me. I'm not going anywhere—and neither are you, at least for the summer."

She folded her arms over her chest, largely to keep them from flapping about like a bird's again. "You want a test?" She shouldn't. But she couldn't think of a bigger one. "I need to get a message to Oliver. Tonight."

He reeled back as if she'd punched him. "Now, that's below the belt."

"Oh, giving up so quickly? I see how determined you are."

"Come on, Benna." He swiped his cap off and smacked it against his leg. "I try to give him a note and he'll be checking it for poison."

"Not a note. Just a verbal message. And this." She pulled the drawing of the coat of arms from her pocket when its presence suddenly flashed into her mind. "Ask him to see if he recognizes it."

He frowned. "Pick something else."

"No." Perhaps seeing him squirm shouldn't be quite so entertaining. But it was. She fluttered the drawing. "Give him this. And tell him another package came for Beth. Think you can remember that?"

He scowled and put his cap back on his head, then snatched the drawing from her hand and put it in his own pocket. "You owe me a picnic lunch for this."

"I most certainly do not."

"You're right. That's not big enough. A dinner. A fancy one, with you in a pretty dress."

She snorted. "In your dreams, Casek Wearne."

"Every night, my 'ansum." He turned to his boat and then went so still that she turned to see what had caught his attention, instead of stomping away like she'd planned.

A boat, its sails a blue that would have matched the sky had it not been heavy with clouds. Small and looking all the smaller for being so far away. "Whose is it?"

"The Hills'."

She raised a hand to shield her eyes from the gleam of sun off the water, but she hadn't a prayer of making out from here who was on it. "I thought Mr. Hill's leg didn't let him sail anymore."

"It doesn't. Must be Perry."

"Well. Nothing too odd about a boy going out for a bit after a squall, is there?"

"Not at all." He shifted back to motion so quickly she had to won-der if it was a lie. He took a few steps toward his boat, then pivoted and strode back to her, not stopping until the toes of his boots were nudging her rain-wet shoes. Leaning down, head angled.

She sucked in a breath, too surprised to leap back. Or smack him, as she should have done.

But he halted a few inches away and grinned that wicked little grin at her. "No. Next time, Mabena Moon, you're going to be the one to kiss *me*."

She stormed away with a growl. And then, at the top of the hill, cursed herself for not at least leaving him with a parting barb. *There will never be a next time.* Or *That's as likely as me growing a tail and becoming a mermaid.*

Insufferable man. Conceited, arrogant oaf. And her—what was wrong with her, letting him get to her like that, render her speechless?

She pushed into the cottage minutes later, flinging her mackintosh onto a chair and kicking off her sopping shoes with a bit too much force.

"Mabena! What's wrong?"

What was *wrong*? She spun toward Libby and waved at the door. "That man!"

Libby sat on the sofa again, the stupid cat curled against her shoul-der. "The one you followed? He didn't hurt you, did he? Or—"

"No." Blast it. She pulled the tie from the bottom of her braid so she could redo it. The wind and rain and hood had surely done a number on her hair. "No, that bloke just got on the ferry."

"Then who?"

"Casek Wearne." She meant to say it with frustration. But she hadn't expected the exhalation would leave her feeling suddenly shaky. She pulled out one of the kitchen chairs and slumped to a seat.

Libby was there in the next moment, pulling out one of the others. "What did he do?"

"What did he *do*?" She squeezed her eyes shut and abandoned the braid in favor of rubbing a hand over her face. "Only all but confessed he was in love with me and then very nearly kissed me, that's all."

"Ah." Libby's tone was every bit as bemused as her expression, when Mabena dropped her hand and could see it. "How . . . terrible of him?"

"It was!" With a groan, she slumped against the table. Never in her life had she imagined having this conversation with Lady Elizabeth Sinclair. Her employer. But then, who else could she ever have told this to? "He kissed me once before. When we were seventeen."

Libby's brows pulled tight. "I thought it was the brother you were engaged to. Mr. Gibson mentioned it," she added when Mabena sat up again.

He never could keep a tale to himself. "It was. This was before."

"And . . . you didn't like it?"

Sweet Libby. Mabena couldn't quite help the low chuckle that tickled her throat. "Of course I liked it. It was Casek Wearne. You saw him, didn't you?"

Her confusion didn't relent. "Then what was the problem?"

"It was *Casek Wearne*." She shook her head. It wasn't something she could just explain to an incomer—even when the incomer was Libby. Not all of it, anyway. "They always told me I was wild as the sea, unbridled as the wind. They always told me I'd need someone to ground me. But Casek—he'd never have done that, and I knew it the moment his lips touched mine. He wouldn't have held me down. He'd have let me fly."

166

If anything, her explanation seemed to make it worse. Libby was looking at her as if she'd lost her mind. "Not that I'm any kind of expert on this sort of thing, but . . . isn't that *good*?"

Self-destructive, that's what it was. Or would have been, had she let it be. But even at seventeen, she'd had more sense than that. "Balance, that's what a couple needs. The wild needs the steady. That's why I opted for Cador. He was always steady. Always got along with everyone and never made me go absolutely mad like Caz did. He was—"

Blast and drat. *Safe*. That's what he'd been.

"I see." Libby squinted her eyes at her. "I don't, actually. But I'll pretend I do, if it makes you feel better."

Mabena's laugh this time at least managed to put her feet back on solid ground. Which reminded her that Casek Wearne wasn't the point of her adventure in the rain. "What was in the package?"

"Paperwork." Obviously eager for the change of subject, Libby sprang to her feet and hurried to the sofa, then back. She held out a sheaf of papers. "They seem to be ships' manifests. Not that I would have recognized them as such, if not for the cover letter."

Mabena took the page from the top and turned it into the light. "It's unsigned."

"But interesting nevertheless. Read it."

You certainly had a point in your last missive; there is no telling whether the articles you're looking for would have been from the Canary *or perhaps another of Mucknell's prey; or a combination thereof, though there is that "John" on the original artifact to lend credence to the* Canary *theory. Regardless, whatever he kept and buried would be something that would not rot. Most likely precious metals. Any Indiamen he took would have been equipped, at the least, with payroll. So coinage is always a safe thing to search for.*

From what we could discern from the archives, however, it's the silver from the Canary *that has never resurfaced and that the rightful owners put considerable effort into recovering. We can find no further information on what sort of silver it was, but if you can find it, it will be the discovery of the century.*

Mabena lowered the page, feeling as though Beth herself had just punched her in the stomach. The first missive had mentioned the *Canary* too. "Mucknell's treasure? Is *that* what Beth has been about?" She shook her head. Tas-gwyn Gibson had been filling their heads with the lore for decades, but surely Beth hadn't believed his tales.

But then, Beth was always disappearing into crevices and cracks of the island that no one else knew. What if she *had* found something? Something that led her to contact whoever this was? Someone in London, clearly, who could access archives of the East India Company.

"Mucknell." Libby tilted her head. "The admiral from Mr. Gibson's story?"

Mabena set the letter carefully down on the table and flipped through the sheets behind it. Lists upon lists of cargo for various ships. "The *pirate* admiral."

Libby sat down again. "I think I need to brush up on my history. What was the *John*?"

"His ship. According to the stories, it was the flagship of the East India Company, the fastest and best outfitted vessel on the seas. Mucknell staged a mutiny on her maiden voyage and eventually came here to offer the ship and his services to the exiled Prince of Wales. Over the next few years, he gathered a fleet of other pirates and wreaked havoc on the shipping lanes. The East India Company especially was hit hard."

Libby frowned. "What happened to the ship?"

"Eventually the Parliamentarians commissioned others to stop him. There was a battle just off the islands here, and the *John* was crippled. No one's certain anymore if it sank at sea, its plunder in its holds, or if it was beached somewhere and unloaded. Either way, everyone knows Mucknell always kept a bit for himself from all his hauls. And they speculate that it's still buried somewhere on the islands."

Libby stared at her for a long moment, mouth agape. "Pirate treasure? Really?"

"So it would seem." Mabena had always just thought them stories. Fables. Fairy tales.

But apparently Beth had a different theory.

The pounding on the door was loud enough and insistent enough that Oliver was on his feet and running for it long before either of the Dawes even rose from their chairs. That kind of knock on a vicar's door could only mean one thing—there was an emergency, and someone needed him.

He was already reaching for his hat as he yanked open the door, the question of "Who? Where?" already perched on his lips, ready to fly at whoever had come with the twilight.

His hand froze when he saw Casek Wearne standing there before him, looking for all the world like an angry, glowering granite statue. Unyielding. Unmoving. Unfeeling.

But as this granite statue did have family that was part of St. Nicholas's congregation, Oliver didn't snap at him. Much. "What is it?"

Casek's gaze burned over him, the sort of burning that could have meant either ice or fire, and it annoyed Oliver to no end that he couldn't tell which it was.

"Another package came for Beth."

It was fire, sure and hot, that swept through him. "What? Are you involved in this? What do you know of my—"

"Ask Benna." Casek took a step away, looking as though he meant to stride off without another word. But he paused, spun, and dug a piece of paper from his pocket. "She said to give you this, too, and see if you recognize it. And while you're at it, tell her I delivered her message word for word. You owe me that much."

"I *owe* you?" Laughable. But at least mention of Mabena had put the fire out. He didn't know why she'd chosen this particular messenger, but she made sense as the sender. He took the paper, though he didn't look down at it.

"It's your fault she ever chose Cador, and don't try to tell me it isn't. You told your sister to convince her I only meant to hurt her."

Oliver's fingers tightened around the doorknob. "You're not going to lay all this at *my* feet. As if Mabena ever listened to a thing I said."

"Which is no doubt why you recruited Beth to help. Like a coward."

If he dug his fingers in any harder, he'd leave dents in the wood. "I did nothing of the sort. But if Beth told her that, then it was because she had eyes to see. Why else would you ever want anything to do with—"

"Because it was *Benna*."

Anguish. Anguish and . . . something else, something even deeper seeped through the granite. Were it anyone else, Oliver would have called it a glimpse of his soul. Of his heart.

But it was Casek Wearne. The one man who would surely never show him such a thing. "What was the package?"

"What?" The abrupt shift dropped confusion over Casek's face, before he wiped it clean and put his usual expression of contempt back on. "You'll have to ask Benna that too. I told you what she told me—not that you've grace enough to thank me for it. But not that I expect anything more of a Tremayne. Too good even to acknowledge us common folk, I know."

If Mother had seen the smile Oliver let tilt his lips, she'd have boxed his ears, and rightly so. "Not all common folk. Just Wearnes."

Casek looked poised to snarl something, but Oliver shut the door before he could hear it. And then squeezed his eyes shut. He didn't need Mother there to box his ears. His own conscience did a fine enough job. "Forgive me, Lord." If only regret was all one needed for repentance. If only one didn't also have to go and sin no more— something he'd yet to master when it came to Casek Wearne.

He turned, jumping when he saw Mamm-wynn two steps away, peering up at him with those blue eyes of hers that he knew so well. "Going to St. Mary's tomorrow, then?"

Exhaling, he steadied himself again. "I suppose I'd better." First, to make sure Mabena had really sent him the message. And second, assuming she had, to see what package had come.

His grandmother nodded. "You might as well stay until Sunday. Mr. Gale would be pleased."

No doubt. The man had been terribly lonely since his own four children had trickled over to the mainland over the last decade. He always said how he enjoyed it when Oliver occupied one of the empty rooms of the vicarage for a night or three. "Did you want to come with me?" He didn't like the thought of leaving her alone, even if she wasn't *alone*.

She chuckled and stepped closer, her small hand slipping into her pocket. "Sunday will be enough of a trip for me, dearovim. But here. Give this to our young lady."

He frowned when he caught the glint of lamplight on the metal she'd pulled free of her pocket. "Mabena? What is it?"

"Not Benna." She laughed again, as if it were a great joke on his part, and opened her palm to reveal a necklace of pearls and gold. "Libby."

Would there ever again be a day when his stomach didn't sink, didn't twist? Though he tried to smile, he also closed his hand over hers. "We're not giving Lady Elizabeth your jewelry, Mamm-wynn."

"She needs it." She turned their hands over and let the gold and pearls trickle into his palm. "Tell her it's a loan if she's not comfortable taking the family jewels yet."

"Mamm-wynn . . ." He needed to tell her Lady Elizabeth wasn't his wife, wasn't his sweetheart, wasn't his *anything*. But if he tried, would she even remember the conversation come tomorrow? Was there any point in insisting upon the truth when her eyes seemed only to see into a reality of her own making? He sighed. He'd just take the necklace for now and slip it back into her things tomorrow, when she wasn't in her room.

She smiled up at him, reached to pat his cheek, and turned. "I think it's time I retire for the night. It's been a long day."

He watched her go, pressing his lips against the quivering in them. Beth should be here, helping him determine what to do. And Morgan—he missed his brother's counsel, that somber wisdom always to be found in his eyes. But he hadn't his brother. Hadn't his sister. Hadn't his parents. His eyes slid shut. *Help me, Father God. You're the only one I have to turn to.*

When he opened his eyes again, he finally thought to look at the paper Casek had thrust at him. A coat of arms, a family crest. Not one that he saw regularly, but . . . but it looked familiar. He stared at it for a long moment before spinning for the stairs and taking them two by two, then running down the hallway until he was at Beth's closed bedroom door.

He had been in here not long ago to put away the items she'd left in the cottage. But he hadn't paid much attention to anything else. Now, though, he aimed straight for the shelves in the corner, full of trinkets she'd collected over the years as she explored the islands or received as gifts from their parents or other family and friends.

His eyes moved over the familiar assortment of baubles and shells and sea glass, looking for the trinket box she'd always kept in a place of honor, ever since Mother had given it to her from her own collection. It was usually right there, on the middle of the middle shelf, proudly showcasing the gold-leafed crest that he *thought* matched the one on this paper. Only empty space stared back.

Oliver's brows knotted. He couldn't remember the wooden box's story entirely—something about a long-gone relative, a noble-born love lost at sea. Beth had loved the story though. It had fueled her own dreams of finding a love with a man from a noble family, he knew.

But it was gone. Along with his sister. Which meant . . . what exactly? That she still had it with her, wherever she was?

That made precious little sense. But then, nothing did anymore.

13

The telegram sat on her dressing table, yellow and watchful. Proof that even from hundreds of miles away, Libby's mother still knew when she was tempted to bow out of an engagement and stay home with her books and microscope. If she didn't attend the Wights' dinner party tonight, Mama would *know*. Somehow she would know, and another telegram would come, or a letter—or worst case, she herself would appear at the door, reproof in every lovely line of her face.

It was a fear bigger than that of sitting through a boring dinner that kept Libby's bottom planted on the stool while Mabena fussed with her hair. And fussed some more. And fussed *again*.

Libby scowled at her friend in the mirror. Nothing made her half so cross as having unending hairpins jabbed into her scalp. "Why are you going to so much trouble? I don't care if I impress these people."

Mabena flicked a gaze to her reflected one, then back to what she was doing. "You've worn nothing but a braid since you arrived. If you're going to dress for dinner, we're going to do it right. Besides." She flashed a grin. "Maybe you'll steal the attention of the one that chatty gossip wants."

"Amusing." As if she'd ever stolen the attention of any man. And as if she'd want to.

"Well, why not? Look at yourself, my lady." Mabena pushed Libby's shoulders into their proper posture, positioned her head just so, and nodded beside her in the mirror. "You're as lovely as any other young lady when you try."

A blatant lie. Other young ladies—like Edith, for example—didn't *need* to try to be pretty. They just *were*. Even when their hair was in a braid and they were wearing cotton.

Or perhaps it was that they always tried. Which sounded exhausting. Libby blinked at her reflection, tempted to screw up her lips to ruin the image. She didn't look like herself. Didn't *feel* like herself in this beaded evening gown. The only thing she liked was that it was purple. And even that only made her smile because it reminded her of Mamm-wynn. "Are you finished yet?"

Mabena rolled her eyes and turned to root through the box of doodads and whatnot on the dressing table. It held all the dreaded hairpins and the ribbons and pearls Libby had begged her not to put into the coiffure, along with bracelets and rings and necklaces.

The digging and shifting went from lazy to panicked. "Where are your necklaces?"

Libby wrinkled her nose at her reflection, tempted to stick out her tongue at herself too. "How am I to know? You did the packing." She sounded petulant. But it was the corset's fault. Mabena hadn't let her keep it tied as loosely as she usually did. Probably because the purple gown wouldn't have fit otherwise. And she'd made her put on the ridiculously long satin gloves. She hated gloves, unless it was cold outside. They made it hard to write or sketch.

A knock came from the front door, bringing Libby to her feet. It would be Oliver, here to spend the evening poring over maps and history texts and every record of the legends surrounding Vice Admiral Sir John Mucknell, pirate extraordinaire. Sure enough, many of the books she and Mabena thought might be Beth's touched on the pirate and had been taken, Oliver was certain, from the Tremayne library.

And though history wasn't Libby's primary interest, she would have far preferred spending the evening learning about the East India Company's rather justified argument with the king and their leaning toward the Puritan Roundheads than going to a dinner party.

She scrambled to her feet while Mabena was still distracted with the hunt for the necklace, before she could decide she needed more hairpins. "I'll let him in."

Mabena was still mumbling about missing pearls and how she *knew* she'd packed a selection of three necklaces as Libby hurried into the main room. She pulled the door open, offering a smile to Oliver, who stood there with a briefcase in one hand, the other hand in his pocket.

And utter stupefaction on his face as he blinked at her. "Pardon me. I must have the wrong cottage."

"You're hilarious." After spending the last two evenings with him, she could very nearly ignore the fluttering he caused in her midsection and focus instead on the tease. Stepping back, she gestured him inside.

He entered, but without taking his eyes from her. Which very nearly made her think the hairpins were worth it. And the corset. Though if he liked this version, which wasn't the real her . . . She pressed a hand to her ribs.

His smile was right at least. Soft. Knowing. Altogether Oliver. "The viscount is going to be completely enchanted."

"I have no interest in enchanting the viscount. Or his wealthy cousin. I'll bore them with talk of Latin nomenclature to prove it."

From the bedroom, Mabena called out, "I thought Miss Gossip said the viscount was fascinated by scientific things."

Libby wrinkled her nose at the memory of when Lottie had found her cottage on Thursday and spent three eternal hours there chattering about people Libby didn't know. Or *want* to know. "Then I'll bore him with talk of pirates."

Oliver raised a finger. "Talk of pirates is never boring, my lady."

She sighed. "I'm sure I'll find some other way to lose their interest then. It never takes me long."

"How could that possibly be?" He slid his satchel onto the table, as he'd done last evening, and the one before. She rather liked how it looked there—so masculine and comfortable. "I could talk to you for hours and be riveted every moment of it."

Heat crept up her neck, and she found herself rather glad that his words had been too quiet for Mabena to hear from the bedroom. He was probably being kind, trying to bolster her confidence before the dinner she'd already admitted she didn't want to attend. He seemed like that sort of man. And Mabena, who knew him better, would no doubt say as much, which would rob it of a bit of its effect.

She also had no idea how to respond to such a compliment. She could only smile her thanks and try to nudge Darling away from the beaded hem of her dress that had been tempting him since she put it on. And then snicker a bit when Mabena came stomping out with obvious frustration, muttering, "I thought for certain I'd packed them. I must have put them down again when I considered adding the silver set."

Oliver turned to greet the newcomer with a grin. "Problem, Mabena?"

"No, I'm muttering for my health."

Libby tamped down a grin of her own. The salt air seemed to have made Mabena more sarcastic. Perhaps she shouldn't have found it so entertaining.

"Anything I can help you with?" Oliver asked.

Mabena gave him a withering look. "Only if you happen to have a pearl necklace in your pocket."

His face went blank for a moment, then a strange look flitted over it. "Actually . . ." He reached for his satchel, opened it, and fished around in the interior pouch.

Coming up with, of all things, a pearl-and-gold necklace.

Mabena just stared at it. "And you're carrying your grandmother's necklace around with you because . . . ?"

"She forced it on me before I left. Said—well, frankly, she said, 'Libby needs it.'"

"How could she have known that?" The oddity made it far more intriguing than it would have been otherwise. Libby stepped closer to get a better look.

It was prettier than hers, honestly. Rather than a simple string of pearls, this one was a double strand, choker length. In the middle, there was a cameo—only, instead of the expected woman's profile, an eight-petaled flower had been carved. Perhaps a *Dryas octopetala*.

But she couldn't accept. All Mama's lessons in etiquette had at least taught her that much. "It's lovely—and lovelier still of Mamm-wynn. But I can't—"

"Of course you can. It will make her happy to know you did so." Rather than hand it to Mabena, Oliver turned to her himself, moving behind her and draping the necklace into place in one swift move. "For Mamm-wynn, my lady."

She touched a finger to the cameo while he fastened it in place, afraid to move any more than that lest . . . lest . . . well, lest she do something wrong somehow. "All right. Anything for Mamm-wynn." Mama never even needed to know.

His fingers were warm as they grazed her skin, probably making her neck and cheeks flush again. His hand moved from her neck to her satin-encased elbow as he stepped around her again. "Would you like me to walk you to the Wights' cottage?"

Yes! She nearly shouted it. Anything to keep his hand on her elbow a little longer, to be at his side a bit more, to . . . "No, thank you. Though I thank you." She was such a dunce. A dunce who needed to clear her head of this lovely, silly haze he filled it with *before* she stepped foot in the Wights' cottage and was introduced to the viscount and his cousin. She certainly didn't want to arrive all moon-eyed and have them think it was over *them*.

Though given the shadow that flashed in his eyes, he probably thought her quick refusal was because she didn't want to be seen with him in said company.

She ought to say something to make it clear that wasn't at all the case. But she had no idea how to say as much without making more a ninny of herself than she already had.

"Here." Mabena broke the tension by coming toward her with Mamm-wynn's shawl in hand and placing it around her. "A perfect complement."

The shawl was a heather purple, light and misty, the dress a deeper, royal hue. Even Libby's eye, untrained in fashion, found the contrast pleasing. She smiled. "Are you certain I can't just stay at home and pretend I forgot it was Saturday?"

"Go." Mabena gave her a helpful push toward the door. "That way you can write to your mother tomorrow telling her you did so, and she'll be pleased enough that perhaps she'll not insist on other engagements."

That was an optimistic thought. "All right. Solve a few mysteries while I'm out."

She stole one last glance at Oliver—for fortification, that was all—and then let herself out into the warm, fragrant evening. It felt odd to be *walking* to a dinner party in this getup, and no doubt it would be a terrible idea to take her usual path through the sand, on the beach. So, she stuck to the main road, telling herself her lazy pace was for the sake of her shoes and not because she didn't really care when she arrived.

Halfway there, a sweet, exotic scent caught her nose, bringing her to a halt. Jasmine? They had a potted variety in the arboretum at home, but with the Scillies' subtropical climate, it was possible—yes! She spotted the distinctive white flowers growing along the backside of a garden fence, their long-throated trumpets releasing their perfume over the entire area.

Libby scurried over to them, breathing deeply as she went. She adored the *Cestrum nocturnum*. It was one of the strongest-scented plants to be found, and she'd always admired it for withholding its fragrance during the day and releasing it only at night. It seemed so secretive, so reserved. Only for those who truly loved it, not just for the casual, daytime passerby.

She reached for her pocket, for the pencil and miniature notebook she always carried, before realizing she was in an evening gown. "Dash it." And she'd almost kneeled down there in the road to better inspect the blooms too.

Where was Bram to shout at her when she needed him? She relied on her brother to remind her of what she was wearing on such occasions. Her lips quirked up at the thought.

"You're late, Elizabeth."

She jumped, spun, and collided with a solid figure. A solid figure who shoved her unceremoniously back around to face the jasmine, holding her in place with iron grips on both her upper arms.

"Don't be a fool. You know the rules. Eyes forward."

To keep from seeing him? A shiver coursed through her, her eyes darting every which way in search of help. She could scream. There were undoubtedly people around within earshot.

But at the moment, he presented no threat. Unless one counted the way his fingers dug painfully into her arm.

"I'm not Elizabeth Tremayne."

Mabena would probably kick her for saying so. But she *didn't* know whatever rules this man thought she did, and she had a bad feeling she could pay for that ignorance.

He snorted an unamused laugh, and he was standing so close that the gust of his breath collided with her hair.

He was tall, then. She stood at five-six without shoes, and if one factored in the heels of her slippers and the height of the curls Mabena had fashioned with too much care, for his nose to be right there, he had to be at least six foot. Perhaps closer to six-two.

"Nice try," he muttered into her hair. "But I've seen no other pretty blondes walking from the garrison cottage to the Wights' this evening at the precise time we were to meet. *Elizabeth.*"

Think, Libby. Think. Her stomach felt so sick she'd have liked to curl into a ball. Why would Beth Tremayne have arranged a meeting with whomever this was? She didn't know, *couldn't* know, and didn't have enough information to pretend she did. But he obviously wasn't going to believe her claim of ignorance. "What do you want, exactly?"

"What game are you playing, girl?" His fingers bit harder. "Whatever it is, drop it before it gets someone else killed."

Killed? Her breath tangled with itself in her throat, nearly choking her. The moon, newly risen even though the sun's last light hadn't yet been claimed by the sea, winked at her in the pane of the window of the jasmine's building.

A reflection. The little house was dark inside, nothing to hinder that glint. She shifted a bit, saw her own wavering form, almost. Barely. She needed to shift them a little more if she meant to get any kind of glimpse of the man. "Sorry," she whispered, for lack of anything more insightful. Then a bolt of inspiration struck. "The last delivery didn't come. It was pouring with rain on Wednesday. I was only trying to make sure that wasn't what you needed just now."

The man growled into her ear and tugged her arms a bit toward her back, straining both her shoulders and her gown's beading. "I don't know or care about any deliveries. You said you could find it—the silver. Will they have to send their own people in?"

The way he said it—*their own people*—brought to mind images of ruffians and lowlifes and criminals to rival any of the buccaneers in Mr. Gibson's stories. And who were *they?* Libby told her throat to let her swallow, told her heart to calm, told her stomach to ease.

They didn't listen. "No," she croaked out, wishing she knew what he was talking about. At least if she knew, she could fight it. Argue. Do something other than stand here, wondering if Beth's secrets were going to get her hurt or killed. "But I don't *have* the silver. Not yet." That much was certainly true. She didn't have it, and unless whatever silver he wanted had been among the things Beth had taken with her when she vanished, she didn't either.

The manifests—the letter that had been with them. That had said something about silver—pirate treasure. Was that what this was about?

He jerked her arms harder, making her squeak a protest before she could stop herself, making a stitch snap somewhere in her shoulder, making her head go light with the scent of jasmine.

"Are you trying to cross them?"

"No! I wouldn't. I just don't—I don't *have* it!"

"Then *get* it. One week."

A week? How in the world were they to put all this together in a week when the last three days had netted them nothing but questions without answers? "I need more than that. A month." It surely wasn't unreasonable. Beth had been planning on spending the whole summer here. Perhaps that was how long she anticipated whatever-this-was taking.

The added pressure against her arms said otherwise. "Two weeks, and no more. Bring it to the large cave at midnight that Sunday. Am I clear?"

He pressed still harder, leaving her little choice but to eke out a pain-ridden "Yes!" She tried to jerk away, needing relief, and managed only to pivot them both a few degrees.

A few helpful degrees. Her gaze flew to the windowpane, and now she could see herself in partial profile—and at least a bit of the man behind her.

Tall, yes. Thin. He wore the garb of a typical tourist—pullover cardigan, white collar beneath it, straw boater in a light shade. Hair dark enough that it blended with the night-heavy glass, and features too much in shadow to be discernible, other than a long, patrician nose.

Enough, perhaps, that she would recognize him if she saw him again.

He shoved her into the fence and its heady bouquet. "Count to thirty before you so much as *think* about turning around."

He was gone, the release of her arms and the pounding of his steps tripping over each other in her awareness. She indulged in a whimper into the white trumpets, rotating her aching shoulders until convinced he'd not done permanent damage.

She didn't count. But she did wait until the last of his footfalls had faded from her hearing before she pushed herself away from the fence. Her shoes were probably dirty now, for which Mabena would scold her. Worse, her hands were shaking.

She stepped back onto the road and turned toward her cottage. Never mind the dinner party and Lottie Wight and viscounts and—wait.

"I've seen no other pretty blondes walking from the garrison cottage to the Wights' this evening."

Had *Beth* been planning to go to the Wights'? How, when Lottie said she'd never met her? Or was she lying—was she somehow involved in this too?

That couldn't be, could it?

She spun to her original path. None of this made any sense. But if she meant to answer that question, she couldn't do it from home, with Mabena and Oliver and comfort. She had to go where that man knew she was going. Where he thought Beth was going. And try to determine why.

Music spilled out into the night long before she neared the cluster of cottages the Wights had let. They must have a gramophone playing as loudly as it would go. Or not, she saw as she drew near enough to see the paper lanterns strung between the cottages and the area set up between. They'd hired a quartet, either from somewhere on the islands or brought over on the ferry.

And it wasn't just the Wights and the two gentlemen Lottie had mentioned laughing and tilting champagne flutes toward their mouths and milling around a makeshift dance floor. There were well over a dozen people crowding the small space, not counting the quartet or the uniformed servants.

She spun away. Forget trying to answer questions, she had no hope of that anyway. She'd go home. Tell Mabena and Oliver about the tall man who'd attacked her and—

"Beth!"

She froze when a hand landed on her sore shoulder, even though it was small and gentle. Turned.

A redhead stood there, laughter evaporating from her lips. "Oh. Sorry. *Not* Beth."

Lottie giggled her way over to them, a nearly empty flute in hand

and its aftereffects bubbling in her eyes. "Em, I *told* you I haven't been able to find Beth. This is *my* friend. Libby. Lady Elizabeth, I mean. Sinclair. I told you about her, didn't I? She left the Château the year before you arrived."

"Sorry," Em said again, offering Libby a sheepish smile. "I've just been expecting to run into Beth every time I turn around."

Lottie laughed again, which made Libby wonder how many other empty flutes she'd already created, and tugged her into their little bower. "Come in, Libby, please. The viscount is dying to meet you. And this is Lady Emily Scofield. Did I mention her to you? I actually convinced her to come and spend a few days with us!"

"Well." Lady Emily fell in on Lottie's other side, gaze darting all about the party. "I've long wanted to visit, and I thought I could see two friends at once."

Lottie leaned closer, eyes twinkling. "Her whole family came," she said in what she probably meant to be a whisper. "Even her *brother*." That last word she sang in a ding-dong tune. "Wait until you meet him. So handsome. Nearly as handsome as *your* brother." Eyes going wide, she giggled again. "No, wait. Maybe I don't want you to meet him. You stick with the viscount; he's too boring for the rest of us."

Libby wrapped the shawl tighter around her shoulders, glad Mabena had thought to give it to her. She hadn't realized they'd be outdoors all evening. Usually she would have enjoyed that unexpected boon, but all the people spoiled it.

Though she hadn't at all minded the even-larger group watching the boat race on Wednesday morning. That had seemed entirely different.

She directed her gaze to Lady Emily. A friend of Beth's, which seemed an odd coincidence to her. But then again, perhaps Beth always tried to lure her friends to the islands for the summer. "How long are you staying, my lady?"

"Oh, just until Monday."

"I'm trying to convince them to come for longer a bit later in the summer. It would be so much more fun with a more diverse company, don't you think, Libby? We've had no one but each other, Em. We'll be bored out of our minds by July." She produced a stage-worthy pout. "Please say you'll come."

Lady Emily didn't look any more comfortable with the theatrics than Libby felt. "That's my parents' decision, Charlotte. All I can do is ask."

"Oh, you can surely convince your father of anything. That's what daughters *do*. Speaking of fathers—there's mine with the viscount. Daddy!"

Mr. Wight acknowledged his daughter with an easy smile and a glass lifted in salute. And he apparently knew what it was she wanted, because he and the man at his side were soon coming their way.

Perhaps the events of the evening had already numbed her, because Libby's stomach couldn't muster so much as a single cramp at the approach of the viscount, even when his gaze swept over her before landing on her face and a smile graced his lips.

He looked vaguely familiar, the kind that came of seeing someone across a crowded ballroom but never being introduced. No doubt they had scores of common acquaintances, and Bram probably knew him well enough to say hello on the street. He may have been a bit older than her brother—or else just looked it due to his receding hairline.

He wasn't a bad-looking man though, not that Libby made a study of the specimens on display each Season, like Lottie did. He was of average height, wore a well-cut jacket that she suspected hid a waist that was thicker than he wanted it to be, and had eyes that, at least, gleamed with intelligence. That was a nice change of pace.

"Lady Elizabeth, so glad you made it!" Mr. Wight boomed. A newcomer might assume it was in order to be heard over the instruments, but she'd met the man before. He boomed *everything*. Perhaps in order to be heard over his daughter's incessant chatter. "Allow me to make introductions! Lady Elizabeth Sinclair, sister of the Earl of Telford! Viscount Willsworth!"

She held out her hand, not regretting having worn the satin gloves that stretched over her wrist and then her elbow, all the way to her bicep. They gave her a bit of insulation between her hand and the stranger's as he took her fingers and bowed over them.

"How do you do, my lady?"

"Very well, my lord. Thank you. And you?"

He straightened again with a warm smile. "My evening just brightened considerably. You're the friend Miss Wight mentioned who is interested in botany? And biology?"

She nodded.

"I suspected as much." His hand inexplicably lifted, hovered, and his brows raised to match. "Excuse me, you've . . ." He reached forward and plucked something off her arm.

A jasmine flower, snagged in the lacework of her shawl. "Oh." She cleared her throat. She couldn't exactly say she'd been shoved into the plant's embrace, could she? "I saw a *Cestrum nocturnum* on my walk here and stopped to investigate."

He didn't seem to find anything amiss in her explanation. He smiled and motioned to her head. Or her hair, specifically. "If I may?"

Libby's lack of reply was covered by Lottie's next burst of giggles, even as Willsworth tucked the bloom into her hair and then quickly retreated.

It probably should have brought heat crowding her cheeks, as Oliver's nearness had. But it didn't. It just left her feeling awkward and ready to go home.

He proffered an elbow. "I believe we've been paired for the meal. If I may lead you to our table?"

Others, she saw now, were meandering toward the cloth-covered tables. Four small ones were set up around the edges of the clear space.

She rested her fingers lightly on his arm. "Yes. Thank you." They walked a few steps before she realized she should probably say something to start an actual conversation. "Lottie mentioned you're interested in science? She didn't know what branch has garnered your interest."

"Paleontology, primarily." He beamed down at her, perhaps as happy as she to be able to talk about something other than who was seen flirting with whom at a dinner party. "My family seat is in Oxfordshire, and I stumbled upon a fossilized bone when I was just a boy. It's since been identified as a *Megalosaurus*. I've been intrigued with dinosaurs ever since and have led many an excavation throughout the area."

"Fascinating." Prehistoric animals had never really interested her as much as living ones did. She preferred being able to observe them in their natural habitats than simply guessing at their musculature and skin and patterns of movement. But she would have been intrigued to discover ancient remains in her own garden, without question. "I had the opportunity to view the skeleton of the *Scelidosaurus* once."

"I've seen it several times. And I was just talking with Lord Scofield about the fossils on display in the British Museum. Isn't that right, my lord?"

Libby looked up to see to whom he was talking and offered a small smile to the older man approaching the same table they were, a woman on his arm who, given the scarlet hair that matched Lady Emily Scofield's, must be his wife. And they her parents.

"We've some of the most remarkable examples in the empire there." Lord Scofield smiled, pride in his eyes.

"Lord Scofield has the honor of presiding over the board of trustees for the museum." A bit of his awe at this seeped into the viscount's voice. "Lord and Lady Scofield, please allow me to introduce my companion for the evening. Lady Elizabeth Sinclair."

To her utter amazement, Lord Scofield's eyes lit with recognition. "Lord Telford's sister?"

"Yes, my lord." Because Lord Willsworth held her chair for her, she sat, a second behind Lady Scofield, who deserved the first honor. "Do you know him?"

He laughed, a jolly rumble in his stomach. "I saw him just last week. Had an energetic conversation with him when we dined together at Sheridan House."

Of course, that explained it. Lord Sheridan, with his love of anything old and encrusted with dirt, would naturally have befriended anyone he could find at the British Museum. He probably was jockeying for a place on the board of trustees himself.

"They mentioned that you and he would be sharing a special announcement soon." Lord Scofield gave her a fatherly wink. "Needed a bit of holiday before all the bustle of wedding preparations, did you?"

Now her face flushed, far hotter than it had with Oliver. And it only got worse when she saw how stiff Lord Willsworth went as he lowered himself to the chair beside her. Not that she cared whether or not he thought her attached, per se. But Scofield had just said she was engaged when Charlotte Wight was within a mile, which meant all of England would hear about it before two seconds were out. And *then* what would she do?

Her fingers curled into her palm, tucked safely away in her lap, under the tablecloth. "I believe my brother may have overstated it, my lord. He may wish for such a match, but—"

"It wasn't your brother who said it, my lady. It was Sheridan himself."

She'd always known she didn't like him. Why didn't he have the gumption to stand up to Bram from the start? He couldn't *want* the arrangement. He didn't like her any better than she liked him—she was certain of it. And while she was confident he'd come to the same conclusion given enough time, that was with the assumption that he wouldn't have bound them both with the fetters of society's expectations in the meantime. Blast him. "Well, there is certainly nothing official, regardless. I haven't even seen Lord Sheridan recently."

Lucky for him. When next she did, she might just borrow a bit of Mabena's salt-inspired surliness and kick him in the shin.

Then she might as well fly to the moon to hide, if she were dreaming of impossible things.

Her discomfort must have been obvious. Lady Scofield interjected herself into the conversation and deftly changed the subject, asking Willsworth about his latest excavation. Given that he went on to describe animal bones and what he was hypothesizing about them based on fusions in the vertebrae—rather than Sheridan's inexplicable fascination with shards of pottery and Druid ruins—it would have been an interesting conversation. If only her mind weren't an absolute muddle and her stomach a matching knot.

Every time she moved, she caught a whiff of the jasmine in her hair, bringing back those terrifying moments on the road. And she'd no sooner shake that off and look over at Lord Scofield than she'd hear Sheridan's name in her mind again and see Bram's self-satisfied smirk as he announced that he had the perfect solution to their woes.

As if the thought of her simply remaining at home unmarried any longer was a *woe*.

The meal finally dragged to its conclusion, which unfortunately meant that the string quartet went from soft serenades to livelier melodies that they'd be expected to dance to.

She couldn't bear that. Not tonight. The moment Willsworth pulled her chair out for her again, she sprang to her feet, excuses ready to trip off her tongue.

"Well, what a pleasure it has been to make your acquaintance, Lady Elizabeth," Lady Scofield said. She wore a gracious smile that said she forgave her for completely failing to hold up her end of the conversation.

"Quite so." Lord Scofield helped his wife to her feet as well. "And when I see your brother next week for our squash game, I'll be sure and tell him you were looking well and happy, that the seaside agrees with you."

Escaping to the moon was sounding better and better. "You needn't trouble yourself, sir." She kept her tone casual—she hoped. Perhaps he'd forget by then that he'd ever met her and Bram would be none the wiser that she was in the Scillies. "I've been giving my mother regular updates."

"No trouble at all, my dear."

Her smile probably looked as weak as it felt. She spun away, mumbling something that vaguely resembled "Excuse me" to Lord Willsworth, her eyes flying over the group in search of Charlotte. She had to get out of here. Now. But if she left without telling anyone, they'd probably send someone to find her.

She eventually spotted her friend laughing with a young man who may or may not have been the wealthy Mr. Bryant. But she managed to catch Lottie's eye and gesture her toward the garden gate she'd entered through, moving toward it herself even then.

Freedom beckoned from the road. A glance over her shoulder told her Lottie was coming, so she secured a bit of that liberty by stepping outside. Then took another step, and another. She was nearly to the road by the time Lottie surged through the gate, her laughter a half huff. "Libby Sinclair, where are you going?"

"I'm not feeling well. Thank you for having me, Lottie. It's a lovely dinner party."

"Well, you can't just leave, not by yourself. We were going to have the Bankses walk with you."

She didn't even know who the Bankses were, but she wasn't about to wait for them. "I'll be fine. It's right down the road."

"But it's full dark now." Lottie edged closer, peering out into the night as if it might scarf her up whole. "And haven't you heard all the stories in town? There's been a ghost prowling lately."

"Lottie." She hadn't, in fact, realized that the stories had made their way to St. Mary's, though she supposed she shouldn't have been surprised. "There's no such thing."

"There has to be something, doesn't there, to inspire the stories?" Charlotte shook her head hard enough to dislodge a curl. "I never discount such tales, not with all the time we've spent in Ireland. I have no doubt at all that fairies are real—and they're nasty little creatures. Scillonian ghosts could well be the same."

"There are no ghosts on St. Mary's. And I can walk the five minutes home without—"

"Please don't." Lottie seized her arm and held it tight. "I'd never forgive myself if something happened to you. Just wait a moment, that's all, and I'll have Daddy take you home."

She didn't want to wait for Mr. Wight. Didn't, frankly, want to walk home with him. She cast a longing look down the road—and nearly laughed with relief at the familiar figure walking their way. "There's Beth Tremayne's brother. He can accompany me."

"Where?" Lottie dropped her arm and turned with her. "What's he doing here?"

"He's giving the sermon tomorrow—he's probably walking to the vicarage or something." She saw no reason to mention that he'd be coming from her cottage. Or that the vicarage was in the opposite direction. She didn't know why he was walking this way, but she wasn't about to complain.

Lottie pursed her lips. "All right, he'll do, I suppose. But I'm going to make sure he agrees before I leave you."

And get a look at him, no doubt. Lottie was nothing if not consistent in her desire to catalogue and rank the handsomeness of all eligible bachelors in England with as much care as Libby had given her study of butterflies when she was fifteen.

Either Oliver recognized her in the light spilling from the garden or he lifted a hand in greeting to every person he saw. Which, come to think of it . . .

But he was smiling as he drew near enough for her to make out his features, and he said, "Lady Elizabeth, good evening."

"Mr. Tremayne." She edged a step away from Lottie. "I wonder if I might impose upon you to escort me back to my cottage? I've a trifling headache but don't want to pull the other guests away."

"No imposition at all." He stopped a step away and held out an arm, nodding a greeting to Lottie. "Good evening."

"Good evening." Lottie didn't make any subtle noises hinting at an introduction, but she did send Libby a look that said, *He's a handsome one, isn't he?* Lottie had perfected the art of saying such things without words—when in a gentleman's presence. She'd put words aplenty to it the moment he was gone.

No, the moment *they* were gone. Let her do her exclaiming to Lady Emily. Libby tucked her hand into the crook of Oliver's arm. "I'm in your debt, Mr. Tremayne. And thank you again, Lottie, for inviting me. Tell your parents it was lovely."

They started back along the road, Libby waiting until she heard the gate latch before whispering, "I don't know why you were coming this way at just that moment, but thank you."

He chuckled. "I've been walking back and forth for fifteen minutes. Mabena said you wouldn't last but an hour before you found an excuse to leave, and I didn't want you walking back alone."

"I really *am* in your debt."

"Nonsense. I love nothing so much as a stroll on a summer night. And it's made all the sweeter with sweet company."

She ought to have indulged that sweet company on the way to the dinner as well. Maybe then the stranger wouldn't have accosted her.

Or maybe he'd have simply been more violent than he was. Maybe he would have hurt Oliver before threatening her. "Something happened on the way there—I'll tell you the details with Mabena, but . . . but we—Beth—a man demanded silver. In two weeks, in the big cave."

"What?" He drew them to a halt and turned to her, searching her face. "Who? Are you all right? Were you injured?" His gaze flew over her, snagging on the jasmine flower in her hair and then down to her arm. Could he somehow see what she suspected were bruises by now, under the shawl and through the moonlight? His hands cupped her elbows in that way of his.

Maybe Mabena was right. Maybe she *had* been doomed by elbow-magic since the first touch. "Nothing serious. And I don't know who it was, but I noted everything I could. I'll write it down when we get in."

"Libby!" The screech came from behind them. Lottie had barreled out of the gate again, though she didn't go beyond the circle of light. "Why didn't you tell me you're engaged to Lord Sheridan?"

Could this night get any worse? "I'm not!" Then, more urgently but more quietly, meeting Oliver's eyes. "I'm *not*."

Lottie simply laughed and went back into her garden. But Oliver smiled and turned her toward home again. "I know."

"You . . . how?" It should comfort her, maybe. But instead, dread curled up in her stomach.

"Mabena mentioned that was why you came to St. Mary's. To escape your brother's planning."

She'd told him that? Despite the fact that it was Libby's to share or not? Despite the fact that she'd known Libby wanted no one to hear of it?

He'd taken her elbow again, so no doubt he sensed how she felt about that. "I'm sorry. It's not my business—I shouldn't have said anything."

"It's fine. I don't mind you knowing."

And she didn't.

What she minded, more than she could possibly articulate, was Mabena telling.

14

Try as Libby might to focus on the new list of Latin names that needed to be applied to her catalogue of flora for St. Mary's, her gaze kept wandering away from her notebook and to the two envelopes resting on the table.

The first had been delivered yesterday afternoon by another anonymous chap asking for Elizabeth. They hadn't opened it, tempted as Mabena had clearly been. They would wait for Oliver to arrive, which he ought to be doing any moment. The second had come in the morning post, and Mama's familiar script had lured Libby into tearing it open straightaway.

She rather wished now that she'd held it for later. She'd expected her mother's usual cheer, perhaps even a note of thanks for doing as she instructed and attending the Wights' dinner party. She hadn't expected the rebuke that kept battering now at her mind.

Did you truly only stay forty minutes, Libby? Mrs. Wight's note sounded most distraught—she was afraid they had offended you somehow. Is that not exactly what I have warned you countless times will happen if you do not make an effort to engage with your peers? I know it is difficult for you. But you must try, dearest. For your own good, you must.

And while I know you will not want to hear this, I find myself compelled to say it: Perhaps you should seriously consider your brother's arrangement with Lord Sheridan. I know you wanted the summer away so that he might "come to his senses" and argue with Bram— but I do secretly hope that instead, you will give it some thought and come home in September ready to make the betrothal official. For all your clashes, Sheridan would not mind your eccentricities. He would indulge your preference for country life. He would respect you. I can think of no better match for you, dearest.

No better match? Libby gripped her pencil with far too much force. How could her own mother think that? Did she deserve—could she *hope* for—no better than a man who would simply tolerate her for his friend's sake?

She squeezed her eyes shut. What would she do if Sheridan didn't object? If she went home at the end of summer and the situation was exactly how she'd left it? No, if it was *worse*. By then, Bram and Sheridan could have spoken to far too many people about their ridiculous agreement. And how in the world would she muster the gumption to argue with *everyone*?

Darling leapt onto the table, batted at the envelope for Beth, and gave a loud meow when Libby picked him up and deposited him back on the floor. Even she had her limits, and kittens on the same surface where she ate pushed beyond them.

As did mothers suddenly taking the side of brothers. But how could she resolve that one?

The knock at the door interrupted those morose thoughts, and she jumped to her feet even as she called out, "Come in!"

Most of the gentlemen she knew would still wait for someone to open the door for them, but Oliver took her at her word and let himself inside with his usual smile. "Good morning, my lady."

Mabena surged out of her room with a scowl. "It's about time."

He lifted his brows. "Am I late? It's scarcely nine thirty."

"She's been a bit impatient." With Mama's words still fresh in her mind, Libby expected to have to dig for a smile. But it came easily to her lips as she motioned toward the envelope on the table. "I insisted we wait for you before we opened it."

Oliver's lips twitched. "You're a brave soul, Lady Elizabeth."

"Here." Mabena snatched up the envelope and thrust it toward him. "It's a fat one, but small. Doesn't seem like it would include pages of manifests again."

With an amused calm that surely covered his worry over his sister, Oliver joined them at the table and took the envelope. He opened it, withdrew the single sheet of paper inside, and frowned as he unfolded it. It took Libby only a moment to see why as a pile of pound notes slipped into his hand.

"Money?" He sounded utterly baffled. "Looks like . . . a hundred pounds."

"What does the note say?" Not that Mabena waited for him to read it. She simply moved to his side to read it over his shoulder.

Tempted as Libby was to do the same, she made herself remain in her place. Mama's voice was still too fresh in her mind and would be scolding her for unseemly enthusiasm in a gentleman's company.

Thankfully, Oliver satisfied her curiosity. "It says, 'Since you never answered as to whether you'd prefer a wire or a bank draft in exchange for the artifact, please find the cash enclosed.' That's all. No signature, as usual."

Mabena's brows were knit as tightly as Mamm-wynn's shawls. "That's a lot of money. But for *what*? What artifact?"

Oliver shook his head. "Clearly Beth found something." Eyes alight, he refolded the money into the letter and slipped it back into the envelope. "I've gone back through everything I can find from the weeks before she declared her intentions of summering on St. Mary's. I've never bothered with a detailed calendar of engagements, but Mamm-wynn has always been meticulous about such things, and she allowed me to check her records. She had jotted down everywhere Beth mentioned going."

Mabena's frown didn't ease any. "Since when does your grandmother track your every move?"

"She doesn't." Oliver chuckled. "But she *did* mention what Beth brought back with her, and from where. You know Beth always brought her a little something—a flower or a pretty rock or a feather." His gaze moved to Libby. "She's been doing that ever since we were children."

Libby couldn't help but smile. "That's very sweet."

"And handy, in this case. It seems that just before she got this notion of a holiday in her head, she was spending quite a lot of time on the uninhabited islands. Perhaps she found something related to Mucknell on one of them."

Mabena blew out a breath. "Which one though?"

"I think we ought to start at Teän. I recall the day she went there—we were having dinner guests that night, and she was annoyingly late getting home."

Libby had studied a map of the islands enough to know that Teän was quite near to Tresco, so it wouldn't have been the sailing that had taken Beth long. "It's one of the larger uninhabited isles, isn't it?"

Oliver nodded and glanced at the clock on the mantel. "And a fair distance from St. Mary's, so if we *do* want to explore it today, we had better be off."

Libby all but bounced. "Let's! I'll just grab my bag." In it she'd already stowed everything she'd wished she'd had with her on Monday, when Mabena had taken her to a nearer uninhabited island called Annet. Pipettes, slides, pincers, and a fully stocked field kit joined her ever-present sketchbook, notebook, pencils, and pens.

While she was grabbing her bag, she checked to make certain Darling had ample food in his dish, smiling when he dashed into her room and under her bed the moment they moved for the door. It seemed that outside was the last place he wanted to go, now that he'd found an indoor home.

Mabena passed her a hat and locked up behind them. She and Oliver were debating which sailboat they should take, the *Mermaid* or the *Adelle*, and Libby was content to let them fight that one without her input. She didn't much care which vessel took them there; she was simply happy to have a day of exploring ahead of her.

"Well, what luck! Lady Elizabeth, we were hoping to run into you."

It took her a moment to place the voice. And frankly, she didn't quite manage it until she'd turned around and spotted Lord Willsworth and Mr. Bryant striding toward them on the street.

Blast and bother. She summoned a smile to her lips, but this one required effort. "Oh, good morning, my lord. Have you met Mr. Tremayne, the vicar from Tresco, yet? And this is my maid, Miss Moon."

Perhaps she took a bit too much pleasure in introducing her maid to the viscount. Not that he did more than nod in their direction and say, "Oh, quite right. I was at St. Mary's the day you filled in for Mr. Gale, sir. How do you do?"

Oliver had scarcely returned the greeting before Willsworth faced her again. "We've just booked a boat for the day to take us to Bryher—we mean to explore the cairnfields. We hoped to convince you and Miss Wight to join us."

"Oh." For a moment, Libby could only blink at him. Never in her life had a gentleman invited her on an outing for no good reason. Perhaps she hadn't managed to scare him off fully at the dinner party after all. She wasn't sure if she was relieved—Mama would certainly be pleased to learn it—or sorry. All she knew was that she had no desire to exchange her current plans for his. "How kind of you to think of me. Perhaps if you had found me sooner, but I'm afraid I've already made plans to explore a different island." She lifted her bag in proof. "I'm cataloguing the flora, you see."

She didn't mention *which* island she'd set her sights on today. One never knew when a gentleman might decide to alter his own plans to be "accommodating." It was just the sort of thing Bram would do, if for no other reason than to needle her when he knew she wanted solitude.

"And if you mean to make it back to St. Mary's this evening, my lady, we had better hurry on our way." Mabena used the same tone of voice she had always employed at Telford Hall—demure, respectful, but knowledgeable. Only upon hearing it again did Libby realize she'd not since they arrived. And that she hadn't missed it, though it was convenient now.

She dipped her head. "Of course, Miss Moon. I certainly don't want to be stranded on a rock for the night. Have a lovely day, my lord. Mr. Bryant. Perhaps another time?"

Not giving them time to answer—or invite themselves along—Libby spun and hurried along the cobblestones.

Thankfully, they didn't follow, though a peek over her shoulder a minute later verified that they were still standing where she'd left them.

Oliver chuckled beside her. "I do believe you put a crimp in their plans, my lady. His lordship looked quite disappointed."

Which would probably last all of a minute before he remembered what a dunce she'd been at the dinner party. "He'll recover. Now, what should we be looking for on Teän?"

"Ideally, pirate silver." Mabena sounded doubtful even as she said it. "Though I'd settle for evidence of Beth's having found something there."

Libby pursed her lips. They could perhaps expect evidence of it if someone had been digging or had removed something—but how would they know it was Beth and not someone else? Or even an animal? There was no shortage of wild creatures on the islands, much to her delight.

It was a question they debated as they made the journey to the small island between St. Martin's and Tresco. They hadn't really come to any solid conclusions by the time they waded to shore, but it hardly mattered. They would simply keep their eyes open, explore everything they could, and hope to come across something that would provide a clue.

Once Libby's feet were on dry sand and she'd put her shoes on again, she turned to survey the grassy hills and rock outcroppings with a grateful breath. Though it lasted only a moment. "Looks as though we're not the only ones here." She should have expected as much, she supposed. Other holiday-goers hopped all about the islands, courtesy of the locals and their boats.

But Oliver and Mabena both frowned when they followed her

pointing finger to the blue sails barely visible over the land, clearly belonging to a boat anchored at another beach.

"The Hills' boat," Mabena muttered. "Have they hired it out?"

"Not that I've heard." Oliver's voice carried a note she'd had yet to hear from him—a bit stern, a bit resigned. "No, I suspect it's Perry, who ought to be at school, not gallivanting about Teän. And no doubt he has a Grimsby brother or two with him."

Mabena laughed. "I did my fair share of playing truant on a fine day. Third term was always the worst."

"Mm." Oliver sighed. "Come on. Let's see where they are."

Libby followed them through the sand and into the grass. The walking was easier than it had been on Annet, which was littered with rocks and holes that were entrances to the underground nests of the seabirds. And she spotted dozens of plant varieties she had yet to catalogue.

Teän had a few ruins she wanted to explore, in addition to her nature hunting. An abandoned cottage, an early chapel, a Bronze Age cairn . . . and they seemed to be walking past one such structure even now. No doubt, because the sound of adolescent voices was coming from within the tumbling walls.

Walls that were covered in a lichen she'd never seen elsewhere in England. Really, everything here was simply remarkable. Different lichen, different bracken, different heather—a whole new world! She could spend a lifetime cataloguing and still never list it all.

"How are we even supposed to know what he was looking for, Perry?" The young voice came from behind the lichen-covered stones, and it sounded none too happy.

An exasperated huff replied, "I don't *know*, all right? But he was here the day before he died."

"So? I bet he also visited the loo. Do we need to investigate *that*?"

"Yeah, Nick." Perry's voice sounded exasperated in the extreme. "That was going to be my next suggestion."

"About as useful," said a third voice that sounded much like Nick's, only a trifle higher.

Mabena and Oliver were creeping silently around the corner, perhaps aimed for a door or something. Libby had no idea what might be on the adjacent wall. She stepped a little closer to the stones, though, fishing into her bag with one hand. A scraping of the lichen would only take a second, and her friends certainly didn't need her to confront lads she'd never even met. She would just—

A scream spilled from her lips when her next step met air instead of ground. Her foot had found a hole that went deep enough that she sank up to her knee, her ankle twisting as it jammed into the uneven bottom. Worst of all, her satchel took the full brunt of her weight as she caught herself on the ground, and something cracked within it. Slides? Her magnifying glass?

"My lady!" Oliver dropped to his knees at her side a moment later, his face contorted with concern and his hands gripping her elbows to steady her. "Are you all right?"

"More surprised than anything." The initial throb in her ankle was already dulling. Or else it was just fully eclipsed by the far pleasanter sensation of his hands on her arms, his face so close to hers. Bother, but she didn't know what to do with these feelings he inspired in her. Or why in the world she was debating it when knee-deep in a hole. She ought to have been embarrassed, flustered by the situation more than that gleam in his eyes.

"Let me help you up." He did so with ease, levering her back to the foot still on solid ground. But he didn't let go. Perhaps because he was conscious of how carefully she put her abused foot down. Perhaps—dare she hope it?—because he enjoyed the nearness too.

Given the way his gaze brushed over her face and lingered a moment on her mouth, she could convince herself of that.

"Are you certain you're all right?" he whispered.

Never in her life had she been tempted to lie, to exaggerate a hurt, just to keep a gentleman closer. Lottie would be proud of her for entertaining such a thought even briefly. Which was enough to make her shake it away.

She plastered on a smile and flicked it from Oliver to Mabena, who had also hurried back. "Quite."

The lads dashed around the corner too, looking stricken and pale. "What happened?" Perry's voice asked. She could see now that said voice belonged to the boy clearly not related to the other two, who looked enough alike to have been twins, if they weren't four inches apart in height.

Someone must have raised these lads right. Had it been schoolboy-aged Bram and Sheridan caught adventuring when they should have been in class, they'd have run the other direction upon hearing another voice, not come to make certain all was well.

She rewarded them with a smile for their concern. "Just found a hole with my foot. A burrow of some kind, no doubt."

"That's no burrow." Though he toed the hole, Oliver kept an arm around her that warmed her far more than the summer sun. "Look. The edges are square."

The lads surged around Mabena and crouched down beside the hole. It wasn't large—just big enough for her unfortunate foot—and grass had crept over the edge, which surely meant it had been dug a while ago. "Bet Johnnie dug it," Perry said.

The taller of the brothers snorted. "It could have been anyone, Perry. Any time."

It could have been Beth. That was surely what Oliver and Mabena were thinking. But how could they ever know?

Oliver cleared his throat and put a stern expression onto his face, though the boys could no doubt see as easily as she did that it was more obligatory than meant. "And what exactly are you three doing here when you ought to be at school? What would Mr. Wearne say if he knew you were here?"

Whether they saw his mixed feelings or not, they reacted as any lad would when faced with the consequences for his truancy. Their faces morphed immediately into pleas. "Aw, come on, Mr. Tremayne! You won't tell him, will you?"

"We'll head right back. We promise!"

"It was such a beautiful day. . . ."

Oliver just lifted his brows. Given the twitching at the corners of his mouth, she suspected he said no more simply to keep laughter from his voice.

The lads huffed out matching sighs and pushed back to their feet, shoulders sagging. The taller of the brothers muttered, "We'll just get back, then."

"You certainly will," Mabena put in with gusto, narrowing her eyes and crossing her arms over her chest. "And you can be certain we'll be watching those blue sails of yours all the way back to Tresco. Now get on with you."

The trio scuttled away, though the wind brought snatches of their murmuring to Libby's ears.

"He wouldn't . . . Mr. Wearne . . . don't even like each other."

"But she's his girl!"

Libby sneaked a glance at Mabena to see what she thought about being known as Casek Wearne's girl by the schoolchildren on Tresco, but she didn't seem to be paying them any heed. She'd moved closer and was frowning down into the hole. "Did you see this, Oliver?"

"The hole?"

"No." Mabena knelt down, reached into the hole, and came up with something thin and colorful dangling from her fingers. "Beth's bracelet."

"What?" Oliver took it from her, his arm drifting away from Libby's back. An absence she felt like a blow. He flipped the beaded length over, fingering the frayed end with a frown. "No surprise it came off—she was losing it all the time. But it isn't dirty. Not like it would be had it been in that hole for months, getting rained on and muddy."

Mabena huffed. "And if it was coming off all the time, why didn't she take it to Mam for fixing?" Her gaze flicked to Libby. "I made it for her—my first attempt, using my mother's jewelry-making supplies. No surprise the clasp wasn't as secure as it ought to have been, but Mam would have fixed it for her."

So Mabena and Beth were good enough friends that her first jewelry-making attempt was a gift for her—another piece to the puzzle Mabena seemed set on keeping her from putting together. Libby made a mental note.

Oliver shrugged. "You know Beth. She hates to part with a trinket she loves, even for a short time."

"And look where that's got her." Mabena took the bracelet back. "So, she was here recently then. Probably since the last rain. But the hole doesn't look freshly dug, so she was investigating one she made earlier, or one someone else—perhaps Johnnie Rosedew—had put here."

Libby stepped around the hole, only wincing a little when she put weight on her foot. The twinge was minor, really. She'd be right as rain in a few minutes. "So that leaves us . . . ?"

"Absolutely nowhere, other than certain Beth's still about—as we more or less knew anyway." Mabena huffed again. "Come on, then. Let's see what else the island has to tell us."

Oliver moved to Libby's side and offered an arm, eyes twinkling. "For support, my lady? We don't want you tumbling down any rabbit holes into Wonderland."

She smiled and tucked her hand into the crook of his elbow. She didn't *need* the support. And he hadn't needed to offer. But he had, so she'd take it.

And she wouldn't even investigate that cracking sound she'd heard from her bag. No sense in ruining the moment.

15

Mabena had lain awake for hours already, her mind twisting and turning like waves in a gale. She tried to calm her thoughts through reason, through willpower, even through prayer. But nothing helped.

And how could it? They had only three days left before Libby was expected to meet that blighter in the caves, and they still hadn't a clue what silver he wanted them to deliver—or how they were supposed to find it. They couldn't even be entirely certain that "the large cave" meant Piper's Hole on Tresco, though it was their best guess, as it was the largest one to be found in the Scillies. They didn't know what he might do if she didn't show up in the right place with the correct silver. They didn't know if Beth actually *had* the correct silver. They'd spent the last two weeks scouring the islands and the books she'd left here, but both searches had been frustratingly futile.

People had been looking for Mucknell's treasure for generations. How could she and Oliver and Libby just snap their fingers and find it? And if Beth had, if she knew where it was, she obviously still had information they lacked.

That was what kept Mabena tossing from side to side, sleep as elusive as a rainbow. With a growl, she gave up and swung out of bed, snatching Beth's shawl from the chair and wrapping it around her shoulders.

She probably should have sent it home with Oliver, as she had everything else. But she hadn't. And though he'd seen her wearing it last Thursday when he'd come by to see if there'd been a new Wednesday delivery, he hadn't said anything.

Leaning into the window frame, she rested her head against the painted wood and let her eyes slide shut. She'd left the window open so she could hear the shushing of the waves, as familiar as a mother's heartbeat. The wind whispered in, kissed her brow. The moon sang a lullaby.

But her heart wept and her mind wouldn't still. They had a collection of clues stored safely on Tresco with Oliver. The letters, the manifests that had continued to show up each Wednesday, the hundred pounds with the mysterious note about it being for an artifact.

What artifact could possibly have been worth so much?

She wrapped one of the corners of the shawl around her hand. Mabena had followed the last few deliverymen too. All different blokes. All simply went straight to the ferry. She'd approached one and tried to talk to him, acting like a concerned friend of the girl in the cottage, but he hadn't said anything useful. Just that he'd been asked to deliver something, so he did. When she asked who'd hired him— because she had no doubt money was involved—he'd just shrugged and said, "Some bloke."

Narrowed it right down.

The ocean's serenade unknit a few of the knots in her shoulders, anyway. She'd missed that sound. More than she'd known.

More than she'd admitted.

A creak snapped her eyelids open again. Maybe it was just something outside, swaying in the wind . . . but the wind was only a breeze. And she wasn't hearing it through her open window. She was hearing it from her bedroom door.

Her breath caught even as her heart pounded. Another creak from the short little hallway connecting the bedrooms to the rest of the cottage. Probably just Libby, needing a cup of water.

But she knew Libby's step. Even Libby's quiet, trying-not-to-wake-her step. This wasn't it. She eased a bit closer to her door, cracked open from habit, in case *she* had to slip out for water. There—a shuffle, like shoes on the wood floor. Libby certainly wouldn't be wearing shoes at this time of night.

Her eyes well used to the dark after hours of staring into it, Mabena skirted her bed and hastened to the entrance, silent as a fish. She wrapped her fingers around the door's slab, pulled it open all at once, as she'd learned that kept it from squeaking. Stepped into the hall.

A figure was silhouetted in the dark, barely more than a shadow. But enough to see that it was no taller than Mabena. Slight build. And reaching for Libby's door.

There was no time for thinking—just for doing. She launched herself toward the figure with a guttural cry, tackling it to the ground. Given the size, it must be a lad. No, given the squeal, it must be a girl.

Whoever it was kicked her, pushed at her, but she held on, flipping them both toward the main room and away from Libby's. She dodged a hand to her face and shoved at the intruder's head. Her hand caught on something knit.

"Meow." The little monster pounced, batted at something. What was he doing out of Libby's room?

The knit thing pulled away, and Mabena saw in the scant moonlight that it must have been a cap, because hair came spilling out. Fair golden hair that she'd know anywhere, any time of day.

Mabena pinned the girl's arms. "Elizabeth Tremayne! What in blazes are you about?"

Beth went still—then pushed her off, eyes wide. "Mabena? What are you doing here?"

"What am *I* doing here? Quite a question from the amazing vanishing girl!"

Beth scrambled to her feet, full panic in her face. The kind Mabena hadn't seen from her in a decade, since the time they were nearly caught while swimming at night in only their knickers in the Abbey Gardens pond. Her gaze skidded from Mabena to Libby's door.

No. To Libby, who stood there with chest heaving and her dressing table stool held up like a weapon.

Beth backed away, hands out. "You weren't to get involved in this, any of you. The cottage was supposed to be empty. I was—no one should be here. But you are, which means you've interfered, as you always do. Where are they?"

Mabena tried not to bristle at the accusation, given that it had a bit of truth to it. "Where are what?"

"The deliveries. If I wasn't here to receive them, they were to drop them for me at—but nothing was there. I need them, Benna, and *Treasure Island* too. Where are they?"

At the *thump-scrape* from her left, Mabena looked over, saw that Libby had put the stool down and sat upon it. And that her ridiculous cat was even now jumping into her lap, the black cap Beth had been wearing between his teeth like a prize.

She turned to Beth again, seeing no reason to give her anything but the truth. "Ollie has it all." He'd insisted on taking it all home and putting it in his safe, and it had seemed the wisest plan. Let her sneak in *there* if she wanted them back.

"No." Beth squeezed her eyes shut, pain flashing over her face like lightning. Then her eyes sprang open again. "You have to leave. All of you. And Mamm-wynn and Tas-gwyn and—everyone. Get them, get them out of here. Quickly. Go anywhere—just make sure it's random."

"Why? What in the world—"

"Can't you just trust me? These people . . . they'll stop at nothing. They proved that with Johnnie." Her voice cracked.

So did Mabena's patience. She lurched forward. "What does any of this have to do with Johnnie?"

Beth jumped away before Mabena could grab her. "Just go. Please. I'll take care of this, I'll—"

"We're not leaving you to handle it alone! We're *family*!"

Beth shook her head and ran toward the front door, still half-open from where she must have slipped in. Mabena wondered fleetingly how she'd gotten past the lock but just as quickly realized she must still have a key.

All of which served only to distract her long enough that she didn't see the kitchen chair Beth tipped down behind her as she ran. It tripped Mabena up, tangled with her arms and legs and shouts. And probably inflicted a few bruises in the process.

Beth, blast her, was already gone by the time she looked up and out the door.

Hands landed on her arms, helping her up, but they weren't Beth's, as they should have been. Libby. "Should I go after her?"

"There's no point." Wincing at the pain in her shin and rubbing at the one in her ribs, she scowled at the door. "She's faster than either of us, and she knows the island inside and out. No one hides like Beth Tremayne. When she doesn't want to be found, you don't find her."

Libby's hands fell away. "You said . . . you said you were family."

She could have claimed she'd meant it metaphorically, as she would have done three weeks ago. But what did it matter now? She sighed. "Cousins. Our mothers were sisters. My family's the one that's dragged the Tremayne name down."

Libby sank to a graceless seat on the floor in a puddle of moonlight from the still-open door. Darling pounced on her again—sans the hat this time—but she didn't even stroke his fur. Just stared up at her as if her name were Judas Iscariot. "Why didn't you tell me? Why did you—you let me think you . . . You knew before we came, didn't you? You knew something was wrong."

"Her letters stopped." It wasn't how she'd meant to tell her. No, that wasn't even it. She'd *never* meant to tell her. She righted the chair, knowing she couldn't right this misstep so easily.

"So you . . . manipulated me. Into coming here. It was never about me and Sheridan and Bram, it was . . ."

The hurt was so heavy in her voice that Mabena had to brace herself against it. Squeeze her eyes shut, even as she pushed shut the door. Maybe the swinging darkness would blind her to the truth she didn't want to see on Libby's face. "Can't it have been both?"

208

"No. If it had been both, you would have *told* me. You would have . . . and you *should* have. Don't you think I would have sent you, or come with you if you wanted? Did you trust me so little that you thought lying was the only way to come and help her?"

Mabena turned, slowly. Too slowly. By the time she was facing her again, Libby was on her feet, speeding toward her bedroom. When the door slammed a moment later, Mabena's new bruises throbbed. "My lady!" She didn't know what she meant to say, and part of her insisted she shouldn't say anything. She should just go to her own room and let it rest. Address it in the morning.

But that was the coward's way. So she limped to Libby's door instead of her own. She didn't knock—it would just give her an excuse to tell her to leave. She didn't try the knob—it was probably locked. She just rested her forehead on the wood. "When I answered your advert—Cador had just left me for some London girl who promised him connections. He said . . . he said I wasn't *good* enough. Not for the life he wanted. That I wasn't fit to be the wife he needed, only a maid to serve her."

How could it taste so bitter on her tongue, even two years later? "So I . . . decided that if that was all he thought I was, that was what I'd be. I saw the advert in a paper a tourist left behind, and I answered it. Beth wrote my recommendation. My family begged me not to go, but I needed to get away."

The only sound from within was the squeak of the bed's springs. She could imagine Libby lying on it, her back to the door, a pillow over her head to try to block out Mabena's pathetic story.

"When I realized that Beth had found some sort of trouble . . . she's my cousin. My best friend. I couldn't just do nothing, my lady, and you had a problem of your own, so . . . It seemed a handy solution. I never meant you to be hurt by it, and I certainly never meant you to get mixed up in whatever *she's* mixed up in."

There. It was the closest thing to an apology she knew how to give, and it was true, every word.

But silence pounded from the other side of the door. And every pulse of it screamed that it wasn't enough. That she wasn't forgiven. That she didn't deserve to be. That it didn't matter what had chased her from Tresco two years ago. It didn't matter what had brought her back now. She'd played it all wrong, and while her family here could overlook it, Lady Elizabeth Sinclair could not.

She sighed and tapped a finger once against the door. Then pushed away. Maybe it wasn't enough. But it was all that she had.

Without another word, she slid back into her own room like a shadow and curled up on the floor under the window. The ocean's heartbeat melded with her own.

Having lived most of his life on an island that was all of a square mile in size, Oliver was no stranger to tension among his neighbors. Sometimes through a stormy winter there was little to do but argue with whomever crossed your path. But he never *liked* sensing that angry rod between two people, holding them six feet apart even if they were standing shoulder to shoulder. The mirror erected between them that kept them from seeing each other and showed them only their own frustrations, their own pains.

After the note that came from Mabena, saying she'd seen Beth, he'd expected her and Lady Elizabeth to arrive on Tresco Saturday evening bursting with whatever story they had to tell. Eager—if anxious—to put the finishing touches on their plan for tonight's visit to Piper's Hole. Instead, they'd stepped out of Mabena's boat with a curtain of silence draping them. The kind that wasn't stiff enough to speak of an argument only minutes past, but whose very heaviness said it had persisted far too long already.

He'd shot Mabena a silent question, but she'd pretended not to see it. As she *always* did when she didn't want to address something. No, she'd just shouldered the overnight bags they'd both brought and said with false cheer that she'd better go and see her parents straightaway. He'd taken Lady Elizabeth's arm and walked with her, but her silence only grew deeper, if that were possible.

Perhaps it was insight that told him she, then, had been the injured party, rather than the injuring one. Perhaps it was bias—he tended to assume that when someone had that windblown, storm-struck look in their eyes, the tempest named Mabena was to blame. Either way, he didn't know whether to assure the lady that it would blow over, leave it alone entirely, or try to wheedle more information out of her.

Twenty-four hours later, he still wasn't sure. He'd gotten to know her fairly well over the last three weeks, he'd thought. They'd gone to the other islands together, searching for Beth. He'd visited them on St. Mary's each Thursday to see what new novelty had been delivered the day before. They'd come to Tresco each Tuesday noon, and he'd met their boat, walked them into town. She'd been at the races each Wednesday morning, cheering him on, offering the same teasing consolation as any islander would when his team lost. Handing out Mrs. Gillis's tea and no doubt the one who tucked pound notes into her jar—no one ever saw her do it, but who else could it have been? And the fact that she did it, but on the sly, that she dressed like the rest of them, that she helped wherever needed, had resulted in his neighbors' all coming to call her "our lady."

It made him smile. She wouldn't know it, but they used the same tone they did when talking about the Dorrien-Smiths—"our Lord Proprietor." They had a way of looking at him—and now at her—as if he belonged to them and not the other way round. Which, really, was as it should be.

He couldn't tell her that, though, when she was cocooned in that silence. Its wall was too thick. Even after church this morning, when such a non-fuss had been made over her that she ought to have been thrilled at feeling so included. Even after an afternoon spent running their plan past the constable, who looked dubious but had agreed to it and hadn't even chided him—much—for not telling him straightaway that Beth was missing.

Even now, as they made their way to the cave. She ought to be nervous. Or excited. Or fearful. She ought to be *something* other than numb. And the fact that she wasn't . . . It was concerning. Yes, if all went well, they'd end this night with the man who'd accosted her two weeks ago in custody. But if it *didn't* go well . . .

His own chest had been tight all day, considering that *if*. If it didn't go well, Lady Elizabeth's life could be in danger. If it didn't go well, *Beth's* life could be in danger. If it didn't go well, any one of them could be hurt or worse.

But she was the one bearing the brunt of the risk. She would be taking on the blame for his sister. She'd offered it, when they first devised this trap, saying it was the only way, since she was the one he'd be looking for. She'd simply offered herself up as bait and then gone on to hum the overture of *The Magic Flute* while she made a tidy list of everything they ought to do to prepare for it.

He'd met a lot of people over the years. Here on the islands, on the mainland, at university. Friends, neighbors, strangers. None of them—not a one—was like Lady Elizabeth Sinclair.

Mabena was already walking a few steps ahead of them, never one to stroll along when she could stride instead. Oliver held Lady Elizabeth back a bit more with a hand on her elbow. "My lady . . ." But that didn't sound right, not now. Not when she was risking her very life for his family. "Libby."

It was a liberty he oughtn't to take without her permission. But if things went wrong tonight, that was the least of his concerns.

She looked up at him, her face traced only by moonlight and his gaze. She looked tired, but it was less because of the shadows under her eyes than the ones in them. He sighed. "You needn't do this." It wasn't what he meant to say.

The corners of her lips tilted up, then drifted back down. "We've been through this . . . Oliver." *Oliver*. Even better than simple permission to use her given name. "Whether I come to the cave tonight or not, the risk to me is the same. I'm the one they think is Beth. I'm the one they'll be looking for, whether they're looking here or at my cottage."

"You could stay here with the Moons and not go back there. Or—" He choked on the obvious suggestion and had to clear his throat. "Or you could simply return to the mainland." She had to at some point. It would be logical to do so now.

But he'd spent a few too many hours tossing and turning these past two weeks, praying she wouldn't. If she left now, when would he see her again? He couldn't exactly come to call at Telford Hall or their home in London—her brother wouldn't allow it. He knew that. She might not be engaged to Lord Sheridan, but she'd marry him or someone like him. Like that viscount who had "stumbled across" them twice already while Oliver was there—and probably many times when he wasn't. A man with a title. Or an estate large and impressive enough that no one minded the lack of said title. Not an island vicar whose holdings on the mainland were as modest as Truro Hall, whose resources had largely been spent on ineffectual doctors for his brother.

And blast it all, but never in his life had he felt the least desire for anything more than what he had. Never the least bit of shame or regret.

But then, never in his life had he wondered if treasure hunting with a lady could be termed courting. And if so, what her family would say about it.

Libby shook her head, and it took him a moment to realize she was responding to his suggestion that she leave the Scillies, not to his silent question about whether this thing between them was a courtship. "I'm not leaving." Flint sparked against the iron in her tone.

She wasn't just saying it to him, he knew, about tonight. She was saying it to the invisible specter of her brother, whom she'd been half expecting to show up and demand she return home ever since the Wights' dinner party. Perhaps Lord Scofield had forgotten to mention her to Lord Telford after all.

They could hope.

"Good. I don't want you to leave." A truth that warmed the back of his neck. Perhaps Enyon had been teasing him incessantly about flirting with her, but the truth was that he was a novice at such things, and while the words came naturally with her, he was also keenly aware of his own awkwardness.

He didn't know how to court a lady. Frankly, he didn't *want* to court a lady. He just wanted to get to know her better, from the inside out. He wanted the right to slide his fingers down her arm and weave them with hers. He wanted her here, at his side, indefinitely.

Heaven help him. This was all Mamm-wynn's fault, putting ideas in his head.

No. It was Libby's fault for being so incredibly and beautifully different from all the other girls in England.

That smile joined the moonlight again, too fleeting. She shifted a bit closer to him with one step, then back to their usual space with the next. "What time is it?"

He didn't have to pull out his pocket watch to know it wasn't yet eleven—he knew when they'd set out from home, after all, and how long it took to walk to Piper's Hole. "We'll have an hour to get into our places." And they'd been down there earlier too, deciding where each of them would be hidden, where she should wait, what she should say to lure the chap into revealing something incriminating so that Constable Wendle had a reason to block the cave entrance and detain him.

Plenty of time. "Won't you tell me, Libby?"

"Tell you what?" But she knew. She had to, and he could hear in her voice that she did.

Still, he'd humor her. "What's broken between you and Benna?"

He nearly regretted the question when he saw the moonlit pearl of a tear drop onto her cheek.

16

Libby averted her face so she could dash the tear away, praying he hadn't seen it. She'd never been the sort of girl to cry over every snubbing or hurt feeling. She couldn't be, otherwise she'd have spent her entire adolescence in tears, crying over each little barb Edith or one of her friends sent her way. The year at finishing school would have been a veritable ocean of waterworks. No, she wasn't the sort for tears, and she didn't want Oliver Tremayne to think she was.

But she'd been so dashedly close to them for the past two days, every time she looked at Mabena and realized everything she'd thought she knew about the woman was a lie. And to hear it put so truly, in a voice so very sincere in its request that she open her heart—even if he *hadn't* been gripping her elbow, her emotions would have surged up.

Broken. The perfect word to describe things. "She isn't my friend." It came out a murmur, one that she prayed the wind wouldn't take to where Mabena strode ahead of them. "I suppose I never should have thought she was. Perhaps Mama was right. Perhaps there can never be true friendship between employer and employee."

Mama had actually expanded it to *"between people of different stations,"* but Libby couldn't go quite that far.

And she felt Oliver's fingers stiffen on her arm. "You can't believe that."

"Not for the reasons Mama said. Not because there's any natural

215

superiority. But because there's something about the nature of the relationship that must make it too hard to trust." She sighed, trying to watch Mabena on the path ahead of them, even though it was hard to see her through the night. "Or maybe it's just me. Maybe she just can't trust *me*."

"You can't believe that either."

"I *must* believe it. What other reason is there?" She might have banished that first renegade tear, but now more stung her eyes, and she had to blink furiously to keep them where they belonged. "I suppose I've never been anything to her but an employer. An unusual one, which is probably why she's lasted this long with me when it's clearly not what she ever meant to do for any length of time. But still. In her eyes, I've never been anything but the reason for her position. An outsider when it came to anything that mattered to her. A—what is it you call tourists? In-something?"

"Incomers." She could hear the smile in his voice, and the sorrow, without looking at him. "What makes you think she thinks of you that way, my . . . "

My lady, he was going to say, as he always did. The familiarity forgotten already. Two words to prove again that she wasn't one of them, didn't belong here, where the only gentry or nobility were tourists, or else a Dorrien-Smith.

". . . Libby?"

A balm. A bandage. And even something that made her lips want to smile. *My Libby*. If only. But that could never be either. She shook her head. "She told me, the other night. After Beth came. She told me the truth. That she's your cousin. That she knew all along something was wrong and that's why she convinced me to come here. After Beth's letters stopped."

She'd assumed he'd known it all, since obviously he knew they were cousins. But his hiss of breath said otherwise and brought her gaze around, danger of tears be hanged. "You didn't know?"

"Suspected." Even in the moonlight she could see his eyes snapping. "But she swore to me it was only that *you* needed to get away."

And so she had spilled Libby's secrets rather than her own. Strange how it chafed in one direction and yet soothed in another. At least Libby wasn't the only one she'd lied to.

"As for the relationship." He pulled her to a halt and turned to face her, angling them both so they could see each other's faces in the silver light. His gaze sought hers and held it as gently as his fingers did her elbow. "I didn't know why she wanted it kept secret. Not from you. But I didn't think it mine to tell. I'm sorry for that, if it's hurt you in the slightest. That's the last thing I meant to do."

She could appreciate that, even as she doubted it. Maybe he didn't want to hurt her more than he wanted to hurt anyone, but facts were still facts. "You've known me only three weeks, Oliver. She's your *cousin*. Your loyalty belongs first to her."

"Does it?" His expression, as he cast a glance toward where Mabena had disappeared, was so very normal in its frustration that she felt a bubble of mirth rise. It popped before it could emerge as smile or laugh, but even so. It was good to know he wasn't as perfectly empathetic and bighearted as he seemed. "Funny, just now I'd rather toss her in the drink and side with you."

"Oliver." It was nearly the same tone she took with Lottie, though far more amused.

"Oh, it would be all right. She can swim. But if I may return to your other point." Did he truly step closer? Lean in? Or did it just seem that way when he returned his gaze to her face? "We've known each other two years, not three weeks."

"Do you really think an hour's conversation two years ago counts?" She hoped it did, given the many times she'd thought of him since. Wondered who he was. None of her conjecture had done him justice though. Because she hadn't known to imagine him *here*, but the islands were such a part of who he was. She hadn't been able to see him clearly without the Scillies as a backdrop.

"When it was a more meaningful conversation than any to be had in a drawing room or on a dance floor, I absolutely do." He stepped to her side again, urging her onward. Making her heart sag again. "It was a seed of friendship, well planted. It needed only a bit of water and sun to sprout and grow, flourish and thrive. The seed may be the plant only in potential, but without it, there would be no plant at all. Ergo, it is without question the beginning of said plant, as you can clearly see."

"Clearly." Though she had to wonder, and chide herself for wondering, if a seed of friendship could grow into something . . . more. She was a fool for even wondering it, she knew. And yet—no, and yet *nothing*. That's what would come of it.

They walked in silence for a few minutes more, her thoughts as restless as the waves that rolled onto the shore a few feet away. The entrance to Piper's Hole loomed ahead of them, blacker than night and far more menacing, given their purpose there.

It had once been a mine, Mabena had said. Hundreds of years ago. Then just a favorite haunt of the locals—a place to explore. In the last several decades, as more tourists came to the islands, it had become a regular place for visitors as well. A boat was always kept at the little pool, and sometimes locals even lit it all up with candles, making a grotto that was quite romantic.

There were no lights tonight. No romance. Just now, all locals thought of when the cave was mentioned was Johnnie Rosedew's tragic death, and they'd even told the tourists it was off-limits.

"They proved that with Johnnie."

She could still hear Beth's panicked voice, the timbre unfamiliar but that note in it undeniable. Beth thought that Johnnie's death was no accident. That it was caused by the very people who were now demanding silver from Libby.

She'd brought some with her tonight—some of what Mama had sent. Just pounds sterling, coins. Nothing special, not all that much. It wasn't what they'd meant—she knew that very well. But it may lure the fellow into spelling out what it was he *did* mean. That was what they needed.

"Libby." Oliver halted her again before they reached the entrance to the cave, into which Mabena had disappeared. He turned to face her again. "Much as we've tried to mitigate the danger to you tonight, there is still some. And I don't want you to step into such a situation with this burden on your shoulders. Please. Tell me what's weighing you so."

She'd said enough that he could no doubt piece it together if he wanted. There was no need to bare her soul to him.

And yet there was no one in the world she'd rather bare it to. She let her eyes slide shut, let her chin dip down. Let all the aches of the last two days—no, of all her life—swim to the surface. "I've never had the sort of friends you have here—Enyon and the others. It was just me and Edith at home, a few neighbors and cousins, but . . . but they never understood me. I never fit with them. I thought when Mabena came . . . I thought I finally had a friend. A true one."

But it had all been a lie, built on nothing but Mabena's desperation to escape her *real* home, her *real* friends, her *real* family. A whole world she'd never breathed a word of. A love gone wrong that Libby couldn't have guessed at. A personality, wild and free, that she'd kept so reined in that the Mabena she'd shown Libby wasn't really Mabena at all.

"I grow so weary of being alone." The whisper, pitiful even to her own ears, scalded the night like the tears did her eyes.

His hand left her elbow, and for one eternal second she felt so incredibly bereft that she thought she might splinter, fracture, fall to pieces. But then, then his warm hand was cupping her cheek, and those fissures closed. "My sweet Libby. You're not alone. You're *never* alone. Even if your family were gone, even if we here who would be proud to be counted as your true friends were never to see you again— even then, you wouldn't be alone."

She knew well that he meant God. It was the vicar in him; he couldn't help but say such things. And she admired him for saying them, for being able to believe them. Still, she had to shake her head. "I'm afraid I don't know how to have that sort of faith, Oliver. I wish I did." Even if she granted that He was necessary, He was still so very distant. She could see Him in the order of things, as Oliver had pointed out weeks ago. God not of the so-called mysteries that weren't mysterious, but of order. But that was just a creator. Not a friend.

He tilted her face up, and she let her gaze follow, expecting to see disappointment in his face. Or even rebuke. After all, what kind of man of the cloth would let someone speak so of the Lord? But for some reason, the moonlight touched on a smile on his lips. "I've heard many people say they wish they had more faith. People who have been broken by life, by disappointments, who can't fathom a God who is good in the face of a world filled with evil. But trying to answer that question isn't the way to make Him known to you, is it?"

"I don't know *how* He could be made known to me. That's the problem." She *wanted* to believe. But no one's explanations had ever made sense. And maybe . . . maybe she wanted it more so she wouldn't disappoint her mother than because she thought she needed that belief for her own sake.

"Is it enough, perhaps, to believe that He knows *you*?"

She blinked, refocused on his eyes. "I don't know what you mean."

He gave her that beautiful smile of his, full of caring and knowing and something a bit more she was afraid to name. "You are a student of nature. You study it and catalogue it. You take the utmost care to put the proper name with each specimen. Why?"

She smiled a bit, simply because it echoed the conversation she'd first had with his grandmother, before she knew she was *his* grand-mother. "Because it's by naming a thing, knowing a thing, that you come to understand it. Only when you see its unique traits can you truly appreciate what it is, and what it isn't."

He nodded. Ducked his head a few inches so their eyes were level. "The islands know your name, Libby—I know they do. You're a part of us here. We will always be your people. Do you believe that?"

Her heart swelled in her chest so that she could only nod.

His smile deepened. "Don't you see, then? It's like that with God, but more. He knows your name. Not Libby, not Elizabeth Sinclair. Your *true* name, the one at the heart of you that has never been spo-ken. He knows you, and He calls you by it. You, in all your uniqueness. You, in everything that differentiates you from others. You, in all you have in common with them. He knows you, and He calls you by name. He knows how you fit into this world."

"Does He?" Her breath wouldn't come, stuck somewhere between her lungs and her throat. It was a thought that demanded more attention than she could really give it right now, with a dangerous man due to arrive within the hour. A thought that, if she emerged on the other side of this night in one piece, she'd no doubt lie awake contemplating. "Would that He would tell me, then."

"He has." Oliver's thumb stroked gently over her cheekbone. "Perhaps you weren't perfectly adapted to the environs into which you were born, Libby. But that doesn't mean He made a mistake in where He put you. It means only that He set you on a journey, like any other migratory creature who needs different settings for different seasons. He led you *here*."

She'd thought it Mabena who had led her here, not God. But Mabena had come back for her own purposes. Libby hadn't been anything more than an excuse to her. Yet coming here—he was right, in the words he didn't say. She belonged here more than she ever had elsewhere. And while instinct hadn't led her on this journey like a bird knowing just where to fly . . . perhaps Someone had. Someone who knew her name. Knew her needs.

"Do you think so? The Lord led me here?"

His nod was solemn. His eyes somehow more intense at midnight than they ever were midday. "To us. To . . . me." The last word was but a whisper.

A whisper that sent a thrill up her spine. He was definitely leaning closer now, and tilting her face up with his hand, and her breath was still caught somewhere in her chest, but she didn't need it anyway. She needed only the feel of his palm pressed to her cheek. His other arm resting gently around her waist. The sensation of his hair, too long for fashion or Mrs. Gillis's tastes, brushing against her a moment before the unbelievable happened.

His lips touched hers. She would have dreamed of this moment, if she'd known how. Would have tried to guess at how it would feel, to hypothesize the effect it would have on her, to understand what she'd done to attract the attention so she could repeat it. But such facts, if they existed, didn't matter in that moment any more than air did. All that mattered was that she felt, for the first time in her life, as if she were exactly where she was meant to be.

She half expected him to retreat after that first light kiss—and to immediately apologize or express regret for it. But instead, he pulled her a little closer, caressed her lips with his again. Smiled against her mouth. "Are you cataloging? Taking measurements? Classifying?"

A silent laugh slipped from her smile to his. "I'd like to. But I'll need a longer example to study."

His fingers moved from her cheek to her hair. "Well. Anything for science."

She'd always wondered what drew a bee to a flower, what allure nectar had that would bring them flying in from miles away for just a taste. Now she knew. She'd fly miles too, if she had the wings for it, for this moment. This taste of melding lips and racing hearts and the certainty that eternity could spin out here and now and she'd never miss the normal tick of time, never need the rest of the world. Her limbs felt like tidewater, flowing and ebbing. Her brain was nothing but fog.

Until a scream shattered it all. Piercing—and then, worse. Silent.

———————◯———————

Mabena plunged down deeper, hands battling against the water, head an explosion of black pain and white distortion and the sudden certainty that this would be her end. She could feel the pull of the very island itself. The heart of its earth dragging her down. The pulse of its waters covering her. The cut of rock. The weight of time. Lungs burning, rebelling against the brine she'd sucked in.

Hands. Hands shoving. Holding. Smashing her head into that rock. It was them she fought, not just the water, but they were only a flash in her awareness before they were gone or she was gone or the world itself was gone.

Forgive me. She screamed it to God, because she knew He was listening. Meant it too for her family, for Beth, for Oliver, for Libby. Perhaps He'd let them know—Oliver had a line directly to Him, it seemed. Surely the Lord could whisper her apology to him for them all. *Forgive me for all I've done. All I didn't do. All I . . .*

Black pain. White distortion.

Hands. Hands grabbing her, and she hadn't any fight left, couldn't make her arms swing or her feet kick. Tas had always said she had salt water in her veins. She had it now in her throat, in her nose, in her belly. If it had always been a part of her, why did it burn like fire?

The water around her lightened, turned to air, but still it was black as tar and held her limbs no less captive. She couldn't open her eyes, couldn't draw breath. Couldn't hear anything but the rushing in her ears.

Pressure on her chest. Heavy, too heavy. Forceful. It shoved down to her very soul. Past her heart and the island rock and all the way to the salt water beneath. It came surging up, bringing her surging with it. Coughing, spluttering, gasping.

Still dark as midnight, but she could blink against it now. Grab at the hands that grabbed at her head.

"Benna! Benna, speak to me. Are you all right, my love?" Those hands probed straight into the heart of pain, making the black flash to white again.

She screamed, or tried to, though it came out as a scratch in her throat more than sound. Tried to turn away from the hands. Casek's hands.

Casek's hands?

It took her a moment to piece together why that was wrong and what would have been right. What had come before the rock and the water and the black and the white and the certainty that it was her last minute to beg forgiveness from the Almighty.

The cave—she'd stalked into Piper's Hole well ahead of Oliver and Libby and lowered herself down to the rocks and the pool, ready to get on with the night. Hoping to battle someone, truth be told, so she could expend some of this frustration that had built up inside like steam in a boiler. She'd been moving toward her prearranged position, had fished the electric torch from her pocket to aid her in the tricky maneuvering.

Then the hands, fast and hard. Grabbing, shoving, crashing. Water, swallowing her up. She coughed again now for good measure and tried to convince her eyes to see an outline of Casek instead of her own pain. "Caz?"

Her torch was still on, somewhere. Its light ricocheted off the cave's walls until it found them, though he was still more silhouette against it than features. He was kneeling beside her, a great hulk of worry.

Then she was part of that hulk, as his arms closed around her and dragged her against his chest, still heaving from his dive into the water after her. Or maybe his fear of losing her?

"Mabena." His one hand stroked her hair, avoiding now the place where pain lived, and the other held her pinned against him.

She saw no reason to argue about that, given how solid and warm and secure he felt after the salt water's deceptive embrace. In fact, his shoulder, as she let her forehead rest against it, was her new favorite thing in the world. "I'm . . . all right." Probably.

"Mabena!" This cry came from farther away and carried with it pounding feet and a new beam from another torch that made her wince when it flashed over her face. "Casek! Get away from her!"

She didn't know how it looked to Ollie, exactly. Though she could imagine, when viewed through his eyes, that *bad* was at the top of his perception. She'd screamed, and he came in to find his lifelong enemy crushing her against him. Still, it took a surprising amount of energy to hold up a hand to halt his assumption. "It's not—" More coughing interrupted her, though only briefly. "Wasn't him. He saved me."

Saved her. She squeezed her eyes shut against that awful reality. She, Mabena Moon, had needed saving.

"You expect me to believe that? That he didn't—"

A crack sounded so loud as it ricocheted with the light that Mabena thought for a moment her skull had given up and split in two. Her ears rang, shouts rang, everything rang. Then water again, though her head didn't go under this time, just under the cover of the rock ledge. It took her a moment, through the muddle of her own head and the chaos of it all, to realize the crack had been a gunshot, and that Casek had dragged her to the safety of the water again, his arms never letting go of her.

And he fairly vibrated with rage. "Did you just *shoot* at me, Tremayne?"

"Don't be an idiot, Wearne!" Ollie's shout sounded even farther away now. He must have retreated back to the entrance of the cave, presumably with Libby. "Who's there? Show yourself!"

"Oh, I don't think so." The new voice made Mabena go still with its very wrongness. It had a clipped London accent instead of rolling Cornish vowels—but not educated London, like Libby had said her attacker had used. And it was punctuated with another crack, followed frighteningly by the ping of bullet off rock and the hiss of it reflecting into the water. Too close. And how close had its rock target been to where Oliver and Libby must be hiding? She shivered and wrapped herself more tightly around Casek, closer to the protective shelf of rock.

"You islanders just won't learn, will you? I didn't think it needed to be said again to come alone. Do I have to teach you the same lesson I taught your young friend? I will *not* be crossed!"

Your young friend. Johnnie.

"I didn't *bring* them!" Libby's voice trembled its way into the cave too. "The cave isn't exactly a private location, you know. I don't see how—"

"So these others are just random neighbors?" A cruel laugh echoed through the cavern, skipping over the water to Mabena like a stone. "Don't bother lying to me, Elizabeth. I've seen you with her. And really, I don't care that you have someone helping you. As long as you have the silver."

Something struck rock. Clinking like coins, softened by a pouch.

Libby must have tossed the purse she'd brought with her down to the rocks. "There's your precious silver. Come and get it."

"Do I look like a fool? You're going to pick it up, my pretty one, and bring it here to me. By yourself. While the giant in the water and his dripping spitfire join your brother outside the cave."

Mabena wished a sliver of light could reach them here so that she could see Casek's face. See what he thought of this, what he intended. As it was, all she could do was hear the rumble of his words in her ear. "We're going to do what he says, Benna. He's shifted a bit—he could shoot us here, if he wanted to."

She nodded, wishing she could keep the trembling from her body. What if he thought it fear rather than the shock of the injury, the cold of the water? The idea of Casek thinking her afraid . . .

He rested his forehead on hers for a moment, sucked in a breath, and tucked her to his side. Even with only one arm, his strokes through the water were sure. She helped him as much as she could, but her limbs were still weak and shaking.

If ever she met that stranger when he didn't have a gun in his hand, she'd delight in cracking *him* on the head.

A moment later they were near to where the boat always waited to row tourists through the pool, and Oliver was there on the rocks, reaching to help them out of the water. Libby too, a few steps away.

Panic clawed at her chest. This wasn't the plan, wasn't the plan at all. He and Mabena were supposed to be hidden in the cave before the stranger arrived, along with the constable's men. But had they even gotten here yet?

This bloke must have had the same idea and positioned himself inside first.

Libby, who'd never even stepped foot in the cave before today, wasn't supposed to be going alone into its darkness. But there she went, one hand on the ever-damp wall, the other now clutching the change purse. The only light within was from the torch Mabena had dropped.

She gripped Oliver's arm. "She shouldn't be in there alone."

226

"You think I don't know that?" His voice was agony wrapped in fury. "He has a gun. What am I to do, exactly?"

"The two of you should have run."

"So he could shoot the two of *you*?" Apparently satisfied that her footing was firm, Oliver pulled his arm from her grasp. "Don't be an idiot. She was inside and dropping down to the rocks before he finished speaking. You're her friend, Benna, whether you realize it or not."

"And what is *that* supposed to mean?"

Casek pulled himself out of the water behind her. "Could you two save the bickering until later? Who is that in there? What's this about? He thinks she's Beth?"

"We don't know who it is." Oliver clambered up the ledge and reached a hand to Mabena. But his eyes were on Libby, and he looked as though he might rush to her side with just a breath of wind to nudge him. "But yes."

Casek snorted and reached for a bag he must have stowed in the shadows. "Leave it to the Tremaynes to bring a mad gunman to our shores."

17

Oliver gritted his teeth and turned his head, ready to sneer, snap, or punch at Casek Wearne as he shoved past him and strode out of the cave. But the moment he turned, he saw movement on the path they'd run up, and his chest tightened even more, somehow.

"The constable's men." He kept his voice so low that he could barely hear it himself and aimed so that the wind and rock and water couldn't carry it inside the cave. "Wearne, I need you to go and intercept them. Tell them not to come this way, or he'll just shoot her."

Casek raised his chin. "*You* go and tell them."

"I'm not leaving Libby in there alone!" he whispered furiously.

"And *I'm* not leaving *Benna* here with *you*."

Mabena should have been bristling at the implication that she needed a protector, but her eyes looked too dull with pain to allow for any bristling. "I'll go with you."

At least *one* of them had sense. Oliver motioned them onward. "Good. You're out of his view now. He won't see you leaving."

Casek relented with a huff, muttering something about fetching the doctor. Oliver stiffened at that—what had happened to Mabena to require a physician? But he couldn't ask. They'd already taken a few steps away, Casek's arm supporting her frame, which meant something must be seriously wrong.

But she was on her feet and moving, so he simply said a prayer and turned back to the cave. Edged, a few inches at a time, more fully into it. Then lowered himself to his stomach so he could see below the ledge.

Libby's progress was slow. Perhaps by design, perhaps because her feet were unaccustomed to the wet stone and her mind no doubt full of the stories of Johnnie slipping and cracking his skull and never rising again.

But not *slipping*. It was him, whoever it was hiding in the shadows in there, that had done it. He knew that now.

Oliver slid a few inches closer to the ledge so he could drop down again if necessary. He didn't know what he could do that wouldn't just get them both killed, but he prayed with every quarter of an inch that the Lord would show him something. Make a way. Send a bolt of lightning or an earthquake or a tsunami or *something* to distract the man long enough for Libby to get back out to him.

She'd made it only halfway to where the voice had come from when it echoed again. "Stop!"

She stopped, hand still braced on the cavern wall.

"What exactly is in that bag?"

Her fingers gripped it tightly. "Silver."

"You're growing tiresome, Elizabeth. What *kind* of silver?"

"Coins." Though this was true, her voice shook just a bit. He couldn't blame her—his would have been shaking if he were approaching a gunman too. Even if he had exactly what the other wanted.

A growl rumbled its way out. "What *kind* of coins?"

He could imagine Libby picking through the answers they'd devised to the possible questions. This one among them, or close enough. "I can only give what I have, sir. Now I'll thank you to let me uphold my end of the bargain so that you can uphold yours and end this nonsense."

Her voice was stronger that time and nearly sounded like Beth's.

They'd schooled her a bit in his sister's intonations and phrases over the last two weeks. Just in case whoever met her tonight relayed her words to someone who actually knew Beth.

If only they really were capable of upholding whatever bargain Beth had struck.

But the man in the cave didn't seem amenable anyway. His voice emerged cold and cruel from the shadows. "If those are modern coins, you'll pay the price for your deception. You know well we want Mucknell's hoard. Nothing less."

Blood pounding, Oliver slid his foot forward again.

Libby dashed the change purse to the ground in the exact fashion Beth would have done, with the right snort of exasperation—they'd made her practice the move that Beth was famous around the islands for. "You don't want it? Fine! I'll keep it myself, and you'll either shoot me and lose all hope of recovering the rest, or you'll give me the time I asked for!"

That *shoot me* part hadn't been rehearsed. They hadn't known there would be a gun involved. And though he was proud of her for the improvisation, he couldn't quite believe how offhandedly she'd tossed that part in.

"Think you're indispensable, do you?"

Given the shift of Libby's head, she must have lifted her chin. "I know I am, or you wouldn't be here. No one else knows these islands like I do, sir. Not now that you've killed Johnnie." Also true, if she were who they thought.

The man took a step forward. Not so far that the splash of light fully reached him, but enough that Oliver could make out his general form. He frowned. The fellow Libby had described from the road to the Wights' was tall, thin. This chap was average height at best, stocky. Either she'd been wrong in her description—which he doubted—or it wasn't the same man.

Which meant what? That the other was lurking somewhere too? Or just that he'd sent someone else to do his dirty work tonight?

"Let me make this clear, luv. If you're going to fail me anyway, then it doesn't much matter, does it? Dead or alive, you'd do me just as much good. Only, making you dead would be considerably more entertaining than just showing up again empty-handed at my employer's. So, you get me the silver the buyer wants. Or I make you dead. Yeah?"

The man couldn't honestly expect Oliver to stay still at that. He surged over the ledge and landed quietly on the rocks, though he was careful to keep his arms out once he landed, proving he had no weapon. "That'll be enough of the threats. She said she'd find what you want if you gave her the time, so *give her the time*. Artifacts don't exactly wash ashore at the behest of men."

"I don't recall inviting you into the negotiations, brother dearest. And now that you've got me irritated again, I'd also like to point out that I don't much appreciate the obvious trap you two were trying to set. I'm thinking a nice bullet to the leg might teach you a lesson."

"Do it," Libby interjected at once, "and you'll be arrested in a heartbeat. We know these caves far better than you, sir. And we have people stationed at the only exit—they may not have been here when you came in, but they're there now, I promise you. Hurt us, and this whole game is over."

Silence echoed. But the man edged backward again. "Do that and you can kiss your commission good-bye."

This was about money? But why? Perhaps Truro wasn't bringing in enough to pay for a house in London for a Season and perhaps they'd been a bit strapped when they were paying for Morgan's treatments, but it provided all their needs, didn't it? And now that they were able to save again, even some of their wants.

"Then it seems we had better strike a quick bargain, sir." Libby edged back a step too. "You give me more time to find the silver you actually want. No one gets hurt. We leave, you leave. Have we an agreement?"

It wasn't what they'd been angling for tonight. They'd wanted to arrest this fellow—but then, he wasn't the fellow they'd expected. And Oliver had a feeling that someone who spoke of the "entertainment" of murder wasn't the sort to spill to an island constable the details about who he was working for or with.

It would do. He would deem tonight a success if no one else got hurt.

The man apparently agreed. "The original date, then. Or I'll be back, and I'll take it out of whoever I must. Your brother. Your grandmother. Your spitfire cousin. Understand?"

"I understand." She bent low and scooped up the coins again. "I'm going now. We'll have everyone cleared from the entrance within a few minutes."

"That's good. Because if I don't report in by twelve thirty, the rifleman aiming through dear Grandmama's window will pull the trigger."

Libby spun at that, flying over the slippery rocks now at a pace that proved her earlier one had been deliberate. She clasped the hand Oliver held out to her the moment she was near enough, accepted the boost up to the ledge above, and they ran together from the mouth of the cave. "Are they here yet?" she whispered to him. "The constable's men?"

"They were just approaching. We'd better hurry."

They ran, hand in hand, up the beach path, and Oliver was a bit surprised to see the entire group still gathered in a knot together. But then, Casek and Mabena had been moving slowly, and the exchange in the cave probably hadn't taken half as long as it felt like it had. They joined the group within a few minutes, breathlessly sharing what had just happened.

Constable Wendle's frown was back in place. "I don't like this. Men like that on Tresco . . . we won't intercept him, but you can bet we're going to see if we can spot him. And ask around to see what incomers are here who match the description. First, though, we'll be visiting any house with a view of yours, Mr. Tremayne. You can rest assured of that. Nothing will happen to your grandmother."

Their tasks set, the five men hurried off, leaving only the four of them. He and Libby, Mabena. And for a reason yet to be determined, Casek Wearne.

Oliver turned to him, all the adrenaline from the preceding minutes surging again. "Now. You. What were you doing there? Are you involved in all this too?"

Casek's arm dropped from Mabena's waist. "I've about had enough of you and your accusations, Tremayne. Last I checked, you didn't own this island, nor the caves."

"So you just happened to be there. Pure coincidence." Oliver took a step closer, even though he knew he was asking for trouble.

Maybe he needed a bit, a bit that he could control. A bit of the familiar sort that didn't involve guns and threats of death.

And Casek was never one to disappoint on that score. He met him, shoved a hand into his shoulder. "I just *happened* to be where my student died over a month ago, yes. Because, apparently, of something *your* sister had cooked up! And you want to turn it on *me*?"

"Johnnie wasn't Beth's fault." He didn't know if it was true. Only that he needed it to be. He shoved back. "She never would have wished him harm."

Casek knocked his hand away, reached into the bag slung over his shoulder, and pulled out something white. Tossed it at him. "It's Beth behind all this, and you won't convince me otherwise. Unless you're going to try and tell me it's your grandmother stalking the shores of the uninhabited islands, getting everyone worked up."

"What?" Oliver caught the white thing, frowning at the feel of silk in his fingers. A shawl, he saw when he let the length unravel. His heart sank like a stone into his stomach as his fingers found the corner. The embroidery. The familiar Tremayne crest there, with its fancy *T* monogram. Mamm-wynn had given this shawl to Beth on her eighteenth birthday.

"Where did you . . . ?"

But Oliver knew even as he asked it.

"On Samson, right after my students were talking about the White Lady being spotted." Looking thoroughly disgusted, Casek shook his head. "I don't know what she's about, but she's deliberately trying to stir people up. And it started after Johnnie. She's behind all this—she

233

caused it—and now we're all left rocking, because a Tremayne never cares for anything but a Tremayne!"

"Casek." The croak from Mabena was more effective than a shout would have been in wheeling Casek around like a stallion brought up short. She had a hand pressed to her head and was swaying on her feet. Libby had reached out to steady her, worry on her face.

Casek knocked *her* hand aside too and swept Mabena up into his arms. "To the doctor with you, dearover."

"I don't need a doctor." Always stubborn, even when she had agony scrawled across her face. "Just take me home. Mam can tend me."

"You want to worry your parents? Tell them all this? At this time of night?"

Her face screwed up even more. "All right. The doctor then."

"And afterward, bring her to my house." Oliver couldn't argue with the logic of not setting the Moons to worrying, especially since the plan had been for Mabena and Libby to stay at his house tonight anyway, given the evening's outing. Though they'd told her parents they were merely going to enjoy a night of games and stargazing. Something they'd done countless times over the years.

Casek, of course, snorted. "Right. Can't trust me with her."

"Well, you're certainly not taking her to your flat."

Wearne rolled his eyes. Probably. Though he'd turned away, so Oliver couldn't see him. "I don't recall saying I meant to."

Mabena moaned. Or muttered something. Possibly a plea for them to stop, though he couldn't be sure, given the way the wind garbled it. Either way, Casek's long legs started eating up the track without a pause for another exchange, and Libby drifted to Oliver's side.

They both watched them disappear beyond the rise before saying anything more. And then it wasn't a word but a touch that had him sighing out the anxiety of the night—Libby's hand on his arm, sliding down to his wrist. Taking his hand, the one not tangled up with incriminating silk.

He wove their fingers together. Foolish, no doubt. But he needed the touch, and he suspected she did too.

234

"Why do you dislike him so much?"

He hadn't been sure whether she'd ask about that or Beth or all that transpired in the cave. But this was by far the easiest to answer. "Because he dislikes me."

"And why does he dislike you?"

He sighed, shrugged. "He always has. The Wearnes and the Tremaynes have never been what one would call friendly."

"Because . . . ?"

"Because . . ." He frowned into the night. And wondered where the stranger was. Deeper in the caves, looking for another way out? Or sneaking out behind them even now? He cast a glance over his shoulder and tugged Libby into a walk. "Because we have holdings on the mainland, I suppose. No one here owns any property. The Wearnes always said we lord it over the rest of them. That we only stay here so we can feel superior to someone, since we haven't enough to do that on the mainland."

"That's ridiculous, from what I've seen."

"Exactly! We're here because we love it here. That's all."

"Which means that's only an excuse." She stepped closer to him as they walked so that their arms brushed with every movement. She wasn't wearing gloves—never did, aside from the night of the dinner party. He found he liked the feeling of her fingers against his. "The real question, I think, is why you've never tried to work past that with him."

"I have." Hadn't he? Surely so, at some point. Or another. Over the years. When they were children, perhaps, or . . . since.

"Really? You've worked your elbow-magic on him, as Mabena calls it? And it's failed?" Somehow a shade of amusement colored her tone. Amusement, after all this.

He opened his mouth. But had to shut it again. Of course he'd never taken Casek Wearne's elbow, nor invited him to open his heart to him. "If I tried it, he'd sock me in the nose."

"That may be. But I think Mabena's wrong." She settled her hand on his arm too. Two connections, which were somehow more than twice as effective at making him aware of her every shift. "The elbow has nothing to do with it. It's you that sees people, Oliver. Sees them truly, sees them clearly. Sees them with purpose—and that purpose is to care."

He glanced at her face briefly, then back to the path. "I suppose he resists me more than most."

"I don't think that's it at all." She squeezed his arm, then let her fingers drift away again. "I think it's that you don't *want* to see him. So you've never really tried."

He winced. Wanted to deny it. But he knew truth when it pierced his soul. "I don't know how to want to. Not with him." Those words would probably make her respect him less, think him petty.

Or make her chuckle. "I think you'd better sort through that. Because he's clearly in love with your cousin, and I think she's leaning that direction too."

"No! He'll only hurt her." The objection emerged from reflex more than thought.

But she angled her face toward his, brow arched, called him on it. "Someone already did, Oliver—but it wasn't him. Not two years ago and not tonight."

He huffed out a breath. "I know." He let silence walk with them for a few paces and then said, "He's always had eyes only for Mabena. But everyone thought Cador the wiser choice, if she liked that particular face."

She snorted a laugh, no doubt at the thought of twins being interchangeable. She would know, better than most, how nature only provided so much of who a person was. "She said Cador kept her grounded, and that's what everyone said she needed." She squeezed his fingers, and he knew well it was a warning. "But she said that Casek made her fly."

A warning he certainly appreciated. He drew in a long, salt-laden breath and let it leak out again. "She told you that?"

"Mm."

"Well." He squeezed her fingers back. "Then I think you have

236

your answer on whether she's really your friend. That's not the sort of thing she'd say to someone who wasn't."

But expecting him and Casek Wearne to ever claim the same would require more than elbow-magic. It would require an outright miracle.

18

"amm-wynn?"

"Mrs. Tremayne? Where are you, dearover?"

Libby blinked awake, staring for a long moment at the unfamiliar wall across from her before the words combined with the image and reminded her of where she was—the Tremayne house, and given the angle of light coming through the window, she hadn't been sleeping in this borrowed bed for more than four or five hours.

She sat up, rubbing her eyes. Still gritty. They'd spent an hour last night talking to the constable. The man from the cave hadn't been spotted anywhere, but they'd determined that no threats lurked in the nearby houses, at least. Then they'd spent another hour waiting for Casek to bring Mabena, talking over why Beth would be trying to scare anyone with ghost stories—and deciding it must be to keep them away from wherever she was, or where she suspected a treasure was buried. Wondering what had been delivered to her before she left the cottage, what she knew that they didn't. What she might have already found. When finally Casek had delivered Mabena to them, it had been with a few short words, saying the doctor had stitched up a sizable gash on her head, given her some aspirin for the pain, and that sleep would prove the best healer.

They'd tucked her into Beth's room, and then Libby had been

shown here, to a guest chamber. It was charming and pretty in blues and whites that whispered of the ocean. And its lovely walls didn't reveal anything now about the whereabouts of the Tremayne matriarch, who had wandered off again.

Libby pushed herself out of bed and quickly changed into the fresh clothes waiting for her, trying to grasp the wisps of a dream as she did so. Something about trees . . . curling bark . . . strange plants . . . with fairies darting among them. The images were too elusive for her to pull back into her mind though. Best to focus on Mamm-wynn.

From what Oliver had told her, his grandmother had taken to escaping Mrs. Dawe several times a week, but she usually only went out to watch the ocean or to the Abbey Gardens. If they were calling for her with that note of panic, it could well mean they'd already checked those places and come up empty.

Not really caring that her braid was frazzled from sleep, she opened the door, charged into the hallway, and barreled straight into Oliver.

He caught her with hands on her arms and a worried, distracted smile. "Sorry. We woke you."

"It doesn't matter." He looked as tired as she still felt, with circles under his eyes and hair as wild as her own. And he had on only shirtsleeves and trousers, no waistcoat or jacket. Unusual for him. "Has she slipped out again?"

"I was about to take another turn through the Abbey Gardens. I already did so once, but perhaps too quickly. I could have missed her somewhere."

"I'll come with you." She turned back into her room to grab her purple shawl, not giving him the chance to refuse her company.

He didn't try anyway, just stood there waiting for her, hands on his hips and gaze unfocused. "She doesn't usually slip out so early, other than on Wednesdays lately, to see the races."

"Could she think it's Wednesday? Perhaps she's confused by Mabena and me being here." She swung the shawl into place and flipped her braid outside it.

"It's possible. We'll check the beach too." He took her hand—not placing it on his forearm as he'd done before but weaving their fingers together. Like last night.

They hadn't spoken of the kiss. There'd been too much else to fret over. But it had been thoughts of that, not the gunman or pirate treasure or poor Mabena's injury or the feud with Casek Wearne, that had lulled her to sleep a few short hours ago. She'd half expected morning to bring with it a return to *My lady* and proper distance between them.

This was promising though.

He led her out a rear door, into his garden, which she'd yet to properly explore. And now certainly wasn't the time, other than for a careful check of all the corners and hidden nooks to make sure they were empty of grandmothers. From there, they hurried to the Abbey Gardens and the side entrance that was unlocked.

He said nothing. Didn't shout for Mamm-wynn. Perhaps because he was keenly aware of the sleepy silence of the rest of Tresco, as she was. Perhaps because the cool, misty morning air seemed to forbid any loud noises. Perhaps because he knew the moment he shouted for her outside, all his neighbors would join in the hunt, and he wanted to reserve that for if and when it became imperative.

Libby's heart squeezed a bit more with each step, each glance that didn't reveal Mamm-wynn. It had seemed harmless enough the other times she'd found the lady away from where she should be. But this early there was no one to keep a watchful eye on her and steer her back toward home. What if her steps faltered and she slipped? Fell? Injured herself?

Her fingers tightened around Oliver's. And she nearly laughed in relief when the sound of something shuffling against the garden path reached her ears. They both took off in the direction of the sound, coming up short when they saw a crouched figure.

But masculine instead of feminine. Mr. Menna. He looked up at their quick steps, brows furrowed. "Mr. Tremayne! And Lady Elizabeth. What brings you—"

"It's Mamm-wynn. She's slipped off again." Oliver shoved his free hand through his hair. "You haven't seen her, I assume?"

Mr. Menna stood, shaking his head. "No, but I'll check the Gardens, if you wanted to look somewhere else."

For a split second, Oliver hesitated. Debating, she assumed, whether to accept the help or insist they could do it alone. But concern must have won out over pride. He nodded. "Thank you. We're going to check the beach, in case she thinks it Wednesday, since Libby and Benna are here."

Mr. Menna stowed his small shovel in the wheelbarrow parked a few feet away and brushed the soil from his hands. "Good idea. You two go ahead. I know all her favorite spots here."

They passed by the Tremayne house again on their way to the beach from which the racers always launched, and Libby pulled Oliver to a halt when a splash of brightest pink caught her eye. Cultivated daisies—*Mesembryanthemum*, a variety she'd never seen outside a hothouse before coming here—lying in the street rather than growing where they ought to be beside the Tremayne front door. She bent to pick them up, frowning at the neat slice on the stalks. "They've been cut, but obviously not long ago or they'd show some wilting. Perhaps she came out to gather some flowers?"

"Seems likely." He accepted the blooms when she handed them to him, a brief smile flitting over his lips before retreating. "Beth's favorite. Let's hope Mamm-wynn left a trail of them, like bread crumbs, for us."

She kept her eyes sharp for any other patches of color along the road, but they weren't so lucky—or Mrs. Tremayne hadn't come this way. Certainly when they arrived at the beach they saw no evidence of a pixie of a woman watching for racers that weren't on the water.

Well, someone was, or was about to be. But he was stepping into a one-man gig. And he spotted them before he launched, which brought his feet back onto the sand. "Ollie!"

"Enyon." Oliver hurried over to his friend.

As soon as they were close enough to see each other clearly, Enyon's welcoming, teasing smile—and the gaze that he'd arrowed onto their joined hands—gave way to a worried frown. "Something's wrong?"

"Mamm-wynn. Again."

Enyon lifted a hand to shield his eyes from the sun painting fire over the water. "Early for her."

"I know." Oliver sighed and scanned the beach. "Mr. Menna's checking the Abbey Gardens. And Mrs. Dawe is checking the house and grounds again."

"I'll hug the coast, see if I spot her anywhere. She's probably just out for a morning stroll. It's a beautiful day."

Though Oliver nodded, Libby could see the tension in his lips. The fight to hold back the words, the worry.

To keep himself from saying that the beauty of a day didn't insulate it from horror. Last night had been just as beautiful, but his cousin was sleeping off a head injury even now, the same sort that had killed Johnnie Rosedew.

To keep from voicing the worry that the constable's men had been wrong and there *had* been a threat lurking in a neighboring house, and it had found her.

Sour fear burned Libby's throat.

"You two walk the south path. I'll start going north. We'll have found her in a few minutes."

Oliver made no attempt at conversation as he moved to obey, and she could hardly blame him. Once you named a thing, after all, it became a bit more real.

She instead let her gaze dart every which way as they walked the coastal path southward, though she saw nothing that seemed out of the ordinary.

Oliver halted her, though, when they reached the turn that gave them a view of Samson. She wasn't certain why, what had knit his brows together, until he pointed out to the water. Or more particularly, to the small sailboat upon it. Its sails were down, and it looked to be drifting. "That's Tas-gwyn's boat."

Her stomach flopped. She was no boatwoman like Mabena, but it didn't look right to her. She didn't see an anchor line, nor could she make out anyone in the boat keeping it where it should be.

Which was probably why it was just drifting there, halfway between the islands.

"Come on." Oliver had apparently thought much the same thing, because he took off at a run back for the beach where they'd seen Enyon, dropping her fingers after they turned.

She tried not to focus on how cool and lonely they felt without his around them. Better instead to focus on keeping up with him, which was trial enough.

Perhaps she needed to spend more of her days moving and fewer sitting around studying slides under her microscope. But she was determined not to slow him down, not when his grandparents were his reason for hurrying. Grateful that she was at least in reasonable clothes that allowed for movement and not the restrictive sort of dress Mama always tried to make her wear, she ran as fast as she could on the path. And fought for breath enough to call out, "Does Tas-gwyn . . . usually go out . . . so early?"

"Never," Oliver answered over his shoulder. "Aside from the Wednesday races, he won't even leave the house before nine these days. Says such hours are for youngsters and fishermen."

Bram would get along with him well, then. Though it was hardly time for thoughts of her brother. "So *both* . . . of them?" She'd meant to say more than that, but they were back to the descent to the beach, and she opted for paying attention to her feet's purchase in the sand instead.

Oliver offered her a hand, and then held on to it again. His dark eyes were troubled. "I do wonder if it's related. Tas-gwyn Gibson is the only one Mamm-wynn trusts to take her on the water these days, other than Beth and me and maybe Mabena. They joke that he is the little brother she didn't know she had until their children married."

But surely Mr. Gibson wouldn't take Mrs. Tremayne out on the water before dawn without telling Oliver. Would he?

He must have been wondering the same. His face moved to the sea again, and he tugged her toward the boathouse. "We'll take a gig to it. I daresay it will be quicker, given how low the wind is right now, even with only one at the oars."

"I'll help row." The words were out before she could stop them, though she wasn't exactly surprised when Oliver shook his head.

"Not necessary, my lady."

And they were back to *that*. "I know how. There's a small lake at Telford Hall, and we went out on it frequently with rowboats. Nothing so grand as to allow for sails, but Bram always made me pull my own weight." Unlike Edith, who swore such sport was unladylike—though Bram had always teased that it was just her excuse for not wanting to exert herself. "Let's strike a bargain, shall we? Test me for a minute, and if I make the going slower, I'll stop. But it seems to me that speed is of the utmost interest just now, so if I *can* help us along, I *should*. Don't you agree?"

Though it was fleeting, he sent her a smile. "Your logic is unassailable."

And more importantly, he wasted no more time arguing about it but simply slid a small gig out of its rack and grabbed two sets of oars. Within a few minutes he was pushing them into the water, leaping in without even wetting his shoes.

She'd never thought herself the sort to admire a man's musculature and physical prowess. But she had to admit, watching him move, that his able form ignited a purely animal response inside her. Not surprising from a biological standpoint, of course. It was the attraction to the fittest that allowed them to survive, by Darwin's theory. They were the ones to attract a mate, to reproduce, to pass their superior traits along to the next generation.

Her cheeks warmed. She'd examined such theories aplenty, but never with the thought that *she* was the mate to be attracted. It made it entirely different.

And entirely irrelevant just now. She was being every bit as silly as Lottie, thinking of a man's handsomeness when she should be worrying over his grandparents. She gripped her oars firmly and, the moment he dipped his, matched him.

Only the slip of wood through water spoke now, and the cry of birds overhead, out for their breakfast. It would have been a serenade if not for the circumstances. Determined to prove herself to him, she matched him stroke for stroke, stridently ignoring the burn that soon scorched her shoulders. A bit of aching later would be worth it if they could find Mr. Gibson and Mrs. Tremayne.

Soon they were knocking against the hull of Tas-gwyn's boat—built, no doubt, by his son-in-law. Oliver stowed his oars and leapt gracefully to the larger craft, a rope in hand to lash them together. "Stay here for a moment, Libby, if you would."

If he kept calling her *Libby*, she'd obey most any dictate. "All right."

A moment later, he was shaking his head. "He's not on here. Perhaps that's good. If he were, but the boat were drifting, it wouldn't be a good thing. Given the current, I'm guessing it drifted from Samson for some reason. Let's sail it back over there and see if there's any sign of them. We'll tow the gig."

She wasn't exactly eager to make the same climb from one boat to the other, but he was there, hand held out to help her, so what was she to do but agree? And though even with his help she was far less graceful than he'd been, she didn't make an utter fool of herself. Her feet were soon planted on the elegant wood planking of the small sailboat, which freed Oliver to tend to the sails and get them moving in the direction he wanted.

She'd yet to go to Samson, though Mabena had told her a bit about it. It was currently the largest uninhabited island in the Scillies, though as little as fifty years ago that hadn't been the case. There were cottages there, abandoned farms that hadn't been productive enough to support the inhabitants. In the 1850s, the Lord Proprietor had moved the last of them, half-starved as they were, to Tresco after too many of their able-bodied men had drowned trying to save people from a shipwreck. Such a tragic, noble loss. He'd tried to turn the island into a deer park after that, but the attempt failed. Now it was simply a place people visited for a few hours to walk or observe the flora and fauna.

And this was *not* the way she'd planned on seeing it, on a hunt for missing grandparents. But Oliver was soon sailing them to a little quay and helping her out onto the damp sand.

The moment she landed, an unusual break in the colors of the grasses caught her eye. "There!" She pointed.

Oliver wheeled around, clearly spotting the legs and shoes too—masculine ones. They both took off at a run.

"Tas-gwyn!" Perhaps Oliver recognized the feet, or perhaps it was just a hopeful cry. Either way, he was soon proven correct as more of Mr. Gibson came into view as they neared. And the legs moved, which was surely a good sign. By the time they reached him, the old gent was pushing himself up with a moan, a hand clutching his head.

"Tas-gwyn." Oliver fell to his knees at his grandfather's side and put an arm behind his back to help him the last few inches to sitting. "What happened? Are you all right?"

"Beth."

Oliver frowned. "What about Beth? Is she here?"

"I don't . . ." Mr. Gibson winced and shaded his eyes from the climbing sun. "She thought so. Said we should go and find her."

"She—Mamm-wynn?" Urgency threaded its way through Oliver's tone. "Is she here too? Where?"

Mr. Gibson looked around him, clearly disoriented. "I don't know. We were together. It was still dark but beginning to lighten. She said something about taking the path to the cottages, and then . . . I don't remember."

Oliver's gaze flicked to Libby. "Will you stay with him?"

Someone had to, and he'd be the better choice for scouring the island. "Yes. Go!" She took his place by Mr. Gibson's side, keeping him from standing with a firm hand on his shoulder. "You stay put, sir. Oliver will find her."

He must have been in quite a bit of pain to relent as easily as he did. She felt his shoulders sag under her hand. "Poor Adelle. I didn't mean to leave her unprotected."

Oliver didn't rush off as she expected him to. He stood there, eyes focused on his grandfather and yet not. Hands clenched into fists that looked as though they were meant to moor him to some invisible line.

Mr. Gibson looked up at him. "Sorry, my boy. We only wanted to find Beth. I shouldn't have . . ."

Oliver crouched down again and rested a hand on the shoulder Libby wasn't already anchoring. "I think, before I go tearing off in search of Mamm-wynn, we had better pray."

Pray? *Now?* When it was so imperative that he find his grandmother as quickly as possible? Libby opened her mouth to tell him that was a foolish idea, but no words escaped her lips.

And she was glad of it, when she heard the words coming from his.

"Father God, here we are before you. On our knees quite literally. Begging you, our Father and our Lord, to walk before us. Lead us. Show us where to find Mamm-wynn and even Beth. We know that you love them both even more than we do. You have numbered the hairs on their heads. You know their innermost thoughts. You call them by name."

Libby drew in a slow breath, silently, so as not to interrupt him. This wasn't the sort of prayer she was used to, with recited words and memorized phrases. This . . . well, this was the sort one took the time to say. Not an anonymous petition to a King or Creator, as she would have made, but an earnest supplication to a Father.

This was a sort of prayer that at once bemused and intrigued her.

"We ask that you guide my steps now to them. That you keep your hand on them, protecting them. We ask for your healing touch upon Mabena and Tas-gwyn."

Oliver went quiet, but Libby's heart added a plea. *I ask that you show yourself to me, God. If you are there, if you are the loving Father Oliver claims . . . please show me. Show me by showing us Mamm-wynn. If anything happens to her . . .*

She wasn't entirely sure it was the right sort of petition to make. Was it testing God? Wasn't there a Scripture that warned not to do that? But Gideon had asked for proof—she remembered that story well enough. Twice he'd asked. And twice he'd been given what he asked for, to know that it was truly God instructing him.

Well, the Lord hadn't called her to lead an army, so He wouldn't answer her as He had Gideon. But if He knew her name, if He loved her, if He really did number the hairs on her head, perhaps He would do this now. Not just to show himself to her, but for Mamm-wynn's sake. For Oliver's. For every Scillonian who loved her.

"Amen." Oliver whispered the word, opened his eyes, squeezed his grandfather's shoulder. Met her gaze.

She had the strangest sensation that he knew exactly what she'd prayed for. That he'd waited for her to finish her wordless petition before he breathed that last word. She dredged up a small smile to offer him.

In her mind, God had always been distant, abstract. But now, here, with these people, she couldn't help but think that He'd come near. Or that *she* had.

With a nod, Oliver stood again. And ran.

19

Oliver didn't slow until he reached the overgrown path that led to the skeletal remains of the cottages, and only then because a spot of orange caught his eye. He stopped, bent, and plucked up the daisy from the path. Cleanly cut, like the ones outside his own garden gate. Beth's favorites. Had their grandmother cut them for her, thinking to come here and give them to her?

But why? And what would make Mamm-wynn think Beth was here, of all places?

The wind danced around him, laughing in his ears. *Why not?* it seemed to say. She'd known Beth was gone, after all, was "not where she ought to be." She'd known Libby needed a necklace and a shawl. Perhaps the Lord had whispered those things to her. And perhaps He'd done so again.

Spotting another too-bright daisy farther along, closer to the cottages, he followed the trail, praying anew with every step. *Lord, help me to find her. To find them. Show yourself to Libby.*

That last one seemed strangely tied to the others, which made precious little sense. Except that he knew that, even having only known her a few weeks, she loved his grandmother too. And her faith—which was really more stale teaching and a newborn curiosity waiting to bloom into proper faith—might just shrivel and turn cold if it was dealt this blow right now. But he wanted more for her. Wanted her to love the Creator with the same boundless fascination with which she loved His creation. Wanted her to trust Him as she had so quickly come to trust Oliver.

Another shock of color that didn't belong with the greens and browns and greys of the cottages stole his attention—a deep scarlet, too big to be a flower, too solid to be a patch of them. But the very color of Mamm-wynn's favorite shawl. He flew toward it, blinking until the shape was close enough to be more than a blur of color. To be shoulders and back and a precious white-crowned head resting on the earth as if it were a pillow. "Mamm-wynn!"

Unlike his grandfather though, she didn't stir at hearing his voice or her name. She just lay there on her stomach, face turned away from him, one arm extended—a bouquet of orange, yellow, and pink daisies still clutched in her hand.

No! His soul screamed it, fear pounding at his ears with every burst of his pulse. "Mamm-wynn! *Mamm-wynn.*"

Still she didn't move, didn't answer. But he was there now, dropping to his knees on the flagstone path to one of the cottages, blown over with sand and stray leaves and petals. He reached out, his prayers too desperate for words now, and touched her face. Warm. Her throat—there, her pulse fluttered, faint but present.

"Mamm-wynn." He said it more quietly now, giving her shoulder a gentle shake. But her eyelids didn't flutter; her breath didn't hitch. What was wrong with her? He guessed Tas-gwyn had been struck on the head much like Mabena, given the way he'd been holding it and wincing. But when he set his fingers on a light probing of her skull, he found no bumps or gashes, nothing to indicate a physical assault. Did he dare try to turn her over?

He hadn't much choice. He couldn't exactly leave her here. Careful to cradle her head with one hand, he eased her onto her side with the other, then onto her back. Though he held his breath against what he might see, no horrors met his gaze. No injuries visible here either. She simply looked like she was sleeping.

But she never slept so deeply that a voice wouldn't rouse her.

He leaned over to take a closer look, reaching into his pocket for his watch so he could get an accurate gauge of her pulse. His fingers brushed against paper rather than metal, giving him pause. Had he not put his watch in his pocket when he flew out of his room upon hearing Mrs. Dawe?

Apparently not. He pulled out what *was* in there—the nub of a pencil and the letter he'd been writing when sleep had abandoned him.

He'd meant it for Beth, though he'd had no idea how he meant to get it to her. It was half angry exhortation to return home at once, half plea to let them help. Full of all the facts that backed up both. That Lady Elizabeth Sinclair had been mistaken for her, that she was paying the price for whatever Beth had involved herself in. That Mabena had been injured last night by an armed man. That they knew Johnnie's death was linked to it, and that the man had threatened Mamm-wynn.

His gaze flitted up toward the sagging door of the cottage that looked like it might sink into the earth at any moment. His sister wouldn't be in there. He knew she wouldn't. But something had convinced Mamm-wynn to come here, whether it be something natural or . . . not. He took the clutch of flowers from her fingers and stood. He hated to leave her there even for a second, but he had a feeling she'd forgive it if it meant possibly finding Beth.

It took a shoulder to shove the door fully open. It dragged against the floor—which inspired him to look behind it and see that there was an arc of cleaner space where someone else had done the same and pushed it wider.

Not necessarily Beth. It could have been anyone. Tourists caught out in the rain, seeking the imperfect shelter of leaky thatch, most likely.

Then his gaze found the rickety, rotting table in front of the window. On which sat a rock. No, not a rock.

A small, water-scarred cannonball.

His heart thudded, though he wasn't sure if it was from hope or more dread. He spun around, taking in the entirety of the cottage in one turn. Was that clean spot there evidence that someone had hunkered down here? Was that water in the ancient sink from use or the holes in the thatch?

Had Beth been here?

Probably not. But . . . but maybe so. And if so, this could be his only chance of getting a message to her.

Thinking it worth the gamble, he pulled the note from his pocket as he strode to the table. He added a line about Mamm-wynn, scrawled Beth's name on the outside of the folded page, put it on the table, and anchored it with the lead. Finishing off the offering with Mamm-wynn's bouquet, he backed away.

Father, draw her here. Let her find this, I beg you.

With that, he spun on his heel and hurried back outside, careful to wrestle the door mostly shut behind him.

His grandmother still hadn't budged. As carefully as if she were made of finest porcelain, he gathered her into his arms and began the trek back to Tas-gwyn, Libby, and the boats.

———————○———————

Evening had found them again, somehow. Right now it was stretching through the house with long arms of sunshine that elbowed their way through the windows, but soon those golden rays would go purple and red and dusky. Then would come the grey, then the blue, then the black.

Oliver raked a hand through his hair and stared out at the familiar coastline, the familiar sea, the familiar vista. Such beautiful colors, when they were painted over the land.

Such hideous ones when they marred the flesh of one he loved. Mabena's face displayed them all today, and Tas-gwyn's head did too. Only his grandmother had no visible signs of whatever trauma had found her.

Only his grandmother still lay in her bed unconscious, the twelve hours since he found her passing in a blur of visits from neighbors and family and the doctor, who had quietly suggested that she'd suffered some sort of apoplexy. They couldn't know for sure, but the evidence suggested that her own body had attacked her rather than some outside force, likely caused by her advanced age or the stress of Beth being missing.

Perhaps he could accept that, if not for the other two injuries in his family.

No. No, he could never accept it, not really. Even knowing that she was mortal and so her days were numbered, he couldn't accept the soft words that said she might never open her eyes again. Might never call him her favorite. Might never laugh that fairy laugh.

He'd been sitting here beside her bed for hours, but he'd promised Mrs. Dawe he would get up by seven o'clock and find something to eat. It was seven now. A few minutes past. But his stomach churned at the very thought of putting food in it. Even so, he leaned over to kiss Mamm-wynn's ever-soft cheek and then stood. He could use a stretch of his legs, anyway. He'd spotted Libby in the garden a few minutes ago. Perhaps he'd go out there with her. Apologize. With Mabena in bed and Mrs. Dawe and him fussing over Mamm-wynn all day, she'd been the one to welcome neighbor after neighbor who'd come as soon as they heard.

It wasn't fair to her—she was just a guest here. She shouldn't have to play hostess. And yet she'd done it without question, without any qualm that he could see. And his neighbors, those who had slipped back here to bring a vase of flowers or put an arm around him, hadn't seemed to think it odd in the slightest. They'd merely said things like, "I'm glad our lady was on Tresco, at least, to be here now." And "Our lady said I could slip back for a moment, to give you this."

He stepped out into the hallway, knowing Mrs. Dawe would take his place within a minute or two—she'd said she'd be in at seven to make sure he kept his word, and she wouldn't grant him more than a few minutes' grace on that count. But rather than going directly down the stairs and out into the garden, his feet hitched before a closed door at the end of the corridor.

It had been months since he'd opened it. Because for as many good memories that lived in that room, there were bad ones too that he hadn't wanted to face. Too many reminders of the last loss to rock their family. Of the years they'd spent fighting an invisible monster eating away at his brother. Of the final battle that Morgan had lost.

His hand found the latch, cool in the shadows of the hallway, and pushed the door open. He didn't enter, but he leaned into the doorframe. So very weary. In body and mind and soul. So very afraid that soon another room would be empty. First their parents', then Morgan's. Mamm-wynn's next? And what about Beth? Why was she not *here*, where she ought to be, instead of hiding somewhere?

His eyes slid shut against the evening light streaming through Morgan's window. He missed his brother with a bone-deep ache. He wanted to talk to him now. To share the worry about Mamm-wynn. About Beth. To glean some of his wisdom. To introduce him to Libby and confess that he'd kissed her, and that he shouldn't have, and that he wanted to do it again. That he loved the way their neighbors had claimed her as their own. That he wanted to do the same, even though all wisdom said it was far too soon to know if he should, and not likely he could regardless.

She was an earl's sister. And he . . .

"Was this your brother's room?"

He didn't jump at her voice. Perhaps he'd heard her step behind him, even though he didn't recall noticing it. Perhaps he was too tired to react so. Or perhaps he couldn't be surprised at her appearing at his side because she felt so right there. Oliver opened his eyes and glanced down to find her in the doorway too, leaning a shoulder against the opposite side of the frame. Inches away. Her gaze focused on Morgan's sanctuary.

"It was, yes." They'd changed nothing in it. It still had the narrow bed in which he'd spent so much time. The books lining every wall, which had been his window to the rest of the world. The desk whose regular chair had been moved aside so he could wheel himself to it instead. And the wheelchair itself, parked beside the bed.

Her fingers found his and wove through them. "You're not going to lose her yet."

He squeezed her fingers, simply because she understood what had brought him here now. "He was sick for so long. It came upon him when he was just a lad, six or seven. I remember him being excited to go to school soon, and then . . . then our whole world changed. He was so ill, and the doctors couldn't determine the cause. Our parents took him to the mainland once, all the way to London. But it didn't seem to matter. The doctors could only alleviate the symptoms. He'd get better, but never fully *better*. And we always knew that each new illness to go round would find him. Eat at him."

He shook his head, remembering all too well the gaunt cheeks that did nothing to detract from the brightness of his smile. "They expected he wouldn't live but a few more years. He surprised them all though. He always fought. Always. Because he knew we needed him."

Libby lifted his hand, wrapped her other around it, and pressed a kiss to his knuckles, knotting him up inside. And unknotting him too. "My father died of consumption," she said. "It was a long process. Terrible. Some days I wished it would just happen quickly, so he wouldn't be in such pain. Other days, I was so very thankful for the extra time with him. The quiet moments at his bedside, when we could whisper together. I think I got to know him better in those two years of illness than in all the years before."

Oliver nodded. "I've wondered if I would have been as close to Morgan if he had been healthy. If we would have been such friends if he'd been able to go his own way. I can never know, of course. This was the only Morgan we really knew. The one who was so very aware of how big a gift each day was. The one who loved us so fully, because we were his whole life." He shook his head. "We didn't have to be. He was the eldest, the heir. And for a few years there, he was stronger than he'd been before. He could have married—there was a girl who was sweet on him. She'd have said yes in a heartbeat. But he said it would be unfair to her. To give her only a year or two and then loneliness. And to risk . . . to risk having a child with the same infirmities."

Her fingers tightened around his. "I daresay this girl would have disagreed."

"Probably, had he ever given her the choice. I could never convince him to approach her. It was while I was at university, and I wasn't home often. Had I been . . ." Another shake of his head. "She left for the mainland right after his funeral. I see her parents still. They tell me she's married, is happy. So perhaps Morgan was wise in his stubbornness."

Or perhaps he'd chosen loneliness not just for Daisy's sake, but for Oliver's. He'd always suspected it. "Honestly, I think he felt guilty for all the money we'd spent on treatments over the years. After our parents died, he refused any more, anything beyond routine. He said he didn't want to squander my inheritance on quacks hawking medicine that wouldn't work. *My* inheritance." He squeezed his eyes shut again, though it only made Morgan's image all the clearer in his mind. Looking at him with that love. That selflessness. "As if any of that mattered more than having him for one more day, one more week, one more month. I'd have given it all for him. And he should have let me. It was his, not mine."

"I can understand his thoughts though. He wanted to provide for his family in whatever way he could. He wanted to leave you with a legacy, not debt or resentments. My father—he apologized over and again for his illness's taking over our lives. As if I would have traded those days with him for a debut Season at the prearranged time."

She had the right of it. Morgan had been that very way. He tugged their joined hands over so he could take a turn at kissing her knuckles. "I don't want to lose her, Libby. Not yet. I'm not ready. And I know I'll never be ready, but . . . but now I'm *really* not."

"I'm not either." A smile trembled its way onto her lips. "I've only just found her. I know I haven't the claim on her that you or your family or the islanders do, but . . . but I want the chance to."

A corner of his own mouth tugged up in response. And his free hand lifted to rest on her neck, under her ear, without his being aware of giving it the command. "She's certainly claimed you. I think that gives you every right to claim her back."

He really ought to drop his hand and step away. But she leaned toward him, and he was helpless to do anything but meet her, lips to lips. Heart to heart. Their fingers untangled, giving him the freedom to slide an arm around her waist, hers wrapping around him.

For those few glorious moments, there was only her and them and this—a primal need to know and be known and belong there with another. There was the simmer in his veins that no one else had ever ignited and the thudding of his heart that said this was right. There was the fog of pleasure that masked, just for a minute, the pain of the last twenty-four hours.

Then there was the aching certainty that it was only that. A minute. A moment stolen from time that it would demand back. An impossibility. He broke away with a sigh and rested his forehead against hers. "You should make me stop doing that." Or better still, he should stop of his own volition.

If he could make himself want to.

"Should I?" Her voice sounded a bit fogged-up still. And made him want to kiss her again, and again.

He resisted, though his fingers protested by flexing against her back. "Libby . . . they'd never approve of me. Your family, I mean. I'm not wealthy enough or titled. I could supply your needs, but nothing more. Not with all we spent on Morgan." And what was he doing, speaking of such things when he barely knew her?

But no, he knew her. Not in terms of time, perhaps, but in terms of heart. He knew her. At least as well as any society gentleman did after a Season of balls and soirees, and no one would have batted an eye at one of *them* proposing.

Not that he was proposing. Not that he dared to.

Her fingers curled into his shirt over his heart. Pressed there. "I don't care about any of that."

No. She didn't. And that was why his heart had melded so quickly with hers. "But you care about your family. Their approval matters."

A truth she couldn't refute. She sighed, and her shoulders sagged.

"You'll win them over. Just take them by the elbow and you'll have them charmed in minutes."

He had a feeling her brother wouldn't be open to that particular tactic. He made himself ease away, though his stubborn hand refused to break contact entirely. It found hers again and held it tight. "For you, my sweet one, I'll try anything. But I don't ever want to cause trouble between you. I know too well how important family is."

She mustered a smile that looked braver than it should have to be when the subject was something as sweet as the first blush of love.

Not that he was mentioning *love* quite yet either. Perhaps it was the only word he could think of to describe this certainty inside him, but he knew once he spoke it, gave it that name, it would take on new power. Power that might try to run roughshod over the promise he'd just made her. That would seek its own bond with her above others'.

"A worry for another day," she said. "Heaven knows today has plenty of its own."

All the reminder he needed to step back into the corridor, tugging her with him. He left Morgan's door open, though, in case he needed the solace of those memories later. For now, that stroll through the garden was a good idea. "Do you need to go back to St. Mary's tonight? I can take you, or Mabena's father would."

His aunt and uncle had been among the visitors today, and they'd been none too happy to realize that their daughter had been injured too, and that they hadn't been informed immediately.

Libby shook her head and fell into step beside him. "I don't think so. Mabena isn't fit for it yet, certainly. My only real concern is Darling. I hate to leave him so long—though I think I left enough food for him, and Mabena fashioned him a sandbox for his business. He refused to go outside when we left. He hid under my bed, and I couldn't lure him out."

Oliver chuckled. Her kitten had strong opinions, that was for certain. "Perhaps you should bring him with you when you come to Tresco."

Libby walked with him down the stairs, her brows raised. "On a boat? Cats don't like the water, do they?"

"Not as a general rule—but how do you suppose they got on the islands to begin with?"

That sweet smile sprang onto her lips. The one that meant she was amused at herself. "Well, I don't suppose they flew here. Perhaps if I tucked him into a basket?"

"He may meow, but he'd be safe and probably quite happy to be wherever you are." And if it resulted in her extending her Tuesday evening stays to Wednesday nights too, and perhaps even Thursdays . . . well, who could blame him for removing her primary need to get back to St. Mary's?

"We'll have to talk to Mabena and see what she wants to do. If she wants to stay longer in general, someone can simply take me over for Darling and some extra changes of clothes. I only really need to be on St. Mary's for the Wednesday deliveries for Beth."

The reminder brought a quick splash of cold water. He'd been half expecting to catch Beth trying to break into the safe and steal back his copy of *Treasure Island*. He'd changed the combination, just in case she tried it. Anything to delay her longer and improve his chances of catching her. "Perhaps you should distance yourself from that too. Given what Mabena reported Beth said the other night, if no one is there, the items will be left somewhere for her."

"Exactly. And then we won't know what they are. It'll all be up to Beth again." She hesitated at the bottom of the stairs, clearly waiting to see which direction he would lead them.

He turned them toward the hallway that led to the garden door. "I certainly don't want my sister to face those men alone, but I can't let you put yourself in danger for it anymore either. Too many people have already been hurt."

"And the perpetrators won't leave me alone now, Oliver—they think *I'm* Beth. Even if she showed up, they wouldn't trust her now. They'd think *she* was the pretender. Like it or not, I'm involved. So we simply need to determine how to solve this mystery, once and for all."

Simply. Sighing, he led her out into the twilight garden. If only anything about this were simple.

20

Never in her life had a trip to St. Mary's been such a cause for argument. And if Mabena's head hadn't still been screaming at her like a banshee, she might have even found it amusing that Casek and Oliver were facing off over which of them deserved the honor of sailing her and Libby to their cottage.

Amusing. But utterly irrelevant. And, headache or not, she needed to tell them so. So she stepped between them—always a dangerous undertaking—and first met her cousin's gaze. "Why are you even arguing about this? You should stay home with your grandmother."

The bobbing of his larynx told her how painful was his swallow. "There's a better pharmacy on St. Mary's. The doctor suggested a few things that might help, but we don't have them here. I'd need to go regardless. I might as well take the two of you."

"Very well, then." It was the *take* that irritated her. She lifted her chin. "I'm not leaving the *Mermaid* here again though. Tas said he'd sail it over for me and then come home with whoever took us."

Casek crossed his arms over his chest. Which drew her attention to the fact that his sleeves were rolled up to his elbows and he'd discarded his jacket after the school day had ended all of three seconds ago. He must have run to the quay to meet them here, despite the fact that she hadn't told him she'd be leaving today.

Her head was enough of a muddle with pain. It didn't need any extra confusion from him and his hovering and those eyes of his that kept staring into hers as if all the secrets of the universe could be found there.

"There's no need to pull your father away from his work, dearover. I'll take your boat for you. You can even come along with me to make sure I do everything just the way you like."

As if he didn't know how to sail her little sloop. And as if it would impress her that he knew well she'd have made such an argument against anyone else handling her on a normal day.

All right, it did. A little. "And then what? Sail home with Ollie?"

He actually winced, which would have made her chuckle if not for the headache. "I'm sure there will be someone else coming this way."

"You can come with me." Something about Oliver's tone—even, firm, steady—drew her gaze back to him. He wasn't flushed with anger as he usually was when going toe-to-toe with Casek. His eyes weren't glinting. He was just standing there, calm as could be, holding Libby's hand as he'd been doing just about every time they were in the same room together.

Looking perfectly aware that only storms waited in that direction. But then, storms thundered over his house too. Storms loomed wherever Beth was. Storms were all he had just now.

Apparently Casek Wearne and his thundering just didn't rate.

She turned back to him, not sure he'd see the same. Or, frankly, that he could be trusted to respect it. But Casek was regarding Oliver solemnly. And after another moment, he nodded. "It'll do."

Well. Mabena exchanged a gaze with Libby—surprised, impressed—before Libby apparently remembered that her complaints against Mabena still stood unresolved and looked away.

She sighed. The lady had been the soul of concern throughout the day and a half since the attack, tending her with care and consideration when she wasn't doing the same for Mrs. Tremayne. But she never quite met her eye.

They'd have to settle things. Soon. For now though, she'd focus on some other settling. She let a hint of a smile touch her lips as she turned to Casek again. "Well then. Let's be off."

He hiked a brow even as he held out a hand toward where her boat was still anchored. "You're not going to argue? Insist you'll go with them?"

She tossed a smirk at where Oliver was leading Libby toward the Tremayne boat. "I don't think they need my company just now."

He grunted. "That's going to end badly. Not that *I* much care, but I'd have thought *you* would, enough to warn them against it."

"Oh, I did. But . . ." She shrugged. "I suppose I'm utterly failing at my chaperoning duties. Her mother will be appalled and no doubt sack me for it. And you know, I don't care a bit. Let them steal an ounce of joy for a summer. They deserve it, both of them."

She expected him to argue about the deserving bit. Instead, he latched on to the earlier statement. "Let her sack you. You don't need to go back to the mainland. Just stay here, with us."

Us, was it? He meant her parents, she supposed, and her siblings and cousins and aunts and uncles and neighbors. Her lips twitched. "I may, at that."

Not what she'd expected to decide when she came back here. Frankly, she expected to grit her teeth through every moment, find Beth, and hightail it back to Telford Hall with Libby. But she'd underestimated the islands, their pull on her.

And she'd certainly underestimated this one's ability to dig down past the sandy layers of hurt and betrayal. To dig straight down to the rock of her and anchor himself there.

He shot her a look, all raised brows and incredulity. Then a scorching smile that burned the disbelief away and left pure pleasure in its ashes. "I expected it would take another month to convince you. At least."

She allowed a little smile of her own. "Flattering. But I think the blow to my skull knocked a bit of my stubbornness loose." And the way he'd dove after her, cradled her so tenderly, spent every possible moment with her since, despite that it meant visiting her at the Tremayne house . . .

They said nothing more just then, since they were nearly to the *Mermaid*. Just focused on climbing aboard, casting off, and getting her under sail. Only once they were in open water—Mabena happy enough to let Casek man the tack and just relax—did he turn to her again with that look in his eye.

"Benna. When I saw that bloke strike you, when I thought I may have lost you . . . I love you. I always have—you have to know that. And I can't let another day go by without saying it, not with that threat still out there."

Her heart was a cormorant, skimming over the waves with its wings spread wide. "Caz." She didn't know what else to say. Maybe there were feelings there, threatening to choke her, but they didn't come with words. Not that she could find.

"I know it's not so simple for you. What with Cador."

She didn't wince at the name at least. That was progress. Instead, she sighed. Just now, she couldn't solve all the bigger problems they faced—the threats and the mysteries and the injuries. But there was one ghost she could put to rest. "Tell me. I'm ready to hear it now. He married her?"

Casek granted her the mercy of a gaze set on the sails instead of her face. "He did. It was, he thought, the quickest way to what he wanted. They eloped, and then they went to London to introduce him to Fiona's parents."

She'd assumed as much. Still, she'd expected that if ever anyone said it outright, it would be a fresh blow to her heart. Cador, her fiancé, the man she'd planned a life with, now someone else's husband.

Maybe it was just because of Sunday night's very physical blow casting its shadow on her, but she didn't feel that other at all. Not more than a twinge, anyway. "Are they happy?" She wasn't sure she was gracious enough to hope so.

But Casek's snort only gave her a *little* bit of pleasure. "Of course not. Her family didn't approve of him, as we all knew would happen. A little nobody from a National School, trying to rub elbows with the intelligentsia?" He shook his head. "They told her it was either an annulment or they'd disown her."

Her mouth fell open a bit. Cador had always been able to charm his way into anyone's favor. He'd even gotten along with the Tremaynes, for goodness' sake, becoming the only Wearne to claim that feat for generations. But there was no wiggle of hope that perhaps he was free again. Nor any devilish glee in the thought of their hasty marriage failing so quickly. "What did she choose?"

Now Casek glanced her way, a warning in his eyes. "Them, at first. Until she realized she was with child. Then she went back to him. From what I can glean from his letters, they're living in a miserable little flat in London, and he's working for a publisher, though not in any notable position. He maintains that it's a start, and that the misery his nag of a wife subjects him to daily is but fuel for his muse." He rolled his eyes at that. "The latest letter said their second child should join them by Christmas."

He said it gently. And she could appreciate his care. But that didn't sting either, not much. The thought of Cador as a father and his pretty, city wife at his side. Little ones that weren't hers squalling for his attention.

She blew out a breath. She didn't wish him misery—and not with the hope that happiness would silence his muse either. She was simply glad his little family was in London and not here. She may have, at some point in these past weeks home, managed to forgive him. But she didn't have any desire to see him. "But you said he was published?"

"Not by the company he's working for—just a little press that did an initial printing of two hundred copies, none of which have sold. Well, one. Mam bought one, of course."

A chuckle tickled her throat. "As she should. And shouldn't you have bought another?"

Casek's eyes flashed. "I told him when he tossed you over that I was on your side, not his. That if he'd broken your heart, I'd wash my hands of him."

He had? "Caz." She ducked under the boom and moved to his side. "He's your twin brother."

"He hurt you. It isn't forgivable."

"And yet if he hadn't"—she lifted a hand and let her fingertips drift over the taut muscle of his forearm—"those would be *my* babies he's writing home about. *Me* he'd be complaining of. Is that what you'd prefer?"

His arm went even tauter. "That isn't fair, Benna."

"What isn't?"

"Asking a question like that when I can't kiss you to prove what I'd prefer. I promised you'd do the next kissing."

She didn't know if it was the sea air or the sunshine or him, but she could nearly forget the pounding in her skull. "Maybe I will."

That smirk she shouldn't like so much tilted his lips. "That isn't fair either. You're in no condition to fully appreciate it—and I don't want you coming away with any negative impressions that are the fault of your injury and not me."

She highly doubted that would happen. But then, Oliver and Libby were within sight, just behind them, and she didn't much fancy having an audience when she kissed him. For that matter, she liked the thought of his arms coming about her, which they couldn't do while his hands were tangled with the tack.

So, for now, she simply stretched up, pressed a light kiss to his lips, and settled at his side. "There. To free you from the promise. So that next time I say something provoking, you can prove whatever you need to."

Even that light touch sent a tingle through her. One that made her think everyone had been wrong five years ago. And Libby had been right—flying would be a good thing indeed.

Libby. A bit of the elation fluttered away at the thought of her. She looked behind them to where the *Adelle* skimmed along on the same breeze. She and Oliver were talking, her arms gesturing in demonstration of whatever she was saying. Ollie was grinning down at her, happy in that moment despite it all.

"What's wrong, my love?"

She faced forward again and leaned her aching head against his shoulder, in the place that she'd come to think of as hers the other night when he'd cradled her there for hours while they waited for the doctor to return from a birthing. "I've a few bridges to mend, that's all. I upset her the other day. Made her question whether we're friends. Maybe because I wasn't certain myself, she being my employer."

"She won't be that for long though, will she? If you're staying?"

There were more questions there than the ones he asked—a probing of whether she'd meant her offhanded agreement earlier. But she had. And he had a point now. "You're right. Without that between us, things will be different. In a good way."

She could call her *Libby*. Not spare so many thoughts to what her mother or brother would say and put *her* first, as she would any other friend. She could let herself fully appreciate all she'd done while here to help with the Beth mystery. The way she'd taken so quickly to the people Mabena held most dear. She could tear down the barrier she'd kept so carefully between them.

But how to tell her so? She debated it the rest of the way to St. Mary's. Fighting with someone was easy enough, but making up? When it required words and not just a mutual decision to ignore the row and move on, as she and Beth had always done? That was altogether different.

She still wasn't certain how best to handle it when they were all on shore at the quay in Hugh Town, but when Oliver declared he'd better hasten to the pharmacy before they closed for the day and Casek said he'd better check at the ferry office to see if any more shipments for the school had come in, she decided there was no time like the present for making the first strides.

And so she linked her arm through Libby's—something she'd never done before—and gave her a smile. "I'm sorry we'll miss the race tomorrow morning. If you want to just collect Darling and go back, we can." It wasn't what she'd said earlier when they'd asked her. Then, she'd simply wanted to escape her parents' good-natured fussing for a few days. But friendship required a bit of self-sacrifice now and then.

Libby softened a bit, though her returning smile was still forced. "It's all right. Oliver doesn't mean to participate anyway. He convinced Mr. Menna to take his seat."

"The things I missed while I slept off a headache!" Mabena gave the slightest shake of her head—all she dared. "Mr. Menna can out-row any of them."

"That's what Oliver said." Libby's smile faded into a sigh. "Though I'll want to go back soon. To see how Mamm-wynn's doing."

"Any time you like. I ought to be right as rain again by tomorrow. What?" she added at the dubious look Libby sent her. "I've the hardest head on the islands. Ask anybody. A little knock on it can't keep me down for long."

Libby shook *her* head with enviable generosity of movement. Let a beat of silence speak for her. Then said, so softly Mabena could scarcely hear it over the breeze, "You're not leaving again, are you? At the end of summer, I mean."

And how could she know that when Mabena herself had scarcely come to the conclusion an hour ago?

Because . . . they *were* friends. She sighed. "I can't. This is home."

Libby nodded. "I don't know how you ever left to begin with. I mean, I *do*. What with Cador and all. But . . ."

"I had to go. I'm glad I did. Glad I met you." She bumped their shoulders together. "I never expected to make a friend, Libby. But I have, and I'm grateful for it. Grateful and . . . and maybe it's the head injury, but I'm beginning to think maybe it was for a greater purpose too. That the Lord meant for you to come here this summer."

The way Libby's brows knit, and the way she took her lower lip between her teeth, made her seem at once a little girl, dreadfully uncertain, and an old woman who had seen too much. "I've never heard you talk so."

"It's not my way—I always left that to Ollie. But that doesn't change the truth of it. And the truth is that I've never seen *you* as you've been since you got here a month ago." She pulled Libby to a halt, waiting until she looked over at her. "You don't have to go either, you know. At the end of summer. I know that was your plan, that this was just a respite to give Sheridan time to come to his senses and strike down your brother's idea. I know you wouldn't want to leave your mother. But there's a place for you here. I wouldn't have believed it had someone asked me before, but that's truth too."

Libby looked away. But not away. Not *from* Mabena so much as *to* the islands. "When you left here, you didn't give up your place. You could go somewhere new and still know this was home." She met her gaze again. "I'm not so certain that would be the case for me, if I chose the Scillies."

If she chose Oliver, she meant. And she could well be right. "You have the rest of the summer to weigh that, then. To decide what you can live without and what you can't. And I'll be at your side to talk it through with you, if you need. That's what friends are for."

Libby gave her a small, mellow grin that felt like a gift. "I imagine I'll take you up on that."

They turned to the path again and walked up it without any more conversation. No doubt Libby's mind was spinning as quickly as Mabena's. About just as many things. And in Mabena's case, it brought the headache roaring to the forefront again. She was rather glad Libby had declined returning to Tresco tonight. She found herself craving a hot cup of tea, some silence, and the bed at the cottage she'd grown accustomed to.

When they turned the key in the lock and stepped inside, though, she knew there'd be no rest tonight.

Not given the two men sitting at their table. In particular, the one with his arms folded like iron gates over his chest.

21

Libby's stomach knotted, her hands clenched, and she fought down the unreasonable urge to spin on her heel and run all the way back to the quay. "Bram! What are you doing here?"

Mabena clicked the door shut behind them—effectively cutting off her escape.

Her brother lifted one powerful eyebrow and kept right on glaring at her. "What am *I* doing here? I'd think that's fairly obvious."

She wanted to be furious, to channel all the churning emotions into some strong response, like Mabena would have made. Instead, all she could think was that she'd never disobeyed her brother before coming here. Never disobeyed their father before him. Not willfully. And this was why. That *look*.

Even so. If she obeyed him now, the *other* man sitting in her sweet little kitchen would be her whole future. She darted one quick glance at Lord Sheridan to remind herself of why that would never do. And lifted her chin. "I'm not going back. I've let the cottage for the summer, and I'm going to enjoy it."

"Meow!" A tiny bundle of stripes came tearing from her bedroom upon hearing her voice and probably would have climbed directly up her skirt if she hadn't bent down to scoop him up. Darling curled into his favorite spot under her chin, butting his head against her and purring loudly. At least *someone* knew how to properly greet her after an absence.

Bram had opened his mouth, no doubt to issue some command she'd have to ignore despite the churning of her stomach, but he huffed out an incredulous breath instead. "Has that thing been here the whole time?"

"That *thing*?" She stroked a hand over the kitten's vibrating back, lest he be insulted. "His name is Darling."

Bram sent his eyes to the ceiling, looking fully exasperated. "Of course it is."

"And what exactly do you mean by 'the whole time'?" There, finally, the kitten's purring was infusing her with a bit of confidence. "How long have you been here brooding and invading my privacy? And how did you get in?"

"Please." He nodded toward the closed door, which made the sun streaming in the windows glint off his honeyed blond hair. "Mother provided me with your landlady's information when she gave me your address. And given that this so-called privacy was purchased with *my* money, though without my knowledge, I don't think you get to complain about . . ." He trailed off, narrowing his eyes at something behind her. No. Some*one*. "Who is—wait. *Moon?*"

She'd forgotten how different her friend looked—the change had been so incremental. And so complete for weeks now. But her new appearance would be a shock to Bram, who'd never seen her in anything but her high-necked, prim-and-proper dresses, her hair neat and severe. Today, the injury had inspired her to keep her hair altogether down, and the wind on the trip had blown it into an absolute fury of curls. She really didn't bear much of a resemblance to the Moon who'd served at Telford Hall, so Libby could hardly blame him for the momentary confusion.

Mabena sighed. "Good day, my lord. Lord Sheridan." Her headache was audible in her voice. "I think I'd better put the kettle on."

Never one to let confusion reign for long, Bram renewed his glare. "Don't bother. We won't be here long enough to need it."

Libby wasn't optimistic enough to think he meant *he* would leave and leave her there.

Mabena ignored him, giving the table a wide berth on her way to the stove. "None for you, then. Very well. Lord Sheridan? Tea?"

"Yes, I—"

"Sher!"

Sheridan sighed but deflected her brother's scowl with a wave of the hand. "That cup at the pub was terrible. Have a little—well, a little pity, Telford. A man can't be expected to go a whole *day* without a decent cup."

Even hearing him speak made Libby's shoulders go tight.

Bram relented. Though his relenting looked suspiciously like anger. "I cannot believe Mother allowed this. No, that she *enabled* it. Sending her daughter off alone with no one but a lady's maid to chaperone her. And you!" He surged to his feet, no doubt so that he could tower over Libby. Yet his voice was surprisingly quiet. "This isn't like you, Lib. Why would you do such a thing?"

"What choice did you leave me?" She dropped her own volume to a whisper, though there was no hope the others wouldn't hear it in the confined space. "You weren't listening to a word I said! Had I stayed, you'd have bullied me into an engagement with *him*." She gestured with her non-Darling-supporting hand toward Sheridan, then felt her cheeks go hot. "No offense intended, my lord."

His green eyes sparked, though it looked strangely more like amusement than anything. "No, no. Of course not. I took it for a compliment."

Mabena, helpful creature that she was, snorted a laugh from the stove.

Bram growled. "You weren't exactly listening yourself. But I've never known you to be so—so selfish and underhanded."

The words bit, as he'd no doubt meant them to. She stumbled back a step. "I am not. Self-preservation isn't the same as selfishness." Was it? It couldn't be. "And there was nothing underhanded about it. Mama knew exactly—"

"And yet I was let to think you'd gone with her to Edith's! I spent the last month pitying you for what you must be suffering in her company, while all this time you were *here*. Which I had to learn from Lord Scofield, of all people, because my own mother and sister didn't see fit to inform me!" He'd tried to pace, but the tight quarters had only allowed him to take a few steps and then pivot.

She stroked a hand down Darling's back again for comfort. "Did you see Mama or just write to her? How is she?"

As if he'd be so easily redirected. "I spent a *lovely* two days there, convincing her to hand over the particulars so I wouldn't be obliged to knock on every single door on St. Mary's. Which I'd have done." He folded his arms again. "Our sister delivered her husband another boy, by the way. Not that you've asked, despite the fact that Mother hadn't let you know yet."

How could she have known to ask? She'd thought it would be another week or so. Still. The queasiness nearly upended her. "I'll send my congratulations straightaway. Edith is well?"

"Is she ever anything but?"

Mabena provided a bit of helpful clatter from the stove. "Strong or weak, Lord Sheridan?"

"Oh." Sheridan didn't so much as flick a glance toward Mabena. "Strong, I'd say."

"You can give her your congratulations in person. When I deliver you directly to her door." Bram's scowl dared her to argue.

She'd never taken him up on his dares. Not before. But this time, he was in for a surprise. "I'm not leaving. I can't."

He waved that away. "I've already spoken to Mrs. Pepper. Given that I wasn't interested in a refund, she doesn't really care if you vacate the place."

"That isn't why I can't." How to explain it to him though? In a way he'd understand and, dare she hope it, approve?

Before she could think of such magical words, a light tap sounded on the door. A familiar tap. The one that was immediately followed by the door simply swinging open and Oliver stepping inside. His gaze was on whatever was in his hands, and he entered as he said, "Benna, I picked you up some of the aspirin the doctor prescribed, and—oh." Here he finally glanced up, or perhaps just sensed too many people in the room. His spine went rigid, his shoulders snapped back, and his chin came up. Then dipped again. "Lord Telford. How do you do?"

Her stomach would never feel right again. Libby pressed her cheek to Darling's side, willing his purring confidence to penetrate a little deeper. "Bram, you remember Mr. Oliver Tremayne of Truro Hall."

Her brother's glower intensified tenfold. "No." Which was a blatant lie—he never forgot a face, nor the name it paired with.

"Sure you do," Sheridan put in happily from the table, making her like him for calling Bram out. A little. "He came—when was it? To Telford. During the funeral, that was it, but not for you. For . . ." Scrunching his face into a ridiculous parody of concentration, he tapped a finger to the table. "To check on someone. A maid or some such. Remember? We were in your study, situating your books when he was introduced. And you said to me, 'Where the devil is Truro—'"

"Thank you, Sheridan." Bram looked like he'd enjoy socking his friend in the nose for his assistance.

Oliver cleared his throat. "To check on Miss Moon." He nodded toward Mabena. "My cousin."

Sheridan still wore that idiotic look of contemplation. "No, that wasn't it."

Mabena snorted another laugh.

It didn't seem to bother him any. "By which I mean, it's not what you said. At the time, that is. Aren't you a vicar? You went to Oxford with my cousin."

Ever calm, Oliver nodded. "I believe I said she was a parishioner, at the time. Also true, and I didn't want it to appear that her family was interfering, not trusting her in her independence."

Maybe he intended it to be a jab at Bram's presence. She couldn't be entirely certain, though she rather hoped it was.

And her brother clearly felt it as such, given the way his posture stiffened still more.

Another shadow filled the doorway, this one the frowning, hulking form of Casek Wearne. "I thought we were meeting at the boat, Tremayne. Why are you . . . ?" He trailed off as he stepped inside. And his frown rivaled Bram's. "Who are you blokes? Everything all right, Benna? My lady?"

Mabena pressed her lips together over what Libby suspected was another laugh. Or at least a grin. She tipped the teapot over a cup and handed it to Sheridan. "Everything's fine, dearovim."

"I beg to differ." Bram looked as though steam might spill out of his ears to match the kettle at any moment. "I don't care for the fact that strange men just waltz into my sister's holiday cottage without so much as a by-your-leave."

Casek didn't shift at all upon realizing Bram was a lord, not just a bloke. He looked, in fact, utterly unimpressed. "*You're* the lady's brother?" She could have hugged him for his sneer. "You don't seem much like her."

"What exactly is that supposed to mean?"

"That she never lords over anyone. Fit right in, did our lady. You seem more cut from Tremayne cloth."

Insulting both him and Oliver in one fell stroke. Libby didn't know whether to be impressed or panicked.

Her brother didn't seem too conflicted. Just annoyed. "Hardly."

"Oh, look, her door's open!" A new voice drifted in from outside and made her decide on panicked. Not Lottie too. She didn't need anyone else crowding in here, and—drat it all, Charlotte Wight never did know when not to stick her nose in. She burst through the open door, the dual shadows of the viscount and Mr. Bryant behind her. "Libby, you're back! I was hoping you would be soon. I have the absolute best news—Emily is returning! Only there are no cottages left to let, so I . . ."

Someday, this would all be very amusing to look back on. Someday, Libby would no doubt laugh at how many times the same pattern was played out, with guests coming in unannounced and then stammering to a halt upon spotting Bram. Someday, perhaps, she would even joke with her brother about the effect he had on people.

Someday seemed very far away just now. Now she just had to marvel at the sheer bad luck of it. And somehow find the gumption to make introductions. She began with a loud clearing of her throat. "Bram, you may recall that I mentioned my friend from the Château. This is her, Miss Charlotte Wight, along with Lord Willsworth and his cousin, Mr. Bryant. Everyone, my brother, Lord Telford. And his friend, Lord Sheridan."

The fellows had crossed paths before, as evidenced by Sheridan's cheerily trying to place where they'd done so. Bram no doubt recalled, but he'd lapsed into a frown again after an obligatory greeting, gaze flicking from the viscount to Libby to Oliver. She could all but read his thoughts—he was wondering if his little sister hadn't managed to find a decent fellow to spend time with after all, and then doubting she had the sense to follow up on it. He'd be noticing how awkward Lord Willsworth looked as he edged into the cottage—into which he'd clearly never stepped foot—versus how comfortably Oliver had let himself in.

While Sheridan chattered at Willsworth and Bryant, Lottie turned to Libby with wide eyes that all but screamed, *Your brother is here!* "Anyway," she said as if she hadn't been interrupted. "Emily. There's nothing left to let on St. Mary's, and our cottages are positively bursting already—my aunt and cousins just arrived, you see, which I hadn't known they'd be doing when I extended the invitation to Lady Emily. So, I was rather hoping you could put her up here? You've two bedrooms, haven't you? And if the maids prefer it, they could room with ours. Or we could lend a couple cots for them, if you prefer they stay nearby. Though to be sure, I hadn't realized your brother was here. Where is *he* staying? Did he find a room somewhere? We've had absolutely no luck finding anything, though perhaps it's because he swooped in and let the last ones."

Bram shifted to Libby's side, fingers gripping her elbow. "Your friend can have the whole cottage. Libby is coming home."

Lottie's face fell. "Oh, but she mustn't! I had such fun planned for the three of us! And it was probably quite a task for Em to convince Lord and Lady Scofield to let her join us and—"

Porcelain clattered as Sheridan's cup met his saucer. Odd, that. He didn't usually lack for grace. "Did you say Scofield? I mean, pardon me. Not to interrupt."

Not that Lottie minded, given the fact that it was another eligible bachelor who did the interrupting. She dimpled, nodded. "That's right. Lady Emily Scofield, one of my dearest friends. Along with Libby, of course. It shall be properly wonderful, having all three of us together!"

Bram had at least turned his narrowed eyes on Sheridan, though his fingers didn't loosen any on Libby's elbow. "I do apologize for disrupting your plans, Miss Wight. But my sister is needed at home."

"No, I'm not." It came out as little more than a squeak though, covered by another loud gush of wordy displeasure from Lottie. Libby squeezed her eyes shut, wincing a bit when Darling's claws bit in as he tried to climb a little higher onto her shoulder. He was no doubt as fond of the crowd as she was.

Sheridan's voice won out next over the din. "Oh, we've been staying in Penzance the last two days, ferrying over. You're right—there's absolutely nothing here to let."

Libby forced her eyes open, trying—and failing—to pull her elbow free from Bram's hand. "Then you had better get back to the ferry. The last one's leaving soon, I believe."

Bram glared down at her. "You're absolutely right, Libby. So you had better start packing. Moon can help you with that, and I'll see to your . . . *guests.*"

"I told you." Not only was her voice still too faint to be heard above the other chatter in the room, but it was quavering now too. "I *can't* leave right now."

Her brother let out an exasperated sigh. Then, miraculously, his face softened. A bit. "You can bring the cat, you know that. Have you a basket or something to put him in? He *is* a pretty little thing."

He *had* always had a soft spot for animals—at least the ones he could claim as pets, as he didn't share her fascination with the wild creatures of the world. But she shook her head, throat going tight. "It isn't Darling, Bram."

His eyes darkened.

"We'd probably have room for one of you—don't you think, Bryant?" Willsworth was saying. "Or, hmm. You probably have your valets with you?"

"Yes, in Penzance still though. No point in them coming over with us every day," Sheridan replied. "And that's very kind of you, my lord. Though—I say, Telly—what do you think? Give your sister a day, couldn't we? We could get along all right for a day without our valets."

All the noise was making her head buzz in a way it hadn't done since she'd escaped the London ballrooms. "A day will not be enough. I need the rest of the summer."

"Absolutely not." Now her brother's gaze scorched the entire company, as if he wasn't sure who to blame but knew one of them must be responsible for this seeming daftness in his usually pliant little sister. "You're coming home."

"I am *not!*" This time she actually shouted. Her—*shouted*. And the whole room fell silent.

Bram stared at her as if she'd grown a second head and named it Alice. Clearly he didn't know what to make of her. Never in her life had she contradicted him about something like this, even when they were children. He cocked his head to the side. "If you're staying . . . then *I'm* staying."

Her stomach positively heaved. "I think I'm going to be sick," she muttered into Darling's stripes. To prove it, her knees wobbled, and she might have crumpled to the floor if not for Bram's hand on her arm.

Oliver was at her other side, somehow. Bram's fingers gone and *his* leading her backward a step, to the sofa. She sank down onto it without quite knowing how he'd performed that magic trick and not really caring. It let her lower her head and drag a few soothing breaths into her lungs.

"It's all right," he was murmuring to her. "You'll be right as rain in a moment. Too many people, I'm guessing?"

Too many people *here*. All wanting something of her, none of which she knew how to give without compromising the one thing *she* needed. "I can't leave. I can't." Her voice was still shaking, sounding embarrassingly near panic. And why? She'd never even felt this flustered at a ball. Close, but there she'd known what was coming. And there, most people ignored her. They weren't all crowding into her rooms, demanding she house this one and leave with that one and abandon the only people who had ever made her feel at home while the dearest woman in the world lay unconscious nearby. "Mamm-wynn."

"Who the devil is Mamm-wynn?" Bram, hovering over her.

Oliver cleared his throat. "My grandmother. We found her unconscious yesterday, and she's yet to awaken. She and your sister took a fancy to each other, my lord."

Bram hissed out a breath. "*That's* why you don't want to leave? For heaven's sake, Libby, why didn't you just say so? Am I such a monster that you think I'd force you from the sickbed of an old woman you're fond of?"

She didn't rightly know. It had never come up.

Oliver stroked a comforting hand over her back, once. Enough to still a few of the tremors. Probably enough to earn more of Bram's ire too. "I'll do what I can here," he whispered to her. Then he stood, cleared his throat. "Lord Sheridan, Lord Telford—you're both welcome to lodge at my house on Tresco for as long as you like. We've the room. For your valets too, if you send for them tomorrow. Miss Wight, I'm certain I can help your other friend find somewhere to let. Why don't you all go ahead home for now, and I'll ask around a bit. When is she arriving?"

"Friday."

"Lovely. That should be enough time. I'll send you word tomorrow. Casek, would you run down to Mrs. Gilligan's and ask if she'd consider letting someone stay in the flat above her shop this summer, since her daughter isn't using it after all?"

Within a few seconds, he'd somehow ushered Lottie, Willsworth, and Bryant out the door—and they were thanking him for it, not seeming at all like they *felt* pushed out. Libby breathed a bit easier when they were gone. Casek went too, though with a bit of grumbling and a snarl that he'd meet Oliver back at the boat.

Oliver also stepped toward the door. "I won't impose any longer. I'll just . . ." He held out the bottle of aspirin as a finish to his sentence and slid it onto the table, his gaze moving to Mabena. "Don't let your headache get out of control, Benna. Take it, and then to bed with you."

Mabena had managed to fix her own cup of tea during the chaos. She leaned against the wall now, sipping it. "I'll be well again tomorrow. Well enough, anyway, to take Libby back over to Tresco to see your grandmother."

"If not, I'm happy to ferry you both. Let's say if you're not there by ten o'clock, I'll come and fetch you, shall we?"

Mabena tilted her head. "That seems reasonable."

It didn't escape Libby's notice that Bram hadn't agreed to Oliver's plan. But even now, with no one left in the cottage but the five of them, he didn't object. He just regarded Oliver evenly for a long moment and then asked, "I suppose your boat is at the little quay in Hugh Town?"

Oliver nodded, and Bram mirrored it. "We saw it when we were exploring the town yesterday. Sher, why don't you go down with Mr. Tremayne now, and give me a moment with my sister?"

Sheridan, of course, agreed easily. He swigged the last of his tea and stood. Oliver nodded his agreement too, shooting one final look at Libby. It said a lot, that look. More than words ever could. And made her stomach settle enough that, after dragging in a deep breath, she could stand again. "Thank you, Mr. Tremayne. For all your assistance." The *mister* felt odd on her tongue after having used *Oliver* for the last few days. Silently she added, *You didn't have to do this. I appreciate that you did.*

He must have received her unspoken message. His eyes twinkled at her. "It's truly my pleasure, Lady Elizabeth."

He and Sheridan departed, and Mabena slipped discreetly to her room. She'd no doubt still hear every word, but it gave them at least a pretense of privacy.

Bram didn't linger long in silence. He sat again, without taking his gaze from her face. "Is it really about the grandmother?"

She sank back onto the sofa. "Yes." It was the truth, if not the whole truth. But she couldn't tell Bram about the mysteries and dangers holding her here—he'd forcibly drag her back to the mainland. And she certainly couldn't tell him that she couldn't imagine leaving Oliver or the islands. He'd have her over his shoulder in a heartbeat, carrying her off kicking and screaming.

He let out a long exhale, eyes still narrowed a bit. "I don't know that I believe you. He walked in here as if he owned the place. And what happened to Moon that he came barging in with aspirin and orders to rest? She's never been prone to headaches, has she?"

She had her doubts that he'd have known it if she were. But she shook her head. "She slipped in a cave and hit her head rather badly. It's why we were on Tresco an extra night." If he'd been chatting with Mrs. Pepper already, he'd have learned that she ought to have been back yesterday. Though with a bit of luck, thoughts of Mabena would distract him from thoughts of Oliver.

Wishful thinking, that. "I knew the moment he showed up at Telford Hall that he was trouble."

Libby rolled her eyes. "You did not. And he isn't. He's . . ." *Wonderful. Dream worthy. The best man I've ever met.* ". . . very kind. He answers all my questions about the flora and fauna of the islands with endless patience."

He grunted. "I imagine he does. But put those thoughts I can see you thinking out of your head straightaway. You're marrying Sheridan, not some—"

"I am *not*!"

"Fine." He waved her words away like he would a fly. "That Willsworth fellow would do then, I suppose. A viscount, isn't he? Interested in paleontology, which ought to suit you. He would do."

Heat seared her cheeks. And, even more humiliating, tears flooded her eyes before she could even feel them coming and blink them away. "Are you that eager to be rid of me, Bram?"

"Now, Libby, don't . . . come now. Here." He pulled out one of his ever-present handkerchiefs and thrust it at her. "You know well it isn't that at all. It's not about getting *rid* of you. It's about making certain you're well cared for."

But she *was* well cared for—at Telford Hall, with him and Mama. Why wasn't that enough? And why, if he was so eager to shove her off on someone else, couldn't he let her choose someone who would actually *like* her? Maybe even love her? Was that too much to ask?

A question she didn't intend to voice. Because, quite frankly, she was a bit terrified of the answer.

22

Oliver breathed in the beloved scent of salt water and breathed out a prayer. Partly for Libby, who he'd sincerely hated to leave when she was in such distress. A little bit for himself and the conversation he didn't know if he should postpone or find a way to have with Casek Wearne. And mostly for Mamm-wynn, who'd been weighing endlessly on his heart since the moment he stepped out of the house.

And for Beth. Had she found his letter? *Would* she find it? Would she learn some other way that their grandmother was ill? *Tell her, Lord, please. Somehow. Tell her to come home.*

His boat bobbed up on the incoming tide, reminding him of the time ticking by while he was here, waiting for Lord Telford to join them. And for Casek to get back. Lord Sheridan had struck up a conversation with a few tourists who had just gotten out of a boat, asking them about Druid cairns and seeming delighted to learn that Tresco was littered with them. Oliver wasn't sure if Sheridan actually knew the people or if he'd just seized on the first chap he'd seen in gentlemen's attire.

"Are we ready?"

Oliver turned at Casek's voice—not quite as snarling as usual. He shook his head. "Telford hasn't come down yet." Which probably meant he and Libby were still arguing. His feet itched to take him back up the path to her door to try to reason her brother into letting her remain here. But no, she had to do this herself. And she knew Telford far better than Oliver did. At the very least, they had a few days to convince him.

Casek grunted. "I suppose his lordship has no concept of inconveniencing the likes of us. Or of me. I suppose *you* aren't exactly a nobody, O gentleman of Truro Hall."

Either the mockery wasn't as heavy in his tone as usual, or all the praying Oliver had been doing over this had built a protective shell around his heart. Or perhaps torn one down.

He sighed. "Actually, I believe he would quite like to inconvenience me, even more than he would you. Because I'm the worst kind of nobody, in his mind. The kind who might think himself somebody, even when he isn't."

Casek snorted what might have been a laugh. Maybe.

Oliver set his gaze on him, let it linger. *Made* it linger, made himself study him as he did everyone else. Made himself try to see him. Not as his rival, not as the man who did everything he could to be a thorn in his side, not as the brother of the man who'd broken Mabena's heart.

He dragged in a long breath. "I owe you an apology."

That certainly got Casek's attention. "Come again?"

It took more effort than it should have to keep his shoulders from rolling forward defensively. But not as much as he'd expected it to take. "Sunday night—you were right. I shouldn't have jumped to conclusions as I did. I know very well you would never hurt Mabena. And if you're right that whatever Beth's involved in got Johnnie killed . . ." He shook his head, nostrils flaring. "Then we'll owe everyone a lot more than an apology."

Something in Casek's face shifted. Just a bit, but enough that Oliver could glimpse the man beneath the stone mask he usually showed him. "Beth may be stirring up ghost stories for some reason—but she didn't kill Johnnie. Even if she had something to do with what took him to the caves that night, she didn't do it."

Oliver knew that. Still, it was a surprise to hear Casek admit it. He nodded.

Casek folded his arms over his chest. "Why are you doing this? Apologizing, I mean? You never would have before."

No, and that was something he'd been wrestling with ever since Libby pointed it out. He preached regularly about the need to forgive, to extend grace to one's neighbor. How could he have been too blind to see where he'd failed at it for so long? He'd always just clung to the *"as much as is possible, live in peace with all men"* verse, telling himself it *wasn't* possible, not with Casek.

But it was. Of course it was. "Because I've been wrong. And because it's high time I admit it. High time we try . . . to be friends."

Casek winced—actually *winced*—when he said it. "About twenty years too late for that, isn't it?"

"I certainly hope not, if you intend to marry my cousin."

His arms were still crossed, but his fingers flexed. A flash of insecurity that he covered by nodding toward the village, where Telford had finally appeared on the path to the quay. "I may intend it. Doesn't mean she'll agree."

He'd always intended it. Oliver had known it; he'd just never liked it—and when Mabena had chosen Cador instead, he'd assumed Casek's infatuation would dissipate. It hadn't though, that was clear. He turned toward the boat. "She'll agree. She said, apparently, that—" now *he* winced, at giving utterance to such words—"that you make her fly."

A miracle happened then. Casek Wearne smiled. Honestly. At *him*. "Did she, now?"

"So I'm told."

"Well then." With a last glance at Telford, Casek fell into step beside him. "You're going to have a time of it with that one. You know that, right? He'll be as hard-pressed to accept you as you've been to accept me."

Turnabout? Maybe. The Lord did have the most ironic ways of teaching His children lessons sometimes. "Even harder, I daresay.

We're at least all neighbors. Giving you my blessing won't mean saying good-bye to my cousin."

"Not that we need your blessing—but you do have a point." Casek put on the scowl that he always reserved for tourists. "Blasted incomers. Your lady aside."

Oliver took the exception as the olive branch it was. "I couldn't agree more. Though speaking of which—Mrs. Gilligan?"

Casek rolled his eyes. "Anything," he said in a high-pitched voice meant to be an imitation of the shopkeeper's, "for the Reverend Mr. Tremayne."

Good. One less problem that would be thrust in Libby's lap.

Telford caught up with them half a minute later, his scowl as dark as the thunderheads hunched on the horizon. "I do hope you chaps are decent hands at sailing. I don't fancy getting caught in that storm."

Did he seriously just question the sailing abilities of islanders? It was like asking a London cabby if he could find Big Ben. Oliver glanced at Casek, who glanced at him too. They both, under their breath, muttered, "Incomers." And Casek was probably wondering, just as Oliver was, how well the Earl of Telford could swim.

Mamm-wynn's eyelids had fluttered open a few times last night. And her fingers, so frail in his, had squeezed his hand now and then. Oliver listed those praises as he knelt in the damp earth of his garden, pulling out weeds and praying for the strength he'd need to get through today. The gladioli were doing well—another praise. And he'd managed to make it twelve hours without saying anything rude to Lord Telford, which was surely a testament to the Lord's Spirit in him, because he'd *thought* about twenty different rejoinders last night as Libby's brother insulted everything he saw with those clever little jabs the nobility were so good at.

"Oh, I see electricity hasn't been run to the islands yet. I suppose it's a relief for someone in your position not to worry with all the upgrades."

"*A lovely meal, considering the limited selection available on the islands.*"

"*Your home is very pleasant, Mr. Tremayne. Cozy. I suppose with such a view, it's worth tripping over one's family every time one turns around.*"

Oliver tossed another weed onto the stack of them and blinked tired eyes. He was glad he'd convinced Mr. Menna to take his seat in the races this morning—he'd have been a liability. Even so, it felt wrong to be in his garden this time of day on a Wednesday instead of skimming across the water with his best chums. But he'd slept fitfully in the chair by Mamm-wynn's side most of the night, and by the time he rose, the race was likely all but over. So he'd come out here to wake himself up as pleasantly as possible.

He glanced up to check the sun in lieu of digging out his pocket watch and getting it dirty. Probably around eight o'clock. He'd finish here and then clean up, and with a bit of luck, he'd miss his guests in the breakfast room. After he finished eating, he'd check on Mamm-wynn again, and by then he should know if Mabena had made the trip or if he should go and fetch them from St. Mary's. The storm, at least, had blown itself out overnight.

And only the first gusts and droplets had caught them last night—not that Telford had thanked him for it, though Sheridan had made a good-natured exclamation about their providential timing.

The fuchsias weren't thriving as they should be. Oliver leaned close, examining the stalks, the leaves. Well-eaten by caterpillars, which was no great surprise. He'd fetch some soapy water to spritz on them to deter the insects.

"Well, how nice. Do you always have your morning tea in the dirt? I think I'd rather like that."

Oliver turned at the voice, glad it was Lord Sheridan who'd just stepped outside and not Lord Telford. His comments last night hadn't been half as acerbic. And given his way of turning every conversation to the next dig he had planned, Oliver suspected he meant this greeting sincerely too.

He glanced at his teacup to see if anything remained in it. It was as empty as it had been the last time he checked. "Not every morning, but several times a week, yes. Mr. Dawe officially manages the garden, but he's not as young as he once was, and it's difficult for him to kneel for so long. And I enjoy it." Not that he had to defend himself—plenty of gentlemen enjoyed nurturing their own gardens.

Sheridan didn't seem bent on judging him anyway. He'd meandered over toward the slab of granite in the corner. "Interesting. I was reading about your Abbey Gardens yesterday while we waited for Lady Elizabeth to return. It mentioned a stone that dates from the Druid days, presumably. Are there many such things about?"

"Here and there. Most of the slabs are just thatch anchors." Not that his roof had thatch. Some Tremayne of generations past had invested in slate. And not that he'd apologize for it if it did.

Well he knew that his house here was small—that even Truro Hall was small by Sheridan's or Telford's standards. Just as he knew that chaps of their ilk usually used the word *cottage* to describe a small mansion, not the holiday cottages on the islands, which they were more likely to call hovels. But he loved this house. Its every stone, its every tapestry, its every stick of furniture meant *home*. And as Telford had insulted it all last night, Oliver had bitten back all those clever retorts he'd wanted to make and comforted himself with that knowledge.

This was home. He wasn't ashamed of it. And if his guests couldn't appreciate that, then it was their own lack, not his.

"I've long wanted to come to the Scillies, you know," Sheridan said. "Beautiful. Even more beautiful than the pictures I've seen. And, of course, the history. I've always been intrigued by it. By the islands' role in England's history, that is."

Oliver smiled, pulled out one last weed, and gathered the pile of them together. "They are rich in history, for certain. Pirates, exiled princes—you name it, we've hosted it." He stood and walked the weeds to the compost pile in the corner.

"Have you any books on local lore? And would you mind if I

borrowed them, if so? Not that I'd take them when we go, of course. While we're here, I mean." Hands in his trouser pockets, Sheridan turned to him again, his smile cloudless.

Oliver returned it easily, glad he'd brought home all of the volumes Beth had apparently borrowed. "You're welcome to whatever I can find. And if it's local lore you're after, I ought to introduce you to my grandfather. He could tell you tales you'd never find in a book." He chuckled. "Some may even have a kernel of truth in them. Though I wouldn't wager anything on that."

Sheridan's face lit. "Jolly good of you. That would be just the way to pass a few days." His lips twitched, though he didn't come right out and smile as he said, "I suspect we'll be here longer than Telly thinks. I've always—if we're being honest—found his sister to be rather hardheaded."

"Have you?" Oliver frowned, though he directed it at his dirty hands rather than his companion. He clapped off what soil he could and then fetched his utilitarian teacup—Mrs. Dawe never let him take the fine china outside, of course. He wanted to ask how well Sheridan knew Libby. And why he'd say she was stubborn when Oliver had found her to be anything but. At least about things that mattered. Why, she was the sweetest, most gentle-natured lady he'd ever met.

Sheridan breathed a laugh. "We argued for an hour at Christmas over where I was excavating. She insisted I was destroying the habitat of something-or-another. As if the relics in the earth know what's nested above them."

"Ah." Oliver smiled too. *That* he could well imagine her getting up enough of a bother over to argue about. "Yes, that does sound like the lady, now that you mention it."

"She's a good sort though!" The words all but exploded from Sheridan's lips, and his cheeks went a bit pink too. "Not saying she isn't. Of course. A bit of stubbornness can be a good thing and all. She'll make a fine wife. I'm only saying—I mean, Telly, that's all. He's underestimated her this time, I think."

Did the man always qualify every sentence like that? A rather odd mannerism for someone of his stature. Usually marquesses owned their opinions and shared them without such worry that their every sentence would be taken the wrong way.

Maybe it was the effect of the too-confident Telford?

No. No, that wasn't it at all. Oliver smiled to let him know he hadn't been offended on Libby's behalf. He wasn't quite sure what it was, but there was a layer beneath the equivocating one. He could glimpse it; he just couldn't see it clearly quite yet. "We brothers are all the time underestimating our sisters, I'm afraid." He certainly hadn't expected his to disappear for so long—or to have uncovered any hints of Mucknell's treasure, come to think of it.

Sheridan meandered toward the door with him, hands still in his pockets. "Mine practically raised me. I've two, one thirteen years my elder and the other fifteen years. We've never had a very typical sibling relationship, I fear, given that they were more mothers to me. Our parents both passed away when I was only four, you see."

"How very sad. I'm so sorry to hear of your loss—though glad you had sisters who stepped into that role for you."

Sheridan's smile was easy—no doubt he didn't even remember those days. "We got on well enough. You've a sister too, then? Not living at home? Elder or younger?"

"Younger. She's . . . on holiday. Though I expect her back any day now." *Please, Lord.* He led the way inside, ducking into the kitchen to wash his hands. He expected Sheridan to have continued toward the dining room, but he was waiting in the corridor when Oliver emerged again, studying one of Mamm-wynn's drawings that they'd framed and hung on the wall. It was a labeled watercolor of an *Echium* plant. It was really no wonder she and Libby got along so well.

"Have you had breakfast yet?" Oliver asked. "Or would you like me to show you to the library?"

"Ah." Sheridan turned his way again, that easy smile on his lips. "No rush, whatever you like. And feel free to just tell me to entertain myself if you've things to do. Telly's doing that all the time. He seems to think I'll just follow him about forever unless he dismisses me."

That self-deprecating twitch of his lips. "No idea where he got that impression."

Oliver chuckled. And it was nice to be able to do so. For all Sheridan's odd foibles—and his seeming acceptance of the idea that he ought to marry Libby—Oliver liked him. "How about breakfast and then the library? You can browse to your heart's content while I check that my grandmother is comfortable again."

Sheridan nodded, but his eyes went curiously serious. Or perhaps not so curiously. "It was good of you. Very. To take us in like this, when you've such concerns. You could have just told us to go back to Penzance, Telly's high-handedness be hanged. And we'd have gone—though don't tell him I told you so. He likes to come off as more ferocious than he really is. A bit like Abbie's pug. That's my sister. Abbie, I mean. Not the pug."

Oliver laughed again and led the way into the dining room, where Mrs. Dawe had porridge and toast and jam set out, along with a bit of bacon. "I won't tell. Telford, that is—if ever I meet this Abbie, I may just imply that you told me your sister was a dog."

They enjoyed a cheery breakfast that only dimmed a little when Telford joined them. Primarily because the man didn't say a word, not even in response to Sheridan's stage-whispered explanation that Telly detested mornings that began before ten and rarely spoke a word before eleven.

Suited Oliver just fine.

He was just finishing up when Mrs. Dawe poked her head into the room. "I see the girls coming up the street. Benna must be feeling better."

"Oh good. Earlier than I dared expect them." They must have decided to come over early so they could get back before the usual Wednesday-afternoon delivery. He stood and moved toward the front door, opening it to receive the morning breeze even though Mabena and Libby were still a fair way off. They were walking at an encouragingly normal pace, though, which told him Mabena must be feeling more herself. And Libby had a basket looped over her arm whose lid she was holding down, which must contain Darling.

Another figure, running full speed up the incline and bypassing the girls with a greeting he couldn't hear from here, had him digging his fingers into the door. "Beth?" It looked like Beth, except that Beth never wore trousers as this figure did, not since she was a slip of a girl, anyway. But then, no one else on the islands had hair so fair, and the braid flying out behind her certainly insisted the person was a female.

A moment later, she was close enough to remove all doubt. Oliver stepped outside, not entirely certain whether he meant to greet her with a hug or a rebuke. Or both. "Beth!" Mabena and Libby were speeding to catch up with her, though there was no one who could do so when his sister was determined to be speedy, as she was now.

As she drew near, the worry etching lines into her face told him why. She dashed up the walk, threw herself into his arms, squeezed him tight, and said, "How is she? Tell me I'm not too late." Then she pulled away again and made for the house.

Oliver pivoted to follow her, knowing Mabena and Libby would join them momentarily. "No, not too late. She seems to be rousing a bit. I hope."

"Oof!"

Oliver pressed his lips against a grin when he finished his turn to find that his sister had plowed directly into Sheridan, who had trailed him to the door. "We have guests," he belatedly informed her. "Lord Sheridan, allow me to present my sister, Miss Elizabeth Tremayne."

"How do you do?" Sheridan steadied Beth with what must be his habitual cheerful smile and slid out of her way.

She shot Oliver a baffled look. "Guests? *Now?*"

"Your brother's most gracious. Also, there was the fact that we— or Telly, rather, I like to think I didn't do it—boxed him into a bit of a corner. Or, no, we boxed Libby. Well, Telly did. And Tremayne here thought to unbox her. Because, as I said. He's most gracious."

Beth had turned back to Sheridan during that explanation, if it could be called such. She blinked at him. Gave her next blink to Oliver, which clearly said, *Where on earth did you dig this one up?* And then, with a shake of her head, she took off again with a muttered, "Do excuse me. I must see my grandmother."

Testament indeed to her worry. In days past, Beth would have been all too eager to make a good impression on any visiting nobleman—not that they'd ever had many of them in their house, other than an occasional distant relative of Mamm-wynn's.

Perhaps whatever she'd gotten herself involved in this summer had rubbed away a bit of that yearning for that Something Else.

Oliver cleared his throat, three different cords tugging at him. He wanted to follow Beth, greet the girls, and get Sheridan tucked safely away in the library and didn't know which to do first. It might be a bit obvious if he shoved Sheridan down the corridor with the front door still hanging open, so he decided to wait. He'd give Beth a moment with their grandmother before following her, and then he would explain everything to her. For now, he held the door open for Benna and Libby, who were at the gate already, and sighed a bit when he saw Casek Wearne alter his trajectory toward them as well. He was still in his rowing clothes, coming up the hill at a jog. Must have spotted Mabena.

Oliver was apparently going to have a houseful this morning.

His cousin's eyes were blessedly clear of pain. And Libby's full of it, though more the emotional sort than physical. She smiled at him, but the smile stiffened and faded when she glanced past him and presumably spotted Sheridan.

Though Oliver of a Week Ago would have taken a bit too much pleasure in closing the door before Casek could reach it, Oliver of Today left it wide as he welcomed the girls inside. "You have a shadow, Benna." He nodded toward Casek, noting the way her cheeks flushed when she noticed him.

It barely even made him sigh. He was making progress.

His fingers found Libby's elbow of their own volition, and he smiled down at her. "I suspect that isn't a picnic in the basket." A woeful meow was his answer, making him chuckle. He tapped a finger in greeting upon the wooden lid. "Good morning, Darling. We'll let you out once the door is closed, and you can come and meet Mamm-wynn."

Mabena didn't seem to know whether to step back outside or dash down the hallway. "Beth?"

"She's gone to see her."

"How is she? Mamm-wynn?" Libby leaned a bit closer to him as she asked—something he might not have noticed had he not been keenly aware of Lord Sheridan standing half a step away and her brother lurking in the dining room.

He ought to let go of her arm, probably. But couldn't convince his fingers to obey. So instead he led her a few more steps into the entryway so they could make room for Casek. "She stirred a bit overnight. Opened her eyes a few times."

Libby frowned at him. "Did you get any sleep at all?"

"Here and there."

Her frown only deepened. "Oliver, you mustn't—"

"*Oliver?*" Lord Telford's voice, gruff and surly, intruded upon them.

Sheridan spun to face his friend with an overly bright look of surprise. "He speaks! And it's before nine! Note it on the calendar, Lady Elizabeth."

Libby just let out a long breath. "Good morning, Bram."

"Remains to be seen." Scowling and clutching his teacup as if it contained the very elixir of life, Telford stepped into the hallway and motioned at Oliver and Libby. "You'll not call him that."

Oliver wasn't certain at first if she'd drop her eyes or roll them. She surprised him entirely by ignoring her brother's directive altogether and turning her gaze back on Oliver. "You need your rest, or you'll be no good to her. Don't neglect your own health."

"I won't. I promise. Especially now that Beth's home—I imagine she'll take a shift tonight." Because if his sister thought she was going to blow in like the wind, spend a few minutes with Mamm-wynn, and then vanish again, she was in for a surprise. He'd bar every door and window if he must, but she wasn't leaving until he had some explanations and their grandmother was back on her feet.

Behind him, he heard Mabena asking how the race had gone, and then the closing of the door. Casek, obviously not shut *out*, laughed. "You ought to bow out more often, Tremayne. My lads routed yours rather handily."

Since facing Casek was no worse than the continued glare of Telford, Oliver turned to the newest addition. "I do hope you didn't gloat in front of Mr. Menna."

"Saved it for you." And he was smiling again. Genuinely. No doubt because he was standing so near Mabena, but still. "Besides, it wasn't Mr. Menna's fault. Enyon looked fit to fall over." His gaze flicked to Sheridan and Telford and back again. "Must have been fairies or goblins in Piper's Hole keeping him up again." He said it with a straight face.

And with a flash in his eyes that Oliver had no trouble deciphering. It wasn't fairies or goblins they needed to watch out for in the sea cave—but whoever had attacked them there before could well still be lurking about. He nodded. "I'll have to pay him a visit later. For now, allow me to show you to the library, Lord Sheridan." With a bit of luck, Telford would follow, and the rest of them could slip out to the garden, where Beth could join them.

He didn't intend to wait much longer for the answers he needed.

23

Libby crouched down in the corner of the small library, placing the basket gently upon the floor. She'd yet to really explore this room and would love the chance to do so, sometime when Sheridan—and her stewing brother—weren't in here. But for now, it seemed like a good place to let Darling out. No open windows or doors for him to fly through. She was a bit nervous that he'd go streaking out of the room and the house and she'd never see him again.

God? It seemed silly to pray for a cat. Wasn't it? But her prayer for Mamm-wynn had been answered, and Oliver claimed he prayed for his plants. Surely a kitten was no worse, so she finished her silent request. *Please keep Darling calm and help him adjust to coming here. I don't want to lose him.*

She lifted the lid of the wicker basket, and Darling scrambled out—directly into her arms. Grinning, she stood again, letting him put his front paws on her shoulder as usual and being rewarded with his loud purr.

"This section here is the local history," Oliver was saying to Sheridan, motioning toward a shelf. He must have been in the garden already this morning—the cuff of his sleeve, though rolled up to his elbow, had a dusting of rich brown soil upon it that made her smile.

And she'd caught a lovely whiff of green things on him when he'd been standing at her side.

Bram was at her side now, looking even grumpier than he usually did of a morning. "Stop."

She lifted her brows. "Stop what?"

"Looking at him like that. I won't have it." He'd folded his arms forbiddingly across his chest—which may have looked a bit more intimidating if he weren't still clutching a dainty, blue-sprigged teacup.

And if her heart weren't still feeling bold and strong from the conversation she and Mabena had enjoyed on the sail from St. Mary's. It had begun with Mabena officially resigning as her maid and then asking if she might keep staying with her as a friend, and from there . . . well, from there it had been like what she'd always dreamed of finding with a friend. Laughter over Casek and Oliver, worry over the mystery, a bit of moaning over the interruption to her nature-watching plans. And the gentle reminder from Mabena that Libby always had a choice. They came with consequences—but they were still her choices to make.

She could stay here, despite Bram's disapproval and the risk of Mama's disappointment and censure. It would come with a cost. But she could do it. She could take her summer, even if she ended up having to stay with the Moons. She could see Mamm-wynn back on her feet. She could enjoy the neighbors she already wished were her own.

She could spend the days with Oliver. Which was her brother's primary objection, and she met it now with a sigh. "Brother dearest, you need a new pastime. May I recommend rowing or sailing? Plenty of opportunity for that around here, and I daresay it'll be a far sight more entertaining than worrying over me."

He grunted, which was about what she'd expected from him at this hour. She was frankly surprised he'd put a few entire sentences together already. But he could be rather eloquent with his expressions. Now, for instance, he narrowed his eyes at where Mabena and Casek were laughing together by the globe and then turned a questioning look on Libby.

She smiled. "I'm afraid my lady's maid has given me her notice. It seems she intends to stay here and marry." Though she said it quietly enough that Casek wouldn't hear. Mabena probably meant to let him chase her awhile yet.

A sudden crash drew her gaze back to Oliver and Sheridan, where the guest had somehow managed to drop an entire stack of books onto the floor. Odd, since he wasn't usually clumsy. But then, he was darting a mortified gaze even now toward the door while he bent to retrieve the tomes.

Libby peered around her brother and saw that Beth had appeared in the doorway, looking like a very different person from the one who had raced past them on the road into Old Grimsby. Instead of the utilitarian braid, she'd brushed her hair into a simple, elegant chignon. The trousers and man's shirt had been exchanged for a day dress in pale blue that perfectly complemented her complexion. She couldn't have spent more than five minutes on her appearance after she'd checked on her grandmother, yet she looked more put together than Libby felt after an hour of Mabena's ministrations.

She almost felt a twinge of jealousy. For half a second. Then she was just glad that this young lady she didn't know had come home, and that it looked as though she meant to stay for a while, if she was changing back into what must be her normal attire.

Oliver accepted a few of the books that Sheridan thrust at him and put them back on the shelf. "How was Mamm-wynn, Beth?"

"Sleeping, it seems. Could I borrow you for a moment, Ollie? I'd like to hear what happened to her. And perhaps Benna can—Casek Wearne?" She frowned, having not looked to her cousin until that moment. "What are you doing here?"

"Gloating," his lips said, though the hand he had on Mabena's back said, *Courting* far more loudly.

Beth's frown only deepened. "Hadn't you better be getting home and cleaned up so you can go to school?"

"School?" Back on his feet with a stack of books helter-skelter in his arms, Sheridan quirked a brow toward Casek.

Mabena smiled. "He's the headmaster." Only a dunce could have missed the pride in her tone.

Beth was apparently no dunce. She blinked, opened her mouth, closed it again. "It seems I missed quite a bit while I was . . . on holiday."

"Mm." Mabena's smile turned to narrowed eyes and pursed lips. "Just a tad. You've had Charlotte Wight and Lady Emily Scofield looking for you on St. Mary's—"

"Emily was here?" Beth lurched a step into the room, eyes wide. With panic, or regret? Libby couldn't quite tell.

"And will be again, we hear, as of Friday. But we can talk more about that in a moment." Mabena gave her cousin a strange look before turning to Casek. "Let me see you out, dearovim, and then—"

"No." He said it easily, but he had a statue-like quality just now. Like his feet were made of granite and weren't about to budge. The smile he sent to Beth looked anything but casual. "I have a few questions for your cousin that I mean to ask before she vanishes again."

Beth's chin ratcheted up. "I'm not going anywhere. Not with Mamm-wynn ill. Though I can't think what business you would have with *me*, Casek Wearne."

"I think you can."

"Johnnie Rosedew." Libby nearly clapped a hand over her mouth after she said it. Why had she spoken? It must be Darling's fault with that purring-induced confidence.

Sheridan fumbled the books again. What had gotten into him? Though he winced as they hit the floor, he didn't bend to scoop them up this time.

Oliver cleared his throat and took a step toward the door. He sent Libby an apologetic look. "Do excuse us for a moment, my lords. My lady. We'll not bore you with our family business. Beth, Casek, Benna—the garden, I think."

She understood the apology in his look now. She wanted to go out with them, hear what Beth had to say. And she'd have had every right to, if her brother hadn't ruined everything with his arrival. But now it was only logical that she keep him and Sheridan out of the way. Oliver and Mabena would just have to update her later. She gave him a small nod to let him know she understood.

Sheridan didn't seem to though. He stepped forward too, an odd expression on his face and a hand held out. "Actually . . . that is, I think you'd better stay here. I mean, I have a feeling—drat it all. Is this about the search for Mucknell's treasure? What with Scofields and Rosedews and Elizabeths, I suspect it is."

Libby knew her own face must register the same shock that the others' did. And a bit of the matching confusion on Bram's and Beth's.

Beth regained herself first, surging another step into the room and slamming the door behind her. "What do you know of that, my lord?"

He gave her a look that was perfectly Sheridan—a bit wincing, a bit self-deprecating, and yet fully committed to whatever path he'd decided upon without a single care to whatever bystanders might be in the way. "Well, you see . . . that is . . . well, I'm the buyer who hired them."

--------○--------

Bram was pacing, still clutching his empty teacup. Sheridan was hunched into a chair at the head of the library table, looking as though he were trying to keep a mental list of the dozens of questions that had already been fired at him. Casek and Mabena had both taken seats too, and Beth had pulled out a chair across from Sheridan but failed to sit in it, gripping it tightly instead as she glared at him.

Libby had stayed where she was, since her spot afforded a view of all the faces at the table. And she was doubly glad of it when Oliver edged his way to her side.

"I can't believe this." A sentiment they were no doubt all thinking for different reasons, but it was her brother who spat out the words at his friend. "You mean to tell me you had ulterior motives for coming here? To check up on . . . on—what exactly? One of your baffling archaeological obsessions?"

"It's hardly baffling. Family history, actually, you know—a bit."

Sheridan huffed. "I've told you before we're descended from Prince Rupert, haven't I? He served with Mucknell during the Civil War. And why did you *think* I was so eager to join you in the Scillies?"

Having reached the opposite wall, Bram pivoted. "To see your fiancée."

"I am *not* his fiancée!" Libby probably shouldn't have shifted closer to Oliver when she said it. It just brought Bram's thundering attention back to her, and it was clearly threatening enough to scare even the kitten. Darling squirmed out of her hold and leaped to the ground, pouncing on a tassel of the rug as if it were a mouse.

Prince Rupert . . . Wasn't he the pirate prince Tas-gwyn had mentioned? She looked over at Oliver, who was clearly piecing the same thing together. Her own mind went from *pirate prince* to the start of Beth's unfinished fairy tale.

Once upon a time, there was a princess. She lived on an island of rocks and bones, with no one to keep her company aside from the fairies. All her life she'd danced with them to the tunes they played on their magical pipes, the tunes echoed by deep voices from the rock itself. One day, however, the music stopped.

"All right," Oliver said in that calm voice of his that could bring order to any chaos—at least when it was a chaos of people. "So, Lord Sheridan, you have an interest in information on Prince Rupert of the Rhine and, by extension, Vice Admiral Sir John Mucknell. Is that right?"

Sheridan nodded. "Ever since I learned of the prince as a lad. Who wouldn't? I mean, a pirate prince! For a relative! I've made no secret of it. That is, I'm always on the hunt for more information. In fact—don't you remember, Telly? I contacted the British Museum years ago, asking if they had anything in their archives that would be of interest. Inspired, actually . . ." He cleared his throat and stole a glance at Mabena, of all people. "Well, when you hired Moon and said she was from the Scillies, it stirred the memory, you know. Of Prince Rupert. That was when I asked the museum for any information."

Bram grunted. "And offered to fund any promising ventures, no doubt."

300

"Well, archaeologists and historians need to eat, you know. Funding *is* required." Sheridan faced Beth again. "It was, oh, two or three months ago that Lord Scofield got in touch. Said—what were his exact words? Oh, never mind. But the gist was that he'd found a lead. You, Miss Tremayne. I expect, anyway. He didn't give me your full name, of course. Just said a friend of his daughter's named Elizabeth—that would be Lady Emily. That she—you, I mean—was from the Scillies and had happened upon something."

Beth's fingers were white around the chair back, and her cheeks ashen too. "You. You're the one they sold it to. Give it back! I never gave them permission to sell it."

Sheridan seemed to know exactly what she was referring to—which was more than Libby could say. He lifted his chin, eyes flashing. "I bought it. It's mine."

"It was no better than stolen goods! I asked them to authenticate it as his crest, not to sell it!"

"Wait." Oliver held up a hand, his brows knit. "What exactly is *it*?"

Beth turned to him. "The old trinket box that Mother gave me, with the gold-leaf coat of arms embossed on it—you remember it, don't you? She said it was passed down through the family, left with some great-great-grandmother when her true love, a nobleman, left and went to sea. The Scofields asked me to keep an eye out for anything with Prince Rupert's coat of arms on it, and they sent a drawing of it. I recognized it at once and sent them the box—to *look* at, not to sell." Here she glared at Sheridan again. "Which I made perfectly clear."

Libby pressed her lips together. Was that the drawing Darling had found under her bed? She'd not given it a moment's thought since that night.

Sheridan folded his arms over his chest. "It wasn't made clear to *me*. I paid good money—"

"Irrelevant! It was not theirs to sell. And they never even paid me—"

"Actually." Oliver cleared his throat. "They sent payment last week."

"Then return it to his lordship, so that he has no argument."

Never in her life had she seen Sheridan look so near explosion. "Now see here—"

"Enough." Casek leaned forward, all menacing muscle. "Who really cares about a trinket box? What do you know of Johnnie Rose-dew?"

Sheridan at least had the grace to look abashed. "Only the name— from a report. Not from Scofield, but . . . ah, I must go further back. You see, I'd been paying another chap to look into a lead in the Caribbean, as that's where Rupert and Mucknell went for a while. Before Scofield, I mean. That my search there was before, not that they were in the Caribbean before. Though, of course, that was *also* before."

"Sher!"

Bram's bark earned a throat-clearing from Sheridan and a splinter of a smile. "He'd found nothing though, and Scofield—or rather you, Miss Tremayne. The first piece you found." His face lit, eyes all but blazing as they always did when he thought a discovery just beneath the dirt on which he stood. "I had a chance to see it when you sent it to them for authentication. It was Mucknell's mark, I'd know it anywhere. And it mentioned the *John*. So the timing is right."

Libby's brows knit. "Which item was this?"

Beth shot her a look but still said nothing.

Sheridan never had any such inhibitions. "A map—an actual trea-sure map! Or, well, maybe. On the treasure part. No one knows what Mucknell did with it, you know. The loot, I mean. But it could be here still, in the Scillies. He lived here for years, apparently. With his wife. Well, not right here in this very spot, of course, but somewhere nearby."

"The *point*, Sher." Bram, naturally.

While the rest of them exchanged a glance. *This* house hadn't been his. But Tas-gwyn Gibson's had been, if his word on the matter could be trusted.

"Ah. Right. Well, you see . . . ." He faced Beth again. "You probably know this already. But no one's entirely certain what happened to the

John. Might have sunk, or he might have got it back to the islands and then scuttled it. Never sailed again though. Of course."

Beth sighed and looked to her brother. "I did a bit of digging. It seems the ship he took right before his final battle was called the *Canary*, and there was something of value on board that the rightful owners spent considerable time searching for to no avail. But if the *John* was scuttled, then it means whatever treasure he carried was brought ashore. And even if not, if it's at the bottom of the sea, there was a lot of loot he'd taken with it beforehand."

"But no one knows what he did with it," Sheridan concluded.

Mabena snorted. "Spent it, most likely."

Sheridan shook his head. "Couldn't have, here—there was nothing to spend it on. I mean, the islands are lovely. Quite the holiday spot *now*. But not then. Just rocks, basically. Barely enough to support anyone. Before the Dorrien-Smiths brought the flower trade here, I mean."

Libby had to give Sheridan a bit of credit. He knew how to do his research.

Oliver sighed. "It's always been a matter of local speculation. From the Scillies he went to the Caribbean, as you said, and he certainly wouldn't have taken any of his personal treasure with him. But he never made it back to England. And his wife clearly didn't take the plunder and use it—she petitioned the Crown for his pension after the war and lived modestly, according to what I've read."

"Exactly!" Sheridan slapped a hand to the table. "Which means it's probably still *here*. Somewhere. Buried."

"Or sunken." Bram stopped pacing and leaned down to scoop up Darling. The little traitor nuzzled his chin and meowed at him. "You'll never find it if it's at the bottom of the sea."

"But it isn't! Or probably. Not, I mean." Sheridan gestured toward Beth. "That's what the map could indicate."

Bram, kitten purring happily against *his* shoulder, leaned against the wall beside Libby. "Get back to your original point, Sheridan. This other person you'd hired, who had been in the Caribbean?"

"Ah. Right." The excitement on his face dimmed to something that looked oddly like worry, though she'd never seen such an expression on him before to know exactly what it looked like. "Bloke by the name of Lorne. I called him off. I mean, even I'm not going to fund something fruitless. Not for long, anyway. Told him I had a more promising lead in the Scillies." He winced. "I didn't mean for him to come here. But he, ah—well, he's butted heads with the Scofields' lads before. In the field, I mean. Quite a competitive game is archaeology, you know. It can get . . . nasty."

Casek's hand, which had been splayed on the tabletop, curled into a fist. "You mean to tell me this bloke came here? That he's the one who killed Johnnie?"

Sheridan eased out a breath. "Can't say. That is, he said the lad was killed in an accident but that it could rouse suspicion. So he was lying low. That's all I know. Honestly. About the young man."

"It wasn't an accident," Casek snapped. "I saw him, saw the blow to his head. He couldn't have got it by slipping and falling, not there. Someone's responsible, and if it's this Lorne bloke, I'll see he's brought to justice. He had to have been involved somehow."

Beth sucked in a breath. "He'd hired him. I found Johnnie poking about in Piper's Hole on St. Mary's, and he admitted he'd been hired by an incomer to find Mucknell's treasure. I thought at first the Scofields had hired him behind my back and was a bit put out—I wrote a rather heated letter to Emily's father." She shook her head. "If I could undo that, I would. But after the . . . *misunderstanding* about the Prince Rupert box, I was quick to suspect foul motives on their part. Regardless, Johnnie went to the cave that night, and he must have told his contact something that displeased him. Perhaps about me—perhaps knowing there was a rival looking for the same treasure angered him, I don't know. But the morning after Johnnie's death, someone left a note at my cottage that said, 'Find the silver or you're next.'"

Sheridan sank back against the bookshelves. "I never would have condoned such tactics."

"Did you forbid it?" Beth drilled him with a glare as cold and sharp as an icicle. "Did you tell them to work together or not at all?"

"Well, ah . . . no." He looked away, rubbing a hand at the back of his neck. "I didn't think to, at first. That is, at first I didn't even realize Lorne had come here. Then, when he sent a report . . . well, sometimes competition works to one's advantage, you know."

"And sometimes people end up dead." Beth's voice cracked. "Poor Johnnie didn't deserve that."

Casek pushed away from the table, not seeming to be calmed much by the hand Mabena rested on his arm. "Which of them did it? This Lorne bloke or the Scofields?"

Beth shook her head. "I don't know. I wasn't there that night, I just—I knew he'd set up a meeting. And then . . ." She squeezed her eyes shut. "I didn't know if they'd come after me next. But I knew I didn't have what they wanted, and they seemed willing to make me pay for that. So I left, and I sent the rest of my rental money to a barrister in Cornwall to set up couriers for the remaining information that the Scofields would be sending to me. They were researching in London, trying to discover what could be *in* the treasure we're looking for. What was on the ships Mucknell took."

She blinked her eyes open again and turned to Libby. "I didn't mean to get you involved, Lady Elizabeth."

"What?" Bram straightened again. "What do you mean, get Libby involved?"

Libby cleared her throat. "These couriers thought I was her. I've been . . . receiving her post, more or less. My cottage had been hers."

"The couriers were just told to look for a young lady, blond, who answered to Elizabeth, or else to leave the items at a specific location if I wasn't at home." Beth gave her a rueful smile. "I didn't realize there'd be another of me at home when I wasn't."

Oliver was shaking his head. "But where did all this start, Beth? On your end, not Lord Sheridan's."

Beth glanced around at the collection of people, clearly not wanting to say in such mixed company. "I . . . you know I've always collected bits of this and that as I explore the islands. Well, one day I found the map his lordship mentioned. I didn't dare hope it was anything as promising as an actual treasure map, so I sent it to the Scofields for authentication. I thought that, with their connections, they could help me determine what it was. And they were quite excited. They sent it back with the promise of a buyer of any Mucknell or Prince Rupert items. I thought . . ." She shifted, dropped her gaze. "You know I'd always wanted to spend a Season in London."

Oliver let out a sigh. "Beth."

"I thought it would be nothing but a bit of fun! Poking around all my favorite spots, trying to match the map to one of the islands—I never for a minute thought anyone would get hurt. Not until they all started focusing on silver." Her fingers knotted together. "Once greed reared its ugly head though, I knew I'd got in too deep."

She still hadn't said *where* she'd found the map—and Libby suspected she wouldn't, even if asked directly. Not to all of them.

Casek didn't look mollified. "And what of your stalking about the islands at night in white, like a ghost?"

Beth visibly started. "What makes you think—"

"I found your shawl on Samson after one of the supposed sightings. It's monogrammed, you know. With the Tremayne crest."

Beth's cheeks flushed. "Much of my prowling about had to be at night. In case anyone heard me or saw me, I wanted them to chalk it up to a story. They'd dismiss it then. Not go looking too deeply."

Mabena rubbed at the bridge of her nose, making Libby wonder if the headache was making its return. "A fine kettle of fish you've cooked up, as my mother would say."

"Well, luckily, his lordship is here to set it all to rights." Casek lifted a challenging brow. "Isn't that right?"

Never in the decade that she'd known him had she ever seen Lord Sheridan look so uncomfortable. "Of course. That is . . . I'll try. Though I don't, to be honest, even know what these men look like. Which is to say, all our communications have been by letter. Or telegram. They wouldn't know me if they saw me. And . . ." He glanced toward the three of them against the wall. "Then there's the matter of Lady Emily showing up. I must say, I'm not sure what that portends."

Bram stroked a hand down Darling's striped back. "So, what you're telling me is this is bigger than you know, you don't know how to stop it, and you didn't even see fit to tell me that we were walking into it, much less that my *sister* was involved."

Sheridan cheered a bit. "Well, I didn't know that part. Your sister, I mean. Can't blame that on me."

Bram hissed out a breath and turned to her. "Pack your bags. We're leaving before *you* get hurt."

"I don't think it's that simple." Since she was experimenting with prayers, she mentally whispered one for courage, since he'd stolen her kitten. And met his gaze. "They think I'm her. They'll probably be watching the ferry, ready for her to try to flee. For *me* to, I mean." And now she was starting to sound like Sheridan. She shook her head. "We have to just see it through, Bram. Put a halt to it."

Bram's jaw ticked he was clenching his teeth so tightly.

"She's right." It was one of the only times she could remember Sheridan being in agreement with her on anything. "So . . . any ideas on how to accomplish that?"

24

Mabena walked as far as the gate with Casek, not quite willing to leave the circle of still-heated conversation inside the library, but also not ready to part from him. The school day wouldn't wait for them to sort matters out here though. And this close to the end of the third term, there were always far too many recalcitrant boys getting sent to the headmaster's office. Well, to be fair, there were no doubt recalcitrant girls too. She'd certainly seen the inside of that office often enough.

It was still strange to imagine this hulking giant folded behind the desk instead of Mr. Morris. Just as it was still strange to think that this hulking giant could be *hers*. She trailed her fingers down his arm, the skin still warm from sport and summer. Cador had been an inch shorter, far slighter. It came of ignoring sports and exercise in favor of books, she supposed. But how had she convinced herself she preferred that? He couldn't hold a candle to Casek.

She could feel his tension in each muscle of his arm though. He wanted to physically put things to rights, pound a few skulls. She could understand the sentiment. But . . . "We'll get it sorted, Caz. Bring to justice whoever killed Johnnie. But it won't bring him back."

"I know." His fingers caught hers and squeezed, but it wasn't her he was looking at. His gaze was toward Old Grimsby. "But if we can stop it from happening again . . ."

308

Her brows knit. "What do you mean?"

He sighed. "Perry and the Grimsby boys—well, Nick and Joseph, anyway. They've been chasing after whatever Johnnie was involved in."

Mabena's breath tangled in her throat. She had hoped they'd given that up by now, after they'd caught them at it on Teän. "Did you warn them off?"

"I've tried, but what could I say? I told them Johnnie slipped, like everyone else was saying. But Perry must have known he was up to something. And you know boys—the more you make something seem forbidden, the more determined they are." He shook his head. "I won't have any more of them getting hurt. I can't."

She touched a hand to his chest, over his heart. His shirt was still damp from the race, but she hardly cared. All that mattered was this man who put on such a front of disdain used it to cover a heart bigger than all the islands put together. "You're a good man, Casek Wearne."

His gaze flashed back to hers, and a grin winked out. "I've been telling you that all your life, Mabena Moon."

"Well, it may be I believe you now." She returned the grin and curled her hand into his shirt, using it to give him a tug off the path. The flowering trellis didn't exactly hide them completely from any prying eyes peering out neighboring windows, but it would obscure them a bit, anyway. She stretched up on her toes.

It was all the invitation Casek needed. His arms came around her, hauling her up the remaining few inches until her feet dangled and her laugh at it was cut off by his lips claiming hers.

It shouldn't make her soul take wing even now, should it? Johnnie Rosedew was dead, likely murdered, and the man responsible was after Beth . . . or Libby. Her cousins' grandmother was still abed, Tas-gwyn had been clobbered as surely as she herself had been, and more lads could be in danger. There was nothing light about this situation. Nothing all that hopeful, even.

But for all that was wrong, this was right. The way her blood trumpeted through her veins, making a glorious symphony of noise in her ears. The way she fit inside the circle of his arms, making her feel as protected as a bird nested in the rocks, yet still as free as one gliding on the wind. The way her heart skipped and jumped and raced.

She pulled away with a little groan, pushing him back a step even though she kept her fingers curled into his shirt. "You need to go."

"Soon." He kissed her again first, bending down this time to accomplish it. "I've a lot of years to make up for."

She laughed. And convinced her fingers to let go of the cotton. "And we've years in which to do the making up. The future's ours, dearovim."

If only it were pure joy in his eyes at that, untainted by all this. "I hope so, my love." He nodded toward the house. "You'll have to be the voice of reason with that lot. I don't trust those dandies to sort things out, not as far as I can throw them."

Her lips twitched—first because neither Sheridan nor Telford were dandies by any definition other than an islander's, and second at the image of him giving them a nice, friendly toss. "How far do you think that is, exactly?"

He chuckled. "If they don't watch themselves, we may find out." He pressed his lips to hers once more, softly. "I'll find you after school. Are you here tonight, or back to St. Mary's?"

It had been ages since anyone asked her questions like that—questions that at once granted her the right to decide for herself how she'd fill her days and yet asked to be a part of them. "Here. Libby wants to be close to Mamm-wynn. We'd originally planned to go back just for a bit this afternoon, to get the Wednesday delivery, but with Beth back, I don't think we need to. Which is fine with me. We brought enough clothes to last us a week." Including evening wear for Libby, much to the lady's dismay—but with two lords in residence and Beth back, dinners would be a formal affair again at the Tremayne house. They'd had two lads carry their bags from the *Mermaid* to her parents' when they landed.

"Good. I'll feel better with you close. And don't let those idiots do anything stupid while I'm at work."

She smiled her promise. "I'm flattered you think me capable of stopping them."

He laughed and stepped back to the gate, opened it. "I think you're capable of anything, dearover." With a wink, he stepped to the street. "Tonight?"

"I'll be either here or at my parents'."

He nodded, lifted his hand, and strode away.

Mabena stood there watching him until he disappeared, arms wrapped around herself even though she was far from cold in the summer morning air. Just . . . savoring. Feeling. Holding it all in.

"Mind telling me how *that* happened?"

Mabena smiled at Beth's voice, turning her head but otherwise not moving. "You vanish for over a month and you miss a few things, cousin." It was a relief, though, to see her back here where she belonged. Strolling toward her with the front garden as a perfect backdrop to her pretty dress, her pretty face. Mabena sighed. "Where have you been? All this time?"

Beth gestured to the southwest. "One of the abandoned cottages on Samson, mostly."

Mabena frowned. "Where your grandmother and Tas-gwyn went to find you? But—how could she have known? Her eyesight isn't so good that she could have spotted you."

"No one would spot me." But Beth frowned. "What do you mean, that she knew?"

She told her briefly about the scare the other day, with the grandparents having vanished, and what Libby and Oliver had told her about finding them. Then added, "It isn't the only odd thing she'd done lately either. She's the one who sent Oliver to St. Mary's the day after we arrived to see where you were."

Beth folded her arms over her chest, her gaze distant. "The veil's slipping."

"What?"

But Beth shook her head, and her eyes refocused on Mabena's face. "Just something she used to say. About her own grandmother. I'm going to go and sit with her for a while. Coming in?"

"I'd better." She sent a look in the general direction of the library.

"I have a feeling the gentlemen aren't coming to any helpful conclusions—and Libby's probably about ready to curl up on the floor with her cat and howl in frustration."

An echo of a smile touched Beth's lips. "She's not what I expected. From your letters."

"No?" What had she written that was wrong? She tried to send her mind back over all the words, but they were a muddle in her mind, confused with the pain she was determined to ignore. She opted for a grin to deflect that truth. "Your brother certainly likes her."

"So I noticed. Not certain what I think about that yet—though it's no secret what *her* brother thinks."

Mabena chuckled and meandered back toward the front door with Beth. "He'll come around or he won't—but I don't think Ollie means to let her go back at the end of summer. And I hope she agrees. They fit." She hadn't thought to expect it. But now, having seen them together this month . . . she couldn't honestly imagine anyone else making either of them happy.

"Well. If *you* say so, I don't dare disagree." Beth bumped their shoulders together, twenty years of friendship summed up in that single touch. "She seems sweet."

"She is. But she has a good dose of salt too—necessary in these parts."

"And she'd be happy here? Because I can't imagine Ollie ever wanting to be elsewhere, even Truro."

Mabena didn't bother holding back her smile. "The islands know her name, according to Mamm-wynn."

Beth's shoulders relaxed as she reached for the door. "That's all I needed to know."

Rather than stepping through the doorway, Mabena paused, her brows knit. "One question, Beth, about all you said in there. The map—it wasn't among the things we found. Do you have it still?"

"I have a copy. But the original is stowed in my—*your*—cottage." Beth's eyes sparkled. "I was hoping to reclaim it when I came to collect *Treasure Island* last week."

She linked her arm through her cousin's before she could think about darting off again. "You're not going back for it alone though, just so you know. We're in this together."

"Mm." Beth's gaze as they stepped inside tracked toward the library, from where too many masculine voices were ringing. "More of us, it seems, than I'd ever bargained for."

It had rained buckets all day Thursday, effectively keeping them Tresco-bound and delaying the gentlemen's intentions of sending for their valets, but when Friday dawned bright and fair, Oliver breathed a prayer of thanksgiving and all but leapt into the day. They'd go back to St. Mary's today—first to meet Lady Emily Scofield's ferry and see her to the room he'd arranged for her above Mrs. Gilligan's hat shop, and then to get the map from the garrison cottage where his sister had apparently stashed it.

And best of all, he might even escape Telford's hovering presence for a few minutes. He'd been a perpetual, stormy shadow since Wednesday, and no amount of politeness or attempts to engage him in honest, heart-seeking conversation had resulted in anything but a glare.

A glare that said quite clearly, *Stay away from my sister.*

A glare Oliver couldn't have obeyed if he wanted to. Dressed for the day, he slipped into Mamm-wynn's room, acknowledging silently what had become all the more apparent in the face of Telford's thunder. He'd fallen head over heels in love with Lady Elizabeth Sinclair, and he couldn't be in her presence without finding his way to her side. Teasing a smile to her lips. Whispering a Latin name or two as their own private joke. *Ira Frater* in response to one of Telford's irritated—and irritating—commands, for example.

And she'd replied to his "angry brother" moniker with a nod toward Beth and *Soror Absit*—"absent sister."

He sat on the edge of his grandmother's bed and took her hand in his. She rewarded him with a fluttering of her eyes, though they didn't focus on him. Just gazed blankly for a moment before her lids swooped down again. More than she'd given them that first day. And the doctor said it was a good sign that she was becoming more alert, and that one side of her body didn't seem to be weaker than the other.

Still. Oliver wanted her awake. Squeezing his hand. Talking to them. "We'll be going to St. Mary's for a while today, Mamm-wynn," he said softly. "Mrs. Dawe will be here, and Aunt Prue means to spend the afternoon with you, I think. Do you need anything?"

How he wished she'd demand a bun from the Polmers' bakery. Or some new yarn for her next project. But she said nothing. He let loose a long breath and lifted her hand, pressed a kiss to the papery skin. "You did what you meant to do, you know. You brought Beth back to us. Thank you for that—but don't think you're finished yet. We still need you. *I* still need you."

He set her hand down again and then leaned over to kiss her forehead. "Rest now, Mamm-wynn, but wake soon. Please."

Sheridan was already in the dining room with his tea and porridge, one of the books of local history open before him—probably to a page that told him something about Mucknell and Prince Rupert. Oliver still couldn't quite believe he was the one behind all this, however inadvertently. But at least the marquess wanted to put it to rights somehow. Not that they could all of them agree on the best course of action to accomplish that.

They had to bring Lorne and whoever the Scofields' counterpart was before the magistrate, that was certain. And at all costs keep them from finding anything of actual worth. Even with their buyer here, on their side, none of them were willing to trust these shady antiquity hunters. If Sheridan tried to call them off and not pay them, who was to say that they wouldn't just find someone else eager for some pirate silver? There was surely more than one gentleman in England willing to pay for it.

It may be wise, as Telford kept insisting, to simply put it all as far from them as possible. To tell the Scofields their search had met a dead end, and to let Sheridan distract their overeager employees with a few other inquiries he had stored up. But that still left the Lorne fellow, and he was a bit of an unknown. Sheridan hadn't seemed at all confident that he'd be able to redirect him. *A bloodhound*, that was how he'd been described and why Sheridan had hired him to begin with. Once he was on the scent of something, he just wouldn't let it go.

And apparently wouldn't let anything or anyone get in his way.

Oliver made it through breakfast without running into Telford and even stole enough time to pay a quick visit to Mr. Menna in the Abbey Gardens before the six of them met at the quay. There had been no debate as to which boat to take, as only the *Adelle* was large enough to hold all of them. He and Beth and Mabena moved in perfect harmony readying her, Libby able to pitch in without getting in the way too.

Their lordships at least had the good sense to stand on the shore and wait until they were called.

Soon enough they were skimming the waves toward St. Mary's, sun and wind spurring them onward. But it wasn't a pleasure cruise, and no one on board seemed to mistake it as such. Shoulders were tense, spines rigid. His sister grew more silent, more anxious with every passing minute.

Oliver prayed his way over the four miles of water. That they would have wisdom. That they would find answers.

That no one else would get hurt in the search for them.

They spotted the first ferry of the day as they neared the quay— and ended up dropping anchor just as it pulled in at the docks. Beth, shielding her eyes against the sun, waved a hand furiously. "Emily!"

Oliver turned, though he had no idea who among the passengers was his sister's friend from school.

"The ginger," Libby whispered, nodding to a young lady whose hair was noticeable even beneath the wide brim of her hat. Not that said lady had been able to hear Beth's shout over the ferry's engines. Either that, or she was ignoring her.

"Well, let's get on with it, then." Looking like he'd rather wrestle a shark, Telford offered a hand to the ladies at large.

It must have been the engines, because as they made their way ashore, it was Lady Emily who did the shouting and rushing forward upon spotting Beth—and to his trained eye, her joy looked genuine, untainted by any devious motives. Not to say she couldn't be hiding them, but if so, she was quite skilled at it. He watched as the girls embraced, Lady Emily laughing and clutching Beth close.

"Oh, I've been so worried!" she exclaimed. "We haven't heard from you in so long, and when I came for a visit, you were nowhere to be found. I confess my imagination began conjuring up all sorts of nightmares. I made an absolute nuisance of myself until Father agreed to let me come back for a longer stay so I could put some genuine effort into finding you."

"You must have been desperate, if you threw yourself on the mercy of Lottie Wight. At least if Libby's stories of her can be trusted." Beth grinned, looking from Emily to Libby. "You've met, correct?"

Hand on her hat to keep the wind from snatching it, Lady Emily turned to smile at Libby too. "On my previous visit here, yes. How do you do, Lady Elizabeth? It's so lovely to see you again."

Libby smiled back and murmured a greeting, but given that the newcomer was noticing the size of their party and seemed a bit taken aback by it, Beth had to interject with those introductions.

Oliver paid especially close attention to her reaction to Lord Sheridan, curious as to whether she knew he was the buyer her parents had lined up for Beth's finds, but she greeted him with the same blank politeness she did the rest of them. No recognition in her gaze for anyone but the two Elizabeths.

"I don't believe she knows much about what's going on." His observation was quiet, meant solely for Libby's ears. Because he'd ended up at her side again, despite the invisible daggers her brother was throwing at him.

"Good." Relief saturated Libby's returning murmur. "I hated the thought that Beth's friend might be party to whatever underhanded dealings are in play."

Mabena must have heard their quiet exchange too. She fell in on Oliver's other side as they all wandered away from the other ferry passengers. "The question, if you ask me, is what she knows that she doesn't even realize. With a bit of luck, it's something that will be useful to us."

"We'll find out soon." Though certainly not out here in public. But Beth knew to lead the way to Mrs. Gilligan's, which would afford them privacy enough for a conversation.

Quick motion in his periphery caught his attention, making his shoulders go tight again. Though only for a moment. A young lady dressed much as Mabena had been when she came home was jostling her way through the crowd, scanning faces rather frantically until she spotted their group and then visibly relaxing. Oliver nudged Mabena. "I think we're leaving without Lady Emily's lady's maid. Would you?"

Mabena chuckled. "Since I'm more suited to the company of maids than ladies, you mean?"

He gave her a helpful shove in the shoulder. "You're the one who decided to prove him right. And now that you've that experience, you ought to at least know how to talk to her without startling her."

She shoved him right back. "I think you just want a moment alone with Libby."

"You call this alone?" But it was as alone as they were likely to be in their current crowd—Beth and Lady Emily, heads together and arms linked, were strolling along the road, the two lords a few steps behind. Neither, for once, paying any attention to him and Libby. He offered his arm with a grin. "My lady?"

"Good sir." She tucked her hand into the crook of his elbow, and they fell in a goodly distance behind her brother and not-fiancé. Though her gaze seemed focused more on Beth and Lady Emily. "I think it's time I give up."

He quirked a brow at her—not sure what she meant exactly, but hearing no defeat in her tone.

She nodded at the girls. "I'm not like them. And I don't enjoy trying to be."

He covered her hand with his. "You don't need to be. You're you, which is absolutely perfect."

Her sigh sounded somehow both happy and resigned. "You're the only one I've ever met who thought so."

Hence why she needed to stay here, with him. He might have said as much had her brother not remembered to send him a scowl over his shoulder just then, and hang back enough that he probably would have heard.

But it was the truth. Why should she spend the rest of her life struggling to fit into a world that couldn't appreciate her? London balls, country house parties, drawing room visits—those didn't make her sparkle, make her come alive. She needed *this*. God's world in all its splendor surrounding her and stirring her curiosity. She needed to chart the tides and the paths of the migratory birds and count the flower species with Mr. Menna each year. She needed to serve his neighbors tea on cool Wednesday mornings and listen to Tas-gwyn's ridiculous stories. *That* would make her eyes shine, day in and day out.

But how to make her brother see that?

They soon arrived outside Mrs. Gilligan's shop, which he could hear Lady Emily declare to be "darling." It was, rather purposefully. All the shops on the islands were so that they might draw in the tourists and the pounds sterling they tossed about without a care.

The flat above it would be far more utilitarian, though Mrs. Gilligan *had* taken care with it, thinking she'd be welcoming her daughter and a newly born grandbabe while her son-in-law was at sea. But Sam had sustained a minor injury last month, so they'd stayed in their little flat on the mainland, and the babe hadn't made his or her appearance quite yet.

"Ah, my dear Reverend Mr. Tremayne," Mrs. Gilligan called out the moment they entered the shop. She *did* sound a bit like Casek's imitation of her, which made his lips twitch up. "I've got the flat pretty as you please for your friend."

"So very gracious of you, Mrs. Gilligan." He stepped away from Libby so that he could greet the middle-aged shopkeeper properly, taking her hand and clasping it between both of his. "Any good news from the mainland yet?"

Mrs. Gilligan's smile was bright, though her laugh was rueful. "Not yet. Any day now, any day. I'm starting at every breeze, thinking it a lad from the telegraph office knocking on my door." Her face went sober. "How's your grandmother?"

"Improving, I think, though not quickly enough for us. We do appreciate any prayers you offer up for her."

"Morning and night, dearovim. Morning and night." She brightened again, her gaze scanning the rest of the group and landing unerringly upon Lady Emily. "Well now. Shall I show you the flat?"

The newcomer offered a dainty smile, as fragile looking as porcelain. "That would be delightful. Thank you, madame."

It was, Oliver saw two minutes later, about what he'd expected. Not large by any means, but fully equipped and decorated with all the ribbons and frills a first-time grandmother with a stockroom full of hat trimmings might be expected to produce. "Charming," according to Lady Emily, and she sounded as though she meant it.

Squeezing them all in even for a few minutes was a tight fit, but the way Sheridan and Telford leaned against the walls somehow made it clear they didn't intend to leave again right away. Mrs. Gilligan did though, after promising to stop up after closing time to have a chat and talk about the logistics.

The door had scarcely clicked behind her before Sheridan said, "Let's get to it, then. Which is to say, no time to lose. Am I right?"

Lady Emily looked baffled. "Get to what, exactly?"

Beth took her friend's hand and tugged her to a seat on the newly reupholstered sofa. "I've a bit of explaining to do. And then some questions to ask. I hope you can help us sort through the last of it, Em."

She laid it all out in a few minutes, but the more she explained, the more troubled Lady Emily appeared. When they got to the bit about someone accosting Libby, she interrupted with horror. "Before the Wights' dinner party? But—what did this fellow look like?"

Libby recited the description she'd put to paper when they'd gotten back to her cottage, which made the lady wash paler still. And mutter, "Well, that can't be."

Libby lifted her brows.

Lady Emily flushed. "Not your description, my lady. I beg your pardon. I was referring to my own immediate thought. It sounds like . . . but it couldn't have been him. He wouldn't." So said her lips, while her eyes said, *Would he?*

Beth scooted closer to her on the sofa. "Who wouldn't?"

Lady Emily's gaze bounced from one of them to the next. "My brother, Nigel," she admitted quietly. "He was here with us, on St. Mary's, but he didn't show up at the Wights' dinner party that night until nearly midnight."

"And he's involved in your parents' archaeological ventures?" Telford asked.

"He's involved in *all* their ventures." She unpinned her hat and held it out, the lady's maid she'd nearly left behind on the ferry springing forward to take it from her. Then she rubbed at her temple. "Far more than I am, which is to be expected. Or so Father says. He says the world of archaeology is too cutthroat for ladies."

Sheridan grunted. "Sometimes. Or at least—it can get cutthroat. And Mr. Nigel Scofield—I've never actually met him, though I've seen him around. Have you, Telly?"

Libby's brother shook his head.

Sheridan mirrored him. "Older than us, a bit. Missed him at school. But I've heard stories. Always thought I'd *like* to be introduced, but perhaps . . . Well, perhaps *not*."

Lady Emily's nostrils flared as she looked to Beth again. "I thought . . . I was so excited when you wrote to me and sent that map. For the first time in my life, *I* had something of interest to them. I thought that maybe, finally, they'd let me be a part of it. Truly a part. Perhaps I shouldn't have wished it at all. I cannot bear the thought that I put you in danger, Beth."

"You didn't, Em." Beth took her hand. "You've been nothing but a friend. It's this rival, I think. Lorne."

"And my own brother. Threatening you, or who he thought was you." The lady looked as though she might faint from the thought of it, which Oliver sincerely hoped she wouldn't do. "I can hardly fathom it. Except . . ."

"Except?" Beth dipped her head a bit to peer into Lady Emily's downturned face.

The lady looked away. "We aren't exactly close. Not like you and your brothers. Hearing your stories, I was always a bit ashamed to think of how much a stranger Nigel has always been to me."

Beth frowned. "I'm sorry. I never meant to upset you—"

"Oh, it isn't *your* fault!" The lady frowned. "It's us. He's just so competitive! I always thought he resented the very fact that I was born and so stole a bit of our parents' attention." She tried to laugh it off, but the laugh burned cool while the flame in her eyes went hot. "He . . . they've had to cover up more than one incident where he let his competitive streak take him too far. Even I don't know all the details, but . . ." She sucked in a breath, held it, let it out. "If he had been involved in the Mucknell treasure, if he realized this other man was too, and if he perceived it as a personal rivalry—there's really no saying how far he might carry it."

Not exactly the news they wanted—but the news they needed, if they meant to keep everyone safe. Oliver stepped forward. "I think the next question, then, is how patiently he'll wait for Beth to get him what he seeks, and when he'll try to get it himself. Because if he and Lorne are both so eager for the silver we've yet to find . . ."

Now it was Beth whose cheeks washed pale. "And while they may at first have been willing to let the locals do the work and take the risks, if we seem to be dropping the ball—"

"Or worse, withholding information." Oliver felt his every muscle go tight. "Their threats could well be carried out."

"What, then?" Sheridan had picked up a whelk shell from one of the shelves and was passing it from one hand to the other. "Do we do, I mean? Let them find it and sell it to me so it's all over? And just have the constable on alert? In case they try to duke it out?"

Lady Emily frowned. "I beg your pardon, my lord, but I don't think it's that simple."

"Oh. Well. It is, though." He cleared his throat. "I'm afraid I'm the buyer."

But the lady was shaking her head. "Not to say I doubt you, but—but I've made it a point to overhear as much as I possibly can about this, given that I'm the one who brought it to their attention for Beth. And they have more than one buyer interested. I've heard them whispering about higher bids and an auction. They've made mention of an American."

"What?" The whelk went flying.

Telford, face placid, snatched it out of the air and slid it back onto the shelf.

Sheridan sputtered for a moment, then his face went positively ferocious. "New plan, then." His gaze moved to Beth, then to Oliver and Libby. "We find it first."

25

One month. One month to the day since that first Wednesday when it had all begun. When the man had found Libby on the beach and handed her the cannonball. One month since Oliver had knocked on her door and demanded to know where his sister was. One month that she'd called this cottage home.

How, in one little month, could her world have changed so fully? Libby trailed Beth through the cottage—hers, then theirs—toward the bedroom they'd both called their own. She'd known all along that someone else had stayed there before her. Many someones else. She'd known this was just a rented cottage that she'd spend a season in and then leave. But it hadn't felt strange before.

It did now, following a former occupant into the bedroom and watching as she knelt down in front of the chest of drawers, reached under it, and peeled something off the bottom of the drawer that had always stuck.

Beth's hand emerged with two pieces of paper. Or rather, one large piece of brown paper that closely matched the wood of the drawer, adhesive tape edging it. And a smaller piece of parchment that the paper had clearly been protecting.

A treasure map, hidden all this time beneath her stockings. Libby sank to a seat on the little desk chair while Beth flipped the parchment over and spread it on the top of the chest.

"If you've retrieved it, do bring it out here so the rest of us can see it, Beth," Oliver called. The gentlemen, of course, hadn't followed them into the bedroom. Which was good, because if they had, this whole situation would feel even more surreal, the place even less Libby's, despite all her things still taking up residence.

Or some of them. Nearly half her belongings were in her room at the Moons' now. And Darling had been curled up happily in Mrs. Moon's lap when they left, seeming to have adjusted rather well to his new mobile life. The only possession still in this room that shouted her ownership was the microscope at her elbow.

This wasn't really her room, wasn't really her life. But being here had made the world of London and Telford Hall seem so far away, so unattractive.

She glanced out the door, catching a glimpse of her brother. He hadn't said anything else about leaving—yet. Not while his best friend was set on finding a pirate treasure, not while Mamm-wynn was still largely unresponsive. But he would soon. He'd grant her a week, if she was lucky. It wasn't enough though. If a month had been enough time to make her think this was where she truly belonged, one more week wasn't enough to satisfy that yearning to curl into her place here. The rest of the summer wouldn't be either. She wanted to see autumn paint its colors over the heather and gorse. She wanted to note the birds that left, the others to come. She wanted to watch for seals and whales and who knew what else as winter winds danced around the islands. She wanted to see fresh life spring up again months before it did on the mainland, covering the fields in flowers that the locals would harvest and send inland.

"Are you coming?" Mabena's hand landed on her shoulder, her voice intruding softly.

Libby forced a smile but barely glanced away from the window she'd been staring out. "In a minute. Go on. I just need to memorize the view a bit more." Who knew when next she'd see it? She meant to stay on Tresco until Mamm-wynn was well. After which Bram would try to make her go home. Try to make her marry Sheridan, who still hadn't had the sense to object. And Mama would push for the same.

But what could she really do to argue? She had no means of her own with which to stay here—her inheritance was all tied to her dowry or held in trust by her brother. She was at the mercy of her family. Which had never been so bad before, but now . . .

She could hear her companions in the other room, their voices an odd collection she'd never expected to hear grouped together. Bram and Sheridan verbally jostled each other—probably as they physically jostled each other for the best view of the map.

"Easy, gentlemen." Beth sounded half-amused and half-impatient with them. "We can't even know for certain if it *is* a treasure map."

"But it has an *X*!" Sheridan's voice, other than being too deep, sounded exactly like a lad's on Christmas morning.

"There are no landmarks though, no outlines to give us a hint as to which island it is." Oliver, his tone contemplative. "How would we know where to begin or what it denotes? It could be leading anywhere. There isn't even a compass rose to tell us how to orient it."

"That was my concern too, hence why I've been using the copy I made of this original in a variety of locations. But up here in the corner—you'll see what looks like 'from the *John*.' And that *M* made me think Mucknell. And look here." A tapping, presumably as Beth pointed to something. "It says *cave*. Or maybe *cavern*—there's a bit of water damage here. Which means, if it's Scilly—"

"Piper's Hole." Mabena let loose a long breath. "On Tresco?"

"That was where I searched first, it being so near home. And I've looked several times since in the last month."

Oliver's huff might have been a laugh. Maybe. "Why do I have the feeling that if we noted when you'd been there, it would align with Enyon's sleepless nights?"

Beth sounded sheepish as she said, "I've tried to be quiet."

"Found nothing though, I assume?" Sheridan again, and the lad at Christmas had turned into one whose promise of his first fox hunt had been ruined by a downpour.

"No."

"What about the Piper's Hole here on St. Mary's?" Oliver again, though not so much musing as enlightened. "That's why you wanted to come here for the summer."

"Well, I couldn't just go poking around in the daytime. There are too many tourists about. I needed to be somewhere that I could easily do my exploring without anyone knowing. Though, again—nothing."

"All right. What about where you found the map? Not that you've told us that bit." Oliver seemed to be striving for patience in his tone, though she could hear its ragged edge. "Was there anything else in the same place that could be helpful?"

A beat of silence that spoke quite loudly. Louder than Beth's voice when next she spoke. "Letters. From Mucknell to his wife. One of them mentioned that he would send her a songbird as a gift. I thought it was code, since that last ship was the *Canary*."

"Secret codes. Perfect." The lad at Christmas was back. "And that was the one with the silver, yes?"

"Yes, but I couldn't find any other clues in the letters."

"Well, get them out! I mean, that is—you could. We could help?"

Beth sighed. "I don't have them here on St. Mary's. They're . . . back in the place where I found them. For safekeeping. But I'll fetch them later."

Libby really ought to go out and join them. And she did want to see the map—not that she'd have any better idea what it might be denoting than the locals did. And if it were water damaged, how could they even be sure they had all the necessary information? With a quiet sigh, she rested a finger on the mirror of the microscope and gave it a twirl. Light flashed over the walls, floor, ceiling. And into her mind.

Water damage—it would have washed away most of the ink. But not necessarily all of it. Just what was visible to the naked eye.

She surged to her feet, gripping the neck of her microscope. Maybe she *did* have something to offer. She hurried into the outer room and to the kitchen table around which the others all huddled. "I may be able to help!"

They turned to her, their varied expressions saying so much about them. Her brother—doubtful. Sheridan—surprised she was still there. Mabena—indulgent. Beth and Lady Emily—curious.

Oliver—perfectly confident in her.

She smiled and moved to the table, nudging Oliver out of the way so that she could capture the light from the window.

He didn't seem to mind. "Excellent thought, Libby. We may be able to see under magnification what we can't normally."

Bram, predictably, snarled. "*Libby?* Her name is Lady Eliz—"

"Really, Bram. Give it a rest." She sat in the chair Oliver held out for her and nudged the mirror until it caught the sunlight and angled it up through her eyepiece. The brilliance brought *Orfeo* springing up, but she'd only managed to hum the first four notes before Bram's snort of laughter silenced her. Clearing her throat, she looked up at Beth. "May I?"

Beth passed the map to her, and her fingers closed around the worn parchment. It certainly felt old, and it looked it too. Having never really studied maps, though, she found the markings on it more scribbles than intelligible clues. How were they to know what the lines meant, and the dashes, and the swirly bits?

They weren't relying on her to decode it though. Just to see if the parchment itself was hiding any other secrets. Praying her light was strong enough to help with that, she started in the corners that were intact and moved the parchment inch by inch to familiarize herself with how it looked.

"Well?" Sheridan.

Oliver chuckled. "Give her some time, my lord. I daresay she hasn't examined much parchment under magnification before. It'll take a bit of getting used to."

She would have paused to shoot Oliver a grateful smile if she hadn't just reached a portion that had some ink upon it. "How interesting."

"What?" Sheridan must have abandoned his chair while she set everything up, because he pushed Bram aside and crowded her left side. "What's interesting?"

"The ink. Under magnification, it's quite interesting. I can see where the iron-gall has rusted and turned brown and still make out a bit of the black base of it as well. And I can see the flow change with the pen strokes. Quite interesting indeed." She moved the map around, rolling the edges gently out of the way so she could trace the path of the long-ago pen.

"How is that helpful? Do you think?"

She sighed. "I said it was *interesting*, Lord Sheridan, not *helpful*. Although—that's odd." She frowned and pulled away, blinked, then lowered her head again. "Probably nothing. But . . ."

"But?"

She slid the map back to the lines that were, presumably, some sort of directions. And then once more to where *Cave* was scratched into the faded corner. "Maybe it's from the exposure to water?"

"*What* is?"

Really, how had her brother tolerated Sheridan for so long? She pulled away again, jumping at how close he was. He looked like he might shove her aside and peer through the eyepiece himself at any moment. Though at her scolding look, he inched away. A little. She cleared her throat. "The ink used on the word *cave* looks quite different from the drawing. It isn't half so rusty."

"Newer, then?" Oliver leaned against the table on her opposite side. "A later addition."

"How much newer?" Beth tapped a thoughtful finger to her lip. "Indication that it's been moved, do you think?"

"Or misdirection." Sheridan straightened. "History is full of those, you know."

They would have a better idea of that than she would, so she kept her attention on the parchment. Which was far more interesting than their conversation anyway. "Well now."

"What? Well what?" Sheridan really did nudge her aside this time and put his own eye to the eyepiece. "What am I looking at?"

Libby scooted her chair a few inches away and sent her brother an exasperated look.

Bram just smirked back at her. "You knew what he was like before you agreed to marry him."

Of all the . . . "I did *not* agree!"

Sheridan waved a hand in her direction. "Right, I know. I'm annoying and displace frogs. You don't want to marry me. All well and good, but what in the world am I *looking* at?"

Beth nearly choked on a laugh. "You displace frogs?"

"With his excavations—he destroys their habitats." Since he didn't appear to be uncrowding her any time soon, Libby stood, which just led to his stealing the chair too. "And you're looking at the parchment. It's been scraped in that section."

"Oh! So it has. That's what those fibers are, I expect. That's how they erased things, you know. Ink, from parchment. With a knife, I suppose."

Libby folded her arms over her chest. "Perhaps that's why I pointed it out."

He didn't seem to hear her mutter. "It does appear thinner there, and the scrape marks don't match the area around it. And what's this other bit? A shadow or . . ."

"Well, I don't know. Someone stole my microscope from me before I could look any further." She didn't honestly expect that to garner any more of a response.

But he pulled back, stood, and waved to her chair with a sheepish grin. "Sorry. Almost. You might need to magnify it more—I daresay if I fiddled with any of the thingamabobs, I might find myself without fingers."

"Smart man." Bram looked far too amused.

Libby huffed and took her seat. She immediately saw what had grabbed his attention, on the side where the water damage began. It could well just be where the ink had washed over it. Or perhaps something more. She adjusted her lens to a higher magnification. And gasped.

"What!" Sheridan sounded frantic, but this time she'd fight him for the eyepiece if she must.

"Another word." She nudged the mirror just a bit, smiling when the extra light shone through. "Yes. It looks like *c-a*—"

"Cave again?" Beth this time.

Oliver sighed. "Let her finish." His hand settled on her shoulder, which was no doubt infuriating Bram. But it also told her that he knew she was on to something, and he trusted her to decipher whatever it was.

"Not *cave*. It looks like—an *f*. But then . . . *t*? That doesn't seem right."

"*F* or *s*, do you think?" Oliver's fingers tightened on her shoulder. "Historically, an *s* in the middle of a word looks more like our *f* now."

And when he made the suggestion, it didn't irritate her at all, just made victory swell in her chest. "Oh, quite right! I'd forgotten that. Definitely an *s* then, making this . . . *castle*."

For a moment, silence descended as she straightened and looked at those gathered round. Then an utter cacophony erupted as everyone started talking at once. Libby stood again, her gaze seeking Oliver's. "How many castles are there, exactly, in the Scillies?"

"Three." He looked much like Beth had when he tapped a thoughtful finger to his lips. "Star Castle here on St. Mary's. Then King Charles's castle and Cromwell's castle on Tresco."

That was a lot of crumbling stone to look through. "How do we know which one Mucknell had a connection with?"

"We don't." Yet he smiled. "But I know who would."

She smiled. "To Tresco then, to visit Tas-gwyn Gibson."

———○———

The evening was one of the finest they'd yet enjoyed that summer, the sun lingering long, the breeze warm and gentle, the temperature perfect. Oliver hated to spend such an evening inside, but he'd been a bit surprised when the entire company took him up on his offer to enjoy their pudding in the garden.

There they all were though, laughing and arguing over the letters Beth had somehow produced, though he hadn't even noticed her slipping away to reclaim them, with his flowers as a backdrop. Evidence, undoubtedly, that her secret hiding place was somewhere nearby.

Oliver drew in a long, fragrant breath and leaned against the stone wall at the garden's edge. Mabena had bowed out of dinner with them. She'd said it was because she'd had enough of the bickering and didn't imagine their lordships really wanted to dine with a lowly former lady's maid . . . but Oliver suspected it was more because she meant to accept the Wearnes' invitation to join *them* for the evening meal. Lady Emily hadn't come over from St. Mary's with them either, which meant it was just Beth and Libby, Sheridan and Telford sitting there now, debating whether they ought to trust Tas-gwyn Gibson's advice and try King Charles's castle first.

The girls both agreed they'd better. The gents were less than willing to trust his grandfather's instincts.

Oliver had already weighed in on Tas-gwyn's side, and he didn't imagine any further argument from him would achieve anything, so he'd gotten up to stretch his legs and come to see how his fuchsias were faring. Though instead of checking their leaves, he found himself just watching the four across the garden.

All right, mostly the one. His gaze kept returning over and again to Libby, as it always did and certainly had been doing all evening. They'd dressed for dinner—though he rather enjoyed the more casual meals he and Mamm-wynn had been having in Beth's absence—which meant that for only the second time, he was beholding Libby in something other than a simple skirt and blouse. And while he appreciated her practical choices and loved that she fit so well with all his neighbors, he had to admit that seeing her in soft color that draped her form, her hair swept up, pretty much guaranteed that he couldn't think of much other than her.

She was as lovely as the blossoms that surrounded her.

She looked his way, a soft smile curling her lips, and murmured something that he couldn't hear from here. No one paid her any mind anyway as they continued to debate whether the drawn map matched the sketch of the castle's layout that his grandfather had unearthed. Libby slipped from her chair and meandered in his general direction, though she paused at the rosebush for a long moment until her brother turned back to Beth and Sheridan.

Oliver met her in front of the thatch anchor and had to clasp his hands behind his back to keep from reaching for hers. "You've proven yourself quite the heroine of the day with your microscope discoveries."

She waved that away, though her eyes still smiled. "We'll see tomorrow if it was any help at all, I suppose. Do you think we'll be able to obtain permission to search the castle grounds?"

He tamped down a grin. "The general wisdom is that what the Lord Proprietor doesn't know about, he can't refuse permission for."

She chuckled. "A fine philosophy for exploring children or tourists—though I'm not so certain it's the best one for the vicar and the headmaster to ascribe to."

"Even so, the Lord Proprietor and I are on good terms. As long as we don't destroy anything, I can't imagine he'll mind. And unless we mean to send a telegram asking for permission or wait for him to get home next month . . ."

"That would suit me fine." She grinned up at him. "If I could convince Bram to let me stay until we saw it through to completion."

If he thought they could keep Lorne and Scofield at bay, he might agree. But he had a knot in his spirit that just wouldn't loosen whenever he thought of them. They wouldn't sit around much longer, waiting for someone else to deliver them what they were after. Not with a second buyer promising Scofield money and the rivalry spurring Lorne on. Oliver had met men like these before—men who would stop at nothing to get the upper hand in whatever they were doing. Men who took the kind of petty tension he'd always had with Casek and magnified it more powerfully than Libby's microscope could do.

Thoughts of Casek brought other thoughts, ones that made that knot cinch tighter. "Lorne hired a local lad before. I suspect he'd do it again—and we can't let anyone else get tangled up in this." The people of Tresco, of all the Scillies, were his responsibility. In part, anyway. And he didn't want to be officiating any more funerals because of this.

"I know." She rested warm fingers on his arm.

She did know. Libby wasn't the sort who would ever put her own desires above another's well-being. Just another reason he couldn't stop looking at her. He smiled down into her eyes, wishing and praying. They hadn't had nearly enough time together to make it seem reasonable to do something like propose. Especially not when she still had a few questions to answer for herself about the Lord—never mind the brother.

"Libby, hadn't you better go in and sit with Mrs. Tremayne for a bit so I can walk you home at a decent hour?"

Or perhaps *not* never mind the brother. He seemed set on making himself a problem. They broke their gazes away from each other to look up at the shadowed face of Lord Telford.

Oliver's gaze darted past him, and he frowned. "Where are my sister and Lord Sheridan?"

"On their way to the library in the hopes of settling an argument with the help of a book." Not that Telford so much as met his gaze when he answered. He kept his eyes trained on his sister, and it was no wonder she'd always found the weight of it intimidating. "Go on. She's your reason for wanting to stay, isn't she? And you need to collect your cat from her bedside, regardless."

Her shoulders rolled back, making Oliver think for a moment that she meant to argue. But then she sighed. "I do want to spend some time with her this evening—and Mabena took far too long on my hair to allow me to slip in before supper."

"Go on, then." Telford's voice had gentled, and he even gave her a smile. "Take your time."

She hesitated a second more and then sighed again. "Good night, Oliver."

"Good night." He watched her until she had the door open, though he knew what came next wouldn't bode well for him.

Shockingly, when he turned back to Telford, he found his face absent of the mask of thunder. It was instead open. Frank. And far too worried. "I don't mean to be an ogre," he said in what must be his normal voice, rather than the one set on intimidating him. "It's just—you're a vicar. And she doesn't even have any use for God."

A perfectly reasonable objection, really. If it were true. Oliver drew in a long breath. "I don't think I'd have any use for the version of God she's been taught either."

Telford frowned. "Pardon?"

"A god who supposedly created a world we cannot understand, yet who himself can be handily put in a little box and tucked into my pocket?" Oliver shook his head. "Our Lord is the opposite of that. He has created a universe of order and rules—but He himself is so much bigger. So full of mystery. Your sister is coming to understand that, I think. And when she does, I have a feeling she'll realize she not only has a *use* for God, but the greatest need of Him."

The fact that Telford didn't immediately respond told him he was letting the words sink in. Still, he sighed. "Even so. Forgive me for having pried, but I know your family spent their fortune on your brother's physicians. I'm not judging you for it." He lifted his hands as if to ward off Oliver's defense—not that he'd intended to make one. "I would have done the same. I'd have paid anything to keep my father with us longer. But still, I have to consider it. Consider what's best for her."

Oliver respected that. But . . . He swallowed, though it did nothing to relieve his tight throat. "And you think that's Lord Sheridan? Despite the fact that they don't even like each other?"

"I think they respect each other, which is frankly more than I can say for any other acquaintance she's made. He wouldn't try to change her. He wouldn't forbid her from being who she is or take her microscope away or grow angry when she resists going to London."

"But accepting and appreciating are vastly different, my lord." His fingers curled into his palm. "And she deserves more than just being tolerated. She deserves to be loved."

334

"At what cost?" Telford cast a critical eye over his gardens and the house Oliver loved so much. "Perhaps she thinks she likes it here, but it's a novelty. How quickly would it begin to chafe when you couldn't afford to buy her new slides or books or allow her to travel?"

He didn't mean to bristle. But he wasn't as broke as all that. "Don't presume to know my ledgers so well, my lord. But even so—I think you underestimate your sister."

Telford blinked at him, shook his head. "I've known her for twenty years. You've known her for a month."

"And Lord Willsworth has had only a few conversations with her, yet I imagine if he came to you seeking your blessing, you'd give it. And why? Because he's titled? Wealthy? Do you really suppose those things will make her happy?"

Rather than answer, Telford studied him for a long moment. Not with the immediate dismissal he'd looked upon him with before, or with the disdain he'd lavished upon him since. He seemed, for the first time, to be trying to gauge the sort of man he was. Then he drew in a long breath and straightened his shoulders. "Again, I don't mean to be an ogre. But she's my sister, and I have to protect her. You understand that."

"Of course I do."

"So then. You know it's with her best interests in mind that I say this, not because I have any particular dislike for you." He took a step back, lifted his chin, and looked suddenly the earl, not just the big brother. "If you propose to her, and if she says yes, she won't get a penny of Telford money. No dowry. No monthly allowance."

A perfectly logical threat meant to dissuade him if he were only interested in her because of the windfall she could bring him. "Understandable. But would you cut her off emotionally as well?"

Telford's brows slammed down. "I beg your pardon?"

Oliver buried his hands in his trouser pockets. "I'm perfectly capable of providing for a wife. But I would never want to be responsible for causing a rift in your family. And so I ask if all you would withhold is your financial support, or if you'd also refuse to speak to her. To visit her? To allow her communication with your mother?"

"I hadn't given it any thought."

Because he hadn't thought it would be an issue. He'd thought the moment Oliver learned she wouldn't come with a dowry he'd lose interest. He'd thought, seeing the size of his house and knowing of the bills that had once stacked up on his desk, that he could be categorized quite simply as a money-grubber.

Oliver lifted his brows. "Well, think about it, if you would, my lord. Because I'm in love with your sister. I think she could be quite happy living here, but I *don't* think she could be happy without you and your mother in her life. So, if you intend to take that away, then I won't speak up. I'd rather lose her than let her lose you."

Telford would be wondering if it was a ploy. A play. A bid for his respect that would lead him to relent on the monetary side as well.

But it wasn't. And the more he considered it, the more he'd surely see that. Because all he'd have to do was say a few words, and Oliver had just promised never to declare himself. He had nothing to gain here but Libby herself. And everything—absolutely *everything* to lose.

26

Our Lord is the opposite of that. He has created a universe of order and rules—but He himself is so much bigger. So full of mystery."

The words kept replaying in Libby's mind as she held Mamm-wynn's hand in her own. She hadn't *meant* to catch that exchange between Bram and Oliver, but how was she supposed to have closed the door when she'd heard her brother state so baldly that she had no use for God? When she'd been so shocked at hearing the words from his lips that she couldn't help but hold the door an inch open to hear Oliver's response to it?

When the question of whether he was right pounded ferociously at her heart?

How had he even known that? She'd never breathed a word of her doubts to anyone at home. Never given voice to her questions, not until she came here. She hadn't wanted to disappoint Mama by asking such things, and Bram—she didn't frankly know how Bram felt about matters of faith.

She has no use for God.

Libby rested her forehead on Mamm-wynn's hand, not sure why that statement made her eyes burn. But it wasn't exactly true. Not given the words Oliver had spoken, which *were*. Perhaps she saw no point to the version of God she'd been taught since childhood, the one who was himself limited to the point of being boring, who wanted only obedience to a set of strict rules and for His children never to question Him. The one who was at war with science and the evolution of human thinking and who demanded one choose between faith and knowledge.

But how could she go on thinking that really was what God was like when she'd seen something far different since coming here? She'd closed the door after that reply from Oliver, but his words had followed her up the stairs and into Mamm-wynn's room.

"How did you know?" she whispered, turning her face a bit so she could look at the lady's. "How did you know where Beth was? How did you know to send Oliver to St. Mary's a month ago? To bring me a shawl, to lend me a necklace? How did you know that we'd . . . ?" She couldn't finish that sentence—because Mamm-wynn was wrong about that part. Perhaps Libby had fallen in love with Oliver, but that didn't mean he'd want to marry her. Why would he, when she, with all her questions, would make such a terrible vicar's wife? Bram was right. She wasn't good enough for the Reverend Mr. Tremayne. She couldn't be what he needed.

Something brushed her head, and she started before realizing Mamm-wynn had lifted her other hand, that she was stroking her fingers weakly over Libby's hair. Her eyes blinked open too, and the corners of her mouth had moved up a few precious degrees. "The veil."

"Pardon?" Perhaps Darling's loud purring from where he was curled up at the lady's shoulder had garbled Libby's hearing. Or perhaps these first words she'd spoken in days were disoriented, confused. But she'd spoken! That was worth shouting about. And Libby would shout it, in a minute. She'd go for Oliver and Beth and let them know. Once she could tear her gaze away from Mamm-wynn's.

Because it didn't look confused and unfocused as it had been. It looked piercing. And yet soft. Like a shaft of light. "The veil is slipping," she whispered. "The one between worlds. As it did for Grandmama."

Though Libby didn't know exactly what she meant, she knew she didn't like the sound of it. It sounded far too much like death. "Don't talk so. You're going to get well."

"Yes." Her lips curled higher. "I will, for a while. But these old eyes are seeing different truths now. Different facts."

Libby shook her head. "I don't understand. There is only one set of facts."

"Is there?" That fairylike chuckle slipped into the room, made Darling shift, curl into a new position even closer to Mamm-wynn, and redouble his purring. "Is that what your microscope has shown you?"

She opened her mouth but then paused. "It shows me that what I assume is sometimes wrong. That what my eye sees is only a partial story."

"Exactly so." Mamm-wynn nodded, her eyes slipping closed again, though only for a moment. "As our eyes always do in this world. We see only in part. But there is more. More to this physical world that your magnifying lenses can show you. And more still beyond it that we need a spiritual lens to see."

Her chest went tight. "The mysteries."

"How an old woman can know where her granddaughter is hiding." Mamm-wynn's fingers drifted back down to rest on the bedcover. "How sometimes the future can be whispered into our hearts. How one Man's blood can take away our sins."

The tightness was different this time than what she usually experienced. Not the anxious squeezing that made her stomach ache. But the kind she felt when Oliver looked at her. The kind she'd known when Mabena had called her *friend*. The kind that had seized her when Mama and Bram presented her with the microscope last Christmas, proving not only that they knew her but that they loved her as she was.

The kind that spoke of truth beyond facts. Of the spirit beneath the cells of her body. Of a God who called her by name and made a place for her in this world where she was allowed to explore it. Of a Son who did the miraculous, the impossible, so that she might live after those cells returned to dust—and so that she might love beyond all reason in the interim, knowing that's where true treasure lay.

That really was the mystery. Not how a plant grew or whether a comet was a chartable phenomenon or a harbinger of supernatural destruction. Those they could learn about and come to understand, as Oliver had said. But how sins could be forgiven, how Jesus could have taken them upon himself with death and then come to life again, how they could somehow partake of a world beyond the physical one she so loved . . . those were the things that belonged to faith. Those were the things science couldn't answer, and didn't need to.

Why, then, had so many people focused on the wrong side of things and taught it to her? Why was the miracle of Christ presented as something simple, something easy, something to be taken for granted and not even thought about overmuch, while so much attention was given to arguing about the things they could easily discover with a telescope or microscope? It seemed to her that there were mysteries enough to contemplate about the divine nature of God and Christ to keep one busy for a lifetime—just as there were things enough to learn about their world through observation, which didn't need to be debated so much as explored.

She'd thought she had to choose one or the other. That she couldn't have both faith in what she couldn't see and understanding of what she could. That if what she learned of the world didn't agree with the things she'd been taught to believe, she must choose between belief and observation. Why had it never occurred to her that the problem wasn't with the beliefs, as Oliver had said, but with the interpretation? That God was bigger than man's finite understanding of Him and of His Word? That it was people, not the Lord, who tried to make her choose?

"There now." The hand she held squeezed her fingers, relaxed again. "I knew you would see. A heart like yours that wants to understand the world around her cannot help but see when it goes earnestly looking."

"I think I'd been afraid to look too closely. Afraid I couldn't accept the answers—that God would demand I accept this world on faith *that* it works and never ask *how* it does."

Mamm-wynn chuckled and let her eyes slide shut again. "But then there are the Daniels in history—the ones who make their fame with both prophetic visions and earthly knowledge. They can be your model. Your hope."

"You're very wise, Mamm-wynn." Libby leaned over and pressed a kiss to her cheek. "I see where Oliver gets it."

That the lens of the spirit was to faith what her microscope was to the world—that was a thought that brought unspeakable peace to her mind. More, it was one that made her crave *both* lenses—the physical and the spiritual. Knowing God didn't mind her understanding the one made her long to know more about the other.

"Will you sing to me?" Mamm-wynn's eyes were closed fully again, and she repositioned herself a bit against her pillow. "It's been so long since I've heard you."

Had she ever? In church, perhaps. But then, Mamm-wynn didn't seem to be limited by what Libby remembered as the past. A mystery she could either call madness or accept as a part of this woman she'd so quickly come to love. "What would you like to hear? A hymn?"

"Mm . . . no." She sighed and nestled deeper. "An aria. Beth will never sing me those—she hates opera. Silly girl."

"So does Bram. He always makes fun of me when I sing them. Or maybe it's because I'm not all that good."

"I love to hear you." Mamm-wynn gave her a small, tired smile. "Sing '*L'amour est un oiseau rebelle.*'"

"One of my favorites. I always sing it when—"

"When you're painting. I know."

She could sit here wondering how, when Libby had never admitted that to a soul here, or she could give her this simple gift she asked for. She chose the second option, launching into a quiet rendition of her favorite song from *Carmen*.

"Love is a wild bird that no one can tame, and you'll waste your time trying to catch it." She'd always loved the first verse. It was no wonder it sprang to mind when she was painting, given how often birds were her subjects.

And how true those words were. Love really *was* like a bird. You didn't know where it might settle, or when. You couldn't tame it, couldn't force it. Couldn't often predict it. You could call and call for it and never would it flutter down. Then, at the most unexpected time, in the most unexpected place, there it was.

Here it was.

By the time she finished, Mamm-wynn had fallen asleep again. For a moment she felt guilty that she'd monopolized her entire waking and hadn't told the lady's grandchildren that she'd spoken, responded, seemed like her usual self, just tired. But she'd go and let them know now.

She scooped Darling into her arms and turned, jumping a bit when she saw Oliver leaning into the doorframe, Bram a step behind him. She expected her brother to give her his usual sigh over the opera or joke about her torturing an ill old woman with it. But he didn't. He didn't say anything.

Neither did Oliver. He just tracked her approach with that watchful look of his, and when she paused in front of him, he looked deep into her eyes. No doubt seeing, because he was Oliver, all the thoughts that had settled. All the peace that had taken the place of the questions inside her. The fresh yearning to learn more about the beyond, as well as the here and now.

And he smiled.

---○---

Mabena turned her face toward the rising sun and let it warm her. She breathed in the scents of salt and sand and sea. Felt the smooth wood of the oars in her hands, the firm seat beneath her. The pull of the water against the paddle. Birds called out to each other, chattering about where the fish were swimming and what predators circled above, no doubt. From the distance came the fading shout of a fisherman.

Home.

"We could just stay right here for the next few hours. I could look at you longer."

Casek's soft voice made her smile and face him again. She'd slipped from the house with the first fingers of dawn on the horizon to meet him on the beach, so they'd have time for a nice row before their days began. She could begin every day like this and be happy.

Well. She'd be even happier after they married. When first she'd wake beside him, and *then* they'd head for the gig, hands entwined. It was a dream that had rooted itself in the bedrock of her soul over the last week. "Somehow, my love, I don't think the world would stop if we did. And I don't think either of us would be happy to let it pass us by—not today."

But Casek didn't dip in his oars again yet. Just kept on looking at her. "I don't care a whit about pirate treasure or princes or maps or silver."

"No." He didn't. That had never been what drove this man forward, brought his fists up, or inspired his world. He wasn't the sort to ever leave her for the pursuit of more. How had she not seen that years ago? That all his volume and bluster were just the waves crashing against the sturdy rock of him. He was the steady one. It was just that, in the Scillies, steady meant storms and waves and winds as much as sunshine and blue skies. "But you care about the lads who have been poking about looking for it."

He sighed and looked to the shore, hands gripping the oars again now. "We lose so many of them. To the mainland. To the sea. To hard living. We can't lose more to this, Benna."

"Which is why we're going to put a stop to it. Today." They dipped their oars in unison, their stretching forms mirror images, since they faced each other.

His face was still clouded though. "I don't know that we *can* stop it entirely. Not if these are just hirelings here now. More will be sent. More lads lured into treasure hunting. More skulls knocked in when they don't deliver what the gentlemen want."

"You think he can't be trusted? Lord Sheridan?"

Casek screwed up his face in dismissal. "Not him. The ones from London, the family of Beth's friend. Them I don't trust. Not if they mean to double-cross Sheridan. He may have his head in the clouds of legend, but I think he's harmless enough. This Scofield bloke though . . ."

"Or whoever he hired. And Lorne." They'd asked around about him last night, while the ladies and gents were having their fancy dinner at Oliver and Beth's house. Settled themselves down at the pub with Tas-gwyn Gibson, who was more than happy to lend a hand. Apparently, when Sheridan had shared what he knew of Lorne yesterday, her grandfather had been convinced he was the one who'd knocked him upside the head on Monday. He had a vague recollection of seeing a little dinghy that he recognized as one the Morrises had rented out for the summer, and of hearing a voice behind him curse in a rough London accent.

They still couldn't be certain if it had been Lorne or the Scofields' lackey that had knocked *her* head in Piper's Hole, but they'd learned more than Mabena had hoped. More than she wished were true. A few islanders had ferried Lorne about here and there until he'd rented that boat for himself, all of them reporting that he seemed keen on learning every facet and rock and crevice on all the islands.

Not that the islanders had told Lorne much—they all had a healthy distrust of incomers whose interests went beyond mere curiosity—but they couldn't exactly stop him from exploring. And they'd been seeing him for weeks, here and there. No one was certain where he was staying. Some thought St. Mary's, others Bryher, others still reported seeing him here on Tresco late enough at night that he couldn't have meant to leave.

Bad news, all of it.

But they'd come up with their own plan to keep Casek's students safe from Lorne's influence. One that wouldn't interfere with the scheduled search of King Charles's castle later today.

"There they are." She nodded to the beach by the Hills' little house, where Perry and the Grimsby boys were even now stealing down the sand toward Mr. Hill's old rowboat. Just as Casek had overheard them planning to do yesterday—to sneak over to Piper's Hole this morning.

Casek had said he'd debated trying to talk them out of it, letting them know he'd heard their plans. Perhaps even warning them away from Lorne directly. But it wasn't so long ago that Casek had been a boy just like them. He'd known that forbidding a thing would only make it more alluring. So instead they'd decided to put themselves here, now.

Enough morning mist hovered over the water to help their voices carry. "That's what Beth said." She recited her agreed-upon line to get them started, turning her head a little to send the words toward the lads, though careful to keep her eyes trained solely on Casek, who didn't so much as glance toward the shoreline.

"I know she's the one who found what silver's been found," he added. "But Samson? Makes no sense."

As they'd hoped, the boys had ducked down beneath the hull of the boat. But they'd be listening. "She says it's where she found the treasure map." It wasn't. She'd yet to say *where* she'd found what she did—an omission that hadn't slipped by Mabena. "She probably has the rest of the crate in whatever cottage she'd been staying in."

"Maybe. But do you really think we can convince her to send it to the Scofields?"

"We have to. If we don't, she could be in danger." They'd debated this tack, too, and decided it was the most likely to convince the boys. "We need to find it, get it to them. If she's too stubborn to save her own skin, we'll save it for her." They'd probably not believe that Mabena meant to undermine her cousin for the sake of silver. But for her own good? Anyone would believe that.

And if they could convince them to go to Samson this morning instead of Piper's Hole, that ought to keep them safely out of the way.

They continued their northward row and their fabricated discussion until they were unquestionably out of the boys' hearing and the caves were within view. They turned into one of the smaller ones, stowing their boat out of sight behind a boulder and scrambling into the small opening. They'd watch a few minutes and make certain the lads didn't still come by and go to Piper's Hole. Inspiring them not to was better—but they'd resort to command if they must.

She turned with a grin to Casek, though he'd not be able to see it in the shadows. "I still can't believe the headmaster has resorted to fibbing to his students."

A beam of light blinded her from deeper within, accompanied by a click that echoed ominously off the rocks. "And *I*," said a clipped London voice she'd hoped never to hear again, "can't believe two such fine prizes wandered in here of their own volition."

"Lorne?" Casek stepped between Mabena and the light, an arm reaching behind him to steady her. "That's your name, isn't it?"

"Ain't you a clever one."

She balled her hands into Casek's shirt to keep from doing anything stupid. They could just slip back out. They'd have to be faster than him, but they knew the caves—that was in their favor. And a moving target would be harder for him to hit than a still one. "It was you on Sunday, then? But I thought it the Scofields' man we were coming to meet."

The rocks and water took his chuckle and distorted it. "You don't know half as much as you think you do, luv. Now. Do as I say, and I won't have to kill either of you. Turn around. Slowly. Hands where I can see them."

Mabena's muscles coiled as they turned back to face the opening. They could make a run for it, scamper over the rocks and back to the boat.

Casek half-turned his face. And murmured in Cornish, "Do as he says."

"But—"

"I can't risk losing you, Benna. Not again. Not for good." She'd never heard his voice so low and tight. His words drifted back to English. "No more lives. It's not worth it."

"See, and on *that*"—Lorne must have prodded at Casek, given his quiet grunt—"we'll just have to disagree."

27

Libby sneaked one more peek around the crumbling stone wall, willing Mabena to appear as she was supposed to do. It didn't seem right to be here without her, keeping a lookout for *her* instead of the tourists she'd been charged with watching for and dissuading from coming up the path through the heather.

Though how she was meant to do that she still wasn't certain. She'd breathed a sigh of relief when the mist had rolled in thicker instead of burning off. With a bit of luck, it would keep holiday-goers inside for a few hours.

"Stop fretting." Bram slid an arm around her shoulders and gave them a squeeze. "Moon is fine. No doubt she's just whiling the day away with her beau."

Oliver's brows looked every bit as pinched as hers felt, and had ever since she arrived at his door without his cousin. He finished rolling up his sleeves and bent to pick up the gardener's shovel he'd brought with him. "I'm inclined to agree with the worry. Casek always tends school business on Saturday mornings and would never miss a day of work."

Bram lowered his arm. "I know you're friends, Tremayne—"

"Ha!" Beth strode by them into the center of the ruins, turning a circle with the map held up before her. "If my brother has an enemy, it's Casek Wearne. They may have declared a truce for Mabena's sake, but a few days of not threatening to sock each other in the nose does not a friend make."

Oliver rolled his eyes. "I *have* missed your optimistic outlook, Elizabeth Grace. Thank you for your vote of confidence in my ability to make peace."

"I didn't say it was *you* I doubted." She turned another twenty degrees. Looked up. Narrowed her eyes. "What do you think, Ollie? Should we align it this way? It's one of the only things in sight that could be our 'north.'" She pointed through an opening that was squared off, through which the tower of Cromwell's castle came and went through the mist.

Sheridan had a second shovel in his hands and looked as though he'd be happy to start digging absolutely anywhere. "Lovely view. But does it work? I mean, if we make it north? Do any of the walls line up with the lines?"

Libby almost wished Tas-gwyn had recommended they try Cromwell's castle first. It looked more properly castle-like, positioned on the water's edge as it was, its main tower bringing stories of princesses and dragons to mind.

She drew her lip between her teeth and reached into her pocket, where she'd stashed the piece of paper she'd read over and again that morning. Beth's unfinished fairy tale had been niggling at the back of her mind all week. She'd meant to ask her for an explanation first thing, but worry for Mabena had taken over the conversation.

She pulled out her copy now though and glanced at it again.

Once upon a time, there was a princess. She lived on an island of rocks and bones, with no one to keep her company aside from the fairies. All her life she'd danced with them to the tunes they played on their magical pipes, the tunes echoed by deep voices from the rock itself. One day, however, the music stopped.

The princess, concerned for her fay friends, set out to find them, only to discover that every fairy on the island had vanished. Far and

wide she searched, high and low. In the treetops she found no friends
. . . but there was a house in the boughs she'd never seen before, one
made of wood creaking and ancient, bearing the name of the fairy
king over its lintel. In the pools she found no friends . . . but there was
glinting metal winking up at her from the depths, the very shade of
the fairies' eyes. Not to be tempted, the princess pushed onward. In
the forest glens she found a wonder that dazzled her eyes. Trees with
fragrant bark peeling in fairy-wing curls. Crocuses with petals like
fairy gowns. Purple-spiked flowers like fairy crowns. But none of her
friends were there.

She kept on, toward the far-looming mountain from whence it was
said that all fairies came. But the closer she drew to the rugged rocks,
the heavier her feet grew. And the louder came the voices that used to
sing along with the fairies' pipes. The very bones were singing, inviting
her to sing with them. She knew, though, that to give in—to sing that
song—would mean becoming naught but bone herself.

So heavy were her feet by the time she climbed up the first rock
that she could scarcely go any farther, and the winds blew cold now
against her. Shivering, the princess tucked herself into a cleft of the
rock and cried for her lost friends.

Still, the voices sang. "Look to the birds," they chanted over and
again. "Look to the birds, Lizza." The princess tilted back her head
and watched an eagle soar overhead. But no help came for her from
his widespread wings.

The story was linked to this as much as the poems had been, she
was certain. Her current guess was that it included the items from the
manifests that she'd been tasked with finding. "Trees with fragrant
bark peeling in fairy-wing curls"—that could be cinnamon, a popular
spice to be imported. The others could be saffron and turmeric. Saffron came from crocuses. And turmeric was gotten from the root of
a plant that was topped with a spiky purple flower.

But parts of it she still hadn't been able to decipher. And there was
no time like the present to clear up the mystery. "Beth? The notes you
had in *Treasure Island* . . ."

Beth's cheeks went pink as she darted a glance at her brother. "Yes?"

"What was the fairy tale?"

Sheridan spun, eyes gleaming. "Oh, are the fairies involved too? Piping from the cave, perhaps? Yes?"

Beth tried turning the map upside down. "It was just a story I made up to catalogue my findings. A princess—me—who lived on an island of rock and bones. The rocks of Tresco—and the bones of the Jolly Roger. Mucknell."

As she'd imagined. "So, the journey in the story was the treasure hunt. The piping and songs represent Piper's Hole. And each of the things the princess finds are symbols of what you were searching for. But what was the bit at the end? The song about looking toward the birds?"

"Oh." Beth frowned. "That was just something from those letters. Didn't you notice? He'd concluded them all with 'Look to the birds, Lizza.'"

No *wonder* the fairy tale had been haunting her! How had she not made the connection immediately? "Look to the birds." Libby met Oliver's gaze, brows up. And then, together, they turned to the east. Toward St. Martin's and the birds that flocked there. Had *always* flocked there, most likely. Because two hundred fifty years wasn't enough to change the migratory and nesting patterns, not on an island that hadn't otherwise changed, where the few residents still lived now as they had then. "This is your north."

Beth didn't seem to follow their reasoning, given the question in her eyes, but she turned too, and held up the map again. She made an interested-sounding hum. "You know, that squiggle almost *looks* like a bird. It doesn't align north to the top of the paper though."

"Don't put it past a pirate to write sideways on his map." Sheridan grinned and turned with the rest of them. "Let's say it *is* a bird. So it's the way to hold the map. How do we know? What we should be facing with it, I mean?"

"St. Martin's! Of *course*." Beth laughed and shoved the map at

Sheridan, who took it eagerly. "We'll assume that square shape at the base is the window that most directly faces St. Martin's. Here." She ran to the remains of a window and patted the stone.

"To your right next then."

Libby trailed behind as Beth led them along the east-facing wall, along what might have once been a rampart before the top levels had fallen in. They turned at the corner, scurried over a low bit of wall, and struck off down the hill. Libby, Oliver, and Bram hurried to catch up.

"Are you ever going to tell us where you found the map, Beth?" Oliver called after his sister.

She made no answer.

"If the key to knowing how to use it was in a letter to his wife, as was the message about treasure from the *Canary*, with that songbird reference," Libby mused as she jumped down from the wall with the aid of Oliver's hand, "then it has to have been somewhere Mrs. Mucknell would have known to find it. Probably not, for instance, in a cave."

Bram snorted a laugh. "You mean most ladies don't go climbing about in caves? What a novel concept."

"You do have a point, Libby," Oliver said. "Perhaps not in her care exactly, since she never hunted it up herself. But a place she'd have easy access to, if she knew to look for it. The church, maybe. The garrison."

She came to a halt. "Their house."

Oliver stopped too, staring at her for a moment with another *of course* look on his face. And then burst into a run. "Beth! Tas-gwyn's? So you fetched the letters while we were there!"

His sister wasn't paying him any heed though. She and Sheridan had arrived at another outcropping of stones whose original purpose Libby couldn't discern, and they'd fallen to their knees behind it. "Shovel!" she shouted.

Oliver delivered it into Beth's hands—she certainly didn't look inclined to move out of the way and let him do the digging for her.

Bram heaved a long breath and leaned against a different piece of wall. "You might as well make yourselves comfortable." As if to prove it, he reached into his pocket, pulled out a bag of chocolate drops, and held it out to them. "Don't let their initial excitement fool you. Sheridan can dig for hours—days—not find anything, and still be convinced he's in the right place, or just a *few* inches off."

"Inches make all the difference, you know." A clod of earth flew up from where Sheridan's voice came. "Off by one and you find nothing."

Hours? Days? Libby reached into the sack and pulled out a chocolate. "We don't have that long."

"We'll have as long as we need." Oliver accepted a chocolate, too, and turned to the sea. "The Lord didn't bring us all together just so that we'd fail."

Bram lifted a sardonic brow. "Does he always speak so?"

Libby smiled. "Yes."

"And you don't find it off-putting? Or ridiculous?"

"Actually, no. I find it . . . encouraging. And something to emulate."

She was rewarded with Oliver shooting her a smile.

"There's something here!" Beth's voice came more quietly than Libby would have expected, almost reverently.

"Probably a stone." Bram shook the bag of chocolates and peered inside. He took a full minute, sometimes, picking the perfect one. Though what made one perfect in that moment, she couldn't say, since he'd end up devouring them all within an hour, each selected with the same ridiculous care.

"Wood, actually."

Sheridan's clarification didn't stir Bram from his study. "An old timber, then. Careful you don't bring some ancient foundation caving in around you, prodding at its support as you probably are."

"It isn't a timber. The size of the planks is all wrong," Beth said.

Libby moved closer, her curiosity outweighing any Bram-inspired doubt that they could have possibly found something so quickly.

They'd dug down only about a foot, and the hole was only a few inches wide. Given how they crowded the hole, she couldn't see much past them, but they were working rather efficiently now—Sheridan loosening the sod with a practiced shovel, picking it up like a square of green carpet, Beth going in underneath and moving the dirt into a neat pile. Soon, enough was visible that Libby could see what Beth had meant about the plank size. This was definitely no ancient timber—it was slender planking, thin, with the wood rotted by soil and moisture enough that the shovels could probably crack it away.

"Look." Beth breathed the word with awe and rocked back onto her knees so they could peer over her shoulder.

It looked like a crate. One with *Mucknell* branded across the top.

Libby gripped Oliver's arm. "It's actually there. Right there."

Bram, chocolate now in his mouth, moved to her other side. "Probably filled with nails. Lead shot. Moldy clothing—"

"Do shut up, Telly." Sheridan scraped more dirt away. "Could break though. If we try to pull it out, I mean. We'd have to excavate all around it. Or . . ." He grinned over at Beth. "Ladies first?"

She shoved the tip of the shovel into the dirt-packed crack between two planks in reply. A splintering sound filled the air, a creak as she levered it. A snap that made Libby wince. What would they do if it *were* just moisture-eaten clothing or a supply of nails that probably would have been much appreciated at the time but was worthless now? Perhaps, from an archaeological perspective, it would still be interesting.

But she had a feeling Lorne and Scofield weren't overmuch interested in that sort of archaeology. And she couldn't be sure the unknown American was either.

When Beth shot to her feet a minute later, though, it wasn't moldy silk or iron in her hands. It was . . . a fork?

Beth frowned and laughed both when she handed one to each of them. "Silver."

"Ware," Sheridan added. "Brilliant. And it's engraved."

It was indeed. Which wasn't unusual. All the silver at home had an ornate *T* upon each and every handle. But this wasn't just the usual single letter, nor even a full monogram. A name was etched into the handle, elegant and flourished.

Elizabeth.

She looked up at Beth. Beth looked at her. And they both grinned.

Birds suddenly took wing on the opposite side of the castle, crying out as they flew up into the mist. Libby's pulse quickened. "Someone's here." And she'd abandoned her post at the castle's entrance. Was it Mabena catching them up? One could hope.

But she couldn't quite believe it. "Stay down, behind that wall. I'll get rid of whoever it is."

She made no objection when Oliver and Bram came with her though. And was doubly glad of their presence when they rounded the second corner and came face to face with Lady Emily, her arm in the iron-looking grip of a man who had to be her brother. They shared the same shade of hair, of eye, of skin. But where Emily looked miserable and frightened, Nigel Scofield met them with a grin that looked absolutely wicked.

"Oh good," he said. "The Tremaynes. And you've finally brought me my silver."

———————○———————

Oliver kept a silent litany of prayers going upward with every step, and he could tell from the occasional movement of Libby's lips that she was doing the same. He oughtn't to have had attention enough to be glad over that, given the circumstances. But he was. Even if things went terribly in the next hour, at least he knew that she'd made peace with her Maker, with the Lover of her soul. The One who called her by name and had led her here, right here and now, to find Him more fully.

Scofield, at least, wasn't brandishing a weapon at them. He seemed to think when he informed them that his associate had Mabena and Casek held nearby that they'd follow along without a peep.

He was right, of course.

"See how simple it's going to be?" Scofield shoved his sister off the path and into the sand with so little care that Oliver had to grit his teeth against a rebuke. "You give me that sample, and I'll return your friends to you. You leave the rest at a prearranged location, and I never bother you again. Tidy as can be. I don't know why you couldn't have done it this way to begin with, Elizabeth."

Libby stepped into the sand without a hitch or a stumble. "I didn't have it until now."

"A likely story."

Where was he taking them? One of the caves, probably. There wasn't much else on the north end of the island.

"And if you *don't* leave the rest for me to take back to civilization, if you think to get the authorities involved, you'll pay for it. I think I'll start with that doddering old woman who interfered with my associate just as he was closing in on you the other day, Elizabeth."

Oliver's hands curled into fists. "You won't touch my grandmother." And what did he mean, she'd *interfered*? Had she been attacked that day as well? She'd had no knots, no bruising. But they still hadn't gotten any answer from her on what happened, despite the fact that she'd been awake and chatty this morning. He hadn't, frankly, thought to press her on it. He'd been too happy to see her alert again, like herself.

Scofield just laughed. An ugly, abrasive thing that didn't deserve the same name as the sound that spilled from Mamm-wynn's lips, or Libby's or Beth's.

He led them directly to the entrance of Piper's Hole, which had Lady Emily pulling frantically away. "No. I won't go in there. You can't make me!"

He let go of her so abruptly she fell backward into the sand. "You are a disgrace to the family name. You know that, don't you?" He scoffed. "Afraid of a cave."

Telford crouched down beside her, slipping an arm behind her to help raise her back to her feet in the shifting sand. He murmured something into her ear that Oliver couldn't hear, and which failed to bring any calm to her face.

Scofield hissed out a curse and turned his hard gaze on Oliver and Libby again. "My sister will be our lookout. The rest of you come with me." He'd already taken the three pieces of silverware they'd held—a fork, a knife, a spoon. Not that they would have been much use as weapons, but Oliver didn't much like the sensation that they were utterly defenseless.

Well, not utterly. They had the Lord on their side. And Beth and Sheridan still out there. Perhaps, if they hurried, they'd have time to fetch the constable—though they wouldn't know for certain where Scofield had taken them.

Scofield gripped Libby's arm in place of his sister's, and a growl slipped out before Oliver could stop it.

Scofield sent him a look dripping deadly amusement. "Down, boy. I won't hurt your sister unless she forces me to. She's proven herself quite useful."

Lady Emily's brow creased. "She isn't—"

"Going in there? I don't mind." Libby craned her neck around to send Lady Emily a smile that said, *Keep quiet*. Then looked from her back toward where they'd come from, pointedly. "I'll be all right, Em. I go into the caves all the time."

Lady Emily nodded, no doubt realizing that her brother's mistake was playing to their advantage. Oliver still wasn't certain who he thought Telford was, but he clearly assumed there was only one Elizabeth here. And knew nothing about Sheridan.

"Don't disappoint me, Emily." Scofield moved his glare from her to Telford. "And who are you, anyway? One of Tremayne's friends, I assume."

Oliver had to give Telford credit—he appeared entirely unruffled by this turn of events and hadn't missed a single beat. Now he returned the glare even as he said, "Older brother, actually. Morgan."

Oliver sucked in a breath. On the one hand, it was a smart move—he and Libby certainly looked like siblings, and his clothing marked him of higher status than most of the islanders. If Lady Emily had told him anything about the Tremayne family, though, if he knew Morgan had died two years ago . . .

But Scofield's sneer looked blessedly ignorant. "The whole happy family, then. Lovely. Now, in we go."

In they went. Past the place where Oliver had kissed Libby less than a week ago—though it felt a century past, so much had happened in the interim. Over the boulders into the mouth of the cavern, down the drop. Beside the pool—though the boat was missing.

A few candles were burning on the rocks though. Enough to show him a grumpy-looking Mabena and Casek sitting there, hands and feet tied with rope that would be chafing at more than their skin. How had their captor, who stood behind them with that pistol leveled on them again, gotten the best of Casek? Wearne must have fifty pounds on him.

But he wouldn't have risked Mabena getting hurt in any scuffle.

"Lorne?" Scofield called out. "It's just me, with the Tremaynes. As planned."

Lorne? This was Lorne, the man from the cave last Sunday? But that must mean . . .

The man's face cracked into a nasty grin. "Hello again, luv. Have you brought us what you ought to have this time?"

Us. Oliver glanced from Scofield to Lorne. Not rivals—or not anymore. They were working together. He wasn't certain if that made them more dangerous or less.

Scofield held up the silverware he'd confiscated. "Engraved with *Elizabeth*, just as we thought. Mucknell must have kept it for his wife. I wonder if he even knew it had once been the queen's?"

"Hardly matters if he did or not. The buyers know, which is all that matters. A queen's own silver, and with the Mucknell lore added to it besides." Lorne smiled, then narrowed his eyes. "More than a single set, I hope."

"There's a crate, she said." Scofield sent them an arched look. "I'm thinking Permellin Carn will be a fine place for you to take it. Lorne, you can beach your boat there, load it up. If we hurry, we can still make the rendezvous. The *Victoria* wasn't in port yet when I left St. Mary's this morning."

The *Victoria*? Some sort of vessel, clearly. But not one owned by a local. If it was a visitor's, it had to be a large enough craft to have come independently from the mainland. Most likely a yacht.

"What do we do with them?" Lorne motioned with the pistol toward Mabena and Casek. Or perhaps to the group of them at large.

Scofield jerked Libby closer to his side. "We'll take the girl with us all the way to the rendezvous with the *Victoria*. Insurance. Let the rest of them go so they can get the silver to Permellin Carn—and then they're free to go afterward."

Telford surged a step forward. "You said you'd let everyone go if we cooperated." Perhaps he wasn't a Tremayne, but he'd have done Morgan proud. He always wished he'd been able to join their adventures like this.

Scofield huffed out a condescending sigh. "No, I said I'd let *those* two go if you cooperated. Really, Tremayne, you have to learn to listen."

Lorne frowned. "He's not Tremayne. It's the dark-haired one that's Tremayne."

Scofield must not have liked being corrected by a mere lackey. He turned his scowl on Lorne. "There are two of them, you imbecile."

Blast it all. Lorne had been on the islands for weeks—he must know that Morgan wasn't with them any longer. And when their house of cards came tumbling down, if these two realized there were more players in the game than they thought, it could go very badly very quickly.

They had to act—fast. But though he met Casek's gaze in that split second, it wasn't long enough to form a silent plan. Just enough to say they needed one. Still, they'd fought each other enough over the years to be familiar with each other's moves. If one of them lunged, the other would know what to do. They just needed an opening. A distraction.

A new light appeared behind Lorne, Casek, and Mabena, floating on the water, casting an eerie glow out from the darkness. And a ghostly white apparition manifested itself on the face of the pool. "Unhand her at once!"

Not an apparition—Mamm-wynn. Though he scarcely recognized her in the fierce shadows, he'd know her voice anywhere.

And questions of how she'd gotten there would just have to wait. Her sudden appearance had made Scofield curse and jump away from Libby, and Oliver could feel Telford coil beside him, ready to attack in that direction.

But Scofield wasn't the one with the weapon. Lorne was, and he didn't do anything helpful like drop it in shock at Mamm-wynn's arrival. He took aim at Casek and Mabena. "You'll not scare me away this time, old woman, no matter *what* you know that you shouldn't!"

Oliver hurtled toward them.

"No!" Casek, somehow, had struggled to his feet. He was effectively between Lorne and Mabena, but Lorne had jumped onto another rock, out of Casek's lunging range. He wouldn't be able to fight the gun from him.

And a look of utter fury had taken over Lorne's face.

Time slowed as Oliver drew near, observed, calculated.

Could he reach Lorne before he pulled the trigger? He had to try. Because if he shot Casek, Casek would tumble backward into the pool and, with his arms and legs both bound, sink straight to the bottom. Likely dead before any of them could drag his hulking form back out, especially if Lorne re-aimed.

There was only one thing Oliver could possibly do. He threw himself in front of Casek, still flying at Lorne, praying he'd have enough time to reach him.

Thunder roared through the cave, and lightning flashed. He heard a million screams, a thousand footsteps, felt the sting of a hundred bees in his side as a bullet kissed him. But his arms closed around Lorne and, when Oliver fell toward the water, he dragged the villain with him.

They plunged into the darkness, cold and silky. Lorne thrashed, pushed against him. But it was only fists hitting him, no metallic death. He must have dropped the pistol, either on the rocks or in the water. Which meant Oliver had a fine chance. He shoved Lorne away, downward, and used the momentum to push himself in the opposite direction, toward the faint glow of candlelight flickering on the surface of the pool.

A hand grabbed his ankle, tugged, but Oliver kicked. Not at the hand, but to the side, where Lorne's head would be. And his boot connected with something, something that made the fingers loosen enough that he could kick away.

Lungs burning, he broke the surface of the water and swam with all his strength away from where Lorne would be, toward the rocks.

Hands grabbed his wrists and hauled him out. It took him a moment of blinking through the water streaming over his face to see it was Libby gripping one, her brother the other. He couldn't see Scofield anywhere behind them. "Where is he?"

"He kicked Bram in the head somehow and ran." Libby, eyes frantic, homed directly in on the burning in his side. "You're bleeding. Mabena, give me your wrap! We can use it as a bandage."

"Never seen anyone move like that," her brother muttered, eyes stormy. "They certainly don't teach that sort of fighting at the clubs."

A splash and a gasp brought Oliver's head around, even as his cousin, still hopping out of the ropes that had bound her feet, balled up an old woolen shawl and tossed it their direction.

Lorne had broken the surface. But the murder on his face froze when Mamm-wynn's boat came closer and the barrel of a hunting rifle pointed directly at him, in the hands of Tas-gwyn. His grandmother held a lantern aloft from her perch on the opposite seat.

Those two might just drive him to insanity. When they weren't busy saving his life.

"I wouldn't try anything." Tas-gwyn kept his face gruff, but to Oliver's ear, his voice had a note of glee in it. He could only imagine the yarns he'd weave about this later. "I'm the vengeful sort, you know, and still owe you for that crack to the head."

Mamm-wynn's gaze sought Oliver. "Are you all right, dearovim?"

"I'll be fine." The gunshot wound couldn't be anything serious, not given that he was far more aware of Libby's citrus scent as she wrapped Mabena's shawl around him than he was of the pain.

Tas-gwyn jerked his chin toward the rocks. "Out of the water with you, Mr. Lorne. Let's keep this nice and friendly."

Lorne looked around, clearly considering his options. But between Tas-gwyn's hunting rifle and the pistol that Casek had claimed, he apparently decided that trying to make a break for it wouldn't go well for him. Grumbling, he moved slowly toward the rocks.

"Rescued by grandparents." Telford moved from a kneel to a crouch, a hand out to help Oliver to his feet. "Sheridan's never going to let me live this one down."

Well. There was no one in the world quite like *his* grandparents. Oliver accepted the help up, wobbling a bit when his head swam at the sudden shift in altitude. Perhaps he was bleeding more than he'd thought.

But Telford steadied him with a hand clasping his arm, and Libby's came around his waist.

Noise came from outside, and a moment later the constable dropped into view, surveying the situation with a sharp eye. "Everything under control in here? Enyon said he heard noises—and not ghosts either."

God bless Enyon.

"More or less." Casek didn't take his gaze off Lorne for even a second. "One got away. Did you see him?"

"We saw someone running in the opposite direction. Enyon's chasing him down."

Lorne snorted. "Good luck. That one's slippery as an eel."

"We catch eels all the time." The constable moved with practiced ease over the rocks toward them, handcuffs at the ready and eyes taking everything in. He frowned at Oliver. "You're injured?"

"It's nothing."

"Nothing?" Telford rolled his eyes. "He was shot. Saving that one." He motioned at Casek.

"Really." The constable looked from Oliver to Casek and back again. "High time you lads learned to get along."

Libby pressed herself a bit closer to Oliver's side. And Telford didn't even scowl at her. Just sighed and said, "I suppose if that's how you treat your enemies, I'm looking forward to seeing how you behave with your friends. And," he added quickly when Libby drew in a breath, "I imagine we'll be taking the rest of the summer here to see it. There won't be any prying Sheridan away now. Nor Libby. So we'll see how patient you really are with that 'as long as you like' offer of staying with you, Tremayne."

Libby made the sweetest little squeak. "You mean it? We can stay the rest of the summer?"

"I suppose."

She abandoned Oliver to dart around him and throw her arms around her brother. Which brought a grin to his lips—and to Telford's too, though he tried to smother it.

"Well." Mamm-wynn accepted Mabena's help out of the boat, onto the rocks. "Perhaps we might continue this conversation in the daylight? It's a bit chilly in here. And I'm famished."

No one objected, so the crowd of them made their way up to the entrance and out into the warm sunshine, the mist having vanished as stealthily as it had descended. The constable and Lorne emerged first, and two deputies took him none too gently in hand. Oliver blinked at the onslaught of light when they emerged, glad to spot Beth, Sheridan, and Lady Emily safely on the sand a small distance away.

Not quite as glad to see Enyon jogging back to them, alone. His best friend was waving a hand and shouting, "Ollie! You all right? When I heard a gunshot, I about charged in then and there! But then when that bloke charged *out*—he was fast! Gave me the slip."

"I'm all right!" More explanation than that he wasn't going to shout for the whole island to hear.

Especially since his sister had just spotted their grandmother and had some shouting of her own to do. "Mamm-wynn! What are you doing out of bed? And *here*, of all places?"

Their grandmother laughed. "Saving the day, of course. I had to. All my favorites were here."

It only took Oliver a few steps to realize that the adrenaline was ebbing away—and his side was absolutely on fire. He pressed a hand to it, wincing, and looked down to see blood seeping through the shawl.

Telford's hand gripped his arm again. "Feeling it now, are you, old boy?"

"Perhaps a bit."

He eased closer. "Well. I don't imagine it's life threatening." He pitched his voice to a whisper too low to be heard by anyone else, given the dozen conversations going on all about them. "Which means you'll be wanting to propose sooner or later this summer. I won't object. And I won't cut her off—emotionally, I mean. I couldn't. She's my sister." He sent a hard glare up the beach in the direction Scofield must have disappeared. "Some of us know what that means."

Libby had taken a step away to answer someone's question about something, but she stepped close again now, smiling up into Oliver's face. "Are you all right? Does it hurt? We'll get you to a doctor straightaway."

He smiled right back at her. "Doesn't hurt a bit." How could it? Telford had just handed him the most precious gift in the world. That sort of joy didn't leave any room for pain.

Libby breathed in deeply of the riot of floral scents on the evening breeze, her gaze feasting on the colors available to it in the Abbey Gardens. Mr. Menna had ushered all the other tourists out an hour ago, but he'd let Oliver and her come in for a stroll, just instructing Oliver to lock the gate when he left.

Her hand was tucked into the crook of his elbow. And pure contentment flowed through her veins. "Do you think they'll come to an agreement while we're gone?"

Oliver laughed and led her onto one of the first paths she'd walked here, with Mamm-wynn. They were moving slowly, as a nod to the wound in his side from two days ago. The bullet had only grazed him, but still. It had required stitches, and he probably should have chosen rest over an evening stroll with her, though she was selfishly glad he hadn't.

"Not a chance," he said. "I think it infinitely more likely that Beth and Sheridan will come to blows first."

Libby chuckled too. It seemed that the more they'd pieced together about the silverware—once a gift to Queen Elizabeth, but which had been purchased by a nobleman in the days of Cromwell for his wife, only to be stolen by the pirate for *his*—the more heated Beth and Sheridan's arguments became. "Beth does have a point, that the silverware has no connection to Prince Rupert of the Rhine, and so why should he have it for his private collection?"

"And Sheridan has a point, that it shouldn't be entrusted to a museum, not given the Scofields' influence in those circles. If what Lady Emily fears about them is true, it may never see a museum display if we were to donate it somewhere. It would end up in the hands of the American willing to pay for it." Oliver shrugged. "We have time to decide. It's safe enough for now."

Safe in the small hidden chamber in Tas-gwyn Gibson's foundation, where Beth had found the map to begin with. Matching the one on the opposite side where the letters had been stashed. Between the two, there was just enough room to store the silverware.

If there was more to Mucknell's treasure, it hadn't been buried in the same spot. But the sheer amount of silver made it a valuable haul, and all the more so when one considered its provenance. More collectors than Sheridan and the American would be willing to pay handsomely for pirate loot once owned by a queen.

"And we have the rest of summer to make our decision." She leaned into his arm, still not quite capable of taking that in. Bram had relented. They were staying here, both of them. Lorne was safely housed in Tresco's single jail cell and would be shipped to the Cornwall magistrate soon, and the authorities would be keeping a keen eye out for any yacht called *Victoria*.

Not that the American who presumably owned it had necessarily done anything wrong, but Scofield could reappear if it did. Thus far no one had reported seeing him, including the ferry operator. But then, he hadn't taken the ferry here that morning either. According to Lady Emily, he had several friends with yachts and had probably come and gone by himself. There had been a pleasure craft docked at the port in Hugh Town for a few hours the other day, which gave credence to the thought.

"I still can't believe that telegram Lady Emily received." Oliver shook his head, eyes troubled. "They can't have meant it, can they? That she isn't welcome home until she's sorted things out with her brother?"

"I can't imagine so. But she certainly seemed to believe it." Libby didn't think she'd ever forget the look in Lady Emily's eyes either. Filled with tears. Hopeless. Dejected.

But she was among friends, at least. They'd see she was all right.

They walked in silence, comfortable and familiar. So much had already been said over the past two days. So much needed to be said still. But for now, it was heavenly just to listen to the chirping of the birds, the buzz of insects, the breeze running its fingers through the Cornish palms' fronds. To be walking here with this man she'd dreamed about for years and who so surpassed all she'd ever hoped about him. This man she loved in a way she hadn't quite thought herself capable of.

The path wound around another grove of trees, and Libby smiled. "This is the way your grandmother and I walked the day we met. I don't believe I've come this way since. There was so much else to explore."

"You'll be needing a new notebook soon, I suspect. I did especially love your painting of the lily of the Nile."

The *Agapanthus* was to be seen all over the islands, and she loved the purple blooms. "Would you like to know a secret?" She tilted her face up, grinning. "I usually sing '*L'amour est un oiseau rebelle*' while I'm painting."

Oh, his smile. She could get lost in it. "Well. Mamm-wynn did try to tell me weeks ago it was one of your favorites. I suppose I should have believed her."

"Did she?" Odd. But she was beyond asking *how* at this point when it came to his grandmother. "You should have indeed, then. You ought to know by now that she's always right."

His laugh was a mere breath, incredulous. "So it would seem." His fingers settled over hers on his arm, as they so often did. And she wondered if he'd kiss her again. There were hundreds of perfect spots here, and they had the Gardens to themselves. It would be the perfect cap to the last few strange days. "What did you two talk about that first day?"

"Well . . . on this part of the path, she told me a bit of the history of the Betrothal Stone. Or the legend, anyway." They were only a few steps away from it now, so naturally they stopped. Libby smiled at the memory. "She mentioned that your parents had a story about it, though she didn't tell it to me."

"No? Well, that won't do." Grinning, Oliver pulled away so he could face her. "It was in the dead of winter, so you'll have to use your imagination there. Most of the garden was dormant, and a fierce storm had just blown through. All the islanders had been hunkered down for days, but on the solstice, the sun was shining again. So my father seized the opportunity to take my mother for a stroll. She'd always been intrigued by the local legends—"

Libby laughed. "Having met her father, I find that utterly astounding."

"No doubt." He set a hand on the slab of granite. It would be warm from the summer sun, but perhaps he was imagining it with a winter chill. "Father had told Mother that he'd read the stone may have had some other ceremonial purpose in the days of the Druids. He said he thought that it was originally aligned to catch the rays of the setting sun on the winter solstice. Which, as you'd expect, was all it took to get her out here at sunset. Even though no one knows where the stone originally stood, she was certain that if she caught the flash of sunset through one of the holes, *something* would be revealed."

She couldn't have held in her smile had she tried. "And I suspect something did."

"Indeed." Eyes twinkling, Oliver shifted behind the stone. "While she was busy investigating, Father slipped back here. And at the exact moment when the rays were stretching through the hole, he reached

366

through." Oliver's hand came through the small, topmost hole. "And he opened his hand." Oliver's fingers uncurled from his palm.

Libby's smile stilled. Her breath caught. His hand wasn't empty. There was a ring sitting there in his palm, the main stone a gleaming purple—or green?—with diamond rainbows sparkling from all around it. "Oliver?"

"I'm only an island gentleman, Libby. I have enough of a living to keep you in microscope slides, though I don't imagine we'll be able to travel the world. If you marry me, your brother says there will be no money from him. But if you marry me, I will devote my life to bringing joy to all your days. It isn't a decision you should make lightly or quickly, so don't feel as though you must—"

"Yes!" She reached into the hole and clutched his hand, trapping the ring between their palms. "I don't care about the money or the travel or any of the rest. I only need you. The islands. Your family and mine and all our neighbors."

"My Libby." He moved his hand under hers, and in the next moment the ring was slipping onto her fourth finger.

She tore her gaze away from his enough to glance at it again. "It's beautiful."

"Alexandrite. As rare as you." Their fingers still entwined in the hole, he leaned over the stone. And kissed her.

She let her eyelids flutter closed and reached up to cup his cheek with her free hand. "I love you, Oliver," she whispered against his lips.

"And I love you, Elizabeth."

"And that's enough kissing until the wedding." Bram stepped into view farther along the path, near where the small back gate let the Tremaynes in and out so frequently, his gleaming eyes belying his stern tone. He must have known Oliver's plan, to have positioned himself so nearby. "Which should be planned for quite a while from now. I'm thinking a year's betrothal. Perhaps two, given how short a courtship you had."

"Bram, really." But she didn't much care how long the betrothal was. A day, a year, a decade—whatever the length, she'd get to pass the time knowing this man loved her. Knowing that she would be his. That she'd found her home, here where the islands knew her name.

Oliver came back around, letting go of her fingers only long enough to step to her side and then catching them in his again.

Her brother stepped to her other side and nudged her into a walk. "Well, we need time to get you a proper trousseau. Sort out how much of your dowry you'll need and how much we should, perhaps, set up in trust for future children. Because really, I don't think you could possibly spend it all here."

Oliver's brows pinched. "But you said—"

Bram laughed and slung an arm around her shoulders. "Is he always so gullible?"

"No." She squeezed Oliver's hand, pulling him along with them. "He always sees straight to a person's soul."

"Mm." Oliver shook his head, though she knew well the pleasure in his eyes wasn't from the promise of a dowry. "And what I saw with you, Telford, was a man who would do anything to protect his sister."

"And don't forget it."

They strolled back in the direction they'd come. Talking. Laughing. Planning. About weddings and families and pirate treasure. About friends and enemies and what the rest of summer might hold.

Libby mostly let the men do the talking. She watched the birds wing their way from treetops to heavens, listened to the night insects as they made their debut.

And could swear that when the wind blew again, she could hear the islands whisper, *Elizabeth*.

Author's Note

This story began, interestingly enough, when my copies of *The Number of Love* arrived. I sat down on the floor with seventy copies stacked around me and all the packing slips at hand for those who had preordered signed copies from my website. I had my purple pen at the ready, and I set about signing, stuffing, and labeling all those orders. As I did, I noticed a trend . . . many of these readers had the same or similar names. By the time I got to the sixth Elizabeth, I thought, *Oh, look! Another Elizabeth!* And something about those words stuck in my head.

Another Elizabeth . . . Over the course of the next twenty-four hours, a story emerged to match the words. A case of mistaken identity . . . a cranky landlady ready to judge one Elizabeth because of what another had done . . . that first Elizabeth's things still in the house . . . and that first Elizabeth's brother showing up at the door, shocked to find some other Elizabeth where his sister ought to be. I ran the idea past my editors, who encouraged me to develop it. So, the next question was where to set this tale of mistaken identity.

My best friend/critique partner and I have long been enamored with what we call "island books," so I decided it would be fun to set Elizabeth's tale on an island. I spent quite a while considering and dismissing the various British options—the Channel Islands?

369

Been done. Isle of Man? So small it would be quite limited. Then I discovered—and fell in love with—the Scillies.

I need to thank Richard Larn, a native of the Isles of Scilly and a prolific writer himself, for taking the time to answer my questions about when things like electricity and automobiles reached the islands, as well as reminding me that no one but the Duke of Cornwall owns any land there and only the house of the Lord Proprietor is really worthy of a nobleman. Most of this I found easy work-arounds for . . . and occasionally I said, "Hey, this is fiction!"

So the Tremayne house is a total fabrication, though other landmarks are described as accurately as I was able to make them. I also wanted to incorporate some modern traditions, like the Wednesday gig races. These haven't been going on for a hundred years, but it's a tradition I thought reasonably *could* have had its start in those days, and it's such a wonderful example of island community that I couldn't resist putting it in.

The Isles of Scilly were, historically, a hugely popular place for pirates and smugglers to congregate, given their location. So of course I had to include a bit of pirate lore! And Mucknell was certainly the most notorious of the Scillies' pirate residents. After decades of working for the East India Company, he seized the excuse of the English Civil War to lead a mutiny, steal the Company flagship, the *John*, and start preying on other East Indiamen with the excuse that it was for the exiled Prince of Wales. And the prince not only gave him his blessing, but he named him a vice admiral . . . of a pirate fleet. How fascinating is that? For many years, no one knew what happened to the *John* after its last battle, nor the haul that it had in its hold. Modern evidence suggests that it was purposefully beached and emptied, but there's still speculation about that booty. Is Mucknell's treasure still buried somewhere? Or did he really turn it all over to the Crown? Well, I have my opinions. . . .

I also need to thank my old friend Meagan Fitzgerald for being open with me about what life is like in a household with mito kids. I knew I wanted Morgan to have had a condition they didn't even have a name for at the time, and as I learned more about mitochondrial disease, I knew this was something I wanted to explore, if only in part. Because not only would Morgan have been hugely affected by the limitations, the illnesses that would always find him, and the always-present fear of an early death, but the whole family would have been altered by the care he required and the monetary output. I wanted a hero who had been forever affected by loving a brother with a debilitating illness—and a brother who had loved *him* so much that he'd selflessly preserved as much of the family legacy as he could so that Oliver would have something to inherit after Morgan's death. Though I couldn't name his condition in the story, I pray the slivers of attention I gave to it honor the families who fight those battles daily.

On a lighter note, while I was developing this story, my husband came across a rather unexpected blessing outside our church—a small tabby kitten in desperate need of saving. We named her Sammy and integrated her into our house (much to the initial despair of our two older cats), and she became the inspiration for Darling. All of Darling's mannerisms are, in fact, Sammy's—though what I didn't manage to work in is our kitten's utter gracelessness. She has the most remarkable ability to *not* land on her feet!

As always, I need to thank all the people who help me in my writing process. Elizabeth (yes, this is for you too!), my England native who checks for Americanisms for me; Rachel, for being the best virtual assistant in the history of the world; Stephanie, who cheers me on from afar with hilarious emojis when our writing retreat is canceled because of a pandemic and I'm forced to closet myself in my office alone; David, for being a superhero of a husband, giving me writing time, and being a brainstorming partner and beta reader; Xoë and Rowyn, for always putting up with a distracted mama; Mom and Dad, Nanny, Jennifer, and Terri, for always being proud of me. The amazing team at Bethany House, who help me transform my manuscripts into something worthy of the readers' time; and finally, YOU—my readers. Your enthusiasm, loyalty, and encouragement make it all worthwhile. Thank you for all the notes you send, the social media photos of my books in pretty settings, and always asking about other possible stories. More than once it's been those questions that have inspired me!

I hope you all enjoyed this introduction to a new world set in the islands and that you're curious about what might come next. Because Beth, Lady Emily, Sheridan, and Telford have their own stories to tell, and I, for one, can't wait to see what legends and mysteries they stumble upon!

Discussion Questions

1. Libby feels out of place in her own family and society. Have you ever felt this way, or do you know someone who does? What have you done to find true community? How have you helped others find their place?

2. Oliver's life was greatly shaped by his brother's illness. How have you seen physical afflictions shape a family? Make it stronger? Break it apart? How can we ensure that these struggles strengthen us and not break us?

3. Mabena came home again solely because of her fears for her best friend and cousin. Has there ever been a place, situation, or person you've avoided because of a past hurt? What would convince you to face them again?

4. Libby struggles to reconcile science and faith. Do you think there's a battle between the two? Must there be, or is it created by the opponents of each? Does knowing which questions belong to which side help reconcile it in our minds?

5. Who is your favorite character? Your least favorite? Why?

6. What did you think of Oliver's rivalry with Casek Wearne? How do you think they'll get along now? Would you have been quicker or slower to move toward a truce?

7. Do you think Mamm-wynn could really see "beyond the veil"? What did you think of her and her eccentricities?

8. The power of names and naming is discussed several times. Do you think names are important? What does yours mean? Your kids'? If you could know the name God calls you, what do you think it would be?

9. Mamm-wynn says to both Oliver and Libby, "The islands know your name." Is there a place that knows you, that you love above all others, that speaks to your soul? Where is it? Do you live there or vacation there? If you haven't discovered it, do you think such a place exists?

10. What do you think is coming next for the characters during their treasure-hunting summer on the islands? Which characters are you most excited to learn more about?

About the Author

Roseanna M. White is a bestselling, Christy Award–nominated author who has long claimed that words are the air she breathes. When not writing fiction, she's homeschooling her two kids, editing, designing book covers, and pretending her house will clean itself. Roseanna is the author of a slew of historical novels that span several continents and thousands of years. Spies and war and mayhem always seem to find their way into her books . . . to offset her real life, which is blessedly ordinary. You can learn more about her and her stories at www.roseannamwhite.com.

Sign Up for Roseanna's Newsletter

Keep up to date with Roseanna's news on book releases and events by signing up for her email list at roseannamwhite.com.

More from Roseanna M. White

A skilled cryptographer, Zivon Marin fled Russia determined to offer his skills to the Brits. Lily Blackwell is recruited to the intelligence division to help the war with her unsurpassed camera skills. But when her photographs reveal Zivon is being followed, his loyalty is questioned and his enemies are discovered to be closer than he feared.

A Portrait of Loyalty
THE CODEBREAKERS #3

You May Also Like . . .

In the midst of the Great War, Margot De Wilde spends her days deciphering intercepted messages. But after a sudden loss, her world is turned upside down. Lieutenant Drake Elton returns wounded from the field, followed by a destructive enemy. Immediately smitten with Margot, how can Drake convince a girl who lives entirely in her mind that sometimes life's answers lie in the heart?

The Number of Love by Roseanna M. White
THE CODEBREAKERS #1
roseannamwhite.com

All of England thinks Phillip Camden a monster for the deaths of his squadron. As Nurse Arabelle Denler watches him every day, though, she sees something far different: a hurting man desperate for mercy. But when an old acquaintance shows up and seems set on using him in a plot that has the codebreakers of Room 40 in a frenzy, new affections are put to the test.

On Wings of Devotion by Roseanna M. White
THE CODEBREAKERS #2
roseannamwhite.com

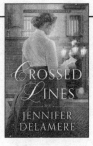

Mitchell Harris is captivated by Emma Sutton, but when his best friend also falls in love with her and asks for help writing her letters, he's torn between desire and loyalty. Longing for a family, Emma is elated when she receives a love note from a handsome engineer but must decide between the writer of the letters and her growing affection for Mitchell.

Crossed Lines by Jennifer Delamere
LOVE ALONG THE WIRES #2
jenniferdelamere.com

BETHANYHOUSE